CHILD
ZERO

OTHER BOOKS BY CHRIS HOLM

THE MICHAEL HENDRICKS THRILLERS

The Killing Kind

Red Right Hand

THE COLLECTOR TRILOGY

Dead Harvest

The Wrong Goodbye

The Big Reap

CHILD ZERO

CHRIS HOLM

MULHOLLAND BOOKS

LITTLE, BROWN AND COMPANY

NEW YORK BOSTON LONDON

Mulholland Books / Little, Brown and Company
Hachette Book Group
1290 Avenue of the Americas, New York, NY 10104
mulhollandbooks.com
twitter.com/mulhollandbooks
facebook.com/mulhollandbooks

First edition: May 2022

Mulholland Books is an imprint of Little, Brown and Company, a division of Hachette Book Group, Inc. The Mulholland Books name and logo are trademarks of Hachette Book Group, Inc.

The publisher is not responsible for websites (or their content) that are not owned by the publisher.

The Hachette Speakers Bureau provides a wide range of authors for speaking events. To find out more, go to hachettespeakersbureau.com or call (866) 376-6591.

All images provided by Pixabay (pixabay.com) and used under the free Pixabay License.

ISBN 978-0-316-29512-3
Library of Congress Control Number: 2021948121

Printing 1, 2022

LSC-C

Printed in the United States of America

For the educators who inspired me to become a scientist,
with special thanks to Susan Morgan and Nick LaPre.

And to the (mercifully few) educators who discouraged me
along the way, it's such a shame I can't recall your names.

Extinction is the rule. Survival is the exception.

—*Carl Sagan*

CHILD
ZERO

1.

Pike and his men reached the encampment's southwest gate at precisely 3:15 a.m.

Twelve minutes earlier, their sleek black SUVs—three in total, armored, tinted, and stripped of emblems, license plates, and VINs—entered the Lincoln Tunnel in Weehawken, New Jersey, having passed the darkened tollbooths without slowing. Two minutes after that, they emerged from beneath the murky waters of the Hudson River in Midtown Manhattan and zigzagged until they reached Eighth Avenue.

The stoplights blinked yellow in all directions. They encountered neither traffic nor pedestrians. *Three years ago,* Pike thought, *these streets would've been bustling—even at this time of night.* Now, thanks to the citywide curfew, they were empty save for police cruisers and sanitization crews.

The former rolled lazily through the intersections, or idled nose-to-tail beside one another so their drivers could converse. The latter clung to the sides of tanker trucks in hazmat suits, or wandered two-by-two with smaller canisters strapped to their backs, spraying bus stops, subway stations, and other public spaces with disinfectant foam. Fresh from the nozzle, it was enough to make your eyes water, but within minutes it dissipated to a lacy film that turned to fine white dust when touched, and smelled like some fragrance chemist's idea of clean.

As squad leader, Pike rode shotgun in the point vehicle. Pike was his call sign, not his name, although he wore it just as comfortably. Despite the illicit nature of their mission, he didn't waste a thought on the police cruisers or sanitization crews, because he trusted the route unfolding on his SUV's heads-up display. It constantly recalculated using data siphoned from the city's surveillance grid to avoid unwanted entanglements, so traversing Midtown unmolested was a simple matter of following the glowing red line projected onto the windshield from the dash.

They took Eighth Avenue to Columbus Circle. Pike felt his weight shift toward the passenger door as they rounded it at speed. At the third right, they continued north, eventually rocking to a halt at the intersection of Central Park West and 65th Street.

"Okay, gentlemen. You know the plan. Let's get to work."

At his command, seven men—Pike among them—exited the vehicles. All wore matte-black body armor and masks to match. Despite the hour, the temperature hovered in the eighties, and the August air was laden with humidity. Pike, sweating, felt a pang of envy toward the drivers, whom he'd instructed to remain inside the SUVs, engines running, AC on.

A tall fence encircled the portion of Central Park between the 65th Street Transverse and Terrace Drive, chain link topped with razor wire. Streetlights glinted off the sharpened coils. Concrete barriers lined the fence on the outside, intended to prevent vehicles from breaking through. They were installed two years ago after a nearby florist—who, despondent at the loss of business and unable to make rent, had unsuccessfully petitioned the city to relocate the park's inhabitants—plowed through the encampment in his delivery truck. Eleven died. Thirty more were badly injured.

Although its light was on, and the endless patter of talk radio drifted out its open window, the guard booth was unoccupied. Pike slipped inside and sat down in the empty chair.

"...*which, my fellow insomniacs, brings us to the topic of the hour: the border crisis. Public health threat or humanitarian disaster? You tell me. Our first caller is Kevin from Wyoming...*"

The desk was dominated by a computer with two oversized monitors. A small fan clamped to one corner pushed warm air around halfheartedly, rustling the paperwork and fast food wrappers scattered around the laminate work surface. A partially eaten donut bled grease onto an old invoice. A frozen macchiato made a puddle of condensation as it thawed.

"...*seems to me, these so-called refugees ain't exactly the innocents the media make 'em out to be. I mean, they slink across the border in the dead of night, carrying God knows what kinds of diseases. They infest our cities, infect our children, and then they have the gall to demand...*"

Pike inserted a thumb drive into the port on the keyboard, then turned his attention to the monitors. One featured a smattering of windows: email, internet radio, diagnostics for the camp's various utilities. The other rotated through an endless cycle of surveillance feeds.

A few clicks of the mouse and the surveillance feeds went black. Another click and the gate buzzed open, wheels squeaking as the chain-link panel rolled aside.

"...*understand, I ain't condoning violence—all I'm saying is, you can't fault these militiamen for wanting to protect their own. And if these people realize the price of entering our country illegally is a bullet to the head, maybe they'll think twice about...*"

Mounted on the wall to the right of the desk was an oversized red button protected by a clear plastic lid. EMERGENCY SHUT-OFF, read the sign above it. DO NOT TOUCH. Pike flipped open the lid and hit the button.

The monitors shut down. Kevin from Wyoming fell silent. The fan at the corner of the desk whirred to a halt. The guard booth's light went out.

As did every floodlight in the camp.

For a moment, Pike just sat there in the darkened booth, waiting for his vision to adjust. Perspiration soaked his clothes and gathered at the edges of his mask. In the sudden quiet, his breathing sounded too loud to his own ears.

When his eyes had fully adjusted, Pike rose, pocketing his thumb drive, and rejoined his men. Then they slipped through the open gate without a word.

Daniel Ballard crouched behind a row of bushes, his heart pounding in his chest.

Until recently, he'd been perched in a nearby oak tree with a partial view of the guard booth, his presence camouflaged by its rustling leaves and his threadbare, dun-colored clothes. When the guard abandoned his post, Dan climbed down to see if he could find out why. Then the military types arrived—tactical knives strapped to their thighs, suppressed compact submachine guns slung across their chests, and strange metal cylinders on their backs—so he hid.

Dan was a lookout. One of four stationed throughout the camp. Six months ago, when Gabriel—a fellow resident—first broached the idea, Dan thought it was a lark, a silly game of cloak-and-dagger that would never actually amount to anything. He'd only gone along because it sounded like a welcome distraction from the monotony of life inside the fence. Climb a tree. Pop a tin of those sardines his fiancée wouldn't let him bring into the tent. Maybe even get a little reading done.

Of course, during the graveyard shift, it was too dark outside to read, but everyone in the rotation took a turn, so there was no point complaining. Besides, the night shift wasn't all bad. The city was peaceful, the park quiet. And nights like this, it was too hot to sleep anyway, so there were worse places to spend them than up a tree, lulled by the whisper of the leaves.

Like, say, hiding in the bushes while masked men with machine guns infiltrated the camp.

Dan was no soldier. Before he wound up in this godforsaken place, he taught grade school in Fort Wayne, Indiana. He was trained to handle unruly ten-year-olds, not armed combatants.

Although his lungs ached for air, Dan forced himself to breathe slowly, to avoid making any noise that might give away his position. Gingerly, he reached into the pocket of his tattered jeans and teased out his contraband cell phone.

When Dan hit the home button, the phone's screen blazed to life. He pressed it to his chest and cast a worried glance toward the men, praying that they hadn't noticed—but the light had wrecked his night vision, so all he saw were green spots dancing in the darkness. Once his eyesight recovered, he cupped his left hand over the phone and tried his best to peck out a text with his right without losing track of the intruders.

That proved more difficult than he'd anticipated. Occasionally, one of the men was swallowed by a patch of shadow or disappeared behind a tree, causing Dan to panic—his gaze darting wildly about, fear uncoiling in his stomach—until he managed to lay eyes on all seven.

Then one vanished and never reappeared.

Don't freak out, he told himself. *You probably miscounted, is all.*

Dan's lips moved silently as he counted again.

Three, four, five, six...shit.

His mouth went dry.

His pulse thudded in his temples.

His head swiveled as he searched desperately for the missing man.

For a long time—thirty seconds? a minute?—Dan couldn't find him. Then a thousand white-hot pinpricks seared his scalp as he was yanked backward by his hair, and he felt the pressure of a knife's edge against his throat.

Dan dropped the phone and batted wildly at his attacker. The man jerked Dan's head to the left, and slid the knife at Dan's neck to the right, before releasing him.

The blade was so fine, so well honed, it took Dan a moment to realize he'd been cut. The scent of iron filled his nostrils. Blood spilled warm and sticky down his shirt. Reflexively, he raised his hands to his neck to stanch the flow.

It wasn't any use. Blood seeped between his fingers. Wind whistled through the gaping hole in his esophagus. Every labored breath drew fluid into his lungs.

Dan's arms grew heavy from blood loss. As he toppled forward, they flopped uselessly to his sides. Unable to catch himself, his cheek slammed into the ground.

Beside him in the patchy grass lay his phone, its screen glowing bluish white. His assailant stomped on it with a bootheel.

Dan gurgled as his body, starved of oxygen, shut down.

His vision dimmed, then failed.

The last thought that arced across his synapses before death claimed him was a fervent hope that, by some fluke, the warning text he'd been composing had sent.

HELP U.S. HELP YOU

Do your part to fight the microbial menace!

Cover Coughs and Sneezes

Stay Home If You're Sick

Report Fevers of 102.5°F or Higher

Obey Local Curfews

And Above All, Remain Vigilant!

———

If you suspect that you or someone you know is seriously ill,
visit www.dbs.gov/reporting.

Together, we can make America well again.

U.S. DEPARTMENT OF BIOLOGICAL SECURITY

2.

Jacob Gibson sat on the edge of the bed and watched his daughter, Zoe, sleep. Her bedroom was, as usual, a mess. The pale glow of the night-light cast long shadows of her toys. Though dawn was still two hours away, the outside air was sweltering, and the AC unit in the window labored to keep up. Its steady racket, and the dry processed air it blew into the room, made Jake's head hurt.

Despite the artificial chill, Zoe's face was slick with sweat, and her cotton nightgown was soaked through. Her furrowed brow and writhing limbs made it obvious to Jake her dreams were troubled. She let out a whimper. Jake dabbed her forehead with a damp washcloth. Her eyelids fluttered, then stilled as she settled.

Zoe was four years old, and looked more like her mother with every passing day. The angle of her nose. The curve of her cheeks. The way she scrunched up her face when she was thinking. The way her eyes gleamed when she laughed.

Every once in a while, Jake was so overcome by Zoe's resemblance to his late wife that he couldn't breathe. Losing Olivia had damn near killed him. Probably would have, if it hadn't been for Zoe. Jake had no idea what he'd do if he lost her too.

She'd been fussy when he picked her up at day care yesterday, and hadn't eaten much at dinner. An hour later, what little she did eat came back up.

Soon after, she complained of achiness. Her forehead felt warm, so Jake checked her temperature. It was a little high. He gave her some liquid ibuprofen and put her to bed—all the while trying his best to ignore the worry that gnawed at his gut.

It's just a virus, he'd told himself. *Kids get them all the time. Come morning, she'll be right as rain.*

The problem was, he didn't quite believe it. Every day, breaking stories of deadly illnesses dominated the news. Last week, a soccer camp in Suffolk County was shut down when a nasty strain of *C. difficile* tore through the dorms, killing three attendees and landing seven more in the ICU. Yesterday, an outbreak of Legionnaires' disease that took the lives of sixteen residents of an apartment building in Turtle Bay was traced back to a contaminated rooftop water tower. This morning, a homeless man was found dead a block from Jake and Zoe's Jackson Heights apartment, so ravaged by leprosy— his face a snarl of bulbous lesions, his hands reduced to twisted nubs, his teeth and gums eaten away—that his corpse was unidentifiable.

On his way to bed, Jake had checked on Zoe and discovered that, despite the ibuprofen, her fever had worsened. Her face was hot to the touch. Sweat plastered her hair to her scalp. He knew then that he wouldn't sleep a wink. He fetched the first of many damp washcloths and cranked her air conditioner so high that his skin prickled with gooseflesh.

Now, the world outside Zoe's bedroom window was bathed in a hazy predawn blue. Yesterday had been a scorcher. Today was forecast to be hotter still. The weatherman said that this August was shaping up to be the warmest on record. He'd been saying that for seven Augusts in a row.

Jake rubbed his bleary eyes with thumb and forefinger. He opened the app on his cell phone that was tied to Zoe's smartwatch and pulled up her biometrics. Her temperature was 102.6°F. Four-tenths of a degree higher than it was an hour ago. One-tenth of a degree above the threshold at which citizens were legally required to report a fever to the Department of Biological Security.

A sudden shiver gripped him. Jake blamed it on the air conditioning.

The Department of Biological Security was founded three years ago in the wake of the 8/17 attack, but the seed was planted several months prior, when new, more virulent strains of common bacterial infections began cropping up all over the globe, impervious to our drugs of last resort.

The DBS's purview included everything from bioterror to border control, disease surveillance to urban sanitization. Its director was beholden only to the president. Last year, its operating costs surpassed those of the Department of Defense.

Jake didn't give a damn what the law said—he wasn't about to rat out his own daughter. Jake was a cop, so he'd seen firsthand how quickly paranoia turned to violence whenever the DBS started canvassing a neighborhood. One minute, field agents were taking cultures and asking pointed questions—*How are you feeling? When's the last time you had contact with the subject?*—and the next, a pack of crazed civilians was dragging some poor soul into the street and setting them ablaze.

Lord only knew how the DBS decided which reports were worth investigating and which weren't, but even if Zoe's illness were ultimately determined to be minor, calling attention to it could prove deadly.

And if she'd contracted something serious...well, everybody'd heard the rumors about the horrifying conditions inside the state-funded sanitariums. Patients left in hallways due to overcrowding. Secondary infections running rampant. Bodies stacked like cord-wood in basement freezers. They weren't treatment centers; they were warehouses. They didn't heal the sick so much as tuck the dying out of sight.

Jake knew he had to tread cautiously until Zoe's fever broke. If he were caught failing to report it, he could lose his job, maybe even go to jail—but that was a risk he was willing to take.

Jake removed Zoe's watch and set it down atop her dresser. Then, to be safe, he deleted the associated app from his phone and cleared his cache.

As he finished, the phone buzzed in his hand, startling him.

It was his partner calling.

He stepped into the hall and answered, his voice a whisper.

"Jesus, Amy—don't you think it's a little late?"

"More like a little early," she replied. "Did I wake you?"

Jake eyed Zoe through the open door. She squirmed in restless, fevered sleep. "No. I was awake."

"Are you at home?"

"It's four in the morning. Where else would I be?"

"Good. Get dressed. There's an unmarked on its way to pick you up. We caught a case."

"You're kidding," Jake said. "It's the weekend, for God's sake."

"So?"

"So last I checked, you and me were off duty—and I've got Zoe to look after."

"Since when does that matter? Did your babysitter finally kick the bucket?"

Usually, when the job pulled Jake away at odd hours, he left Zoe in the care of his next-door neighbor, Mrs. Jimenez. Zoe liked her, and Mrs. Jimenez—who'd lost her husband to pneumonia last year—seemed happy for the company. But Mrs. Jimenez was a worrier, a busybody, and Jake was pretty sure she was the one who'd reported Sunil from down the hall.

One morning, after they'd all run into each other at the mailboxes, she'd asked Jake if he thought Sunil had looked unwell. That afternoon, a pair of DBS agents knocked on Jake's door with a handful of sterile cotton swabs and a clipboard full of questions. By nightfall, Sunil was gone, and his apartment was sealed shut with bright-red quarantine tape. That was more than a month ago now, but the tape was still intact, and no one in the building had seen him since.

"Your concern is touching," Jake replied, "but as far as I'm aware, Mrs. Jimenez is just fine. All I'm saying is, Lutz and Mason are on call. They oughta be the ones dragging their asses outta bed."

"No argument here. Problem is, they already did. A floater washed up in Hell's Kitchen a couple hours ago."

"Busy night for dying, I suppose."

"Nice to know we're at the top of the captain's call sheet, at least."

"Must be why I feel all warm and fuzzy," Jake replied. "So what're we looking at?"

"Honestly, I'm not sure. Cap was a little light on details. All I know is something bad went down in Park City. Now the whole place is on lockdown and no one's allowed in or out until we arrive. I reached out to a couple of my old uniformed buddies to see if they could buy me a vowel. They wouldn't say much over an unencrypted line—word is, the brass threatened to dismiss anyone caught leaking—but one of 'em told me the scene was, and I quote, pretty effing gruesome."

Jake doubted her buddy actually said *effing*. Amy was the only cop he'd ever known who didn't curse. "This just gets better and better."

"Quit grumbling, old man. You know you live for nights like this."

"Old man? I'm only thirty-seven!"

"Saying *only* doesn't make you any younger. Get a move on. Your ride will be there shortly."

Amy disconnected, leaving Jake with his own racing thoughts.

What the hell am I gonna do with Zoe? He'd be insane to trust Mrs. Jimenez to look after her, and he couldn't exactly leave a sick four-year-old home alone. The problem was, he didn't know who else to call.

Then Jake realized that was bullshit.

He knew *exactly* who to call—he'd just been hoping he wouldn't have to.

Jake scrolled through his contacts until he found the one he was looking for. His finger hesitated over it a moment—his jaw flexing, his mouth a bloodless line.

Then he took a steeling breath and tapped the screen.

3.

Hannah Lang pushed through the double doors and stepped into the overcrowded waiting area. More a widening of the hallway than a proper room, it smelled of stale coffee and unwashed bodies, beneath which was the whiff of phenolic disinfectant. Threadbare carpet tiles delineated the space. Banks of garishly upholstered chairs were crammed wherever they'd fit.

It was a little after 4 a.m. Despite the hour, nearly every seat was occupied. Ditto the spots on the floor nearest the outlets. A television mounted on one wall played a rerun of an old sitcom, its laugh track shrill and jarring under the circumstances, but no one seemed to pay it any mind. Many of the waiting area's occupants wore headphones. Some read. Most stared blankly at their device's screens. All of them had drawn expressions, rumpled clothes, and tired eyes. To a one, they looked haunted, stretched thin.

For a brief, blissful moment, nobody noticed Hannah standing there in her pale-blue scrubs and white lab coat. Then the doors clacked shut behind her and twenty-four hopeful faces turned her way.

Hannah resisted the urge to shrink from their attention. After several grueling hours of surgery, the bulk of which was spent debriding necrotic tissue, her nerves were shot and her limbs were heavy from exhaustion. Hannah was thirty-six, and had spent most of her adult life in hospitals, the last seven years as a surgeon. As such, she was inured to all manner of awful sights, sounds, and smells—but one thing she'd never grown accustomed to was the reek of dying flesh. It permeated every inch of the operating theater. Gowns and gloves were no match for it. All she wanted now was a hot bath, a stiff drink, and a few hours of uninterrupted sleep. First, however, she had a job to do—a loved one to update.

Hannah cleared her throat. "Mrs. Isler?"

Twenty-three faces dropped. One showed surprise. It belonged to a slight, birdlike woman in her midforties with long legs, a slender neck, and wide, searching eyes. She rose stiffly to her feet and headed toward Hannah, her forehead creased with worry beneath a tangle of auburn curls.

"Are you Ronald's nurse?" she asked.

Hannah struggled to master a surge of indignation. The mistake was far too common for her liking. "No, I'm his surgeon, Dr. Lang."

The woman colored. "Oh. Forgive me. I...I'm not my best today. It's just...I've been waiting here so long, and no one will tell me anything." Her voice was tremulous. Tears welled in her eyes.

"It's fine," Hannah lied.

"Is Ron awake yet? Can I see him?"

"Mrs. Isler—"

"Please, call me Michelle."

"Michelle," Hannah amended, "how about you and I find somewhere private so we can talk?"

"I don't understand. Did something happen? Why won't you let me see my husband?" As she spoke, her pitch and volume increased, sending waves of agitation through the crowd.

"Your husband's still unconscious," Hannah replied. "If you'd just come with me—"

"No." Michelle's body stiffened. Her hands made fists at her sides. "Whatever you've got to tell me, you can tell me here."

Hannah sighed. She'd seen this sort of thing a thousand times before. Patients' loved ones digging in as if a forceful enough denial could bend the universe to their will. Sadly, it was never any use.

Ronald Isler was a mechanic with the Metropolitan Transportation Authority. Three days ago, he was trying to loosen a sticky bolt when his wrench slipped and he scratched his right forearm on the undercarriage of the bus that he was working on. The wound was barely deep enough to break the skin, so he slapped a bandage on it and got back to work.

The next morning, his arm was sore and stiff. At the time, Ron didn't think much of it. Soon, though, he was unable to bend his right elbow, and the skin around his wound was red and swollen. Michelle insisted that Ron get checked out. Come Friday, he relented, so they set out for NewYork-Presbyterian's ER on 68th Street.

NewYork-Presbyterian was the last remaining nonprofit hospital in Manhattan. Thanks to the implosion of the insurance industry, the rest had either gone private or gone under. As funds dried up, the hospitals that survived were forced to make hard choices. Many elected to close their emergency rooms and cater only to those who could afford their services. NewYork-Presbyterian tried its best to care for the rest.

The ER was swamped when Ron arrived, so he wound up waiting eleven hours to see a doctor. By then, he was visibly in pain. When the doc removed Ron's bandage, a chunk of skin came off with it, revealing an ulcerous wound of mottled red and black. Michelle shrieked. One of the medical students shadowing the doctor passed out. Ron panicked and had to be restrained.

Fortunately, Ron's doctor recognized his wound for what it was. He isolated Ron in an examination room, ordered the ER closed until it could be decontaminated, and had a nurse page Hannah. Michelle was escorted from the emergency room, and hadn't been allowed to see Ron since.

"Michelle," Hannah said, "I'm afraid your husband has necrotizing fasciitis."

"I...I don't know what that is."

"It's an aggressive bacterial infection that typically enters the body via a cut or burn and attacks its soft tissues. Until recently, it was quite rare—maybe a thousand cases a year, nationwide—and not terribly contagious. It typically affected only people whose immune systems were already compromised. Now, unfortunately..." Hannah trailed off. As if anybody needed reminding how much the world had changed.

It began four years ago with a worldwide uptick of bacterial infections. Meningitis in Frankfurt. Tuberculosis in New Delhi. Cholera in Johannesburg. Gonorrhea in DC.

Though the outbreaks spread aggressively and proved resistant to any antibiotics that were thrown at them, public health officials initially dismissed them as unrelated.

They were wrong.

In their defense, antibiotic resistance was nothing new. Penicillin debuted in 1941, and penicillin-resistant infections were seen as early as 1942. Back then, the medical community assumed that they were caused by patients failing to take their full course of medication.

By the late 1950s, however, doctors began seeing infections that were resistant to drugs that patients had never been treated with before, and slowly, a horrifying truth took shape. Like humans, bacteria are susceptible to viruses, but their viruses—called bacteriophages—have a funny habit of picking up genes from one bacterium and depositing them in another, in much the way that bees cross-pollinate flowers. Thanks to bacteriophages, any bacterium that bumps into an antibiotic and survives has the potential to confer that ability to other bacteria—even those of different species—and relatively harmless strains can learn to kill.

By the year 2000, drug companies were cranking out millions of tons of antibiotics every year, and multidrug-resistant bacteria had begun cropping up in hospitals around the world. In retrospect, it was only a matter of time before a chance encounter between virus and bacteria shattered our defenses. But when it happened, we were woefully unprepared.

The virus responsible—named ArBGR01 by the researchers who first isolated it, owing to its Arctic origin and broad genus range, and dubbed the Harbinger virus by the press—was ruthlessly efficient. Released by climate change from the Siberian permafrost, it infected bacterial populations worldwide in a matter of weeks, and trans-ferred genes between them at an alarming rate. Soon, it was thought to be the most common virus on the planet. Its prevalence allowed bacteria to adapt with terrifying speed. New drugs, no matter how promising, were overrun in record time.

As the antibiotic era collapsed, diseases long thought beaten came surging back. The risk of postsurgical infections made organ trans-plants and implants of any kind—hip, knee, cosmetic—a thing of the past. Steroid treatments, radiation, and chemotherapy were off the table too, because they ravaged the immune system. Even the most basic of surgeries became life threatening, as did childbirth. An impacted tooth—or, hell, a paper cut—could kill you. The death toll skyrocketed.

Before the Harbinger virus hit, Hannah was a promising young cardiothoracic surgery fellow. Now, all surgeons were trauma sur-geons, and Hannah was a soldier on the front lines of a war—one humanity was losing.

"This, um—" Michelle began.

"Necrotizing fasciitis," Hannah prompted.

"Right. Necrotizing fasciitis." She emphasized each syllable, like a child sounding out an unfamiliar word. "Is it fatal?"

"Left untreated, yes."

"But you got it in time—you *must* have."

"It's too soon to say for sure, but I hope so."

"Then what's the problem? Why can't I see my husband?"

Hannah looked around. "Are you sure you want to discuss this here?"

"What's it fucking matter where we discuss this?" Michelle snapped. All throughout the waiting area, people stared, unease etched into their faces.

"Look," Hannah replied, irritation creeping into her tone, "I get that you're upset, but there are a lot of people within earshot who're worried about their loved ones, and I'm not about to let you cause a panic. If you'd like to continue this discussion here, that's your call, but I'm going to need you to calm down."

Michelle appeared chastened. "You're right. I'm sorry. But I get the feeling there's something you're not telling me."

Hannah sighed. "A few years ago, cases such as Ron's would have been treated very differently. We would have given him broad-spectrum antibiotics and performed a series of operations, over a period of weeks if need be, to debride the wound. Now that antibiotics are off the table, we no longer have that luxury. We always attempt to remove as little tissue as possible, but unfortunately, Ron's infection was quite advanced—so we were forced to take drastic action to halt its spread."

Her words were clinical, dispassionate. The image in her mind's eye was anything but. Ron's arm flayed open like a frog in high school science class. Foul black tissue shredding beneath her forceps.

"Meaning what?" Michelle asked.

The high-pitched whine of the oscillating bone saw echoed in Hannah's ears.

"Meaning amputation."

"You took my husband's *arm*?"

"Yes, as well as portions of his shoulder, neck, and ribcage."

"You took my husband's arm," Michelle repeated, though it was less a question this time than a thudding, horrible certainty.

"Please understand, I had no choice."

"Bullshit," she spat. "There had to be *something* you could do to save it."

"There wasn't. I tried."

"Do you have any idea what you've done?"

"Yes. I do. I saved your husband's life."

"Ruined it, more like. My husband's a *mechanic*, for Christ's sake. How's he supposed to do his job with one arm?"

"He'll adapt."

Michelle laughed then, shrill and barking. "You make it sound so easy—like you have any fucking clue."

Hannah knew better than Michelle realized. She'd lost the bottom third of her left leg to an infection ten months ago, after being bitten by a patient who'd turned violent.

It took a while for her to adjust to her prosthetic—for a time, walking was awkward and exhausting, and her residual limb still chafed maddeningly in its socket during long surgeries—but, eventually, she'd learned to manage.

Sure, her sleep was often interrupted by nightmares, and she broke out in a cold sweat whenever memories of that fateful day resurfaced, but it was nothing she couldn't handle.

That's what she told herself, at least.

"I never said it would be easy," Hannah said, "but I promise you, it's possible."

Michelle's features twisted with contempt. "Save your promises. I want to see my husband."

"You can't. He's still sedated. Ron's not out of the woods yet—his body's been through a lot, and he's at risk of developing secondary infections. We've placed him in a hyperbaric chamber to promote healing, and we'll be monitoring him carefully for the next several hours. Curfew's over soon; you should consider going home to get some rest."

"Don't you *dare* tell me what to do, you incompetent bitch. I'm not going anywhere until Ron wakes up. And if he doesn't, I swear I'll dedicate the rest of my life to ruining yours."

Michelle stalked back to her seat, every pair of eyes in the waiting area upon her. For a few stunned seconds, Hannah just stood there watching too. Then she turned and slunk back through the double doors.

Her hands trembled.

Her eyes watered.

Her face burned.

Hannah's physical reaction to the encounter blindsided her. She knew that she'd done everything she could to save her patient, just as she knew that Michelle needed someone to blame for what had happened to her husband. Still, she found herself haunted by the phantom stench of rotting meat—and the bone saw's angry buzz, like a hornet's nest disturbed, rattled against the inside of her skull.

A pair of orderlies rounded a corner down the hall, headed toward Hannah, so she ducked into a darkened storage room to compose herself. Once inside, she leaned heavily against a set of utility shelves stacked high with medical supplies, and took several measured breaths. As she shifted her weight off her prosthesis, her residual limb began to throb in time with her heartbeat.

Eventually, she noticed a rhythmic hum emanating from her lab coat's right pocket. Her cell phone, she realized. She wiped her eyes and took it out, its pale glow pushing back the darkness around her, but when she saw Jacob Gibson's smiling face on the screen, she hit Ignore.

The phone rang again immediately. That damned photo of Jake felt like a mocking reminder of better times. Hannah cursed herself for not deleting it three months ago, when he'd abruptly broken up with her.

Anger rising, she jabbed the screen with her index finger—hitting Answer this time—and started talking before the phone was to her ear.

"Jesus Christ, Jake, how many times do I have to tell you to stop calling me? I get that you feel shitty about how things ended, but that doesn't give you the right to tell me so every time you tie one on."

"I know. I'm sorry. Please don't hang up—I swear, that's not what this is."

Well, he wasn't slurring at least. That struck Hannah as progress of a sort.

"Okay, you have ten seconds to tell me what's so important that you'd call me at four thirty in the morning, when I made it clear I never wanted to hear from you again."

"I didn't know who else to turn to," he said, his voice tight with worry. "It's...it's Zoe."

Adrenaline surged through Hannah's veins. Her exhaustion evaporated. For all Jake's faults, and there were many, he'd never use his daughter as an excuse to call. That meant something was really wrong—and since he was calling Hannah, odds were Zoe was sick.

"Jake," Hannah replied sharply, "don't say another word. You can fill me in when I get there." The Wellness Act, which breezed through Congress in the weeks following the 8/17 attack, granted the Department of Biological Security unfettered authority to monitor any electronic communications for "words and phrases deemed relevant to the continued health and safety of the American people." No one outside the DBS knew what, specifically, that entailed, but it stood to reason that mentioning an unreported illness over an open phone line was a bad idea.

"Then you'll come?" The relief in his voice was palpable.

"For Zoe? Of course."

"But the curfew—"

"Is almost over," she said, "and even if it weren't, that's why God invented doctor's plates."

"Hannah," Jake replied, "I can't thank you enough."

"You can try. Hang tight—I'll see you soon."

4.

Mateo Rivas shuffled barefoot through the darkness, moving as quickly as he was able. Absent any light to guide his way, he dragged a hand along the wall of the storm sewer to orient himself. The ancient bricks were cool and slick against his fingertips. The mortar between them felt like sodden chalk, its outer layer crumbling at the slightest touch.

The air inside the tunnel was rank. Creatures skittered all around him in the dark. The sewer floor was rounded, like the walls, and coated with several inches of greasy muck that oozed between his toes with every step. It made the going slow, the footing slippery and treacherous.

Blood thundered in Mat's ears. Steel bands of panic wrapped around his chest. No matter how hard he tried, he couldn't seem to fill his lungs or slow his rapid, shallow breaths. White spots danced at the edges of his vision, only to vanish as he turned his head to look at them. Their false light seemed to him a cruel hoax, like heat shimmers in the desert that beckoned thirsty travelers.

Not long ago, Mat had been sleeping peacefully inside the Park City tent he shared with his uncle, Gabriel. Then, without warning, Gabriel yanked him from his cot and dragged him, stumbling, through the copse of trees that bordered their village. Mat—who wore a pair of shorts so threadbare he'd relegated them to pajama duty, and no shirt—wasn't exactly dressed for the occasion. Branches lashed at his exposed skin. Rocks and roots jabbed his bare feet. Still half asleep, he grumbled about being put through yet another pointless drill, but Gabriel shushed him with such force, he was jolted to wakefulness by the realization that this was nothing of the kind.

The forest, if you could call it that, terminated in a paved drive. The lights that lined the drive on either side were out; the only source of illumination was the city's glow reflecting off the clouds. Mat and Gabriel hunkered in the underbrush a moment to be sure no one was coming, and then headed for the nearest storm drain.

Gabriel removed the grate, which had been loosened for just this purpose, and lowered Mat into the sewer. Mat was twelve years old and small for his age—the result of early childhood malnutrition— but the aperture was so narrow that its edges scraped his ribs as he went through, and the tunnel was small enough that he was forced to duck. There was no way a grown man, Gabriel or otherwise, could've followed him—which was, of course, the point.

From his pocket, Gabriel produced a small package, wrapped in waxed cotton and bound with twine, which he pressed into the boy's hands.

"Take this, mijo, and keep it close," said Gabriel in rapid-fire Spanish. "Do you remember your directions?"

Mat nodded. He'd memorized them forever ago.

"Good. Follow them as quickly and quietly as you can. Someone will be along to collect you shortly."

"What about you?" Mat replied. His own Spanish was more deliberate, owing to the fact that he'd spent nearly a third of his life in the United States, but tinged with the same Salvadoran accent as Gabriel's.

"Don't worry about me. I'll be fine. Now go!"

Mat did as he was told. When Gabriel replaced the grate and covered it with leaves, Mat was plunged into a deeper darkness than he'd ever known. He wished he had a flashlight, a book of matches, *anything* to light his way, but his uncle had insisted it was too risky—that even the scantest illumination might reveal his position.

Instead, Mat swallowed hard and inched cautiously forward, his neck cocked to one side so that he wouldn't hit his head, his eyes so useless that he couldn't tell if they were open or closed.

One of his uncle's favorite aphorisms bubbled to the fore of his mind: *Trust your training. Trust your instincts. Trust yourself.*

Down here, that trust was proving more elusive than anticipated. Though Mat had spent countless hours poring over schematics and pacing out the route on lines Gabriel had drawn in the dirt, everything seemed different belowground. Intersections cropped up when he least expected them, or failed to crop up when he did.

Mat supposed he shouldn't have been surprised. As Gabriel had repeatedly made clear, Manhattan's underground was an endless, tangled warren of tunnels, pipes, and chambers. Some were new, their routes precisely plotted by GPS, but many were as old as the city itself, their long, winding paths often mislabeled or misremembered. Still others were abandoned prior to completion and therefore appeared on no maps, their existence a surprise to sewer workers and excavators alike.

He told himself he'd been through worse, but—even though he'd experienced more hardship on his journey northward from El Salvador than most would in a lifetime—he wasn't sure that he believed it. Doubt chiseled away at his defenses. The only thing that kept him moving was the thought of being trapped down here forever. He repeated Gabriel's advice like a mantra, concentrating on the words until they lost all meaning, until they blotted out his thoughts, his worries, his fears.

When the wall dropped away beneath his fingertips, Mat felt a surge of relief. He'd been looking for this turn for half an hour.

The pipe—clay, by the feel—was narrower than he'd anticipated. Barely wider than his shoulders, in fact. It was set into the wall a few feet from the bottom of the tunnel in which he stood, likely intended to prevent an overflow. Its interior was dry and dusty, which suggested that no water had passed through it in some time.

Mat took a steeling breath and climbed into the pipe. Airborne particles prickled in his nostrils, causing him to sneeze. Somewhere ahead, a rat squeaked in alarm.

He wriggled forward—an awkward belly crawl, his arms extended, his bare feet kicking—and tried not to think about what he was inhaling. The pipe was buckled here and there, jagged cracks roughening its walls, fallen shards as sharp as glass collecting at its nadir. Soon, blood flowed freely from scratches on his arms, his shoulders, his chest.

Fifteen feet or so into the pipe, Mat gripped the walls with his toes and pistoned his legs, just like he'd done two dozen times before— but this time, he didn't budge. He tried to pull himself forward with his hands, but there was nothing to grab on to, just a stretch of smooth, unbroken pipe.

Mat was stuck.

Something snapped inside him, then. Mat thrashed and kicked like an animal caught in a trap. Dirt rained down from above as fresh portions of the pipe caved in. Clay shards sliced into his exposed flesh.

He didn't realize he'd managed to free himself until he spilled out the far end of the pipe. One second, he thought he was still pinned inside, and the next, he was tumbling through a chill, dark void.

Mat plunged headfirst into a pool of stagnant water clotted with leaves. For a terrifying moment, he feared it'd prove bottomless, but then his head hit concrete, setting off a firework of pain inside his skull.

Mat surfaced—gasping, flailing. Once he got his feet beneath him, though, he discovered that the water was no more than three feet deep. He stood woozily, a lump forming on the crown of his head, and patted his front pocket to ensure that he hadn't dropped the package Gabriel had given him. Then he began to feel his way around his new surroundings.

That proved harder than it sounded. Mat was disoriented from the fall, and more freaked out than he cared to admit. He felt like he'd been underground for days or weeks instead of hours. His mouth was parched. His stomach, empty. His limbs were bruised, bloodied, and so leaden from his journey that he felt like he was sloshing through oatmeal.

As near as Mat could discern, he was in some kind of well, its base a five-foot square. At this depth, it didn't seem to have any intersecting pipes.

Despair, abject and unrelenting, overwhelmed Mat. For the first time since Gabriel woke him, he began to cry. Any way he looked at it, his predicament was hopeless. He was entombed inside a cold, wet hole deep beneath the city, with no way out and no way to call for help.

Mat wasn't sure how long he stood there, sobbing, before a low metallic scraping overhead stopped him short. He looked toward it, and saw a crescent of blinding white that seemed to split open the world. His eyes watered as he squinted against the glare.

An arm descended through the aperture—a manhole, it seemed, some fifteen feet overhead—and panned a flashlight around the concrete chamber. Its beam glinted dully off a set of metal rungs sunk like staples into the wall. An access ladder, Mat realized. He must've missed it by a hairsbreadth when he felt his way around.

"Oh, thank God—*there* you are. I gotta tell you, buddy, you scared the hell outta me when you didn't show up at the rendezvous point. I've been backtracking along your route all morning, prying up manhole covers and praying like crazy that I'd catch a glimpse of you."

He wore a hard hat, safety goggles, and disposable respirator mask that marked him as a sewer worker and rendered him unrecognizable. His voice, however, was familiar.

"Brian? Is that you?"

Brian Agren was once a resident of Park City—among the last, in fact, to be cleared for release before the Department of Biological Security put an end to the practice. He'd grown close with Mat and Gabriel during his tenure in the camp, and left owing them both bigtime. Mat should have realized he's who Gabriel would send.

"Last I checked!" Brian's tone aimed for cheery, but missed. As it echoed off the concrete walls, he glanced around with evident concern. "But listen, I'm feeling kinda exposed up here, so howsabout we put a pin in the reunion stuff until we're somewhere a little less public?"

"Okay."

"Cool. Now, are you hurt or can you move?"

"I can move."

"Then what're you waiting for?" Brian trained his flashlight on the ladder. "Let's get outta here before some busybody calls my boss and finds out there ain't a service call within twenty blocks."

Mat, shaken and exhausted, began to climb.

THE 8/17 COMMISSION REPORT
APPENDIX A

The following is an archived snapshot of https://www.shadowvox .net/endtimes as it appeared on October 24, 2027, 04:24:00 GMT. Said web domain is now defunct, the result of a federal seizure order executed on August 23, 2028. Username PlagueDoctor has since been positively identified as Spencer Aaron Brutsch (deceased). Username thewhiterider remains unidentified. For a comprehensive list of all known /endtimes users, see Appendix N.

https://www.shadowvox.net/endtimes

ShadowVox: Speak Freely

CAPNTRIPS (10M): you see this bullshit? https://www.nytimes.com/2027/10/24 /health/who-insists-multidrug-resistant-epidemics-unconnected.html

APOCALYPSEWOW (9M): suuuuuure they are......

REDQUEEN (7M): meanwhile: www.cnn.com/2027/10/24/world/previously -unidentified-superbug-linked-to-72-deaths-in-brazil.index.html

ICE69 (5M): damn whats that- four new outbreaks this WEEK?

PLAGUEDOCTOR (3M): tip of the fucking iceberg, dude. people gotta wake up, realize this genie's never going back into the bottle. you can only push the planet so far before it pushes back.

THEWHITERIDER (1M): maybe they need help

THEWHITERIDER (30S): waking up i mean

5.

When the uniformed officer rapped against the passenger-side window of the unmarked Ford Interceptor, Jake jolted upright in his seat. Until that moment, he hadn't realized he'd dozed off. Worried as he was about Zoe, he was amazed that he'd been able to. Then again, he knew she couldn't be in better hands.

The last thing he remembered was resting his head against the warm glass and listening to the tires' rhythmic clatter against the Queensboro Bridge, sunrise blazing orange in the side-view mirror. His thoughts had wandered as the car weaved autonomously westward through the early morning traffic—its steering wheel adjusting of its own accord to Jake's left, its electric motor nearly silent—until exhaustion overtook him.

Police barricades blocked off Central Park West north of 63rd Street. The Interceptor idled just south of them. An Art Deco apartment building dominated the view out the driver's-side window. Jake's window faced the park. Its thick canopy of leaves blanketed the avenue in undulating shadows, as if the trees were trying to prevent the slanting light from breaking through.

Jake gave the officer outside his window a look that straddled the line between sheepish and annoyed, then fished his gold detective's shield out of his sport coat and held it up for him to see. The cop nodded to a buddy, who slid one of the barricades aside, and waved Jake through. Jake tapped the touchscreen on the dash and the car rolled forward once more.

North of the barricades, Central Park West was eerily empty, although the unmarked remained dutifully in its lane. The sky above was tinted gray by smoke. A police drone zipped by overhead, its tiny rotors whirring as it snapped pictures of the gawkers who had gathered at the barricades. Amy's doing, Jake suspected. It was a good idea, if something of a long shot. While the old saw about criminals returning to the scene of the crime was often true, most of the crowd wore protective masks, which limited the efficacy of facial recognition software—and, despite alarmist social media posts to the contrary, the drone's microphone was all but useless for mass surveillance. Aloft, the mic was overwhelmed by the sound of the propellers; at rest, noise pollution made isolating intelligible audio from a crowd next to impossible.

Crime scene technicians congregated around Park City's southwest gate, taking photographs and dusting for prints. Jake figured this must be where the perpetrators gained entry to the camp. The Interceptor rolled by without slowing, so he was forced to crane his neck to take in the scene.

The gate was one of several secondary entrances intended to provide speedy access to first responders in the event of an emergency. As such, it was supposed to be staffed at all times. Yellow evidence markers dotted the pavement just outside—indicating tire tracks, most likely—but Jake saw nothing to suggest they'd found a body. He supposed the guard booth could be hiding one from view, but if not, he was curious to speak with whoever'd been on duty last night.

The encampment's main entrance was opposite West 67th. A clot of vehicles sat just outside: ambulances, police cruisers, fire-and-rescue. The cruisers were empty. The fire-and-rescue vehicles, too, compartments flung open to access their supplies. The ambulances faced away from the gate, engines idling, for easy loading and rapid egress — but the drivers inside looked bored and edgy. Whatever had happened, there didn't seem to be a lot of injured people in need of transport.

Jake's unmarked pulled in beside the vehicles and chimed to indicate they'd reached their destination. Once he climbed out, it drove away, automatically recalled to God knows where.

Jake headed toward the open gate, eyes burning from the acrid smoke, thick enough here to render the world in jaundiced tones. The concrete barriers that lined the fence on either side of the main entrance were tattooed with layer upon layer of graffiti, some hasty scribbles, others improbably elaborate. The most famous, and most photographed, was a large rectangular piece in the style of an old postcard. *Greetings from PARK CITY*, it read, the all-caps letters oversized and filled with apocalyptic images of Manhattan in ruins.

Park City was created in the aftermath of the 8/17 attack, by necessity and with the noblest of intentions. The encampment's proper name was the Sheep Meadow Emergency Refugee Center, but no one ever used it anymore. It had outlived its formal designation just as surely as it had exceeded its mandate.

Three years ago, on the morning of August 17, a twenty-six-year-old Canadian national by the name of Spencer Brutsch left his third-floor walkup in Washington Heights and boarded a southbound 1 train at the 168th Street station. An hour later, surveillance cameras placed him at a breakfast joint on Lexington Avenue between 39th and 40th. He ordered waffles and appeared to be in good spirits. Credit card records indicated that he overtipped.

Between home and breakfast, Brutsch committed the most heinous act of terror the world had ever seen.

Brutsch was a doctoral candidate at Columbia University's Department of Microbiology and Immunology. Unbeknownst to his advisor and his fellow grad students, he was also an active member of Shad-owVox's controversial /endtimes forum. Authorities believe that's where he was radicalized. The site's fanatical devotion to anonymity made it a breeding ground for extremism of all kinds.

Brutsch, working in secret, used university resources to culture a multidrug-resistant strain of *Yersinia pestis,* the bacterium responsi-ble for bubonic, septicemic, and pneumonic plague. Bubonic and septicemic plague—which take root in the lymph nodes and the blood, respectively—require an animal vector for transmission, but pneumonic plague—which attacks the lungs—spreads from person to person through the air. One to three days after infection, you develop a fever, headache, and weakness. Then pneumonia sets in and breathing becomes a chore. Your lungs try in vain to clear them-selves, spreading pestilence to those around you with every painful, racking cough. By the time shock sets in, it's almost a relief. Many patients die within thirty-six hours. Without timely access to effec-tive antibiotics, no one with pneumonic plague survives a week.

The route Brutsch took on August 17 passed through the two bus-iest subway stations in Manhattan, Times Square–42nd Street and Grand Central–42nd Street, at the height of the morning rush. As usual, several trains were running late that day, so the stations were shoulder-to-shoulder with commuters.

In each station, Brutsch left a rudimentary aerosol device of his own design. He was a better microbiologist than an engineer; the nozzle of the Times Square device clogged within moments of activa-tion. His Grand Central device, however, worked precisely as intended—dispersing a fine mist of aerosolized plague throughout the crowded platform.

That was Thursday.

By Friday morning, the first patients had developed symptoms.

Come Friday afternoon, there were more than seven hundred confirmed cases of pneumonic plague in the greater metropolitan area, and dozens of patients were in critical condition. The mayor declared a state of emergency and suspended all mass transit. Bridges and tunnels were closed.

Manhattan was locked down.

Inside the cordon, panic spread as quickly as the disease. Grocery stores and pharmacies were looted for supplies. Barricades were overrun. Friday night, the president deployed the National Guard, who patrolled the streets in hazmat suits and shot rioters on sight.

By Saturday, the infected began dying. Brutsch was almost certainly one of the first to go, having inhaled enough plague to kill a hundred men while activating his devices. When the FBI kicked down his door, they found his bloated corpse reclining on the couch, his laptop still logged in to ShadowVox—a VPN hiding his IP address and spoofing his location.

He'd died bragging via private chat about the mayhem that he'd wrought.

As the death toll rose, New Yorkers were instructed to shelter in place. Many in the outer boroughs ignored the edict and gridlocked the streets in their attempts to flee. Manhattan hotels refused to rent rooms to those stranded by the quarantine, so temporary shelters were set up in Central Park's Sheep Meadow to accommodate them. FEMA provided supplies enough to house three thousand. The encampment quickly swelled to four times that, forcing the authorities to expand its borders.

The outbreak raged for weeks before martial law and public education finally brought it under control. By then, nearly one hundred thousand people were dead—Jake's wife, Olivia, among them. Another million left the city as soon as they were allowed. Wealthy

New Yorkers turned their buildings into hermetically sealed citadels and hired private armies to protect them. The poor, for want of options, soldiered on as they always had.

Once the city settled into a new normal, the encampment became a liability. After a month of overcrowding and poor sanitation, its conditions were abhorrent—a tiny Third World nation in the heart of Manhattan. Everything from shigellosis to typhoid fever ran rampant, and cases of bubonic plague were not uncommon. In addition to its human victims, Brutsch's attack had infected countless rats, creating a simmering reservoir of plague beneath the city, which was transmissible to humans via fleas. Outside the camp, exposure was unlikely; inside, it was unavoidable.

Panicked lawmakers, backed by a terrified public, ensured that no one was allowed to leave the camp unless they'd been demonstrably healthy for forty days—a near impossibility under the circumstances. Then one detainee who cleared that hurdle turned out to be an asymptomatic typhoid carrier. He sparked an outbreak that left three dead, after which the screening program was suspended. The remaining inhabitants of the camp—4,721, by last count—have been in limbo ever since.

Jake suspected that number was a little lower today.

The camp's administrative offices were located just inside the main gate, in the building formerly occupied by Tavern on the Green. Brutsch's attack had proved devastating to the city's tourist trade, and locals were uninterested in eating overpriced American cuisine while looking out upon a shantytown, so the iconic restaurant went under years ago, and was subsumed by the encampment not long after. Now the structure's faded opulence seemed at odds with its function.

A second fence separated the administrative offices from the interior of the encampment. The parking lot between the fences teemed with police, firefighters, and EMTs. Some wore uniforms. Others wore Tyvek coveralls of white or powder blue. Still others wore shock-yellow hazmat suits. Between the fences, the protective gear was unsullied, because it was all single-use, and reentry from the encampment was tightly regulated. A decontamination tent had been set up on the other side of the inner fence for those returning from the crime scene. Jake watched a group of firefighters enter at its far end, their hazmat suits stained brownish-gray like the sky. Another exited its near end in their station uniforms, having removed their hazmat gear inside.

Jake spotted his partner, Amy, among the crowd and headed toward her. She glared at him as he approached.

"Where have you been?" She spoke at an angry whisper to avoid being overheard. "I called you more than two hours ago."

Amira Hassan was a fresh-faced, dark-skinned twenty-seven, with bright eyes and an easy smile, the latter of which was nowhere to be seen today. She barely came up to Jake's chin but still somehow managed to look imposing in her tailored gray pantsuit and black hijab. Her detective's shield was affixed to her lapel. Her jacket was cut loosely to leave room for the gun on her right hip.

"I know," Jake said. "I'm sorry."

"Oh, good. You're sorry. That makes me feel so much better about putting my career on the line by lying to the captain when he asked where you were."

"You didn't have to do that."

"You're right. I didn't. You've seen firsthand what I go through on the daily. Half the force is chomping at the bit to see me fail. So howsabout you return the favor by telling me what's going on?"

Jake glanced warily around. "I can't. Not here. But I promise that I'll fill you in as soon as I'm able."

Something in his tone caused Amy's expression to soften. "Okay," she said, "but I plan to hold you to that."

"I'd expect no less."

"Do me a favor, though, would you?"

"Name it."

"Next time you leave me hanging, take an extra ten minutes to shower and shave. You look like hot wet garbage."

Jake smiled despite himself. She wasn't wrong. His shirt was rumpled, his hair a mess. His jaw was dusted with stubble. The canvas sport coat he'd grabbed on his way out the door to hide his shoulder holster was creased at the elbows, and the tie he'd found stuffed into its right front pocket was unwearable thanks to a blotchy stain down the front—mustard, by the look of it.

"So," he said, "you wanna tell me what we're doing here?"

A haunted expression flitted across her face. "It'd be easier to just show you," she replied. "But we'll have to suit up first."

She led him to a canopy tent, open at the sides. At one end was a folding table piled high with disposable protective gear. Safety goggles. Nitrile gloves. Respirator masks. Tyvek coveralls with matching booties. The goggles and masks were purportedly one-size-fits-all. Everything else was arranged from extra small to extra large.

Amy went down the line grabbing stuff. Then she shrugged out of her coat and began to put the gear on over her clothes. Jake did the same. The humidity made wriggling into the coveralls a pain, and the coated fabric didn't breathe, so he wound up pouring sweat. He had no idea how Amy made it look so easy. She geared up in seconds flat and then watched with an eyebrow cocked until he finished.

They cleared the checkpoint at the second fence, manned today by New York's finest rather than employees of the private security firm that managed the camp, and climbed into one of several four-wheel-drive utility vehicles that were lined up on the other side. Amy got behind the wheel. Jake rode shotgun. The thing looked like a glorified golf cart, but it had a surprising amount of pickup. Jake was pinned to his seat as they lurched forward and quickly left the pavement behind.

At its height, Park City was an unbroken sprawl of solar-powered FEMA shelters and military surplus tents. Over time, as the population dwindled and the original structures began to fail, it evolved into several clusters of patchwork tents and shanties—villages, in the parlance of their inhabitants—connected to one another by well-worn paths of dirt. Jake and Amy's vehicle now jounced along one of them, headed northeast across Sheep Meadow.

These days, the fifteen-acre field was largely abandoned, its flat expanse a wasteland of collapsed shelters, dead campfires, and piles of trash. Anything worth scavenging had been taken by the villagers long ago. The rest had been left to rot.

Here and there amid the rubble, a handful of ersatz domiciles still stood, their inhabitants too paranoid or misanthropic to live alongside their fellow detainees. Dirty faces peered at Jake and Amy around flimsy doors and dangling tent flaps as they passed. Some looked stricken. Others, suspicious. One woman appeared to Jake as if she were wearing war paint until he realized the lines of white from cheek to jaw were made by falling tears.

At the northeastern edge of Sheep Meadow, the footpath cut through a line of trees. This close to the source of the smoke, the air was foul, and visibility was poor. An old snack shack briefly emerged from the haze as they rolled by, its facade smashed all to hell, and just as quickly vanished from sight.

The trees gave way to a small clearing. Amy braked to a halt at its edge between a pair of fire trucks and killed the engine. Gray water dripped from the branches overhead, beading up on Jake's safety glasses and dyeing his coveralls an ugly shade. When he climbed out of the vehicle, his feet sunk into an inch of dark mud.

Before him was the ruins of a village. Every tent was torn to pieces.

Every shanty was destroyed. Slashed bedding and emptied footlockers littered the grass, their scattered contents soaking wet and streaked with ash. The wooden shelter that housed the village's showers had been knocked down. The chemical toilets beside it lay on their sides, doors flopped open, seams leaking pungent blue. Even the communal garden had been uprooted, its vegetables trampled.

Whoever'd done this had been looking for something, Jake thought—*but what? And why aren't there any bodies? Where the hell had all the residents gone?*

Jake wandered through the wreckage, Amy trailing close behind. The village was arranged around an ad hoc town square, which, at present, housed the remains of an enormous bonfire—extinguished but still smoldering, ghostly tendrils coiling toward the sky. It was clear from the scorch marks on the nearby tents that it had burned for quite some time, but even still, the pile of charred wood left behind was ten feet high. A swarm of hazmat suits surrounded it, shiny yellow streaked with black, the suits' occupants rendered faceless and inhuman by their masks.

Jake watched them dismantle the pyre log by log, Amy eyeing him significantly all the while. At first, he didn't understand what it was she wanted him to see. Then, at once, he did.

They were loading the spent logs into body bags, because they weren't logs at all. They were corpses. Shriveled. Blackened. Limbs burned down to stumps.

Jake no longer wondered where all the residents had gone.

6.

President Marshall Whitmore was eating a bowl of cereal on the damask sofa opposite the television when the director of biological security, Lionel Mercer, entered the Executive Residence.

It was a little after 8 a.m. Whitmore's wife, Thalia, had taken their kids home to Montana for the weekend, so the White House's living quarters were quieter than usual and the president less formal. He wore a Stanford T-shirt and faded jeans. His bare feet were propped up on the antique coffee table.

Yet somehow, Lionel thought, *the asshole still manages to look presidential.*

Whitmore's sandy blond hair parted impeccably of its own accord and featured just enough white at the temples to erroneously suggest that his boyish good looks belied a deeper wisdom. His eyes were brilliant blue and flanked by laugh lines that lent his face a cheery cast. And he carried himself with an easy grace that managed to convince farmers and ironworkers he was one of them, despite a net worth of more than forty million dollars.

Well, technically, the money was Thalia's, but it was easy to see why Whitmore was the horse she chose to back, and why the party elders had been willing to overlook the fact that he was a preening narcissist with little interest in governing.

For a time, their decision appeared prudent—lucrative, even.

Then, as Whitmore's languid first term drew to a close, Spencer Brutsch's despicable act of bioterror sent the country into a tailspin.

It was as if fate, tempted, had intervened.

Whitmore struggled to formulate an appropriate response, and would have surely buckled were it not for Thalia, who was determined not to let him squander her investment. At her urging, he fired the director of the FBI and the secretary of homeland security for failing to prevent the attack. Then he pressured Congress to pass the controversial Wellness Act—which, among other things, established the Department of Biological Security and placed dozens of agencies under its control. Critics decried it as a dangerous expansion of federal authority that violated several constitutionally protected rights and could easily result in martial law.

Whitmore was reelected in a landslide.

Before Whitmore tapped him to run the fledgling DBS, Lionel was a supervisory special agent in the FBI's Weapons of Mass Destruction Directorate. He'd spent years warning an attack like Brutsch's was inevitable, which made him an ideal candidate for the job. A climber with political aspirations, Lionel welcomed the promotion, although he realized that it was not without its risks—chief among them becoming Whitmore's next scapegoat should anything go wrong on his watch.

Lionel mitigated that risk by ensuring that his fate and the president's were intertwined. He cultivated an image as Whitmore's wartime consigliere, his go-to guy, his confidant, his friend. He made a habit of personally delivering the weekend threat briefing at the White House residence whenever Whitmore was in town. And if the paparazzi took a few photos of him on the way in, who was he to complain?

The press and public ate it up. Whitmore, too, as near as Lionel could tell. Their relationship was the envy of the Beltway. It was such a shame he couldn't actually stand the man.

"Lionel," Whitmore said. "It's good to see you." His voice was as friendly and authoritative as a TV dad's.

"And you, Mr. President."

"Are you hungry? I can have the kitchen send something up."

"Thank you, Mr. President, but I'm fine."

Whitmore gestured toward the tray on the coffee table. It contained coffee, yogurt, guava juice, half a grapefruit, and a side of bacon, most of it untouched. "Help yourself to some of this, at least. Seems my eyes were bigger than my stomach."

Lionel frowned, but said nothing. Prior to the emergence of the Harbinger virus, factory farms consumed 80 percent of all antibiotics produced. When those drugs failed, livestock populations crashed, and the world's fruit supply was decimated by blight. Vegetable and grain cultivation was less reliant on antibiotics, but drought and rising sea levels conspired to slash yields, so farmers struggled to meet demand. Now famine roiled across the globe. Even in the United States, fruit, meat, and dairy were luxury items, produced in tiny quantities at great expense. Whitmore's leftovers probably cost enough to feed a family of four for a week.

The president jabbed his spoon at the television. "You see this shit?"

"I caught enough to get the gist," Lionel replied.

The TV was tuned to CNN, which was airing highlights from Ethan Rask's most recent public appearance. Rask was the president and CEO of the pharmaceutical giant ProTx. He'd been touring relentlessly of late, ostensibly in advance of his company's long-awaited initial public offering, but the tenor of his recent remarks had sparked rumors of a White House run.

"*...I know the challenges we face today seem insurmountable.*

45

Most challenges do, until we rise to meet them. To me, the question isn't whether we'll survive, but how. The problem is, we've lost our way. To paraphrase Saint Thomas Aquinas, our fear has blinded us to the suffering of others. As a result, the United States has become a nation of closed borders and closed minds, so terrified of what lies beyond the edges of the map that we stand idly by while vigilantes murder helpless refugees on sight. But there is hope on the horizon. Despite the current administration's best efforts to ensnare us in red tape, the trailblazers at ProTx are making tremendous strides in several promising arenas, such as phage therapy and genomic editing. We've even begun to unlock the awesome potential of the beneficial microbes that comprise the human microbiota . . ."

"Comprise the human microbiota," Whitmore muttered, turning off the TV in disgust. "Jesus. Rask is as pompous as he is sanctimonious."

"He certainly enjoys hearing himself talk."

"That makes one of us. Every time he opens his mouth, my approval ratings plummet. To hear him tell it, you'd think I'm prowling the border with a goddamn M16."

"Speaking of, I bring good news."

"I'm all ears."

"My field team sent along their preliminary report on the thirty-six illegals shot dead outside of Laredo on Thursday. As you might expect, they were riddled with disease. Tuberculosis. Hansen's. Syphilis. Pneumonia. Not to mention a grab bag of exotic parasites and viruses."

"Any chance that information is going to find its way into the hands of a friendly reporter?"

"Already done," Lionel replied. "I wanted to be sure we beat the deadline for the Sunday papers."

"Thank God. It's high time we gave the media something to chew on besides me. Are we any closer to figuring out who's responsible?"

"The smart money's on either the People's Army or the New Confederacy—but the former's members have all gone to ground, and many of the latter's have already alibied out."

"I don't have to tell you an arrest would do wonders for my numbers."

"No, sir. You don't. But without more to go on—"

"I know, I know. Your hands are tied." Whitmore sighed. "Anything else I need to be apprised of before Monday rolls around?"

"There's been an uptick in listeriosis deaths in California. My people are digging into it. Ditto a staph outbreak in an Alabama nursing home. FBI agents operating on my orders raided a facility in New Mexico rumored to be an underground clinic, run by the so-called Resistance, that caters to illegals—but if it ever was, they've since abandoned it. And SIGINT indicates there's been a recent spike in online chatter among several known Endtimes groups, the Soldiers of Gaia chief among them."

Whitmore's face scrunched up with puzzlement. "Endtimes groups?"

"Brutsch acolytes," Lionel clarified. "Your standard 'Man is the disease' types."

"Ah. Right. I've given up on even trying to keep the lingo straight. You think these nutjobs are a genuine threat?"

"Hard to say. The press likes to paint them as death cultists, because sensationalism generates clicks. They tend to fancy themselves radical environmentalists who believe the planet would be better off without us. But the truth is, most of them are disaffected white kids trying nihilism on for size. Still, with the anniversary of 8/17 right around the corner, I'm keeping my ear to the ground."

"Please do," Whitmore said. "I may be termed out, but I've still got a legacy to protect, and I'll be damned before I hand the keys over to the likes of Rask. That means we can't afford another shitshow like this border mess."

On that, he and Lionel agreed.

There was a knock at the door, after which Lionel's chief of staff, Noel Coughlin, poked his head into the room. "Excuse me, Director?"

Lionel waved him over — a horrific breach of protocol in the presence of the president, much less inside the president's private quarters. Whitmore, for his part, seemed to neither notice nor care.

Coughlin, a reedy man with wire-rimmed glasses and busy hands, leaned over and whispered in Lionel's ear. Lionel nodded and then stood.

"Is something wrong?" Whitmore asked.

"Nothing you need concern yourself with, Mr. President," Lionel replied mildly, although internally, he was far from calm. "But I'm afraid I have to go."

He turned and headed for the door without waiting for the president to dismiss him. Whitmore once more failed to register the slight.

When I'm president, Lionel thought on his way out, *I'll fire anyone who treats me half as disrespectfully.*

WE CONTAIN MULTITUDES

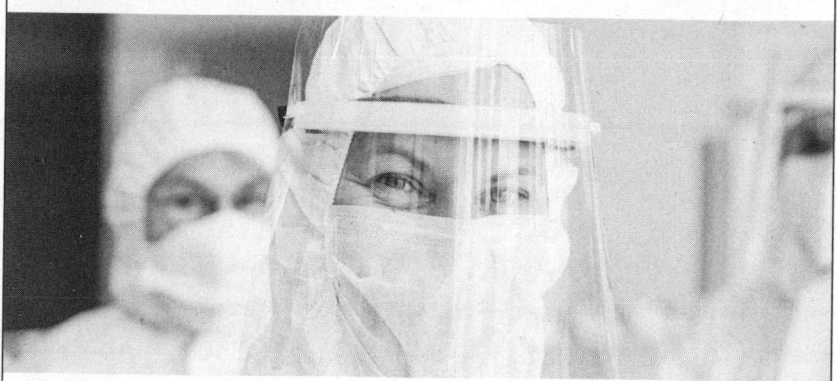

Did you know that more than half of the cells in your body aren't human?

It's true! Each of us is home to a thriving ecosystem of microorganisms known as a microbiota. Your microbiota is influenced by where you live, what you eat, and the people you spend time with—which makes it as unique as a fingerprint.

A healthy microbiota aids digestion, improves mood, and even protects against disease. That's why the wellness experts at PROTX are committed to unlocking its full potential. It's one of many ways we're working toward a better tomorrow. To learn more, ask your virtual assistant about PROTX.

PROTX: WORKING TOWARD A BETTER TOMORROW

7.

Jake watched in silence as crime scene technicians removed blackened corpses from the heap with almost ritual care. Though Amy knew the trail grew colder with every passing minute, she resisted the urge to hurry him along. The scene had taken her some time to wrap her head around as well.

When he finally spoke, Jake's voice was hoarse with emotion. "How many vics?"

"Our best guess, based on the population of the village and the size of the fire, is somewhere in the ballpark of one hundred, but it'll be a while before we know for sure. Whoever did this used a lot of accelerant. The bodies at the bottom are little more than ash and bone."

"Why can't we just take a head count of the remaining residents and see who's missing?"

Had any of Amy's prior partners asked that question, she would've assumed they meant it condescendingly. Thanks to her faith, her gender, and the color of her skin, a lot of guys on the force blamed affirmative action for Amy's rapid ascent to detective and assumed she couldn't pull her weight.

Jake was different. He respected Amy's intellect and instincts. He didn't waste time needling or second-guessing her. If he was asking, it's because he genuinely wanted to know. That's why, despite the bind he put her in by flaking out this morning, she'd cut him a little slack—and why she hadn't pressed him when he refused to tell her what was wrong.

"We're having trouble getting ahold of someone with access to camp records, on account of it's a weekend," Amy replied, "and a proper census is going to take time. There's almost a hundred twenty acres to cover, and many of the residents are understandably squirrelly today."

"Can't say I blame them. If I were in their shoes, I'd have a dim view of authority figures too." Jake's gaze traveled to a nearby utility pole, which was topped with a pair of loudspeakers, a bank of floodlights, and a solar-powered security camera. "You take a look at the surveillance feeds yet?"

"Funny thing about that," Amy said. "Every camera in the park went dead at three fifteen last night, and when we finally got them back online, we discovered their hard drives had been wiped. Some kind of computer virus, I'm told."

"You're right," Jake deadpanned, "that's hilarious. What about witnesses?"

"Obviously, we're questioning every resident we can find, and I've got unis"—cop slang for uniformed officers—"canvassing nearby buildings with a view of the park, but so far, nada. Could be people are scared. Could be they legitimately didn't see anything. Whoever killed the cameras cut the lights as well."

"Sounds like the perpetrators knew exactly what they were doing," Jake said.

"You thinking inside job?"

"Right now, I'm just thinking. You?"

"Can't say it hasn't crossed my mind."

"I'm guessing the perps entered via the southwest gate?"

"Looks that way," Amy replied.

"What about the guard? When I rode by, I didn't see a body. Has anyone talked to him?"

"I wish. He's nowhere to be found."

"You think he's in the wind?"

"Either that or in the pile."

A police drone skimmed above the treetops, taking photographs and lidar images of the crime scene below. Jake watched it thoughtfully for a moment, eyes narrowing behind his safety goggles.

"You check traffic cams to see if any caught these assholes coming or going?"

"No, because I was born yesterday on the back of a turnip truck. They went dead last night too, as did the CCTV feeds for every bridge and tunnel onto the island."

Jake sighed. "Of course they did."

"I sent unis to scour footage from the outer boroughs and looped in local PDs in Newport, Weehawken, and Fort Lee to do the same. Maybe we'll get lucky."

"Maybe," Jake said without conviction. "You like anybody for this?"

"Hard to say. I'm of a couple minds. My first thought, when I saw the burning bodies, was death squad—but the wiped hard drives argue otherwise. I mean, when's the last time you saw a frightened mob pull off anything that slick? Then I started wondering if it was an act of terror, but if so, who are they trying to terrify? Awful as it sounds, most New Yorkers see these people as a burden, and wouldn't be too broken up if the whole camp burned. And there's another thing I just can't square."

"What's that?"

"Death squads burn the sick because they're worried about infection, but—"

"—whoever did this also tossed the victims' stuff." Jake's eyes widened as he completed Amy's thought.

"Bingo."

"So, okay, they were looking for something."

"Yeah, but these people live in squalor. What could they possibly have worth killing for, much less make ransacking their belongings worth the risk?"

"Beats me. I just got here." Jake attempted a smile, but it flickered out as soon as it appeared—and anyway, his mask rendered the expression moot.

A small flatbed truck emerged from the smoke and braked to a halt beside the pyre. Two crime scene techs began to load it up with body bags, their brisk efficiency suggesting no shortage of practice. When the bed was full, one of them banged on the roof of the cab, and the driver headed back the way he came.

"Where are they taking those?" Jake asked.

"An empty warehouse across the Meadow. We aren't legally allowed to remove the bodies from the premises until the medical examiner certifies that they pose no public health risk, and we couldn't very well just leave them here."

"Who drew the short straw at the ME's office?"

"Nguyen."

"You two chat yet?"

"What, and let you miss out on *all* the fun?" Amy tried a smile of her own. It went about as well as Jake's had.

"Gee, thanks." Jake sighed. "I suppose we may as well go get this over with."

The warehouse was a large windowless box of cinder block and corrugated steel, both painted taupe, with a rooftop full of idle air conditioners, and oversized bay doors on either end. It was nestled in the southwest corner of the encampment's grounds, far from the administrative offices and remaining settlements, although its bland utilitarian design would have appeared more at home in any suburban industrial park. Unlike the other buildings in the camp—which, in an abortive but officially sanctioned beautification effort, the residents had blanketed with elaborate murals—the warehouse's exterior featured only the occasional, tentative graffito.

Nearly fifteen thousand souls were stranded without shelter when Manhattan was quarantined in the aftermath of the 8/17 attack. Most of them took refuge in what's now known as Park City. Many developed symptoms of pneumonic plague soon after. FEMA brought in mobile patient-isolation units to house the sick, but their HVAC filtration systems were quickly overwhelmed by the summer heat, so a structure was erected to protect them. Residents soon dubbed it the Farm because, like beloved childhood pets, no one sent there ever returned.

Six months after the outbreak ended, the private contractor that took over management of the camp built a proper health center on the former site of Tavern on the Green's South Terrace. Once it was up and running, the isolation units—too contaminated for repurposing—were destroyed, and the Farm was decommissioned.

Until this morning, it hadn't been used since.

Although the bay doors were open, the air inside the warehouse reeked of burned hair, rendered fat, and hydrocarbons. Lights in wire cages dangled from steel rafters high above. The floor was sealed concrete, glossy mostly, but worn dull in regular rectangles where the isolation units had once rested. Today, the space was dominated by dozens of body bags, arranged in loose concentric circles.

Dr. Xuan Nguyen was supervising the unloading of the flatbed truck when Jake and Amy arrived. Jake caught Nguyen's attention with a halfhearted wave, and Nguyen shuffled over, hazmat booties rasping against the floor.

"Morning, doc."

"Is it still?" they replied, yawning. "I feel as if I've been here for days."

"I hear you." Amy gestured toward the body bags. "What's all this about?"

"We're trying to re-create the scene as best we can. Blood spatter indicates that most of the vics were killed in or near their shelters, then dragged and stacked. The bodies are so badly burned, we won't know who lived where until our PCR results come back. Based on the overlapping drag marks, however, it's safe to assume that those closest to the square were brought there first, and those farther away were piled atop them, so we're arranging the remains based on the order in which they were removed."

"You're saying they were dead before the fire was lit?" Jake asked.

"Looks like."

"What's the preliminary cause of death?"

"It varies. Some had their throats slit. Others were shot. At least two bodies exhibit signs of torture—fingers broken, teeth extracted, hands and feet denailed—but it's unclear, at present, if those injuries were severe enough to do them in."

"Jesus," Jake muttered.

"Yeah. It's not pretty."

"Awfully risky of the perps to put themselves in such close contact with the vics' bodily fluids," Amy said.

"You'd think, wouldn't you? Then again, maybe they knew something that you don't."

"Such as?"

"Whenever my office responds to a call, our first order of business is ascertaining the health risk any bodies and/or fluids might pose. As such, we run a series of diagnostic field tests to screen for common infections. Now, they're not perfect, but they give us a ballpark idea of what we're dealing with, and . . ." Nguyen trailed off, momentarily lost for words.

"And what?" This from Jake.

"So far, it appears none of the victims were sick."

"I don't understand," Amy said. "Nearly half the city's sick with *something*, and most of them have indoor plumbing at their disposal. How'd these guys manage to beat the odds?"

"That's just it. It makes no sense."

"And yet," Jake said.

"And yet," Nguyen agreed.

Amy frowned. "Are you sure the tests are accurate?"

"Quite. The control samples are functioning as expected, and our baseline employee screening, which the DBS requires us to administer prior to processing any scene, revealed three latent infections of which my staff were unaware."

"What about the camp's remaining residents? Are they healthy too?"

"I asked myself that same question, which is why I instructed my people to test several volunteers from elsewhere in the camp. They exhibited as many illnesses as you'd expect. Whatever kept our victims healthy appears to have been specific to this village, much like the attack itself."

The flatbed truck, now empty of cargo, backed out of the warehouse, beeping.

Nguyen sighed.

"You'll have to forgive me, but I need to get this batch of bodies sorted before the next load arrives."

"Of course," Amy replied. "If you find anything else of interest, please let us know."

"I'll do that."

"So," Jake said to her as Nguyen left, "we've got a mass grave in a filthy slum, and a bunch of vics who died in perfect health."

"Seems like whoever did this *knew* they were healthy, and burned the bodies in an attempt to obscure that fact."

"Sure does."

"The question is, what prevented our vics from getting sick? Were they sitting on some kind of miracle cure? And if so, why keep it secret when it could save countless lives, not to mention make them rich?"

"Beats me," Jake replied, "but whatever they were hiding, *somebody* found out, and will obviously do anything to get their hands on it."

"Will?" Amy asked. "What makes you think it's not in their possession already?"

"Maybe twice a week, I lose my wallet, and wind up tossing my apartment trying to find it. Thing is, once I do, I stop looking—"

"—but this village has been razed to the ground," Amy finished. "So, okay, where'd it go?"

"I don't know—but wherever it is, I'm betting our perpetrators aren't far behind."

8.

The city looked nothing like Mat remembered.

His first glimpse of New York was through a scratched oval of plexiglass as his flight descended toward Newark—a place that he knew nothing about, where he'd be living with an uncle he'd never met.

Mat, who was eight at the time, had never been on a plane before, much less flown unaccompanied. Although his case worker at the Office of Refugee Resettlement had assured him it was perfectly safe, every clank and ding made his heart race, and his guts churned with every tilt and dip.

Then Manhattan swung into view, its skyline gilded by the morning sun, and Mat had smiled despite himself.

Still, adjusting to his new reality wasn't easy. The grueling journey northward—and everything he'd lost along the way—had left Mat sullen, traumatized, withdrawn. If it hadn't been for his uncle, Gabriel, he might never have recovered.

Gabriel took note of Mat's fascination with the city, and brought him whenever their respective schedules allowed. They bonded over pastrami at Katz's, hot dogs at Feltman's, pizza at Di Fara. Cracked jokes in Spanish as they walked the High Line, an elevated park perched atop a disused railroad spur. Marveled at the treasures in the Museum of Natural History, the Guggenheim, the Met.

When Gabriel scored cheap tickets to a Friday matinee of *Black Panther* on Broadway, Mat couldn't believe his luck. Online lottery aside, the show was sold out for months. The two of them watched, rapt, from the second row, and emerged from the theater buzzing— only to find Midtown engulfed in chaos. Mass transit had been suspended. Roadblocks prevented access to tunnels and bridges. Armed men in hazmat suits patrolled the streets.

Rumors spread like wildfire, like disease.

Of a dirty bomb. Of sarin gas.

Of plague.

Mat and Gabriel were instructed, via bullhorn, to make their way to Central Park's Sheep Meadow, where temporary housing was being set up for those stranded by the quarantine. Once it was lifted, said the tinny disembodied voice, they'd be free to go.

That was three years ago. Mat hadn't set foot outside the park again until today.

He worried Gabriel would never get the chance.

After Brutsch's attack, the city's population plummeted, and no borough was hit harder than Manhattan. The subway system, already in a horrendous state of disrepair, was consolidated, and several lines retired. Once-vibrant neighborhoods withered and died. Entire city blocks were abandoned to the squatters and the rats.

Mat was shocked how precipitously Tribeca had declined. It used to be a playground for wealthy hipsters, but now its pricey lofts sat derelict and empty, and many of its storefronts were boarded up. Trendy bistros and boutiques had given way to pawn shops and payday lenders. Several buildings within sight were nothing more than burned-out husks.

Automobile traffic in the neighborhood was light, but peddlers lined the sidewalks, displaying their wares on blankets and card tables. Prostitutes, driven offline by sex-trafficking laws, vied for corner space with drug dealers. Beggars held out hands toward any-one who happened by, their faces caved in by disease.

Mat had cleaned himself up in the city truck that Brian drove for work. Because the truck was equipped with GPS, they'd ditched it two blocks north of Canal Street and entered the neighborhood on foot—Brian leading, Mat following several paces behind. Brian claimed that he was leery of being seen with Mat because an older white guy and a young mestizo kid made for a conspicuous pair. Mat thought that he was way more likely to attract attention walking alone, but he was so afraid that Brian might abandon him, he didn't dare complain.

After three years in Park City, the streets were far too crowded and chaotic for Mat's liking. He felt like every passerby was staring at him, like he'd be recognized and reported any minute. He did his best to avoid eye contact and tried to hide his face from any cameras in sight, but there were so many to keep track of. They perched on streetlights and huddled beneath cornices. They lurked inside cell phones, smart cars, and ATMs.

Mat knew what Gabriel would say if he were here—*head down, eyes up, ears open*—but it's tough to fade into the background when the hand-me-downs you're wearing make you feel like a circus clown. The shirt, a faded Giants tee purchased long before the NFL dis-banded, hung to his knees and left his collarbones exposed. The jeans scuffed along the pavement when he walked, even though he'd belted them and rolled them up. And all the shoes Brian had brought along were way too big for Mat to wear, so he remained barefoot, which forced him to watch where he stepped.

They'd been winding through Tribeca for a while, Brian peering at the numbers on the buildings they passed. When he led them down the same street for a third time, Mat sighed. Then, without warning,

Brian reversed course so quickly, he had to grab Mat by the shoulders to keep them from colliding.

"What's wrong?" Mat asked, alarmed.

"Wrong? Nothing's wrong! We're here."

The brittle enthusiasm of Brian's tone grated on Mat's nerves. He regarded the dilapidated building Brian had brought him to with suspicion. Seven stories of mottled gray brick that slouched menacingly on a corner lot, it might not have been the shittiest on the block, but it was definitely a contender. Water-stained plywood covered many of its windows. Shattered glass and fallen masonry littered the ground outside. The front stoop was crumbling and uneven. Its double doors hung crooked and gapped slightly, revealing the fact that they were padlocked from the inside.

"Are you sure?"

"Sure I'm sure," Brian said. "Just hang back a minute while I call my cousin so he can let us in, okay?"

"Okay." Mat's tone betrayed his skepticism.

"Hey. Don't worry. Everything is gonna be just fine. I promise."

For all his bluster, Brian sounded twice as nervous as Mat felt.

Mat couldn't help but wonder which of them he was trying to convince.

9.

Peter Levy eyed Amy from across the tiny conference-room table. Perspiration darkened the armpits of his brown-on-brown security uniform. His fingers tapped the cheap woodgrain.

"Should I, uh, call my union rep?" Levy swallowed hard and looked from Amy to Jake, who stood leaning against the wall behind her. "Or a lawyer?"

"That's up to you, Peter," Amy said, her voice soft, her expression warm, "but understand that it'll change the tenor of our conversation. Right now, we're just talking—one law enforcement agent to another."

"Pete," Levy said, flashing a smile that came off pained. "My friends call me Pete." He placed one hand atop the other and his tapping ceased. Beneath the table, his knee began to bounce.

Levy worked for Cerberus Correctional Services, the private security firm that managed the Park City encampment. As CCS's name implied, prisons and juvenile detention centers comprised the bulk of its business.

According to his file, Levy had been with CCS for fourteen months. In that time, he'd proven himself to be an adequate, if undistinguished, employee. He'd been a C student in high school and had twice failed his NYPD entrance exam before going the rent-a-cop route. Amy had seen his type a thousand times—and been resented by at least half of them. The only remarkable thing about him was that he wasn't dead, given that he was stationed at Park City's southwest gate at the time of last night's incursion.

Forty-five minutes ago, Levy was found wandering the camp in a daze, his face and clothes caked with ash. Once he'd been photographed, swabbed, and disinfected, a pair of unis escorted him back to the administrative building for questioning. For sanitary reasons, guards were forbidden from wearing their work clothes off premises, so the facility was well stocked with uniforms. Levy was given a clean one to change into.

His gun, however, was not returned.

Amy responded to Levy's smile with one of her own. "Pete it is. Why don't you walk us through what happened last night, Pete?"

"There's not much to tell," he said. "For the most part, my shift was pretty quiet."

"If your shift was quiet, Pete, then why the hell did you abandon your post?" Jake used his name as if it were an epithet.

"I didn't abandon anything! I was, uh, reconnoitering the perimeter."

"Reconnoitering the perimeter?"

"Yeah."

"Why?" Jake asked.

"I...thought I saw somebody slinking around inside the park."

Amy struggled to maintain a benign expression. She was sorely tempted to roll her eyes. Levy was an artless liar. She could practically hear the gears turning in his head.

Jake, beside her, scoffed. "Didn't you just say your shift was pretty quiet?"

"I did! I mean, it *was*." Levy sighed, collected himself, and tried again. "Look, tenants aren't supposed to be out after curfew, but the fact is, they sneak out all the time. Usually, we let it go, but last week, management sent out a memo saying they wanted to crack down on people smuggling contraband into the park."

"What kind of contraband?"

"All kinds of stuff," Levy replied. "Drugs. Twinkies. Handheld gaming systems. These people get bored, you know? So when I saw, or thought I saw, somebody walking around, I figured I'd better go check it out."

"Protocol dictates you radio your superior before leaving the booth, right?"

"That's right."

"So, did you?"

"No."

"Why not?"

"I dunno. I guess I didn't want to look stupid if it turned out to be nothing."

Jake frowned. "Tell me you remembered to lock the booth behind you, at least."

Levy feigned indignance, poorly. "Of course!"

"Pete," Amy said gently, "why don't you tell us what happened after you left the guard booth?"

"I...I don't remember."

"You don't remember?"

"Believe me," Levy said, "I wish I did. Best I can figure it, some-body must've jumped me from behind and choked me out."

"Here's the thing, Pete. I *don't* believe you. See, we've got footage that proves you're full of shit."

For the briefest moment, Amy held her breath. This was the moment they'd been building toward. A bluff, of course, but Levy had no way of knowing that.

"What? How? I thought the cameras—"

"Went dark? Yeah, they did, although I'd be very interested to hear how you know that, since we sure as hell didn't tell you. Thing is, while your friends managed to blank all the cameras in the park, they failed to account for the CCTV feeds of the buildings across the street."

Levy's face fell. "I...I didn't—"

"Didn't what? Didn't know what you were signing on for when you agreed to let them in? Didn't think that you'd get caught? At least a hundred people died horribly thanks to you. It turns my stomach that I still don't know the exact number—it feels, I dunno, disrespectful—but they were so badly burned, we've been forced to count the skulls as we collect them. You wanna hear something funny? For a while, we thought we'd find you in the pile too. That you died trying to protect the people in your charge. But you're no hero, are you, Pete? You're just a venal little shit who looked the other way to line his pockets."

"It wasn't like that." Levy's voice was small and childlike. His gaze never left the surface of the table.

Amy placed her hand on his forearm reassuringly. "Then tell us, Pete. What was it like?"

"For starters, I had no idea...I mean, they never told me they were gonna..."

Tears spilled down Levy's cheeks. His body was racked with sobs. Amy let the moment stretch and then uttered one careful, quiet syllable, as gentle as a lullaby: "Who?"

Levy's eyes went wide, as if he hadn't realized until just that moment what he'd let slip. "No one," he said. "I mean, I don't know."

"It's a little late to walk that back now, Pete."

Amy flashed Jake a warning look. He eased off. Gave her space to do her thing.

"You know what *I* think?" This from Amy. "I think you *do* know, but you're too frightened of what they'll do to you if you tell us."

"It's not just me I'm worried about," Levy said.

"What do you mean? Did they threaten someone close to you?"

Levy nodded. Teardrops smacked against the laminate table.

"My mother."

"Imagine what it will do to her when she finds out her son is an accessory to mass murder."

Amy hadn't changed her tone, but her words detonated inside Levy's head regardless.

"Mass murder? But all I did was leave a door open!"

"That's more than enough for a jury to convict," Amy said. "But it's not too late for you to make this right."

"How?"

"By telling us everything you know about the people who hired you."

Levy licked his lips. Beads of sweat ran down his face and mingled with his tears. He nodded toward the conference room door, toward the uniformed officers standing just outside the double panes of crosshatched safety glass. "Could I, uh, get a glass of water first?"

"Of course," Amy replied. She and Jake exchanged a glance, after which he opened the door a crack and relayed Levy's request to the officers outside.

A few moments later, one of the officers entered the room with a paper cup of water in his hand. When he saw it, Levy—hoping, Amy later realized, for real glass—deflated. Then he tensed and lunged.

Amy had to give it to him: Levy might not be the brightest bulb, but he was fast. A human blur, he slid across the table, grabbed the officer by the throat with his right hand, and removed the young man's sidearm from its holster with his left.

Amy kicked back her chair and drew her service weapon. Jake, beside her, drew his too. Both were Glock 17s, identical to the one the uni carried, the one in Levy's hand.

They too were fast, but not quite fast enough; Levy ducked behind his hostage, robbing them of a clean shot.

"Tell my mother that I'm sorry," he said.

Then—Jake and Amy screaming "NO!"—Levy put the gun to his own temple and pulled the trigger.

10.

"For God's sake, Lucas! I don't have time for your bullshit today. Just get down here and unlock the fucking door!"

Brian reddened as he yelled at the man on his cell phone's screen. A nearby street vendor scowled at him. Several passersby swung wide. Mat, who loitered a few paces away, fixed his gaze on the sidewalk at his feet.

"Easy, cuz," Lucas Hanley replied. "If I was you, I'd be real careful about issuing demands. You came to me, remember? And since I haven't heard from you in I don't even know how long, I think I'm entitled to know why before I let you in."

Though they couldn't be more than a hundred yards from one another, their connection was so tenuous that the audio lagged, creating awkward pauses in their conversation, and the video kept glitching. Brian figured Lucas must've somehow rigged his phone so that his calls couldn't be traced. Even as a child, his cousin had a knack for gadgets, and twenty years of petty crime had made him paranoid.

"You're right," Brian said, softening his tone by force of will. "I'm sorry. I promise, I'll explain everything as soon as you let us in."

"*Us?* What do you mean, *us?* Who the hell did you bring with you, Brian?"

"Like I said, if you'd just—"

"—let some stranger into my building, sight unseen? Not fucking likely, dude. You wanna come inside, you're gonna hafta prove you didn't bring the five-oh to my door."

"Jesus, Lucas, do you even hear yourself? I'm a sewer worker. Why on earth would I show up with the police?"

"Hey, you tell me."

"You know what? Fine. If it'll make you feel better, I'll play along." Brian snapped his fingers and waved Mat over. Then he held the phone so that Lucas could see him. "Does he look like a cop to you?"

"Uh, Brian—whose fucking kid is that?"

"Long story."

"Does that story involve you...*taking* him?"

"What? No! I'm just helping out a buddy in a bind. Now would you please come let us in?"

"Shut up a sec, would you? I need to think." Lucas set down his phone, filling Brian's screen with grainy black. As soon as Brian began to wonder whether Lucas had forgotten about them, he returned. "Okay, fine," he said. "I'll be right down."

A few agonizing minutes later, Brian's cousin appeared in the gap between the broken double doors. They'd been pried open at some point, their latching mechanism destroyed, and now bent outward where they once joined. A steel chain, looped around the inside handles and fastened with a heavy padlock, prevented them from swinging open more than a few inches. Lucas unlocked it with a key that hung around his neck, removed the chain, and yanked the doors wide.

"Well? You two coming in, or what? I ain't gonna leave this open all day."

Mat and Brian trotted up the crumbling steps and through the open doors. Lucas reaffixed the padlock as soon as they were inside.

Even in the dim light of the squat's lobby, Lucas looked worse than Brian remembered, pallid and dope-skinny. Truth be told, he didn't smell too good, either, his breath and sweat tinged with the pungent scent of methamphetamine. He wore a dingy pair of matchstick jeans and a sleeveless undershirt yellowed at the edges. His lank hair had been cut into a haphazard mohawk some time ago and left to grow out. His eyes were sunken and bloodshot, the flesh around them the color of a fading bruise.

"Sorry for the runaround," he said, "but me and mine can never be too careful. We ain't exactly paying rent on this place, and some of our business is...delicate."

"Delicate?" Mat asked.

"He means illegal."

"No, I mean *delicate*—but that don't mean it ain't both." Lucas winked at Mat conspiratorially. "So, kid, you got a name?"

When Mat hesitated, Brian said, "*Kid* is fine for now."

"Suit yourself," Lucas replied. "You know he ain't got no shoes on, right?"

"Gee, I hadn't noticed. Thanks for calling it to my attention."

"There's no need to get snippy, dude. I thought maybe I could help, is all. What size shoe you take, kid?"

Mat looked to Brian, who nodded encouragingly. "Seven, I guess. Sometimes seven and a half."

"But a grown-up seven, right? Not, like, kid-sized or whatever?"

"Yeah," Mat replied. "I'm twelve," he added, as if that clarified anything.

Lucas smiled. "Cool. I can work with that. Follow me."

He led them down a winding hallway strung with fairy lights past a series of doorless rooms. Some were original to the building, while others had been carved out via haphazard demolition that exposed wiring and the occasional load-bearing support. One held nothing but an enormous pile of broken furniture, stacked like Tetris pieces from floor to ceiling. In another, cheap metal utility shelves were stocked with lab equipment and chemicals in brown glass jugs. The largest of the rooms they passed was crammed with grubby men and women hunched over jury-rigged computers, some typing furiously in chat windows, others engaged in heated conversations with the angry voices emanating from their headsets. One of them—a burly guy whose face was knotted with bluish scar tissue from eyebrow to jaw, the result of an infected tattoo—scowled at Mat and Brian as they shuffled by.

"Lucas," Brian said, "what is this place?"

"Impressive, huh? Especially considering we're totally off-grid. I wired the building for solar myself."

"That's not really what I meant."

"Oh." Lucas's face fell. "We like to think of ourselves as a crypto-anarchist collective."

"Yeah? Do all crypto-anarchist collectives make their money cooking meth and running malware scams?"

"Hey, man, we're just trying to get by, the same as anybody. Besides, it's not like you're in any position to judge."

"What's that supposed to mean?"

"Calm down. All I'm saying is, if you were on the right side of the law, you wouldn't be here."

That was fair enough, Brian supposed. Still, he and Lucas used to be close, so it sucked to see how far his cousin had fallen.

Eventually, they came to a room stacked high with stolen goods: toys, clothes, jewelry, electronics. Some were in their original packaging. Others were clearly used. Along one wall were dozens of shoe boxes from a variety of brands. Vans. Nike. Adidas. Balenciaga. Lucas gestured toward them with a flourish and said, "Help yourself, kid!"

"Really?" For a moment, in his unbridled excitement, Mat looked like a typical twelve-year-old. "Thanks!"

Mat combed through the boxes and made a stack of any shoes that might fit him. Lucas watched with obvious amusement. Brian, beside him, fidgeted uncomfortably.

"So this stuff, what? Fell off the back of a truck?"

"Sure, if it'll help you sleep at night." Lucas shrugged. "But either way, the kid needs shoes."

"Listen, Lucas... I've got a favor to ask of you."

As the words left Brian's mouth, a young woman with glazed eyes stumbled into the room and began slipping jewelry on at random.

"Not here," Lucas muttered. "Once the kid's finished, I'll take you two somewhere private so we can talk."

Mat eventually settled on a pair of multicolored Nikes that looked ridiculous to Brian and probably cost more than a month's rent. Once he'd put them on, Lucas—apologizing that the building's solar panels didn't generate enough electricity to power the elevators—led them to a stairwell, and they began to climb.

Brian was grateful that Lucas had given Mat shoes first, because the stairwell was littered with broken glass and discarded needles. The landings' vinyl flooring was buckled and uneven, creating depressions in which mysterious puddles pooled. Here and there, junkies too far gone to worry about blood poisoning nodded off, the track marks on their forearms angry red.

Lucas's room was on the fifth floor. Padlocked, like the doors downstairs, and likewise unlocked with a key that Lucas wore around his neck. A former office, by the look of it, no more than eight by ten. A bare mattress pocked with cigarette burns lay against the left-hand wall, a tablet computer atop it, liquor bottles scattered all around. On the wall opposite the door was a window, beneath which was a camp stove, saucepan, and several cans of soup. In lieu of blinds or curtains, an old beach towel blocked the light of day from coming through.

"Make yourself at home. Mi shithole es su shithole." Lucas brushed the towel aside, fetching a pack of cigarettes and a tarnished Zippo from the windowsill. He struck one up and took a drag, his

71

gaze drawn momentarily to the street below. "Now, you wanna tell me what the hell you two are doing here?"

Brian fished his phone and a pair of earbuds from his pocket and handed them to Mat. "Entertain yourself for a few minutes, would you, buddy? Me and Lucas have some business to discuss."

Mat glowered at him. "You know I'm not a baby, right?"

"I never said you were!"

"No, you're just *treating* me like one."

"C'mon. That's not fair."

"I'm just saying, if Gabriel was here—"

"Yeah, well, Gabriel's not here, is he?!"

Brian regretted the words the moment they left his mouth.

Anguish warped Mat's features. Tears sprung up in his eyes.

"I'm sorry," Brian said. "I didn't…"

But he let the sentence die on his lips, because Mat stuffed the earbuds into his ears and flopped onto the bed, his gaze boring a hole in the phone's screen.

"Touchy kid," Lucas muttered.

"He's had a rough day," Brian replied. "We both have."

"You said you had something to ask me?"

Brian wiped his hands on his pants, leaving streaks of sweat on either thigh. "Yeah, but first, you have to promise me you'll keep this to yourself. If anyone were to catch wind—"

"Hey. We're family. You have my word."

Brian hesitated. Took a deep breath. Then dove in. "The kid's name is Mat. He and his uncle Gabriel are friends of mine from my Park City days. In fact, I owe them my life. If it weren't for them, I never would have survived the camp, much less been released. Anyway, last time I talked to Gabe, he made me promise that if anything were to happen to him, I'd deliver Mat to the Resistance."

"You're shitting me." Lucas's eyes widened. "The Resistance?"

"Yeah."

"Why?"

"I dunno," Brian lied. "I never asked."

Family or not, there were limits to his trust.

Lucas filled his lungs with smoke again, then exhaled slowly. "I still don't get what you're doing *here*."

"The truth is," Brian said, dropping his voice to ensure Mat couldn't overhear, "I'm out of my goddamn depth, and you're the only person I can think of who might be in a position to throw me a line."

"Yeah? How do you figure?"

"I haven't the faintest idea how to contact the Resistance—I mean, they're criminals, so it's not like I can just google—but I'm willing to bet *you* do."

"Maybe I do," Lucas demurred, "and maybe I don't."

"Meaning what?"

"Meaning it depends on what you're willing to offer me for my trouble."

"Are you serious?"

"As pneumonic plague." Lucas peeked around his makeshift curtain again. "Sure, you and me go way back, but you've gotta understand what you're asking. The guys you're looking for ain't just criminals, they're enemies of the fucking state, and my record ain't exactly squeaky clean to begin with. I get caught consorting with the likes of them, I'll probably land my ass in some government black site with no hope of ever getting out."

"I'm not asking you to *consort* with anybody. All I want is a way to contact them. And why the hell do you keep looking out the window?"

Lucas, chastened, let the towel fall. "It's just, I dunno, a nervous habit."

"Uh, Brian?" Mat said, too quietly for it to register.

"A nervous habit, huh? What, exactly, are you so nervous about?"

"Brian?" Mat repeated.

"Easy, dude. You're getting squirrelly. Jumping at shadows. Seems like maybe you ain't cut out for a life of crime."

"*BRIAN!*"

"Jesus, Mat—what is it?"

"We have a problem. I was trying to find out about last night's attack, but there was nothing on the news feeds, so I checked social media. That's when I saw this."

He handed Brian the phone. On it was a Trill profile—no bio, no avatar—comprising dozens of identical posts, each time-stamped five minutes after the last, that read: *H4VE Y0U $EEN MY B0Y? 4PPR0X. F1VE F33T T4LL. BL4CK H41R. BR0WN EYE$. M1XED/MED1UM BR0WN $K1N. L4ST $EEN 1N M1DT0WN M4NH4TT4N. N0 P0L1CE. $l00,o0O REW4RD F0R 1NF0RM4T10N LE4D1NG T0 $4FE R3TURN*, followed by a phone number, a URL, and a slew of local subject tags.

"I don't get it. What the hell am I looking at?"

"It's a spam account, brand new today. There are others like it on Locus and Bangarang. All they do is post the same thing over and over. By now, half the city must've seen it."

"Did you look up the phone number?"

"Yeah. It's a VOIP. Disposable, probably."

"And the link?"

"Sent me to an online banking thingy I didn't really understand," Mat replied. "I think it started with an *E*."

"Escrow?"

"Yeah, that's it! What's it mean?"

"In this case, I think it's supposed to prove whoever's behind those posts has enough money set aside to cover the reward." Angry blotches spread up Brian's neck. "Lucas, tell me you didn't do what I think you did."

For a moment, his cousin looked as if he might deny it. Then his face dropped and his shoulders sagged. "Sorry, cuz. I wish I could. I made the call before I came downstairs to let you in. Guy I talked to said to keep you busy until they arrived."

"You son of a bitch. You sold me out!"

Brian grabbed Lucas by his sweat-stained tee and drove him backward into the wall.

The camp stove toppled. Soup cans scattered across the floor.

Lucas flailed, yanking down the towel in the process. Daylight flooded the room.

"But they're not even after you!" he protested. "All they want is the kid!"

"That's supposed to make me feel better?"

"Hey, it's nothing personal. Like I said, me and mine are just trying to get by — and a hundred grand buys an awful lot of getting by."

"Only if you're alive to spend it, dipshit."

"What are you talking about?"

"Jesus! You really think the dude you talked to is a concerned parent? Because I promise you, he's not. He is, however, almost certainly one of the guys who set fire to Park City last night. You figure when he shows up at your shithole squat full of druggies and burnouts, he's gonna knock politely?"

"Crypto-anarchists," Lucas insisted.

"Tell 'em that. I'm sure you'll be just fine." Brian released Lucas, who slumped against the windowsill. "C'mon, Mat. We're leaving."

"You're too late," Lucas said. Brian followed his gaze through the bare window as a pair of large black SUVs screeched to a halt at the intersection outside. "They're here."

11.

"Listen, Cap –"

"I'm sorry, Detective," Ian Bavitz snapped, "but what part of 'in my office' did you not understand?"

The bullpen fell silent. Every cop in earshot looked their way. Jake, face burning from the sudden attention, raised his hands in surrender and followed Amy into their captain's office. Ian fell in behind them and slammed the door so hard, it knocked the pictures on the wall askew.

Ian gestured to the two chairs opposite his desk. "Sit."

Once they complied, Ian rounded the desk and dropped heavily into his own chair.

"Now," he said, "you wanna tell me how the hell you could've let this happen?"

In the bullpen, the captain's indignation had boiled over, but now he'd dialed it back to a simmer, delivering the question in an angry monotone that Jake struggled to decipher over the ringing in his ears.

In the frenzied moments before Levy pulled the trigger, Jake's veins had coursed with adrenaline. He'd long since crashed. Now his head ached and his nerves jangled. Pinpricks of dried blood spatter made his skin itch. A smell like spent fireworks clung to the inside of his nostrils.

"There's not much to say," Jake replied. "We were questioning the suspect. When he realized Hassan had tripped him up, he panicked."

"That's it?"

"That's it," Amy confirmed. "The fact is, sir, neither Gibson nor I thought that Levy posed a threat, to himself or anyone else, until it was too late."

Ian nudged the items on his desk into square, a nervous habit.

"I'm not sure you two understand the world of shit you're in. Park City is a jurisdictional nightmare, not to mention a political land mine, so this investigation has been under a microscope from the outset. Now add to that the fact that our only goddamn suspect died in custody. Top brass is pissed. Rival agencies are sharpening their knives. I'm doing my best to shield you from the blowback, but you've got to help me out a little. Did Levy give you *anything* before he offed himself?"

"Obviously, the guy was terrified," Amy said. "He claimed the perpetrators threatened him and his mother both, so we're digging into them to see if any pressure points leap out. Maybe it'll give us a handle on how Levy wound up on our perps' radar. We're also combing through Levy's financials to see if they offered him a carrot as well as a stick."

"That's not much," the captain replied.

"It's what we've got," Jake said.

Ian closed his eyes, set his glasses on his desk, and pinched the bridge of his nose. "Christ, what a mess. Valente pissed himself when Levy pulled the trigger, you know. Thought he was a goner, I guess. Kid's only six months out of the academy — barely even old enough to drink — and I'll be shocked if he returns to active duty."

"Maybe that's for the best." Jake, uncomfortable talking shit about a fellow officer, cleared his throat and dropped his gaze. "His failure to properly secure his sidearm damn near got all three of us killed."

"I'll admit, the thought had crossed my mind."

A knock at the door, three sharp raps, less a question than a demand. Ian looked at his wristwatch and winced. "I'm sorry. I thought we'd have more time." Then, dejectedly: "Come in."

Two men of the same make and model entered the room. Dark hair, dark eyes, and dark suits, with ties to match, and postures as starched as their white shirts. Their countenances were implacable, save for an imperious upturn at the corners of their mouths, so subtle you might convince yourself it was imagined. They weren't wearing badges, not that it mattered. Jake would have pegged them as DBS at a hundred yards.

The latter of the two shut the door behind them. Both remained standing just inside, forcing Jake and Amy to twist awkwardly in their seats. It was a power move, intended to make them ill at ease. In Jake's case, at least, it worked.

"Agents Paget and Medina, I presume?"

Medina nodded almost imperceptibly. "Captain Bavitz."

"Uh, Cap?" Jake said. "What's going on? Because if this is a fix-up, I wish you'd told me ahead of time, so I could've worn a nicer outfit."

Amy shot Jake an admonishing look that he chose to ignore.

"I take it you haven't informed them yet," Paget said.

"I was getting there," the captain replied testily.

"You know that we can hear you, right?" Amy doubled down with a glare so withering, it would've stopped a charging bull, but Jake was having none of it, because he could see where this was going.

"Agents Paget and Medina are from the Department of Biological Security. They'll be taking over your investigation, effective immediately."

"You're fucking kidding me," Jake said.

"Jake," Amy cautioned, "don't."

"You should listen to your partner, Mr. Gibson," Medina said. "This is well above your pay grade."

"Detective," Jake corrected.

"Excuse me?"

"My title is Detective."

Medina's expression split the difference between amusement and annoyance. "My apologies, *Detective*."

"C'mon, Cap. This is horseshit. You're not seriously gonna reassign us, are you?"

"Actually," Ian said, "in light of this morning's events, the department thinks it'd be best if you two took a little time off."

"Meaning what?"

"Meaning you're both on administrative leave pending an internal investigation of Levy's death."

"We're being suspended?" Amy's tone was calm, but quavered with what Jake recognized as rage barely contained. "But we didn't do anything wrong!"

"Which means you have nothing to worry about," Ian replied. "Don't think of this as a suspension. Consider it more of a vacation."

"An *involuntary* vacation," Jake amended.

"With all due respect, Captain," Paget interrupted, "my colleague and I have neither the time nor inclination to deal with your petty staff squabbles; we have a job to do."

Jake laughed, shrill and humorless. "Sucks for you, pal, because apparently all I've *got* is time, and I'm not about to step aside without a fight."

"Careful, *Detective*. I'm certain you're aware that the Department of Biological Security has the authority to assume control of any investigation that may involve a public health risk—just as I'm certain you're aware that impeding a DBS investigation is a federal offense."

"Are you threatening me?"

"No. I'm merely pointing out that you have no cards left to play. I suggest you go home and enjoy this lovely summer weather. Perhaps you could take your daughter—Zoe, is it?—out for ice cream."

At the mention of his daughter, Jake sagged.

"You know what?" he said. "On second thought, some time off sounds like a great idea."

NEWS

Undaunted: Asylum seekers face long odds as they set sail for New Zealand

Two months ago, the *Dauntless* was a retired fishing vessel left to rot in a Sydney, Australia, boatyard. Then it was purchased at auction by the members of an online survivalist group, who spent weeks restoring its seaworthiness as best they could. Now, they've set sail for the island nation of New Zealand, with the intent to request biological asylum. What will happen when they get there is unclear.

For decades, New Zealand's government has maintained the most aggressive biosecurity measures on the planet. Its policies — originally intended to protect the island's unique ecosystem, the result of 80 million years of geographic isolation — have recently been co-opted by the ascendant FreeNZ party, a nationalist organization that seeks to prevent nonresidents...CONTINUE READING

Related Stories

New Zealand closes borders as Harbinger virus spreads

An Island Unto Itself: How geographic isolation and an unwavering commitment to biosecurity transformed New Zealand into a modern Eden

12.

Brian watched in horror as, five stories below, armed men in tactical gear poured out of the SUVs. Pedestrians fled, screaming. Beggars retreated into the shadows. Hawkers abandoned their merchandise and scattered.

"What's going on?" Mat asked. He was perched on the edge of Lucas's dingy mattress, too far from the window to see anything but buildings and sky.

"No time to explain," Brian replied, hauling Mat to his feet.

Two of the men scaled the front steps carrying a heavy metal cylinder with handles on either side. Shortly after they disappeared from the window's line of sight, a loud *gong* shook the building, accompanied by a screech of rending metal.

"Shit. They just breached the front door. We gotta go."

"Sorry, cuz. You're welcome to leave, but the kid stays."

While Mat and Brian were distracted by the commotion outside, Lucas had crept to the far end of the room. Now he stood blocking the door, a grimy kitchen knife in his right hand, its handle wrapped with duct tape.

Brian yanked Mat backward, putting himself between the boy and his cousin's blade.

"Lucas," he said, "put down the knife."

"And let a hundred large walk out the door? Not fucking likely."

"C'mon, man. Do you really think these assholes brought a battering ram so they could bust in and cut you a check?"

"Guess we'll find out when they get here."

Lucas, not lowering his blade, fumbled blindly for the doorknob with his free hand and yanked open the door. As he hazarded a glance down the hall in the direction of the stairwell, Brian knelt and gripped the saucepan at his feet.

"Hey, Mat?" Brian's tone was quiet, focused.

"Yeah?"

"Run."

As soon as the word left Brian's lips, he launched himself at Lucas, swinging the pan like a cudgel. The sound it made when it struck Lucas in the face would have been comical were it not for the blood that sprayed from his mouth as his head jerked sideways from the blow.

Momentum carried Lucas backward into the hall. Brian tumbled after. They went down in a tangle of limbs, the saucepan sandwiched between them, the knife clattering to the floor.

For a moment, Mat was too stunned to move. Then Brian, winded from landing hard atop the pan, gasped, "The roof! Go! I'm right behind you!"

Mat's paralysis broke. He headed for the stairs, dodging people in various states of sobriety and undress. At first, Mat thought that Brian and Lucas's fight had drawn them out, but as he turned the corner toward the stairwell, he heard a terrified shriek reverberate upward from one of the floors below, followed by a firecracker *pop-pop-pop.*

The shriek stopped short.

The confusion in the hall gave way to panic.

Mat rounded a corner and ran into a crush of frightened squatters, all much larger than he, all headed in the opposite direction, away from the stairwell and the threat of violence fast approaching. He tried to bob and weave between them, to no avail. He was swept along by the current, his feet barely touching the ground.

An elbow caught him in the temple and he fell. Then a bootheel dug into his back, squeezing the air from his lungs. Pain blossomed as a torrent of footfalls rained down.

In actuality, the trampling continued for thirty seconds at most, but Mat felt as if it would never end. He curled into a ball and covered his head with his forearms until the onslaught ebbed.

Get up, mijo.

Mat flexed his limbs experimentally. They felt bruised, but not broken, so he rose gingerly to his feet. As his wits returned, a sudden dread gripped him, and his hand flew to his front pocket with alarm. Gabriel's package was still there, thank God — dented, but intact.

The hallway was nearly empty now, doors open here and there on either side, the rooms they led to abandoned. The sound of gunfire drew closer. Mat fought the urge to shrink from it, instead sprinting to the stairwell and peeking carefully around the jamb, since the door — like many in the squat's communal spaces — had been removed.

When no one shot at him, he crept through the doorway, but froze as a man began to speak three landings down.

"Pike, this is Apollo. Second floor's clear. No sign of the kid so far. Any chance Burbank and Jester are having better luck?"

In the silence that followed, Mat held his breath — afraid that any sound, however slight, might give away his position.

"Yeah, that's what I figured. So, where to next?"

A bead of sweat trickled down Mat's nose, tickling maddeningly. He grit his teeth and did his best to ignore it.

"Copy that." A pause. "Fancy, do you read? Pike says Burbank and Jester are on three, so you and me are taking four. I'm headed there now."

The man reloaded his weapon and began to climb. Broken glass crunched underfoot as he entered the fourth floor hallway.

"Come out, come out, wherever you are..."

A frightened yelp.

A deafening report.

Then nothing but the patter of the man's footsteps receding down the hall.

Mat listened until they were too far away to hear.

Then he released the spent air from his lungs and sprinted upstairs toward the roof.

Lucas groaned and rolled onto his side. His eyes fluttered open and he spat blood onto the floor. Then his gaze lighted on Brian, who lay sucking wind nearby, and the dazed expression on his face gave way to naked malice.

Lucas snatched the saucepan off the floor and clambered onto Brian, straddling his chest. He raised the pan high overhead, and swung it downward like a mallet, aiming for the bridge of his cousin's nose.

As the pan arced through the air, however, Brian bucked beneath him. Lucas pitched forward, sprawling across the floor. The rim of the pan carved a semicircular divot in the vinyl tile, an inch from Brian's left ear.

A sound like hoofbeats filled the hallway. Brian raised his head and saw a roiling mass of people bearing down on him. He curled into a ball—absorbing blows to his shoulders, ribs, and kidneys—and hoped, selfishly, that they pummeled Lucas into oblivion.

Once the stampede passed, Brian straightened and looked around.

Lucas sat, beaten and bloodied, maybe six feet down the hall.

Improbably enough, he was smiling.

A moment later, Brian spotted the reason for his cousin's good cheer. The knife Lucas had dropped in their tussle lay on the floor between them, nearer to him than it was to Brian.

"I've gotta tell you, cuz," Lucas said, "it's been a pleasure catching up."

"No, it hasn't," Brian replied.

Then both men dove as one for the blade.

13.

Mat shouldered open the bulkhead door and spilled onto the sun-baked roof. Its patchwork surface scorched his palms and left behind a tarry residue. He dragged his hands across his sweat-soaked shirt, then rose unsteadily and looked around.

Vents and HVAC units dotted the rooftop at regular intervals, a hodgepodge of mismatched solar panels wedged between. A low wall bordered the roof on three sides. The fourth was flush with the brick face of a much taller neighbor.

Though Mat wanted nothing more than to hole up until Brian arrived, he couldn't shake the notion that his uncle would disapprove. *Remember, mijo,* Gabriel often told him, *chance favors the prepared mind—so we must endeavor to always be prepared.* That philosophy had driven Gabriel to post lookouts at the camp's perimeter, and run drills until Mat had memorized every aspect of his escape.

At the thought of his uncle, grief wrapped itself around Mat's throat and squeezed.

He wasn't stupid.

He knew that Gabriel was probably dead.

But Mat refused to let him die in vain.

He crept to the southwest corner of the roof and peeked over. Two SUVs idled at the intersection below, both with drivers at the wheel.

Another two men were positioned in the streets the building fronted, keeping an eye on the windows and exits.

With all that armor and equipment, there's no way those SUVs could hold more than four guys apiece, which means there can't be more than another four inside.

Mat was surprised by how calm and collected the voice in his head was—and how much it sounded like his uncle.

He retreated from his vantage point and inspected the northern wall, at the rear of the building. It was separated from the back of the building opposite by a narrow corridor that blurred the line between air shaft and alley. By a stroke of luck, the buildings were roughly the same height, but the gap appeared too wide to jump.

Find something to bridge it, and you could crawl across.

In the shadow of an HVAC unit, he discovered a paint-spattered drop cloth, beneath which were four cans of primer, a pair of rollers, and some paint trays, all dried solid, as well as a wooden ladder. Working as quietly as he was able, Mat freed the ladder and dragged it to the building's northern face. It was spongy from water damage, so he had no idea if it would support his weight, much less Brian's, but the roof wasn't exactly brimming with alternatives.

Before laying the ladder across the gap, he peered cautiously in the direction of the street. Then, limbs tingling from a surge of adrenaline, he ducked behind the border wall. One of the men below had a clear line of sight to the corridor between the buildings, as well as Mat's position.

Shit, shit, shit, Mat thought. *Did he see me?*

Mat's instincts screamed at him to run. Instead, he forced himself to count to ten and looked again. The guy's attention seemed to be directed elsewhere, thank God.

Still, his presence was a wrinkle in Mat's plan.

To escape the roof unnoticed, he and Brian were going to need a diversion.

14.

"**Pike, this is** Burbank. Me and Jester finished sweeping the third floor. Nada."

"Wish I could say I was surprised," Pike replied. "So far, Apollo and Fancy have rolled a donut too. I swear, this op is starting to feel like a goddamn snipe hunt."

Even filtered through their radio's encryption software, the irritation in Pike's tone was unmistakable. He'd lobbied hard for a clandestine approach—a few operatives in plainclothes, with backup out of sight nearby—but the guy who signed their checks had insisted they go in hot.

Problem was, the building's air conditioning was nonfunctional, which rendered thermal imaging useless, and the squatters had altered its internal layout so much, the blueprints they'd obtained were woefully out of date.

Not that bitching would do any good. Their job was to deliver results, not excuses, and they were well compensated for it. But after the mess they'd made of the Park City exfil, there'd be hell to pay if they failed to retrieve the target a second time.

Burbank thumbed the wireless push-to-talk button on his modified MP7 submachine gun and said, "I hear you, pal. How are Crank and Hopscotch faring?"

Crank and Hopscotch were off-site, running down a lead on

89

another of their boss's obsessions, code name Shadow Reckoning. A woman named Jessica Vandermeer was rumored to have firsthand knowledge of the operation, but thus far, she'd proven particularly difficult to locate.

"Hopscotch traced the shell company that redirected George Vandermeer's death benefits to a lawyer in Nyack. He and Crank are en route to the guy's house now. We'll know where those payments wound up soon enough."

"Finally, some good news. Here's hoping it's contagious. Speaking of, what floor are me and Jester taking next?"

"Survey says: five!"

"Good as any, I suppose."

"Happy hunting," Pike said. "Watch your six."

"Wilco, brother." Burbank switched channels. "Jester, do you copy?"

"Loud and clear," said his teammate in the building's other stairwell.

"We're a go for the fifth floor."

"Copy that."

Burbank exited the stairwell at the next landing. Beads of sweat rolled down his sides. Trapped breath soured the air inside his mask. His right index finger rested lightly on the trigger of his gun.

The hall was gloomy, quiet, still. Paint flakes dangled from the ceiling. Jagged swaths of wallpaper were missing from the walls.

"Show yourself, you little shit," he muttered. "We haven't got all day."

One by one, Burbank cleared the rooms, most of which were either abandoned or padlocked from the outside. He was forced to pop two hostiles who fired on him when he opened an unlocked door. A third, he found unconscious with a needle in her arm, and left behind. The man in charge told them no witnesses, no evidence, but Burbank didn't think she qualified as either.

Motion ahead. Burbank halted, eyes narrowing. His trigger finger twitched, then stilled.

Someone was waving frantically at him from down the hall.

"Hey! Army dude! Over here!"

It was an adult male, hunching slightly, so his height and weight were hard to judge. His right arm flailed madly. His left, he held tight to his side.

Taking aim at him, Burbank shouted, "Both hands where I can see them—now!"

"No can do," the man replied. "I'm hurt!"

Burbank approached slowly, mindful of a possible ambush from the rooms on either side. As he neared the guy, it became clear he wasn't lying. Blood seeped through the fingers of his left hand and soaked his pants down to the knee. His face was waxen. His eyes were glazed. He wobbled slightly as if his legs were on the verge of giving out.

Hell, Burbank thought, *there's a chance I won't even have to waste a bullet on this scumbag,* though doing so meant nothing to him either way.

"You Phreak_Scene?"

The man smiled, showing bloody teeth. "That's me."

Burbank thumbed the button on the foregrip of his gun. "Jester, this is Burbank, do you copy?"

"I hear you, buddy. What's good?"

"I made contact with our friendly."

"About damn time. I'm on my way."

With his weapon, Burbank gestured toward the man's flank. "Why are you bleeding?"

"Me and my cousin had a little disagreement."

"What about?"

"He thought the kid should leave with him. I didn't."

"Where is this cousin now?"

"Handled."

"And the kid?"

"Somewhere safe. Where's the money I was promised?"

"You'll get it as soon as he's in custody, but not before," Burbank lied. When the boss man said no witnesses, no evidence, he'd made it clear a snitch with a fat bank account counted as both.

"Scout's honor?"

Burbank grinned behind his mask. "Sure."

After a moment's hesitation, the man said, "I guess that'll have to do. C'mon, I'll take you to him."

"Nice and slow," Burbank admonished. "No sudden moves."

"Right, 'cause I look like I'm about to break into a soft-shoe."

The man turned and shambled down the hall, keeping pressure on his wound with his left hand. Burbank followed cautiously behind. Eventually, they stopped before a closed door, its padlock hasp unfastened. As the man reached for the knob, Burbank jabbed him with the barrel of his gun and said, "What the hell do you think you're doing?"

"You want the kid, right?"

"Yeah."

"Well, this is where I stashed him."

"Tell him to come out, then."

"He can't. He's bound and gagged."

Burbank frowned. "Then we wait."

"For what?"

"For my backup to get here."

"You think this is some kind of setup?"

"I think I haven't survived this long by being careless."

"Suit yourself. As long as I get paid, it's all the same to me."

When Jester arrived, Burbank instructed him to hang back and provide cover. Then he grabbed the man by the back of his shirt and shoved him toward the door. "Listen up. When I say so, you're going to open that door and step inside. If you get cute, I'll put a bullet in your head. In the event that I'm unable to, my buddy here has my permission to kill you slow. Do you copy?" When the man failed to reply, Burbank gave his shirt a yank. "I said, do you copy?"

"Yeah, okay, I fucking copy!"

"Good. Now go."

He did as he was told.

Burbank, still holding a fistful of the guy's shirt, followed on his heels.

The room was small and spare, one window, no furniture but a mattress on the floor. Nowhere for a pack of would-be assailants to hide. No sign of the kid either. The only people in the room were Burbank and the injured friendly.

"I don't get it. Where is he?"

"Over there," the man said, jerking his head to indicate the corner obscured by the open door.

Burbank released the man and closed the door partway. Behind it, he found not a child, but a scrawny meth-head with a ratty mohawk, lifeless eyes, and a grungy kitchen knife buried in his neck.

"What the hell?"

Burbank wheeled to find the friendly smiling back at him. His left hand was no longer pressed to the wound in his gut, which flowed freely in its absence. Instead, it held aloft a small rectangle of tarnished brass, slick with gore.

A Zippo lighter.

Burbank's finger tightened on the trigger. Thanks to his mask—which, in addition to protecting against biological agents, filtered out a wide array of chemicals—he failed to register the significance of the room's soft background hiss until too late.

15.

Brian Agren was a man accustomed to failure.

As a child, he drew obsessively, and aspired to one day illustrate comic books. His mom and dad — practical, blue-collar folks who'd worked hard to drag themselves out of poverty — didn't approve.

Over their objections, he set his sights on attending Manhattan's prestigious High School of Art and Design, as many of his Silver Age heroes had done. Secure in the belief that being accepted into so competitive a magnet school would convince his parents that his ambitions were neither fleeting nor frivolous, Brian slaved over his portfolio for months, interspersing figure studies with meticulous reproductions of his favorite covers and splash pages.

Auditions for prospective students with last names beginning with letters *A* through *L* fell on a cold Saturday in December. Applicants, regardless of discipline, were required to attend, so Brian schlepped his portfolio from Staten Island to East 56th Street in Manhattan. An arctic wind roughed up the harbor. Low clouds spit occasional flakes of dry snow.

The session was packed; the talent on display, astonishing. For as long as Brian could remember, he'd been the best artist in his class, his grade, his school. Here, however, he felt unsophisticated, inadequate, and ill prepared.

By the time they called his name, his palms were sweaty and his hands were trembling. As he rose from his chair, he dropped his portfolio, scattering its contents. Someone nearby laughed—at his clumsiness, most likely, although in the moment he was sure they were responding to his work—causing others to join in.

Shamefaced, Brian collected his belongings and fled into the bitter cold.

He walked aimlessly until his extremities went numb and his tears froze on his cheeks, stuffing his portfolio into a trash can along the way. Then he took a bus to the ferry terminal and headed home.

His parents never even asked him how it went.

After graduation, Brian went to work for his old man's plumbing business—first answering phones, then apprenticing, and eventually becoming a competent, if unenthusiastic, plumber. He told himself it was a stopgap, a way to make a little money while he plotted his next move, but the truth was, in those days, he spent more time smoking weed with his cousin Lucas than he did drawing.

Four years ago, when his dad passed, Brian inherited Gold Star Plumbing and the mountain of debt that it was buried under. He limped along for a few months, supporting himself and his mother both, until an unfortunately timed subcontracting gig stranded him in Manhattan during the quarantine.

Compared to many, Brian was lucky. He survived the epidemic and only spent a year inside Park City before his petition to leave was granted. But in that time, the family business went under, his childhood home was repossessed, and his mother was diagnosed with pancreatic cancer. Had she fallen ill a few years prior, chemotherapy and surgery could have prolonged her life, but the Harbinger virus had put an end to both. Brian buried her three weeks after his release.

At least, thanks to Mat and Gabriel, he was able to be at her side when she died.

It was a debt that he'd do anything to repay.

Finding residential plumbing work once he got out proved impossible. Though he'd been given a clean bill of health, his internment was a matter of public record, so potential customers were uncomfortable letting him inside their homes. That's how Brian wound up a sewer worker, liposuctioning the city's fatbergs for the Department of Environmental Protection.

He should've known when he promised Gabriel he'd keep Mat safe that he'd somehow find a way to fuck it up. Still, he never would've guessed it would involve getting stabbed by his own cousin.

Lucas reached the knife first and plunged its blade into Brian's gut. In the moment that followed, Brian felt nothing but surprise. Then pain washed over him in nauseating waves. He crumpled to the floor, pawing uselessly at the knife hilt, crimson bubbles frothing on his lips.

"Easy, cuz," said Lucas with surprising tenderness. "What's done is done. Struggling's only gonna make it worse."

"Lucas?" Brian croaked, eyes wide and searching.

"Yeah?"

"I . . ." Voice faltering, he licked his lips. "I need . . ."

Brian's head lolled. His eyes closed.

"What is it, buddy? What do you need?"

". . . c-closer . . ."

The word was a scant suggestion of a whisper, a gentle sigh on a windy day. As Lucas placed his ear to Brian's lips, Brian removed the knife from his side and drove it into his cousin's neck.

Blade bit bone—clavicle or vertebrae, Brian wasn't sure—and Lucas reeled backward, slamming into the wall. Then he slumped against it, limbs twitching, eyes flitting. Soon after, his movements ceased, and blood stopped pouring out around the blade.

"Easy, cuz," Brian spat. "What's done is done."

A cursory examination of his wound convinced Brian he wasn't far behind Lucas, but he was determined to hold on for a little while, at least. The way he saw it, if he couldn't keep his promise to Gabriel, the least he could do was give Mat a fighting chance to get away.

Brian dragged Lucas back into his room and propped him in a corner. Then he closed the door and opened the valve on the camp stove's gas tank.

A few months ago, while working underground, he'd nearly blown himself to smithereens because a nearby gas main had ruptured and his mask had filtered out its trademark stench. If he'd fired up his equipment before noticing the hiss, he could've taken out a whole damn city block.

The people hunting Mat had deep pockets and fancy toys, so he was willing to bet their masks were at least as sophisticated as his crappy, city-issued one.

Brian found Lucas's Zippo on the floor beside the window and, after pondering where best to secret it, opted to palm it against his side for easy access, in the guise of keeping pressure on his wound.

Burbank and Jester reached the fifth floor soon after.

Though dizzy from blood loss and propane fumes, he played his part with aplomb, and those two asshats bit hard. Honestly, why wouldn't they? Even without a mortal injury, Brian looked soft, guileless, and weak—the kind of guy who's so accustomed to losing, he'd never even think to fuck you over.

Brian was delighted that they'd underestimated him, and that his intuition about their masks had been correct. Flicking open his dead cousin's Zippo, he felt mighty, triumphant.

His last thought, as he thumbed the lighter's flint, was that it was awfully nice to go out with a win.

16.

"Hey, Jake! Wait up a second, would you?"

NYPD headquarters was a fourteen-story brutalist monstrosity overlooking a large plaza in the heart of Manhattan's controversial Civic Center Pedestrian Zone.

PeZe—which, in the local parlance, rhymed with *please*—had its roots in the slapdash perimeter erected around police headquarters immediately following 9/11. It was expanded six years ago, in response to the Foley Square shooting, and again three years ago, after 8/17. Now PeZe was roughly ten blocks by five and encompassed dozens of government facilities, including city hall, several courthouses, a federal detention center, and the New York field offices of the DBS and FBI. Subway service to the area was diverted. Concrete barriers and security checkpoints restricted automotive access. Dedicated shuttle buses ran on weekdays to pick up the slack. Pedestrians, while nominally allowed, were subject to random searches, so on the weekends they were few and far between.

Jake exited One Police Plaza at a trot, ignoring Amy, who chased after him. As he approached the curb, he tried to summon one of the department's autonomous vehicles using the app on his cell phone, only to discover that his permissions had been revoked.

He cursed and headed west across the redbrick plaza, toward the nearest open subway station. Amy followed, undeterred, although she struggled to match his long stride.

"Where are you going?" she said breathlessly. "I'm talking to you!"

"Home."

"Yeah, but what's the rush? I thought maybe you and I could grab a bite or something first."

"I can't. I've got a train to catch."

At the center of the plaza was an enormous steel sculpture, five interlocking circles of weather-beaten red, intended to represent the city and its boroughs. Today, as Jake strode past, he thought it looked more like a blood clot.

"So we're not going to talk over what happened back there?"

"What's to talk about? We fucked up and got benched. End of story."

"Jake, c'mon"—Amy's tone was growing tetchier—"you're being ridiculous. It's a hundred degrees out, easy, and the nearest station with weekend service is fifteen blocks away."

"Yeah, no shit," Jake replied. "I was gonna have an unmarked take me home, but it seems the captain yanked our privileges already. If only the prick was half as efficient when it came to approving overtime."

"Still, that's no excuse to give yourself heatstroke. Lemme buy you a cup of coffee."

"Last I checked, coffee's hot."

She rolled her eyes. "Not if you order iced."

"I'm strung out enough already, thanks."

"How about a drink? There's gotta be an open bar around here somewhere."

"Amy, you don't drink."

"That doesn't mean I can't buy you a round—and after the day we've had, I kinda wish I did."

"No offense," Jake said, "but if you think doing midday shots in some shitty dive bar while my goodie-two-shoes partner watches is gonna make me feel better, you're sorely fucking mistaken."

Amy grabbed Jake by the arm, forcing him to turn and face her. "Listen, asshole. I'm going to let that goodie-two-shoes crack slide on account of something's clearly going on with you—but, suspended or not, I'm still your goddamn partner, so it's high time you tell me what it is."

Jake recoiled as if slapped.

In all their time together, he'd never once heard Amy swear.

"You're right. I'm sorry. But we can't have this discussion here." He eyed a nearby surveillance camera pointedly.

"Okay," she said, "let's go somewhere we *can* talk, then."

They walked awhile in silence, side by side. When they reached the zone's perimeter, Amy gave the officer manning the guard booth a halfhearted nod, but he barely spared the two of them a glance.

Beyond the checkpoint, the neighborhood declined precipitously. On a block so desolate that even the beggars had abandoned it, Jake guided Amy to the recessed entrance of a vacant storefront. Its security gate had been defaced by the stenciled image of a globe wearing a gas mask, the symbol of the Soldiers of Gaia.

"And to think you turned your nose up at a dive bar," she snarked.

"Sorry, but this is delicate, so I can't risk being overheard. Zoe's sick."

"What do you mean, sick? Sick how? Is she okay?"

"Honestly? I wish I knew. It started last night, with an upset stomach, when I picked her up from day care. Then her temp spiked, and nothing I gave her seemed to touch it."

"Her fever," she said, "is it . . ."

"Past the reporting threshold?" Jake said. "Yeah."

"You didn't, though, did you?"

"Of course not."

"Good. Who's with her now?"

"Hannah."

Amy cracked a smile, wan and fleeting. "Wow. You called your ex? Now I *know* it must be serious."

"What the hell was I supposed to do? I wasn't about to leave her with our neighbor, and I didn't know who else I could trust. I mean, it's not like—"

Jake fell silent and cocked his head.

"Uh, hello? It's not like what?" Then her eyes widened as she heard it too—a rapid, overlapping *rat-tat-tat* from somewhere nearby.

Gunfire.

Multiple shooters, by the sound.

As a result of their suspension, they'd been forced to relinquish their service weapons, but that didn't mean they were unarmed. Jake knelt to retrieve his backup piece—a Glock 26 subcompact, consistent in design and function with his duty pistol—from the holster on his ankle. Amy carried hers—an impossibly tiny Glock 43—at the small of her back, so she was quicker on the draw.

They followed the sound of gunshots northwest through Tribeca, to a dilapidated corner midrise. A pair of sleek black SUVs blocked off the intersection just outside. Jake and Amy bounded overwatch toward them as they'd been trained, one advancing low and fast while the other provided cover from a sheltered position. Bystanders looked on, petrified, as they ran past.

Half a block from the vehicles, Jake left his hiding place behind a decorative pillar, only to leap backward as bullets pitted the sidewalk at his feet.

Amy squeezed off three rounds in response, but they slammed uselessly into the SUV the shooter was stationed behind.

Armored, Jake thought. *Figures.*

"NYPD!" he shouted, and received another volley in reply. This time, when Amy attempted to return fire, a second shooter peppered her position.

"Hassan!" Jake said. "Are you okay?"

"Yeah, you?"

"Still breathing."

"Good. Keep it that way."

Easier said than done, Jake thought. They were pinned down. Trapped. In need of backup.

He fished his phone from his pocket and hit Emergency on its lock screen.

"Nine one one," the operator answered. "What is your emergency?"

"This is Detective Jacob Gibs—"

But before he finished identifying himself, the squat's fifth floor exploded, raining fire and chaos on everything below.

17.

When Mat's eyes fluttered open, he was on his back. His head throbbed. His lungs ached. His face felt taut and hot like a fresh sunburn.

Ugh, he thought. *How long have I been out?*

He sat up, dazed, and looked around. The pain in his head intensified. Noxious smoke blurred everything in sight.

Right. Not a sunburn—an explosion.

The blast had thrown Mat clear across the roof. All that had prevented him from falling off was the low brick wall at its perimeter. The HVAC unit he'd been crouched beside was now a blackened heap of gnarled scrap metal. The stairwell enclosure and much of the rooftop surrounding it had collapsed. Flames licked at the jagged edges left behind.

He watched the fire spread through welling tears. Even if, by some miracle, Brian had survived, there was no longer any way for him to access the roof—which meant that Mat was on his own.

As he climbed to his feet, he realized he was bleeding. A gash on his forehead spilled a drying slick down the left side of his face. Another on his right arm ran down his wrist, blood pooling in the meat of his palm. He wiped it on the hem of his T-shirt and was relieved to discover that the package Gabriel had given him was still wedged in his front pocket.

A crack like falling trees, like breaking bones, and another section of the roof gave way. Embers drifted skyward as it crashed into the floor below. Within seconds, the rooftop itself caught fire.

If you don't get out of here soon, mijo, you likely never will—so move.

Deep down, Mat knew the words weren't his uncle's, but his own.

Still, he heeded them as if they were an order.

As he headed toward the rear of the building, the conflagration growing behind him, he took comfort in the fact that at least there was no way those paramilitary dicks could follow him now.

Apollo lay gasping in the shadow of a solar panel when the boy that he'd been sent to capture darted past. Apollo reached out toward him with a trembling hand, only to collapse, exhausted, onto the tarry surface of the roof. Black smoke rose from his body armor. Burn holes marred the fabric between its protective plates, scorched edges framing blistered skin beneath.

He'd been headed to the sixth floor, per Pike's orders, when a noise farther up the stairwell caught his attention. It sounded, to his ear, like a rusty fire door being opened against its will.

Leery though he was of breaking protocol, his instincts told him it was worth checking out, so—quick and quiet as a rumor—he slinked up the stairs.

The stairwell terminated in a wooden structure, furred with dust and cobwebs, that reminded Apollo of a garden shed. A heavy door of rust-streaked gray led to the roof. Sunlight showed along its right-hand side. Someone had left it ajar.

He inched toward the jamb and peeked through the narrow gap. Once his eyes adjusted to the glare, he saw a rooftop clogged with machinery and solar panels. There wasn't anyone in sight, but that didn't mean much, since the terrain provided ample cover.

Using the barrel of his submachine gun, he slowly teased open the door. When he'd created a wide enough gap to slip through, he withdrew into the shadows and waited, ears straining for any indication that someone outside might've taken notice.

For a long while, he heard nothing.

Then a sound like rolling thunder pierced the silence.

The building shuddered, throwing Apollo to his knees. Debris rained down as the stairwell shed collapsed atop him. A ceiling joist slammed into his helmet from behind. His face mask hit the floor so hard it cracked, and consciousness abandoned him.

He was roused by gunshots, dangerously close.

No, not gunshots—the ammunition in his weapon igniting.

The remains of the stairwell shed were on fire. His submachine gun lay beneath a smoldering pile of wood and shingles nearby. As it heated, the cartridges inside exploded one by one.

Though his thoughts were foggy and his brain concussed, he knew he had to move. His mask was ruined, its lenses shattered, so he ditched it. Then, worried they'd blow too, he stripped his tactical vest of spare magazines. They popped like popcorn as he clawed his way out of the flaming shed, trying his damnedest to ignore the searing agony and sickly stench of his flesh burning.

When he reached a portion of roof untouched by flames, he flopped onto his side in the lee of a solar panel. The rooftop shuddered as the section he'd just crawled across caved in.

Not long after, the boy passed by, his back to Apollo as he sidestepped through the narrow gap between the panels. Apollo, short of breath, was too weak and slow to grab him, so instead he waited until the sound of his footsteps was swallowed by the fire's roar and then radioed in.

"Pike, this is Apollo, do you read? I've got a twenty on our target."

His voice was like a blade against a whetstone. He scarcely recognized it as his own.

"Pike, if you copy, please acknowledge!"

Still nothing. He switched channels.

"Fancy, this is Apollo, are you there?"

Static was his only reply. He cursed and threw his earpiece in frustration.

With blackened fingertips, he removed a foil packet from the first-aid pouch on his belt. After a moment's consideration, he took out two more. He tore them open with his teeth and shook their contents, two tablets apiece, into his mouth. Then he ground them to a bitter paste between his molars and choked it down.

They were go pills. Synthetic stimulants designed for military use. Each packet contained a single dose intended to keep a soldier focused and alert for fifteen hours straight.

Apollo's scalp tingled as they kicked in.

His vision sharpened.

His aches and pains gave way to a euphoric hum.

Fuck it, he thought, awash in chemical enthusiasm, *if no one's gonna help me catch this little shit, I'll do it my damn self.*

Mat, at the rear of the building, peered over the low rooftop wall, looking down the narrow corridor at the center of the block, toward the street. Smoke billowed from the squat's windows, filling the corridor and obscuring his view—but, as near as he could tell, the lookout was gone.

Thankfully, the fire hadn't yet reached this portion of the roof. If it had, the wooden ladder Mat had stashed here would've gone up like so much kindling.

He stood the ladder on its end, which proved more difficult than he'd imagined. It was heavy, ungainly. A gust of wind threatened to topple it backward into the fire. Carefully, Mat walked it into position, and—using the wall as a fulcrum—lowered the far end toward the rooftop of the building opposite.

When it clanged against the flashing on the other roof's lip, Mat breathed a sigh of relief. The ladder was long enough to span the gap, if barely.

See? That wasn't so bad. Now all you have to do is climb up there and crawl across.

He took a few deep breaths to steady himself, then clambered onto his makeshift bridge. Paint flaked off everywhere he placed his hands and knees, revealing splintered wood beneath.

The view, whenever the breeze disturbed the smoke, was dizzying: seven stories down to a narrow spit of buckled pavement strewn with trash and overrun with weeds. As he shuffled forward, the ladder bounced, and when he stopped, it bowed beneath his weight.

Halfway across, Mat's hand slipped and he pitched forward, sprawling across the rungs. Heart galloping, he closed his eyes and waited for the ladder to stop moving. His legs ached from gripping the rails so tightly. Saliva flooded his mouth as his stomach threatened mutiny.

Slowly, slowly, the ladder settled—but before Mat could muster up the courage to continue onward, it began to shake once more.

His eyes flew open. His hands tightened on the rungs. His head swiveled as he looked over his right shoulder, toward the squat.

Something had followed Mat onto the ladder.

Rationally speaking, Mat knew it was a man, but it looked as if it had crawled straight out of a nightmare. Its hands were blackened, cracked, and bleeding. Its face was glistening pink and warped by blisters. Its eyes were wide and manic, with pupils small as pinpricks and whites dyed red from broken capillaries.

When they locked gazes, it smiled toothily.

"Olly olly oxen free."

Its words spurred Mat to action. His nausea forgotten, he scampered forward—the ladder oscillating madly—while the thing behind gave chase.

It swiped at Mat, trying to grab him by the ankle. Mat kicked it hard enough to leave a mark.

The creature rocked back. Mat jetted forward, reaching the far end of the ladder and tumbling onto the intact building's roof. Then he sprung to his feet, grabbed the ladder by the nearest rung, and shoved.

The damn thing didn't budge.

"Good thought, kid," said the thing on the ladder, "but no way were you gonna move this baby with all my weight bearing do—"

At that moment, the ladder—brittle, overtaxed—snapped in half.

18.

"Amy!"

Jake charged blindly through the billowing smoke, headed toward his partner's last known position. His voice was hoarse. His mouth tasted of ash.

The air was thick with particulates. A spasmodic coughing bout doubled him over until dark spots swam before his eyes and he thought that he was going to puke. Once the fit passed, he spat gray onto the rubble-strewn street and called to Amy again.

"Amira!"

Jake was lucky. The decorative pillar he'd taken cover behind had absorbed the brunt of the explosion. At least one of the shooters was less fortunate. He lay facedown beside his vehicle, his head staved in, his body peppered with debris. Jake had no idea how Amy, across the street, had fared.

Could be she was badly hurt. Could be she simply didn't hear Jake, or he her, as a result of the deafening blast. Either way, he was determined to get to her before anyone else did.

After the explosion, the fire spread quickly through the building, causing secondary detonations—meth labs and moonshine stills, most likely—that rattled windows up and down the street. Given the decrepitude of the surrounding structures, it was only a matter of time before the whole block was ablaze.

At least the gunfire had ceased, although God knew for how long.

The sedan Amy had sheltered behind materialized from the smoke so quickly, Jake nearly walked into it before he could stop himself. It was beige, empty, and parked along the curb, a chunk of masonry embedded in its windshield.

Jake rounded its rear fender and found himself staring down the barrel of Amy's Glock. When she saw that it was him, she sagged against the car's bumper, her gun hand flopping to the pavement beside her.

"You okay?"

It was a stupid question. Jake could plainly see she wasn't. The left arm of Amy's pantsuit was a bloody mess. A piece of gore-streaked shrapnel lay in the street between her knees.

"Never better," she said through gritted teeth. Her face had gone gray. Beads of sweat ran down her forehead from beneath her hijab.

Jake knelt and examined her wound. Arterial blood pulsed out of it with every heartbeat.

"What's the verdict?" Amy asked.

"Barely a scratch," Jake replied, his levity as brittle as candy glass. "I've done worse shaving."

"That's what I figured."

Amy's words were a little furry around the edges. Jake worried she was on the verge of bleeding out. He removed the stained necktie from his sport coat's right front pocket and a ballpoint pen from its inside left. Holding the pen against her upper arm, he looped the tie around both and made a simple overhand knot.

"Sorry," he said. "This is gonna suck."

Then Jake cinched the knot so tight that Amy screamed.

Ignoring her cries, he tied a second knot to hold his makeshift tourniquet in place and used the pen as a windlass to further tighten it until the bleeding stopped. Then he immobilized the pen as best he could with the tie's loose ends.

As Amy's breathing returned to normal, a pair of fog lights pierced the murk, first swinging toward them, then receding slightly and halting. It looked to Jake like the men who'd attacked them were collecting their wounded—and given the direction the vehicle was facing, at least one carload of them would be headed this way once they did.

"Can you walk?"

"I...I think so."

"Good," Jake said, helping Amy to her feet, "because we've gotta move."

Mat watched, stunned, as his pursuer and the broken ladder were swallowed by the smoke that poured from the squat's rear windows. His body trembled from exertion. His heart fluttered like a trapped bird against his ribcage.

Eventually, the heat of the approaching fire jarred Mat from his stupor, and his thoughts turned once more to escape.

The new rooftop on which he found himself was spartan, its only features an access hatch and four turbine vents, all blackened by decades of pollution. Mat tried the hatch. It was locked from the inside.

Don't panic. Work the problem.

The building's corner lot was a mirror image of the squat's. Streets bracketed it to the north and west. An adjacent high-rise prevented Mat from heading east.

Before the blast, there'd been a lookout stationed to the west, so Mat went north, toward the front of the building. He peeked over the edge, half-expecting a cadre of bad guys to be staring back at him from ground level.

Instead, to his delight, he saw a fire escape.

The problem was, it didn't extend to the roof; its highest landing jutted from beneath the windows of the floor below. Mat estimated the drop at twelve to fifteen feet. Twelve to fifteen feet onto a rusty iron cage the size of a military cot, bolted to a wall of tumbledown brick seven stories above the sidewalk.

Mat let out a breath, then swung his legs over the roof's edge, slowly extending himself until he dangled straight-armed by his fingertips. His head swam when he looked down to spot his landing, so instead he closed his eyes and rested his cheek against the wall.

He mouthed a prayer—to God or Gabriel, he wasn't sure.

Then, every instinct arguing to the contrary, he let go of the roof.

His sneakers clanged against the landing. The impact jolted up his legs. His knees buckled and he pitched backward, slamming into the railing. The masonry around the anchor bolts began to crumble. The platform lurched, canting awkwardly.

Mat laced his fingers through the landing's metal grating and scrabbled uphill toward the stairs, the bolts protesting all the while. When he reached the stairs, he heaved a sigh and climbed to his feet, only to discover he'd rolled his ankle when he landed.

Not broken, he told himself. *Just sprained.*

It hurt like hell, though, and seemed reluctant to accept his weight, so he was forced to lean on the handrails for support. As a result, his descent was awkward, halting.

Eventually, Mat reached the lowest landing of the fire escape, which was on the second floor. A drop-down ladder provided access to street level, but its latch was rusty, stiff. He yanked on it for a good minute to no avail. Finally, with a shriek of metal against metal, the ladder deployed. It hit the sidewalk hard enough to chip the concrete and vibrated like a tuning fork until he climbed on, stilling it.

The street was eerily empty. Mat limped eastward alongside. Ash fell from the sky like dirty snowflakes. Smoke blanketed the neighborhood in false twilight and made it hard to breathe.

There was an intersection up ahead, its stoplight glowing ominously through the haze. He approached it cautiously, a hand against the storefront to his right—a lunch counter, as near as Mat could tell. Its only signage was a tangle of neon that read CASH ONLY. Cloudy windows of cheap bulletproof glass graced its two exterior walls. Its entrance was notched out of the right angle where they would have joined.

Through the window, he could see the restaurant was empty, but hadn't been for long. The overhead fluorescents were on. Half-eaten plates of mofongo and frituras sat atop cheap laminate tables. A shattered coffeepot had left a steaming puddle on the floor. The people inside must've scattered when the shooting started. Mat felt a pang of envy at the thought.

When he realized that looking diagonally through both windows might offer him a bleary view of what lay around the corner, Mat rested his forehead on the glass and cupped his hands around his eyes.

At first, the filmy panes distorted everything to abstraction.

Then he recognized the blurry outline of two figures slinking toward the corner, guns drawn.

He ducked reflexively. His guts went loose and watery with dread. They were only seconds away—and, as the throbbing in his ankle reminded him, he was in no condition to run.

If you cannot run, then hide. And if you cannot hide, then fight.

The words, another of his uncle's favored sayings, were a comfort. Also, a plan.

Mat spotted a broken bottle nearby, its label faded and unreadable. He grabbed it by its neck and slinked toward the corner of the building. Then he crouched and waited. His muscles twitched. His nerves hummed. Adrenaline dampened the ache of his sprain.

A gun barrel peeked around the corner, followed shortly by the arm carrying it.

Mat leapt.

As Jake rounded the corner, he was greeted by a guttural scream, a glint of bottle green. A blur of dirt and ash flew toward him, teeth bared, a cylinder of jagged glass angled toward his throat.

Jake spun and brought his gun up from low ready, but he was too slow to squeeze off a shot. As the broken glass neared his exposed neck, his left forearm smacked into his assailant's wrist, deflecting the blow. The bottle hit the wall of the building to Jake's right and shattered.

His assailant released the bottleneck and clawed wildly at Jake with his free hand. Jake backpedaled and saw, as if in slow motion, fingernails caked with grime rake the air an inch from his face.

Recipe for an infection, he thought.

Jake, off-balance, lost his footing and landed hard on the sidewalk, dropping his weapon in the process. His assailant scrambled for it. Jake kicked him in the stomach and he staggered backward, giving Jake a chance to recover his gun.

He rose, bringing it to bear once more—barrel trained on center mass, finger tightening around the trigger.

Then Amy screamed, "JAKE, NO!"

Amy had been a couple paces behind Jake when he reached the corner, and had since circled wide to cover him. Now she stepped unsteadily into his line of sight, her injured arm held tight to her chest, her tiny backup piece in her good hand—though, unlike Jake's, it was pointed skyward, her index finger nowhere near the trigger.

Amy was small of stature, which forced Jake to realize with a start that his assailant was smaller still. Not a man, as he'd assumed, but a boy of ten or so. Latino, by the look of him. His clothes were filthy and ill fitting. His eyes were wide and afraid. His narrow chest heaved as he sucked wind.

"Easy," Amy said to him. "We're not going to hurt you."

The boy's gaze darted between Jake and Amy, his expression dubious, unsure. Jake took his finger off the trigger and raised his hands, palms out, as if in surrender. A wave of nausea hit him at the thought that he'd nearly shot an unarmed child.

"What's your name?" she asked.

The kid blinked, said nothing.

"I'm Amy. The ugly white guy's name is Jake."

For a second there, the kid almost smiled.

Then, south of them, an engine roared, and his look of fright returned.

"Whoever these guys are, they're on the move," Jake said to Amy, "and there's no telling whether they'll be heading this way. I'd rather not still be here if they do."

"You...aren't with them?"

The boy's voice was shaky, his English unaccented. He looked as surprised as they were that he'd spoken.

"No, we're not," Amy replied gently. "We were responding to the gunfire when they attacked us. Do you know who they are or what they're after?"

Suspicion clouded his features. "Are you two cops?"

Jake opened his mouth to respond. Amy silenced him with a look.

"We're off duty," she said, "and only here to help—so if you're here illegally, it's none of our concern."

A crunch of tires on grit. Headlights swinging northward in the murk.

"Much as I hate to force the issue," Jake said, "can we continue this discussion elsewhere? We've gotta get out of here, now."

"I can't," the boy said. "My ankle's hurt."

"Lean on me if it'll help," Amy said.

"Amy, don't be ridiculous. The amount of blood you've lost, I'm amazed you're still upright as it is."

Jake knelt. Returned his pistol to its ankle holster. Gestured toward the kid.

"What're you waiting for?" he said. "Climb on."

The boy looked questioningly at Amy.

Amy nodded.

Then he climbed onto Jake's back, and the three of them took off down the street.

19.

Lionel Mercer was scowling at the oversized monitor on his midcentury office desk when his chief of staff, Noel Coughlin, slipped into the room. Lionel had spent the better part of the day poring over what little surveillance footage his people had obtained of last night's Park City infiltration. Partial views from blocks away. Still images from passing satellites. Private feeds that weren't connected to the city's surveillance grid. Each more useless than the last.

For a long while, Coughlin said nothing—he just stood there, waiting to be acknowledged, his hands clasped in front of him to keep from fidgeting. Coughlin was the sort of man who remained slender by virtue of constant anxiety, a fact that was evident by the hunched, submissive way he carried himself; the bland but tidy clothes he wore, calculated to neither stand out nor offend; and the creases etched into his face, which suggested a grimace even when he wasn't wearing one.

Eventually, Lionel removed his glasses and set them on his blotter with a sigh. "Please tell me you come bearing good news."

The grimace Coughlin's lines alluded to came out in full. "News? Yes. Unfortunately, it's mixed."

"I'm listening."

"Per your instructions, we've assumed control of the investigation. That said..."

Coughlin swallowed hard.

Lionel frowned.

"For Christ's sake, Noel, just spit it out!"

"There's been another incident."

"What do you mean, another incident?"

"The situation is still developing, so details are scarce, but there have been numerous reports of shots fired in Tribeca, as well as some kind of explosion. It's too soon to say for sure that they're related, much less connected to the Park City assault—"

"—but you have reason to believe they are, or you wouldn't be here."

"Yes."

"Why?"

"Because a few minutes before the reports began, every camera in the neighborhood that's connected to the city's network went dark."

"Son of a bitch," Lionel muttered. "What are our people on the ground saying?"

"Nothing yet, sir. I've reached out, but they haven't called me back."

Lionel's blood pressure doubled. After decades of painstakingly maneuvering himself within striking distance of the presidency, this was turning into the kind of public clusterfuck that could ruin a career.

No.

He refused to let it.

He'd worked too hard.

Risked too much.

Sacrificed too many.

"When they finally deign to," Lionel said, "tell them they're not to speak of this to anyone until I arrive. In the meantime, get me on the next plane to New York. Commandeer one if you have to."

"Sir?"

"You heard me. From here on out, I'll be overseeing this investigation personally."

20.

Tribeca Park was a checkmark-shaped patch of green carved out by the awkward intersection of Beach Street, Walker Street, West Broadway, and Sixth Avenue, a block east of the old Fourth Precinct house.

The precinct house, a gorgeous limestone structure in the Renaissance Revival style that once featured working stables for the police department's equine officers, was now used primarily for storage, its fusty halls a labyrinth of dented filing cabinets and yellowed banker's boxes.

The tiny park had likewise lapsed into neglect. Wooden benches, too long unpainted, had succumbed to rot. Leafy trees cast shade on stone pavers buckled by the root systems beneath. Overgrown shrubberies jockeyed for position with long grasses and invasive weeds. Litter clogged the spaces in between.

Jake, Amy, and the boy—who hadn't spoken since he'd tentatively agreed to come with them—crouched amid a stand of bushes and watched the dusty SUV drive past. All around them, sirens wailed, first responders heading toward the fire to their southwest, their light bars painting windows blue and red as they raced by. Though they never came any closer than a block or two, the kid shrank from them nonetheless.

Unlike the first responders, the SUV didn't appear to be in any rush. It rolled through the intersection at ten miles an hour, as if the men inside were looking for something—or someone.

Jake held his breath and prayed they wouldn't stop to search the park. His Glock was still fully loaded, but Amy's only had two rounds left, so she'd quickly be defenseless in a shootout. And if they were forced to make a run for it, they wouldn't get far. Amy was woozy from blood loss. The kid's ankle was swollen and purple. Jake was spent from carrying him piggyback.

Thankfully, the SUV continued onward.

When it finally disappeared from sight, Amy sighed and said, "That was closer than I would've liked."

"You ain't kidding," Jake replied. Then, to the boy: "Who, exactly, are these guys?"

The boy shrugged.

"They're after you, though, aren't they?"

A hesitation, followed by a nod.

"Why?"

Another shrug.

"Does it have anything to do with what happened last night at Park City?"

The boy looked away. His eyes moistened. His lip quivered.

Amy put a hand on his shoulder. "Hey. Listen to me. We're on your side, I promise, but we can't help you unless you talk to us, okay?"

He swallowed hard. "Please don't make me go back."

Jake and Amy shared a look.

"We won't," she replied. "Not while these men are still after you."

"Even if they're cops too?" he asked.

Jake's face darkened. "What makes you think they're cops?"

"Oh, come on," Amy said. "You've seen their tech, their methods, the way they breezed through here like they owned the place. Is it really that much of a stretch to think they might be government operatives?"

"I hear you—but, last I checked, the government isn't in the habit of slaughtering its own people."

Amy regarded Jake incredulously. "You know, in all our time together, that's gotta be the whitest thing you've ever said to me."

The boy snorted with laughter, surprising all three of them.

"Whoever they are," Jake said, "we should get outta here before they decide to circle back."

"Agreed," Amy replied, "but I'm not gonna make it far on foot—and, no offense, but you can't carry the both of us."

"What're we supposed to do, then, hail a ride? We're two suspended cops—"

"Suspended?" The kid's brow furrowed. "You said you were off duty!"

"—fleeing a crime scene with a material witness in a DBS investigation. Until we find out who these assholes are working for, we'd be crazy to do anything that leaves a trail, digital or otherwise."

"Fair point. Speaking of . . ."

Amy took out her phone, removed the battery, and put both back in her pocket. Absent a power source, it was impossible to track or activate remotely via Wi-Fi or cellular network.

" . . . you still have yours?"

"No. I dropped it when the building blew."

"Bummer."

"Least this way, it can't be traced back to us." Jake paused a moment, thinking. "Hey, how long were the surveillance feeds down last night?"

"The park's internal cameras remained off until we manually reset them. The public feeds were down an hour, maybe less. Why? You think they knocked 'em out again today?"

"Stands to reason, doesn't it? You said yourself they breezed through here like they owned the place. Maybe that's because they knew they weren't being recorded. How big an area around the park did they black out?"

"A few blocks in every direction, plus several potential egress routes."

"So, assuming I'm right, all we've gotta do is find someplace nearby to hole up before the cameras come back on, and it'll buy us time to figure out our next move."

"The only problem," Amy said, "is where?"

Jake smiled. "Actually, I have an idea."

"I can't believe I let you talk me into this."

"Oh, come on," Jake whispered. "It's perfect!"

They stood outside a small two-bedroom on the fourth floor of a prewar tenement a few blocks north of Tribeca Park. Getting into the building had been a simple matter of pressing buttons on the intercom until a resident buzzed them in.

The building had been updated in the early nineties, but not since. Dark carpeting, worn paler down the middle, and busy wallpaper swallowed light cast by shaded sconces. A scuffed white chair rail girdled the hallway at waist height.

"I don't think that word means what you think it means," Amy said, trying and failing to muster a smile.

Truth be told, she didn't look too good. Her headscarf was soaked through with sweat. Her face was a tense, bloodless gray. Pain deepened the lines around her eyes.

At the boy's insistence, Jake had supported Amy's weight for most of the way here, while he hobbled alongside. Though the set of his jaw and his awkward, lurching gait made it clear how badly his ankle was bugging him, he never once complained. Jake felt a pang of sorrow that such a good kid had somehow gotten mixed up in all this—which, in turn, made him wonder for the millionth time since he'd left home how Zoe was faring.

"Tell you what," Jake said. "Let's get you inside. Then you can mock me all you want."

He handed Amy off to the boy, who slid wordlessly beneath her good arm, and jiggled the doorknob. It was locked, as he'd suspected it would be.

Jake glanced around the hall to ensure he wasn't being watched, then removed a folding knife from his front pocket and wedged the blade into the damaged jamb, above the lock. A little wriggling, and the latch gave way. He pushed the door open and they shuffled inside, after which he closed and locked the door behind them, setting the chain and deadbolt so no one else could gain access as easily as he had.

Until recently, the apartment belonged to Harold and Marjorie Crozier. Jake had no idea who owned it now, since, to his knowledge, they had no next of kin.

Eleven days ago, one of the Croziers' neighbors heard gunshots and called 911. The responding officers knocked awhile to no avail before deciding to pop the lock with a prybar.

The apartment was cluttered, but immaculate. The rugs were striped from recent vacuuming. The parquet flooring gleamed like wildflower honey. The wooden furniture was freshly polished, the shelves and baseboards dusted, the throw pillows on the sofa fluffed. Even the trash can and recycling bin had been emptied.

It was cold inside, too, every air conditioner set to max and left to run. A large glass bowl of potpourri perfumed the chilly air.

The officers found Harold and Marjorie atop their queen bed, fully clothed. Marjorie lay on her back, her right hand a loose fist on her chest, a single gunshot wound in the center of her forehead.

Harold sat beside her, his shoulders against the headboard, his brains spattered on the wall behind. A snub-nosed .38 was on his lap, two bullets gone.

Jake and Amy were assigned the case, such as it was. Harold hadn't left a note, but his motives weren't a mystery for long. Two days prior, he and Marjorie lost their only daughter and her young son to scarlet fever. Marjorie wore a silver locket containing photos of them both around her neck. She'd been clutching it when she died.

At least she went out on her own terms, Jake supposed. *It beat the alternative, if only by a smidge.*

Still, for days afterward, the cleanliness of the Croziers' apartment haunted him. He couldn't shake the feeling that they had tidied up because they didn't want to be a bother, even in death.

Once the apartment had been processed and the bodies relocated to the morgue, the crime scene was released—or, at least, it would have been, if there were anyone to release it to. The Croziers owned the place outright, and with their daughter dead, they had no obvious heirs. Eventually, if nobody came forward to claim it, ownership would revert to the state. Until then, it was in bureaucratic limbo—and as good a place as any to hide out.

Today, the cramped apartment was warm and still. The cloying scent of potpourri remained, but beneath it was an unpleasant note that reminded Jake of churned earth.

He crossed the room, opened the curtains, and fired up the AC. Then he returned to help the boy maneuver Amy to the couch.

"We've got this," she said sharply. "Why don't you go close the master bedroom door?"

Jake did as she requested, soon discovering the reason behind her urgent tone. The crime scene cleaners had yet to come, if in fact they had been contacted at all. The Croziers' bed linens were caked with dried blood. Desiccated gray matter speckled the wall nearest the headboard.

Early on in Jake's career, he'd been surprised to learn that property owners were responsible for cleaning up the aftermath of violent crime. Now he carried business cards for several reputable biohazard remediation services as a matter of course. He should have realized that, with both Croziers gone, there was no one left to make that call. He should have recognized the lingering smell of death for what it was.

Jake shut the door and said to the boy, "That room's off-limits, okay?"

"Okay," he replied.

"How's our patient?"

"Eager to get some feeling back in my left hand," Amy said. "You think maybe we can lose the tourniquet?"

"I'm not sure that's such a good idea."

"Neither is leaving it on until my arm falls off."

"I'm just saying, maybe we should get you to a doctor."

"Sure, because ten hours in a germ-infested waiting room is exactly what I need right now. Besides, I gave my word we'd keep our new friend safe. If we head back out, there's no telling what kind of attention we'll attract, and I refuse to be the reason those jerks in black catch up to us."

Jake ran a hand through his hair and weighed his options.

"Okay," he said, "but if we're doing this, we're gonna do it right."

He and the kid set about gathering supplies: duct tape, towels, kitchen shears, sterile saline, a wooden spoon, a cashmere scarf. With the kitchen shears, he cut the towels into strips. Then he flushed the wound with sterile saline, and used the strips to pack and dress it. He fixed the strips in place with duct tape, and used the scarf and spoon to make a second tourniquet, which he placed above the first, but didn't tighten.

"Uh, Jake? Not to question your math skills, but I said I wanted *no* tourniquets, and that's *two* tourniquets."

"Relax. It's just a backup, in case you bleed too much when we release the first one. Put your arm along the couch back for me, so it's above your heart."

She did.

"Good. Now," he said to the boy, "I need you to put pressure on the dressing, like so. No matter what, you don't let go until I say, okay?"

The boy nodded gravely.

Amy scrunched up her face as he bore down.

"Here goes."

Jake snipped the knots holding the ballpoint pen in place. It pinwheeled as the tourniquet unwound. He held his breath and watched for bleeding through the dressing.

Thankfully, he saw none, and Amy's arm pinked up as oxygenated blood began to flow through it once more.

"Well?" Amy asked through gritted teeth.

"Looking good so far, but to be safe, I'd like to keep the pressure on for several minutes." Then, to the boy: "Can you handle that, or do you need me to take over?"

"I think I'm good," the boy replied.

Jake nodded. "Lemme know if that changes. Once we're sure she's stable, I'd like to clean your cuts and scrapes, if that's all right."

"Yeah, I guess. Where'd you learn to do this stuff?"

"I haven't always been a cop. Once upon a time, I was a medic."

"Like, in the army?"

"Exactly like in the army."

"Cool!"

Jake wished he shared the boy's enthusiasm. The fact was, his skills were rusty, and his training likely obsolete. He'd been taught that open wounds should not be treated with harsh antiseptics, for fear of damaging the tissue, but that was a long time ago, when antibiotics could still be counted on to keep infections at bay. Without them, there was nothing more he could do for Amy than wait, watch, and worry—emphasis on *worry*.

"You know, kid, you're not too shabby in a crisis yourself. Plenty of guys I served with would've fainted doing what you did."

"Mateo."

"Come again?"

"My name is Mateo. But my friends mostly call me Mat."

"Nice to meet you, Mat. I'm awfully glad I didn't shoot you."

"Yeah." Mat smiled. "Me too."

21.

When Agents Paget and Medina returned, Ian was in the bullpen, chatting with Detective Mason about the floater she and her partner fished out of the Hudson River the night before.

"Captain Bavitz," Paget interrupted, "a word."

Ian suppressed an expression of distaste. Although, in truth, he was relieved the DBS had taken the Park City disaster off his hands, he wasn't wild about their methods or the way they threw their weight around.

"Of course. Give me a minute to wrap this up, and I'll be right with you."

"You misunderstand. I wasn't asking, and we're in no mood to wait. Whether we talk here or in your office is up to you, but I suspect this is a conversation you'd prefer to have behind closed doors."

A flush crawled up the captain's neck. Irritation seeped into his tone.

"Fine. My office it is."

The walk across the crowded bullpen seemed interminable. Ian led the way, pulse thrumming in his ears. Once he'd closed the door behind them, he said, "Now that you've knocked me down a peg, you wanna tell me what the hell is going on?"

"Funny," Paget said, "we were going to ask the same of you."

"I'm afraid you'll have to be a little more specific."

"If you insist. What, specifically, are Detectives Gibson and Hassan playing at?"

"How should I know? You were here when I suspended them, and we haven't spoken since."

"Then you have no idea where they are now?"

Ian shrugged. "Home, I'd imagine."

Paget and Medina shared a look.

"What?"

"I take it you haven't heard about Tribeca, then." This from Medina.

"I heard there was some kind of an explosion," Ian replied carefully.

"An explosion that was preceded by a gunfight in which Gibson and Hassan were involved."

Ian's stomach roiled. "What do you mean, involved? Involved how?"

"That's what we're attempting to ascertain. Moments before the explosion, Detective Gibson dialed nine one one. Unfortunately, the call was disconnected before he could say why, but GPS data indicated he was within half a block of the blast site."

"Jesus. Is he okay?"

"Presumably." Medina sounded unconcerned. "We recovered his phone, but he was nowhere to be found."

"What about Hassan?"

"We tracked her too, of course. She and Gibson were together for a time. After the blast, she headed northeast, likely on foot. Seven minutes later, her signal vanished."

"Any reason to suspect foul play?"

"No," Paget replied. "A search of her last known position revealed a small amount of blood consistent with her recorded type, but no evidence of a struggle."

"Maybe her phone died," Ian offered.

"Or maybe she intentionally deactivated it."

"What are you implying?"

"I'm not implying anything. The evidence indicates your people have gone to ground."

"That's ridiculous. I'm sure if you check the surveillance feeds—"

Medina grimaced. "Unfortunately, the neighborhood's surveillance feeds were temporarily disabled."

Just like the ones around Park City, Ian thought, *which explains why Paget and Medina are on the case.* "Gibson and Hassan are good police. What possible reason could they have to run?"

"An excellent question. You know them better than we do. Why do *you* think?"

"I have no idea."

"Does Detective Gibson ever talk about his time in the military?"

"Some. Why?"

"Chalk it up to idle curiosity. What about his wife? I understand he lost her to 8/17."

"A lot of people lost a lot of people thanks to that day."

"Indeed," Medina said mildly. "In that respect, Detective Hassan was lucky. Her family was spared. Although several of them have since overstayed their visas—a fact that she has thus far failed to report."

"Where the hell do you get off digging into their private lives?" Ian snapped.

"Several Tribeca residents report seeing a man and woman matching their descriptions flee the scene with a young boy, possibly against his will. Do you have any idea why they'd do such a thing, or who that boy could be?"

"No," Ian admitted, "but if they did, I'm sure they had their reasons."

"As am I," Paget replied, his tone hardening, "and we would very much like to find out what they are."

He and his partner shared another look, after which Medina removed a business card from his inside coat pocket and laid it on Ian's desk with a snap.

"Thank you for your time, Captain. Should you happen across any information that might be relevant to our interests, do be in touch."

Fat chance, Ian thought.

They turned to leave, but as they reached the door, Paget paused.

"Oh, and Captain? If we discover you've been less than forthcoming with us—"

"I haven't."

"—we'll have no choice but to charge you with obstruction."

Paget and Medina exited Ian's office. Medina shut the door behind them. Ian stared daggers at their backs through the glass until they disappeared from sight. Then he plucked his desk phone from its cradle and jabbed at an extension with a forefinger.

"Hey, it's me," he said. "Listen, I need you to send a team apiece to Gibson and Hassan's addresses. No, it's better if I don't tell you. Call me the second you have eyes on 'em, and for God's sake, keep their names off of the paperwork."

He hung up, a sharp pain taking root behind his eyes. In his desk drawer was an expired bottle of Tylenol. He shook two tablets into his hand and dry swallowed them.

Whatever you morons are up to, he thought, *I hope you know what you're doing—because I haven't got a fucking clue.*

22.

As evening fell, the lights of Pell Street flickered ablaze.

The buildings of Chinatown huddled close to one another, blocking the scant breeze, which left the night air warm and thick. Humidity cast halos around the glowing signage.

Curfew was still a few hours off, so the sidewalks were crowded with vagrants, hookers, and street vendors, their combined scents a fug of spice, sweat, and cheap perfume. A steady stream of pedestrians snaked between them, most sporting earbuds and dead-eyed glares to make it clear they weren't interested in anything on offer. One slinked hunch-shouldered from shadow to shadow—a baggy jacket on despite the heat, a Mets cap pulled low over his eyes, a paper mask obscuring his face.

Jake had ransacked the Croziers' belongings to cobble this outfit together. He'd intended it to thwart the city's recognition software, which analyzed gait and body shape as well as facial features. In the relative safety of the dead couple's apartment, it had seemed a sensible plan. On the streets, he was less sure.

The Jade Dragon was sketchy in a vaguely promising way. A narrow space with tacky neon, dirty windows, and a leaky air conditioner above the door, you'd have no trouble believing it served some of the best Chinese food in town, provided it was busy. But until Jake pushed inside, the restaurant didn't have a single customer.

Its interior was done up in black lacquer and red paint, and layered with a scrim of grease. The aquarium beside the host station was lit, but empty of fish. Long strands of algae undulated in the current generated by its bubbling pump.

A man in a silk button-down glared at Jake from behind the bar. Jake removed his mask, approached him, and laid a diamond necklace he'd purloined from Mrs. Crozier's jewelry box atop the varnished wood.

"I'm here for the tasting menu."

"We don't make change," the man said as he inspected the necklace. Though he was Chinese by extraction, his accent was pure New York.

"I wasn't expecting any," Jake replied.

The man secreted the necklace beneath the bar. Then he nodded toward the swinging double doors that separated the dining room from the kitchen.

After the semidarkness of the dining room, the kitchen's glare was blinding. Stainless steel, white tile, fluorescent light. Steam billowed from massive pots. Vegetables sizzled in enormous woks. Jake wondered who all the food was for. Deliveries, maybe.

Unsure of the protocol, Jake opened his mouth to speak, only to be shushed by an older Chinese woman in chef's whites. A twenty-something guy in a filthy apron opened the kitchen's microwave, which contained a smattering of personal electronics.

"Please place any smart devices inside."

"Excuse me?"

"Smart devices," he repeated. "Phone, watch, that sort of thing."

"Due respect," Jake said, "but that wasn't the part I found confusing."

"Relax. We're not gonna nuke 'em. It's not even plugged in."

"Then why?"

"You ever heard of a Faraday cage?"

The look on Jake's face was answer enough.

"The oven blocks all signals in or out. You can collect your stuff when you leave."

"Oh," Jake said. "I'm not carrying anything electronic."

The guy rolled his eyes and said something to the woman in what Jake supposed was either Mandarin or Cantonese. They shared a laugh at Jake's expense, after which the woman mimed to indicate that Jake should lift his arms. When Jake complied, the guy wanded him with a device that he produced from beneath his apron, then nodded to the woman.

She smiled and gestured toward a nondescript door half-hidden behind a set of wire shelves. Jake opened it and saw stairs heading down into the dark. Vape fumes wafted upward from below, a noxious mix of weed and cotton candy.

The basement was lit by a chevron of pink neon on the ceiling, and the dull glow of a couple dozen computer screens. A teenage girl snapped her gum at Jake when he reached the bottom of the stairs and said, "Welcome to the Dragon's Lair. You're machine seventeen." Her cadence was a master class in performative disinterest.

Time was, a burner phone—cheap, prepaid, disposable—would suffice to protect you from eavesdroppers, but the Wellness Act's erosion of the Fourth Amendment and advances in monitoring technology had rendered burners obsolete. Hence the need for modern speakeasies like the Dragon's Lair—illegal hacklabs that sold anonymous, encrypted access to the internet by the hour.

Patrons were scattered throughout the space. None looked up as Jake walked by. Machine seventeen was a heavily customized computer in a carrel of its own. Several sets of initials were carved into the carrel's desktop. Stickers and marker scrawls dotted its interior walls. The keyboard was tacky and smelled of artificial cherry flavoring.

Could be worse, Jake thought.

He sat, tapped some keys, and followed the onscreen prompts to place a video call. When Hannah answered she looked puzzled, then relieved. "Jake? Is that you?"

"Yeah. It's me."

"Where the hell are you calling from? The caller ID was garbled nonsense. You're lucky I picked up."

"That's . . . complicated."

"Are you okay? Because, honestly, you don't look so great."

"I've been hearing that a lot today."

"Then maybe take the hint."

"I'll book a spa day just as soon as things settle down," he deadpanned. "How's—"

"Same," Hannah replied tersely, reminding him that, while his end of the call couldn't easily be traced, their conversation was still vulnerable to eavesdropping.

"Can I see her?"

"She's resting. I'd rather not disturb her." Hannah paused, pursed her lips. "So, do you want to tell me what's going on? Your virtual assistant's been ringing off the hook—and, unless I'm mistaken, there's an unmarked police car watching your place from across the street."

"Honestly, I wish I could, but I'm not so sure what's going on myself."

"Are you in some kind of trouble?"

"Maybe. I don't know yet. And I can't risk coming home until I do."

"Jake, if those guys across the street come knocking . . ." She trailed off, but he got the gist. Law enforcement officers were obligated to report signs of illness to the DBS.

"I know," he said. "They won't. They're probably just waiting around in case I show up. As long as I steer clear, they'll have no reason to come inside."

"I hope you're right about that," Hannah said.

"Yeah. Me too." Jake cleared his throat. "Hey, listen. One more thing. Under the bed is a lockbox. The combo is Zoe's DOB. Do you remember it?"

"Of course, but—"

"Good. If anything gets your hackles up—anything at all, no matter how small—open the lockbox, grab Zoe, and get the hell out of there, you understand?"

"No, I don't understand. If you'd just—"

"I'm sorry. There isn't time for me to explain."

"Where would we even go?"

Jake fell silent a moment. "Remember where we had our second date?"

"Our second date," she said. "Wasn't that the one—"

"Yeah. If anything goes wrong, we'll meet there."

"When?"

"Whenever you wish." He spoke slowly, emphasizing each word, in the hopes she'd take the hint.

"Whenever I...okay, got it. How will you know we're on our way?"

"Your Bangarang account's still active, right?" In truth, Jake knew it was, because he'd drunkenly scrolled through Hannah's social media profiles countless times in recent months.

"I guess. I haven't used it in forever, though."

"Good. I'll check in on your feed as often as I'm able. If you post, I'll know you need me to come get you. Just keep it innocuous, so it doesn't arouse suspicion, and be sure to ditch your phone afterward, so it can't be used to track you."

"Jake, you're freaking me out."

"Don't worry. I'm sure I'm overreacting," he said, hoping it sounded more convincing than it felt.

The girl at the bottom of the stairs met his eyes and pantomimed a telephone, holding her hand to her head with thumb and pinkie extended. Then she tapped her wrist where a watch would be if she was wearing one. Jake, struck by the notion that both gestures had outlasted the objects they referenced, caught her meaning. Even VPNs and anonymizers couldn't hold off government tech forever. If anyone was listening in, it wouldn't be long before they pegged his location. "Look, I've gotta go. Tell Zoe that I love her."

"Of course."

"And Hannah?" Jake swallowed hard. He wanted to say the same to her. But, after all they'd been through—after all he'd *put* her through—he couldn't muster the words.

Thankfully, Hannah let him off the hook.

"I know," she said. "Me too."

Jake stared at her a moment, as if committing her face to memory, then disconnected.

His next call—audio only, this time—was to police headquarters. Jake told the woman who answered that he needed to speak to Captain Ian Bavitz, and doggedly refused to give his name.

"Hello? Who is this?"

"Hiya, Cap."

"Gibson? Jesus—where've you been? I've been trying to reach you all goddamn day!"

"Last I checked, I was suspended."

"Yeah? Then why's the DBS all up my ass about some witnesses who place you running toward a shootout earlier today, and leaving with a kid?"

Ian's question had stamped out the last ember of optimism Jake had been clinging to. This wasn't some big misunderstanding: he, Mat, and Amy had been right to run.

"I don't know what you're talking about," he said. "They must have me mistaken for someone else."

"Uh-huh. That's why you called in from a secure line."

Jake sighed. "What do you want me to say, Cap?"

"I dunno. How about 'I haven't fucking lost it.' Or maybe 'I know how it looks, but I wouldn't dare wade into the middle of a DBS investigation.'"

"If that's what you need to hear."

"What I need to hear is the truth."

"The truth is, me and Amy were damn near killed today by folks who looked an awful lot like government operatives, and seemed hell-bent on abducting a frightened child, even if it meant waging war in the middle of Manhattan. Now I don't know what the fuck is going on, or who to trust."

"That's . . . a lot to take in," Ian said.

"I know how it sounds," Jake replied, "but that doesn't mean it isn't true."

"All the more reason for you to come in."

"I can't."

"You'd better," Ian snapped, "before the DBS decides to rain hell on you and Amy both."

"And if it turns out they're involved?"

"Christ, Gibson, do you even hear yourself right now? You sound like one of those paranoid Endtimes bugfucks on the internet. Why the hell would the DBS be involved?"

"I don't know. I'm just saying, I don't trust them."

"I'm pretty sure the feeling is mutual. Do you still trust *me*?"

"Of course," Jake said, "but not the people you report to."

"Hey—you report to them too."

"Reported," Jake replied. "Past tense."

"If you've got no intention of coming in, why call me?"

"I guess I wanted to get a sense of how much trouble we're in. To tell you our side of the story, as best I can. And to feel out the odds of Amy winding up arrested if I drop her at a hospital somewhere."

A pregnant silence stretched across the wire.

"Is she…okay?" Ian asked.

"Honestly? I don't know. She took some shrapnel when the building blew, and yanked it out before I could stop her. I got her bleeding under control, I think, but I'm scared to shit about infection, and smart enough to know my training's out of date."

"You've gotta realize that if you bring her in, you'll probably both get nabbed."

"Yeah. Unless…"

"Unless what? Unless I help you put one over on the Feds? Sorry, pal, but I've got a family to support. Just tipping you off like this could cost me my job. My marriage too, maybe, since Stuart's got his heart set on another kid, and adopting ain't exactly cheap. If I stick my neck out any further, I could go to jail."

"That's what I figured. Still, it was worth a shot."

"Maybe, if you had concrete evidence of your claims—"

"Cap, forget it. I understand."

Ian sighed. "You can't run forever, you know. And the longer you try, the worse it's gonna be when they find you."

"I know."

"Do me a favor. Try not to get you or your partner killed."

"Sure thing," Jake said.

"And if there's anything you need—"

Jake cracked a smile. It was an old joke between them, even if it didn't seem like one today. "Call someone else."

"You got that right," the captain said, and hung up.

TattleNYC 2m ago

EXCLUSIVE

Man in Viral Video of Tribeca Abduction Identified as Disgraced NYPD Detective

Federal law enforcement sources, speaking on the condition of anonymity because they are not authorized to discuss ongoing investigations, identify the man caught on video absconding with a child after holding him at gunpoint as NYPD Detective Jacob Reinhold Gibson, who was recently suspended from (continue reading)

23.

The Croziers' building was twenty minutes' walk from the Jade Dragon—longer, if you were trying to avoid surveillance cameras. Jake returned shortly before curfew. The streets were haunting in their emptiness.

He located the button on the building's intercom with CROZIER printed alongside, and pushed it three times without speaking, as he and Mat had previously agreed.

Mat buzzed him in, then unlocked the apartment so Jake could slip inside without knocking. As he traversed the halls, he heard televisions nattering, and the ebb and flow of several unintelligible conversations. Jake—whose imagination conjured prying eyes behind every peephole, and insisted that the Croziers' neighbors were gossiping about the strangers in their midst—kept his hat and mask on until the door was bolted shut behind him.

The kitchen ran along the wall nearest the entrance. It was separated from the living area by a small island. Thanks to an abundance of bookshelves, the living area was barely large enough to accommodate a couch and a recliner. Amy lay on the former beneath a multicolored afghan. Mat was curled up in the latter with a novel. A lamp on the table beside him provided the only illumination in the room.

Mat nodded at the plastic bag in Jake's hand. "What's that?" His voice was scarcely louder than a whisper.

Jake matched his tone, but ignored his question. "How's she doing?"

"She dozed off a little while ago. I put a blanket over her so she wouldn't freeze. Before she fell asleep, she seemed okay. What's that?" he repeated.

"Change."

Jake set the bag on the kitchen counter and unpacked several cartons of Chinese takeout. He had no idea what was inside—the man behind the bar had handed him the bag without a word as he was leaving—but they smelled so good, he'd salivated the whole walk back. Mrs. Crozier's necklace must have been worth more than he thought.

He asked Mat to rustle up some plates and utensils, then went to check on his partner. Amy's sleep appeared untroubled. Her breathing was slow and regular, her expression serene. Careful not to disturb her, Jake lifted the afghan to take a peek at her dressing, and was relieved to see no blood showing through.

As he turned to rejoin Mat, he saw the paperback the boy had chosen, lying spine-up in the pool of light the lamp cast on the side table. It had a white cover with red lettering and black artwork of a *T. rex* skeleton in negative. A smile of recognition split Jake's face. He'd loved that book when he was Mat's age.

The kitchen island featured an overhang, beneath which were tucked four stools. He and Mat each took one, the boy's feet dangling well shy of the floor, and started opening takeout containers. Egg rolls. Dumplings. Lo mein. Fried rice. A variety of stir fries. Several dishes Jake couldn't identify. No meat or poultry—these days, only the swankiest restaurants in the city could afford to serve chicken, pork, or beef—but a few dishes contained seafood.

They dug in silently, but with gusto. Jake hadn't realized how hungry he was, or how long it had been since he'd last eaten. When he'd first laid eyes on all this food, it looked like enough to keep them going for a week. Now, he and Mat struggled to pace themselves so there'd be some left for Amy when she woke.

Eventually, they ran out of steam, and stacked the quarter-full containers in the fridge. Then Mat yawned and stretched. His gathered brow and glassy eyes put Jake in mind of Zoe when she stayed up past her bedtime.

"It's late," Jake said. "Why don't you lie down in the guest room and catch some Zs?"

The guest room—if you could even call it that—was maybe six by eight, and done up as an office, but it contained a futon chair that folded out.

"You take it. I'd rather stay out here."

"You sure?"

"Yup. The armchair's plenty comfortable for me."

"Okay, but go wash up first. There's an open pack of spare toothbrushes on the vanity, and a stack of clothes that I thought might be useful in the guest room. T-shirts, sweatpants, that sort of thing." Jake had gathered up the clothes prior to leaving for the Jade Dragon, when he was rooting through the Croziers' bedroom to assemble his disguise. He'd found the toothbrushes while ransacking their medicine cabinet for the painkillers Amy refused to take.

"Fine," Mat said unenthusiastically, but he headed to the bathroom as instructed. Jake took the opportunity to pull up Hannah's Bangarang feed on the Croziers' tablet, and was relieved to see her most recent post was weeks old.

Maybe I really am *overreacting,* he thought.

Mat returned to the main room a few minutes later in a plain white tee and a pair of drawstring shorts. He'd ditched his dirty clothes somewhere—hamper or garbage, Jake supposed—but carried his sneakers, now wiped clean, in one hand, and a small rectangular package, wrapped with waxed cloth and twine, in the other.

"What's that?" Jake asked.

Mat shrugged. "Just . . . stuff."

When he failed to elaborate further, Jake was tempted to follow up, but—Amy's prior admonitions ringing in his mind—he decided it was better not to push.

Mat set the package on the side table, the shoes beneath. Then he climbed into the recliner and reached for the light.

"You need blankets or anything?"

"Nope," Mat said. "I'm good."

Mat twisted the lamp's switch. The room went dark.

"Okay. Good night."

"G'night."

24.

Hannah was in the kitchen, making herself a chik'n salad sandwich, when a strangled cry echoed through Jake's apartment.

She rushed down the darkened hall to Zoe's bedroom, a chef's knife clutched in her right hand, three half-moons of celery still clinging to the flat of the blade. She'd left the door ajar, and now barreled through, flicking the light switch just inside. Zoe was alone, thank God, but she lay rigid on her bed—her face dusky, her tortured wail rapidly dwindling to a low, wet gurgle.

Though Hannah's pediatric rotation was ages ago, she recognized a febrile seizure when she saw one. Feeling foolish for having brought the knife, she set it on the dresser, rolled Zoe onto her side, and slid a pillow under her head—only then daring to glance at her watch, so she could estimate the episode's duration.

Soon after, convulsions wracked Zoe's tiny frame. Hannah crouched beside her to ensure she didn't fall off the bed, and murmured empty words of comfort in her ear.

Three minutes later, Zoe stilled. Her eyes fluttered open, but they were glassy and unfocused. Hannah smoothed her tousled hair. Her skin was hot and sweaty against Hannah's fingertips.

Febrile seizures, while terrifying for the uninitiated, aren't dangerous in themselves. They are, however, triggered by a spike in body temperature, which troubled Hannah, because it meant that Zoe wasn't getting any better.

Eventually, Zoe drifted back to sleep. Hannah rose, yawning, and shut off the bedroom light. It was pushing 1 a.m. Jake had caught her at the tail end of a twenty-eight-hour shift, so she'd barely slept in days. Her eyes itched. Her hair was lank and greasy. Her residual limb rubbed uncomfortably against its prosthesis.

Hannah massaged a knot of tension in her neck with one hand and parted Zoe's curtains with the other. The surveillance detail's unmarked sedan was still parked beneath the maple tree across the street, same as it had been the last five times she'd looked.

She wondered if they'd thought to bring food with them, or if they'd assumed the detail would be over before curfew shuttered every corner store and take-out joint in town. She wondered what would happen if they had to pee. Tired and punchy as she was, she had half a mind to bring them down a pot of coffee and find out.

As Hannah let the curtain fall, a blur of motion outside caught her attention. Pulse quickening, she closed one eye and peered through the narrow gap between the curtains with the other. Two figures in dark clothing had emerged from the shadow of the maple.

No, she thought, *not clothing—body armor.*

Crouching low, they flanked the unmarked car from behind, approaching in its blind spots left and right. Black masks obscured their faces. A pair of handguns, elongated by suppressors, rose as one to target the officers inside.

Hannah fought the urge to warn them somehow. Screaming, maybe, or banging on the window. It wasn't fear that stopped her, so much as the knowledge that Jake had entrusted her with his daughter—and the queasy realization that she would gladly let two strangers die if it meant keeping Zoe safe.

The reports were muffled, but still louder than movies had conditioned her to expect. Three shots each, so coordinated that they overlapped, reminding Hannah jarringly of microwave popcorn. The men in the vehicle pitched forward. The car horn bleated briefly, then silenced as the driver's body slumped onto the center console.

Not one light in the surrounding buildings came on.

Hannah didn't wait to see what happened next. She sprinted for the master bedroom. Knelt at the left side of the bed, the side she still thought of as Jake's. Flailed blindly underneath it for a moment. Retrieved the lockbox Jake had stashed there.

The combination lock comprised six dials, each displaying numbers zero to nine, embedded in the side opposite the hinge. Hannah input Zoe's birthdate with shaking hands and thumbed the latch release. Inside was Jake's old backup gun—a 9mm SIG Sauer P229 he'd carried when his service weapon was a P226—and two spare magazines.

The smell of gun oil brought her back to her first time at the police range, to the unfamiliar weight of this very pistol in her hands. *I'm not really a gun person,* she'd told Jake then. Given the number of gunshot wounds she'd treated in her career, that had been putting it mildly.

Jake's reply surprised her. *Neither am I,* he said, *but if you're serious about sleeping over, you'll be more comfortable—and we'll all be safer—if you know your way around one.*

Just like that, a lousy date became a romantic gesture. And, to Hannah's mild annoyance, she even wound up having fun.

Now, she removed the handgun from its case, ejected the magazine to confirm that it was loaded, then reinserted it and racked the slide to chamber a round. The spare magazines she stuffed into the back left pocket of her pants. They stuck out like her phone did from the back right.

As she returned to Zoe's room, the power went out, plunging Jake's apartment into darkness. Silence descended as air conditioners shut down, electronics ceased humming, and fans whirred to a halt. Streetlights still shone through the windows, though, and TVs flickered in the building opposite.

The outage was confined to Jake's building.

Back when she and Jake were serious—before his ultimatum and the hurtful words she wished she could take back—Hannah had spent enough nights in this apartment to navigate it in the dark with ease.

Panic threatened nonetheless. Her breaths were short and shallow. Her palms were slick against the pistol's textured grip. Her heart didn't beat so much as vibrate in her chest.

Easy, Hannah. You can do this. There are only two of them. If there were more, they would have cut the lights and stormed the building the moment their buddies took out the surveillance team.

She wasn't sure if she believed any of that, but she had to try.

Jake was counting on her to protect his little girl.

Hannah forced herself to take a long, slow, steeling breath. Then she slipped into Zoe's bedroom, the hasty outline of a plan forming in her mind.

When the last two digits of his watch read double-zero, Fancy popped the lock on the front door with an electric pick and slipped into the apartment. He and Deacon had gone radio silent, but a tinkle of glass from the direction of the living room suggested his new partner was inside as well.

To Fancy's left was a hallway, which his mask's night vision optics rendered in ghostly shades of green. He took it. Blueprints indicated it led to two bedrooms and a bath, all of which he'd been tasked with clearing, while Deacon swept the kitchen, living room, and dining room.

Orders were to apprehend anyone they came across, with the thought that they could be used as leverage in negotiating the surrender of the primary target. If, by some miracle, the primary target was present, apprehension of secondary targets would be unnecessary, in which case they would be liquidated.

The first door he came to was ajar, and decorated with a smattering of stickers. Stars, unicorns, rainbows. He pushed it open slowly, the barrel of his weapon panning across the room's interior in parallel to the door.

A little girl—Zoe Rose Gibson; age: four; father: Jacob; mother: Olivia, deceased—slept fitfully atop the covers. He slinked toward her, hoping to clamp a hand over her mouth before she woke.

As he reached her bedside, he heard a noise that made him pause—the *zzzzt-zzzzt-zzzzt* of a cell phone set to vibrate, coming from the closet to his left.

Fancy turned, smiling. Trained his weapon on the closet door. Reached for the knob.

As the door creaked open, Hannah struck.

When Hannah heard the living room window shatter, she tapped the button on her phone's screen, tucked it into the pocket of Zoe's winter coat, and eased the closet door shut. Then she shimmied under Zoe's bed, SIG Sauer in one hand, chef's knife in the other.

Thirty-seven seconds later, one of the men entered Zoe's room. He approached the sleeping girl slowly, as if not wishing to disturb her.

Take your time, asshole, Hannah thought. If he grabbed Zoe before her phone's timer went off, her plan was toast.

From beneath the bed, she eyed his leather boots, and the armored plates he wore at thigh, knee, and shin.

One minute after the men entered the apartment—twenty-three seconds after this one stepped across the threshold into Zoe's room—Hannah's phone began to vibrate.

The man turned toward it. As she'd hoped, his armor was held on with simple nylon straps, leaving the backs of his legs unprotected. Hannah lashed out with her blade, aiming for his inside left pant leg, just above the boot—or, more accurately, the posterior tibial artery not far beneath.

Knife parted fabric and flesh before hitting bone. The man screamed and fell, blood gushing from the wound. His gun discharged, pocking the far wall. Zoe awakened and began to cry.

Hannah slid out from under the bed and stabbed him again, this time burying the knife in his right thigh, severing his femoral artery. Soon, both his legs were drenched in blood.

Within seconds, he lost consciousness.

He was dead before his buddy reached the open bedroom door.

Hannah squeezed off three quick shots. The second man toppled backward into the hall. She followed, aware his armor had likely stopped all three, and determined to keep shooting until he stayed down for good.

Before she got the chance, he swept her legs, and sent her sprawling. She slammed onto the hardwood floor, her gun sailing down the hall toward the front door. It glinted like a beacon in the filtered streetlight.

When Hannah scrabbled toward it, the asshole grabbed her foot and yanked.

Too bad for him it was the wrong damn foot.

With her free leg, she kicked him in the face, knocking his mask askew. His grip on her foot slackened, but held. That was okay. She didn't expect him to release her. She just needed to stun him long enough for her to flip over.

She didn't quite manage—ending up on her side, rather than her back, as she'd hoped.

Eh, Hannah thought, *close enough*.

She did an awkward sideways sit-up and, through her pant leg, pressed the pin lock to release her prosthesis.

Then she threw herself once more toward the gun.

This time, she managed to grab it.

Hannah rolled onto her back and pulled the trigger. Savage delight coursed through her as the muzzle flash created a snapshot of her assailant trying to understand how her foot had just come off in his hand. Then blood spattered her exposed skin, and she was glad he'd killed the lights before she shot him in the face.

Her ears rang from the gunshots, shrill and insistent, like a patient coding. Her body trembled, instinct lagging behind intellect in realizing the threat had passed.

She wrested her prosthesis from the dead man's hands, hiked up her pant leg, and reaffixed it. Then she returned to Zoe's room and scooped the girl up in her arms.

Zoe, hot as a furnace, buried her face in Hannah's neck and cried.

"Honey, listen. I know you're scared right now, and not feeling well, but we've got to take a little trip, okay?"

"Where are we going?"

"To see your daddy," Hannah replied.

THE 8/17 COMMISSION REPORT
APPENDIX D

The following is an archived snapshot of a private https://www
.shadowvox.net/messages chat as it appeared on November 22, 2027,
07:31:00 GMT. Said web domain is now defunct, the result of a federal
seizure order executed on August 23, 2028. Username PlagueDoctor
has since been positively identified as Spencer Aaron Brutsch
(deceased). Username thewhiterider remains unidentified. For a comprehensive list of all known /endtimes users, see Appendix N.

---

https://www.shadowvox.net/messages

ShadowVox: Speak Freely

PLAGUEDOCTOR (1H): hey, man. can i ask you something?

THEWHITERIDER (56M): sure whats on your mind

PLAGUEDOCTOR (55M): do you mean what you've been saying lately

PLAGUEDOCTOR (54M): about people needing a push to wake them up?

THEWHITERIDER (51M): depends whos asking

PLAGUEDOCTOR (49M): just a friend who wants to know if you're serious or
shitposting.

PLAGUEDOCTOR (48M): no judgment here either way.

THEWHITERIDER (46M): you wanna know what i think

THEWHITERIDER (46M): i think most people are sheep

THEWHITERIDER (45M): mindless consumers

THEWHITERIDER (45M): fuckin zombies

THEWHITERIDER (44M): all they care about is there own bullshit

THEWHITERIDER (44M): which means they wont be easy to wake up

PLAGUEDOCTOR (42M): so you're serious, then.

PLAGUEDOCTOR (41M): provided we could generate a big enough push.

THEWHITERIDER (38M): yea i guess

THEWHITERIDER (37M): but itd have to be the redpill of all redpills

PLAGUEDOCTOR (34M): believe me, dude, it would be.

THEWHITERIDER (31M): i admit you've peaked my interest

THEWHITERIDER (30M): *piqued

PLAGUEDOCTOR (29M): even if it means some people have to die?

THEWHITERIDER (27M): seriously???

THEWHITERIDER (27M): youre not a cop are you

PLAGUEDOCTOR (26M): i dunno. are you?

THEWHITERIDER (24M): lol fair enough

THEWHITERIDER (23M): lay your big idea on me

PLAGUEDOCTOR (21M): i mean, i can't promise anything, and even if we agree to do this, it'd take me a while . . .

THEWHITERIDER (20M): jesus bro just spit it out

PLAGUEDOCTOR (19M): okay . . . what if i told you i could get my hands on enough plague to wipe a whole damn city off the map?

PLAGUEDOCTOR (16M): hello?

PLAGUEDOCTOR (10M): you still there?

THEWHITERIDER (7M): youre sure youre not a cop

THEWHITERIDER (7M): or fuckin insane

PLAGUEDOCTOR (6M): i'm not. i swear.

THEWHITERIDER (5M): ok then why approach me?

PLAGUEDOCTOR (4M): because you're smart.

PLAGUEDOCTOR (4M): a true believer like me.

PLAGUEDOCTOR (3M): and because i need help figuring out how to disperse it.

THEWHITERIDER (30S): shit why not count me in

25.

Ethan Rask hunched, panting, over his handlebars. A narrow ribbon of asphalt unspooled haphazardly before him, all hairpin turns and grueling upslopes until the mountain's summit, eight kilometers ahead.

The route wended around outcrops of snowcapped rock. Runoff slicked the roadway. This high up, the air was thin, which made the sky a vibrant shade of blue, and the sun a pale white disk with little scatter at the edges.

Ethan had been riding for an hour and a half. His legs quivered with every pedal stroke. His lungs burned with every ragged breath. Still, he knew the worst was yet to come.

The Col du Galibier's northern ascent was among the most revered and reviled in all of cycling. Nearly thirty-five kilometers, all told, during which you climb two mountains and more than two thousand meters in altitude—some of them twice, thanks to a brief downslope on the backside of the Col du Télégraphe. The final eight kilometers, which Ethan now stared down, featured a series of vertiginous switchbacks and an average incline around 9 percent.

Galibier first featured in 1911's Tour de France, when single-gear bikes were king. Only three riders made it to the summit without walking. Even on a modern road bike, Galibier was an exercise in masochism.

154

As Ethan faded, the incline sapping his momentum, a bearded vulture rode an updraft high above the valley to his left — first matching his altitude, and then surpassing it.

Ethan grinned.

Game on, motherfucker.

He downshifted and rose from his bike saddle, bringing his full weight to bear on every downstroke. His bike lurched toward the mountain's peak.

Somewhere, at once distant and nearby, a door banged open. A woman exclaimed, "Hey! I said he's busy! You can't just—"

"Damn it, Hailey!" Ethan stripped off his VR headset and hung it from the handlebars of the stationary bike to which it was wirelessly linked. "I told you I wasn't to be interrupted!"

"I'm so sorry, Mr. Rask! I couldn't stop him!"

Tears brimmed in Hailey's eyes, but when Ethan recognized the man who'd barged in on his virtual ride through the French Alps, his face relaxed into an expression of amusement.

"Don't worry about it, Hailey. Thus far, Congress hasn't figured out a way to stop him, either, although I'm not sure if that places you in good company or bad." Then, to his uninvited guest: "Good morning, Lionel. How nice of you to drop by."

"Like hell it is," he snapped.

"Hailey, perhaps it would be best if you excused us. Please tell Kristof I'll be taking breakfast earlier than anticipated."

She eyed Lionel suspiciously. "Shall I have him make enough for two?"

"No need," Ethan said. "Director Mercer won't be staying long."

Hailey left. Lionel watched her go.

"Cute kid. What is she, thirteen?"

"She's twenty-seven, and has an MBA from the Sloan School of Management."

"Good for her." Lionel inspected Ethan's private gym with the contemptuous air of a potential buyer who found it lacking. When his gaze lit upon the molded leather pouch that rested on a floating shelf not far from Ethan's reach, he quirked an eyebrow. "My God, you really *do* take that thing everywhere, don't you?"

The pouch contained an autoinjector designed and manufactured by Ethan's company, ProTx. There were only five like it in existence. One had been purchased by the House of Saud. The Knowles-Carter family was in possession of another. Abigail Bettencourt, founder and CEO of Bangarang, had one too—as, per the terms of their divorce, did her ex-husband.

The president, notably, did not.

Each autoinjector contained a single-dose, broad-spectrum antibiotic to which no bacteria outside ProTx's BSL-4 labs had ever been exposed. As soon as any of the five were used, the remaining four would be presumed compromised. Until then, they were a break-glass-in-case-of-emergency guard against infection.

"I don't see what business it is of yours," Ethan replied.

"Funny; you didn't clam up when *Time* asked you about it last year, or when the *Wall Street Journal* ran a fawning article on its development the year before. Why the change of heart? Did your pollsters warn you that your golden healthcare parachute doesn't play well with the proles in the flyover states?"

"Aw. Have you been reading up on me, Lionel? I'll admit, I'm touched. I had no idea you were such a fan. If you remind me, I'll have Hailey fetch you a signed copy of my autobiography on your way out."

Ethan unzipped his jersey to his navel, exposing a dark thatch of sweaty chest hair, and swigged water from the bottle mounted on his bike. Lionel crinkled his nose with distaste.

"How long have you been on that thing?" he asked. "It smells like a goddamn monkey house in here."

"Be that as it may, it's my monkey house, and you are but an uninvited guest."

"The Wellness Act is all the invitation I need," Lionel countered. "You should take a gander at it sometime."

"I've read it," Ethan said, "which is more than the cowards your boss extorted into voting for it can say."

"Doesn't matter how it passed. The law's the law."

"Laws change. So do administrations."

"Not fast enough for you to throw me out of your apartment, I'm afraid."

Ethan admired the glib dismissiveness of *your apartment,* as if his Elysian Tower penthouse weren't among the most desirable and expensive pieces of real estate in the city. Even the building's base units fetched eight figures, due in large part to its exclusivity and its unprecedented commitment to the safety and privacy of its tenants.

"Speaking of, neat trick, waltzing in here unannounced," Ethan said. "Damn few people on the planet have the clout to pull that off. Makes me wonder if you intended it as a threat."

Lionel smiled, showing teeth. "A threat? Goodness, no. More like a friendly reminder that our respective positions on security are not as oppositional as you've repeatedly made them out to be."

"Sure, except the United States isn't a luxury high-rise, and prosecuting trespassers is a far cry from shooting them in the street."

"What happened at the border was an unfortunate act of vigilantism—"

"—spurred on by your boss's wildly irresponsible rhetoric, and perpetrated by members of his base."

"You're one to talk about wildly irresponsible rhetoric," Lionel spat. "And since there aren't any reporters within earshot, don't insult me by pretending you actually give a shit about a few unwashed illegals—or the residents of Park City, for that matter. We both know you're only making waves in the hopes they'll carry you into the Oval."

Ethan laughed. "Wait, is *that* what this is about? You broke into my home to dress me down over a fucking op-ed?"

The piece, titled "The Latest Failure in the War on Bugs," was featured in this morning's *New York Times*. Ethan was quite proud of it. His ghostwriter, a hungry young poet whose own work invariably met with critical acclaim and commercial indifference, had truly outdone himself.

"Of course," Lionel, thrown by Ethan's amusement, replied. "Why else would I be here?"

"If you don't know, I'm sure as hell not going to tell you. Still, I figured you as thicker skinned than that."

"You accused my department of covering up a heinous crime in Central Park, and stopped just shy of implicating us in the explosion in Tribeca."

"Oh, come on. I said no such thing. All I did was pose the question. Readers are welcome to draw any conclusion they wish."

"Yes, you were very careful to avoid being sued into oblivion while all but endorsing the extralegal activities of the Resistance."

"If you don't like what I wrote, offer evidence to the contrary, and I'll retract it. But if my piece was so off base, what are you doing in my Manhattan penthouse at seven thirty in the morning on the very day that it was published, when you live outside DC? I find it hard to believe you hopped a plane before sunrise just to chew me out, which means you were already in town. The question is, why?"

Lionel ignored Ethan's line of inquiry. "You know what your problem is, Rask?"

"Right now, I want to say 'the asshole who barged in on my workout,' but that's probably not the answer you're looking for."

"The fact is, you've been rich so long, you're out of touch. You like to brag you came from nothing, but you have no idea what nothing looks like these days. How could you? The world you knew is gone — killed by the Harbinger virus — and its replacement is uglier than you could possibly imagine."

"Maybe so, but I've got no trouble recognizing fascism when I see it."

"And, what, you fancy yourself some kind of freedom fighter?" Lionel laughed. "Please. It's one thing to take potshots from the safety of your ivory tower. It's quite another to crawl around in the muck where things get done. I doubt you have the stomach for it."

"You have no idea what I'm capable of," Ethan replied, "but you have my word, you'll find out soon enough."

"Tread carefully, Ethan. Threatening a DBS agent is a federal offense that carries a sentence of ten years."

"Oh, don't worry. By the time I'm through with you, you'll no longer be in the agency's employ."

Lionel cocked his head and eyed Ethan appraisingly. "What, exactly, do you think you have on me?"

"More than enough to cast a shadow on your political ambitions, I'd reckon."

"Is that so." Lionel smiled. "Seems to me, if you'd stumbled into something really juicy, you would've used it by now — which means you haven't got a goddamn thing." He made a show of checking his watch. "Hmm. Loath though I am to cut short our little tête-à-tête, I'm afraid I have pressing business to attend to."

"Pity," Ethan said wryly. "I'll summon Hailey to walk you out."

"Don't bother; I know the way. If I were you, though, I'd have her lock up tight behind me. Otherwise, there's no telling who might wander in."

Elysian Tower

There is no greater luxury than peace of mind.

Amenities include:

Keyless, biometric access control

Spacious layouts in a host of thoughtful configurations

Floor-to-ceiling bullet/blast-proof windows, which offer stunning views of Manhattan

Granite countertops, stainless steel appliances, and UV sterilization cabinets in every kitchen

24/7 access to our spa, concierge, fitness center, and private in-house medical clinic

Optional access to our rooftop terrace, meditation garden, and helipad

Hermetically sealed construction and HVAC system featuring DBS-approved biofilters

Full lockdown capabilities, including one month's emergency food/oxygen stores

ZeroInfil® Active Countermeasure System to prevent unauthorized entry

Complimentary one-year subscription to XODUS® Aerial Evacuation Service

---

An oasis of calm in the heart of the city that lets you leave the outside…outside.

TO LEARN MORE, CONTACT YOUR REAL ESTATE AGENT.

26.

Jake awoke, groggy and confused, to the sound of laughter.

He lay on his side atop a flimsy mattress in a dark, windowless room, illuminated only by the stripe of daylight between carpet and door. The wooden frame supporting the mattress pressed uncomfortably against his shoulder, hip, and knee. The dry, conditioned air smelled of potpourri and oxidized blood.

Right, Jake thought, *the futon in the Croziers' spare bedroom.* He never imagined he'd have a weekend so shitty that breaking into a dead couple's apartment would momentarily slip his mind.

His back was sore. His neck was stiff. His joints popped as he stretched. A yawn escaped him, at which point Jake realized the smoke he'd inhaled yesterday had scratched his throat raw.

Creakily, he climbed to his feet and opened the bedroom door.

The curtains in the living room were flung wide.

Jake squinted in the sudden daylight, and shielded his eyes with a raised forearm, vampirically.

"Oh, good!" Amy smiled. "You're up!"

"You two wanna keep it down a little? Or have you forgotten that we're trying to lay low?" His voice sounded like a rusty hinge.

"Don't mind him," Amy told Mat, "he's always grumpy in the morning."

The two of them were on the far side of the kitchen island, facing

Jake. A large mixing bowl, some measuring cups, and a bottle of vegetable oil occupied the work surface, most of them dusted white.

"What's all this?" Jake asked.

Mat beamed. "We're making pancakes!"

Jake's gaze met Amy's. "Seriously?"

"Not from scratch or anything," she replied. "Just a mix I found in the cupboard. It's like a year expired, but still. Seemed a more appropriate breakfast than leftover stir-fry."

"A mix," he muttered, shaking his head. Then, to Amy: "You lost a lot of blood yesterday. Shouldn't you be lying down?"

"Honestly, a little soreness aside, I feel fine. Better than fine, even, as long as I remember not to move my arm too much."

"No redness? Swelling? Discharge?"

"None."

"What about fever or malaise?"

"Jake, look at me: I'm *fine*."

He absently massaged his jaw. Two days' stubble rasped against his hand.

Amy cocked her head, eyes narrowing. "What is it?"

"What is what?" Jake replied.

"Oh, come on. I've been your partner long enough to know when something's bugging you."

"Nothing's *bugging* me, exactly. I'm glad you're feeling better. It's just . . . you remember my buddy Tom Stearns?"

Amy seemed puzzled by his apparent non sequitur. "From your time at the academy, right? Works a precinct up in Harlem?"

"That's the one."

"What about him?"

"Last week, he had to have a toe amputated, on account of an ingrown nail. Meanwhile, you yank a chunk of derelict building from your arm and wake up smiling."

"Thanks to you."

"That's just it. Much as I'd love to take credit, all I did was patch you up. I have a feeling you have someone else to thank for your wound not getting infected."

Jake eyed Mat pointedly.

The boy reddened and looked at his shoes.

Amy scrunched up her face as she tried to square Jake's implication. "How —"

"I don't know, but think about it: Park City's raided. Mat flees, leaving behind a village full of detainees in perfect health. The perps chase him to Tribeca, where we bump into him. Then, last night, when I offer him the futon, he insists on sleeping in the living room with you — and you wake up feeling better than I do."

"My partner spins a decent yarn," Amy said. "Is there any truth to it?"

Mat chewed the inside of his cheek and said nothing.

"If there is," she continued, "you can tell us — we won't get mad."

Eyes downcast, he mumbled something too softly to hear.

"I'm sorry," Amy said, "what was that?"

"I said my uncle made me promise not to tell!"

Jake and Amy shared a glance.

"Tell what?" Amy asked.

The boy, not falling for it, rolled his eyes.

"Maybe we can guess, so you don't have to," Jake said. "Would that be okay?"

Mat shrugged.

Jake adopted a thoughtful expression. "Does it have anything to do with the mystery package you've been carrying?"

Mat shook his head.

"Are you sure?" Jake pressed gently. "It's important that you tell the truth. Even the best medicines can be dangerous sometimes.

That's why doctors have to get permission from the patient or their family before treating them."

"You think I don't know that?"

"I'm just saying, I know you meant well, but if you gave Amy something last night while she was sleeping—"

"I swear I didn't give her anything!"

"Look, Mat, I want to believe you, but you just admitted—"

"No, I didn't." Mat folded his arms across his chest. "You *assumed*."

"Oh, please. That package is the only thing you brought with you from Park City. Before bed, when I asked you what was in it, you deflected. Now, Amy's made a miraculous recovery, and you're all kinds of defensive. What else am I supposed to think?"

"Beats me, but I'm telling you the truth." Mat's face was a challenge. "Go ahead and open it if you don't believe me."

Jake's temper flared. "You know what? I think I will."

He crossed the room and snatched the package off the side table. It was small, rectangular. Wrapped in stiff waxed canvas, bound with twine. Jake picked at the knot until it came loose—Mat scowling at him all the while—then peeled back the fabric to reveal a rusty, dented tin that once held tea.

"Jake, c'mon," Amy said. "If he says there's nothing in there, there's nothing in there."

"Are you willing to bet my daughter's life on that? Because I'm sure as hell not. If there's even a tiny chance he's hiding something that could make Zoe better, I have to look."

Jake popped the lid and tossed it aside. The tin's contents were enclosed in a resealable plastic bag, fogged with moisture. He fished it out, broke the seal, and emptied it onto the coffee table.

He wasn't sure what he'd expected. Vials? Capsules? Syringes? Instead, the bag contained a smattering of photographs and handwritten letters, the former yellowed with age, the latter soft and blurry from repeated handling.

"I don't understand," Jake said. "What is this stuff?"

"That's all I have left of my family," Mat replied, the bitterness in his voice imperfect camouflage for his pain.

Jake's face burned with shame. He opened his mouth to apologize, but the words wouldn't come.

Amy, taking pity on her partner, approached the table and nodded toward the photographs. "May I?"

"Sure."

She plucked a photo from the table by its edges and examined it.

"Is this your mother?"

Mat nodded.

"She's beautiful. And the boy beside her . . ."

"That's me." A faint smile touched his lips. "I was four."

"Who's the baby on her lap?"

"That's my little brother, Sebastian."

"Where's your dad?"

He shrugged. "Dunno. Jail, probably. Growing up, it was mostly just the three of us."

"Your mom and brother . . . are they back home?" The question spilled from Jake unbidden. He wasn't sure he wanted Mat to answer.

Mat's lip trembled as he shook his head.

Amy squeezed his arm affectionately.

"Dad turned up at my eighth birthday party with a bunch of his buddies, said I was almost old enough to follow in his footsteps, to run with La 18. We left town before sunrise the next day."

He swallowed hard, his Adam's apple bobbing.

"It took almost a month for us to reach the US border. Sometimes, we walked. Sometimes, we hitched. Once, we stowed away in the back of a flatbed truck, hiding between giant spools of wire. In

Reynosa, we met a man who said he knew a spot where we could cross. He drove us into the desert, handed us a rubber raft, and told us to start walking north. It was dark out when we reached the Rio Grande. There wasn't enough room for all three of us on the raft—it was really just a pool float—so Mom decided Sebastian, being youngest, would ride on top, while she and I held on to the sides and paddled."

Mat's eyes welled.

"I still don't know how Sebastian fell in. I just heard a splash, and he was gone. Mom let go of the raft so she could grab him, and the next thing I knew, I was alone. I climbed onto the raft, and shouted after them until my voice gave out, but…"

His chest hitched, but he composed himself.

"I don't remember reaching the far bank, but I must have, because that's where Border Patrol found me."

Tears spilled down Mat's cheeks.

He wiped them away with the back of his hand.

"When I met my uncle Gabriel, I found out Mom sent him letters once a month, and included photos of the three of us whenever she could. He didn't keep every letter, just the ones he thought were important. He kept every single picture, though. Three months after we got stuck in Park City, our landlord threatened to evict us, so Gabriel asked a neighbor to retrieve them. Then he bribed a guard to smuggle them into the camp. Now I really wish that he was in the pictures, too, because—"

Mat broke down then. Jake put an arm around him, haltingly, unsure if it was welcome. The boy buried his face in Jake's shirt and cried.

When his sobs abated, Jake said, "I'm so sorry. I didn't know."

"It's okay," Mat replied, sniffling.

"Still, Amy was right. I shouldn't have gone through your stuff like that—but you've got to understand, my little girl is very sick, and there's nothing I wouldn't do to save her." Jake paused. Changed direction. "Hey, can I ask you something? You don't have to answer if you don't want, or if it violates your promise to your uncle."

Mat shrugged. "Sure."

"If you're not carrying some kind of miracle cure, why are the assholes in the black masks after you?"

The boy pursed his lips, as if deciding how, or whether, to answer. He was silent long enough that Jake was certain he wouldn't. Then—quietly, carefully—he said, "Because of what I can do."

"What does that mean?" Amy asked. "What can you do?"

Mat didn't answer. It was obvious he'd said all that he was going to on the topic.

Eventually, Amy forced a smile and said, "Okay, then. Who wants pancakes?"

Both Mat and Jake responded tepidly, but she hurried off to make them nonetheless. Moments later, Mat trundled after to assist. Jake figured two pairs of hands were plenty, so he snatched the Croziers' tablet off the coffee table, opened its browser, and typed in the address for Hannah's Bangarang feed.

At the top was a new post, its time stamp an hour or so after he fell asleep.

In desperate need of a vacation, it read. *Think I'll get out of the city for a while.*

Jake bolted to his feet, the tablet falling from his hands. It hit the coffee table hard enough to leave a mark.

"Jake, what's wrong?" Amy asked, alarmed.

"I have to go," he said. "Hannah and Zoe are in trouble."

27.

When the young men slowed to intercept her, Hannah set her jaw, lengthened her stride, and held the sick child she was carrying a little tighter to her chest.

Hannah had been watching them amble north along the Hudson River in the shadow of the West Side Highway since she and Zoe reached the pedestrian ramp that passed beneath the elevated thoroughfare. Because the lengthy ramp descended northwest from West 68th Street and Riverside Boulevard to the water's edge, she'd realized their paths would intersect, but she'd been praying they'd ignore her and continue on their way.

Instead, it seemed that she and Zoe had piqued their interest, probably because they looked so out of place. These days, few New Yorkers dared avail themselves of the city's public parks, and even fewer were foolish enough to bring their children.

Shame, Hannah thought. *This place must have been beautiful in its prime.*

Riverside Park South owed its existence to an unlikely collaboration between a future president with grandiose plans to develop the defunct 60th Street Rail Yard—then the largest tract of unused land in Manhattan—and the wealthy Upper West Side denizens who opposed him.

For decades, Donald Trump believed transforming the old rail-yard into "a city within a city" would be his legacy. Aghast at the artless cluster of skyscrapers he envisioned, local residents—including feminist icon Betty Friedan, actor Christopher Reeve, and comedian Jerry Seinfeld, as well as future Trump administration gadfly Jerry Nadler—organized against him.

Eventually, Trump capitulated, scrapping his outsized ambitions in favor of a more palatable development plan that included ample waterfront greenspace. The West Side Highway was relocated. Riverside Park was extended south. The railyard's decrepit pier was rebuilt for public use.

At the time, the park was hailed as a triumph of urban planning, but since 8/17 it had fallen into disrepair. Its paths were uneven and overgrown. Its athletic fields were patchy and strewn with litter. Its pier—once host to fairs, concerts, and outdoor movies—had been surrendered to the criminals and indigents.

These three were almost certainly the former. Though they appeared to be in high spirits, jostling one another playfully as they walked, Hannah took no comfort in their exuberance, because she recognized their kind.

They were Endtimers.

Soldiers of Gaia, to be precise.

Hannah guessed that they were in their early twenties, although their emaciation made it hard to say for sure. Two had shaved heads. One had dreadlocks held in place with a bandanna. All were pale, greasy, and unbathed. Even from a distance, they stank of body odor and patchouli.

Their clothes were a baggy mix of thrifted items and army surplus, which they'd customized with myriad patches, pins, and buttons celebrating everything from antinatalist philosophy to animal liberation. Their jackets bore a stenciled image of Earth strapped into an old-timey gas mask. Bedraggled canvas sneakers, mended with duct tape, graced their feet.

Ten months ago, an adolescent male of the same description was wheeled into Hannah's ER with severe head trauma, multiple fractures, and acute respiratory distress. When she attempted to treat him, he went berserk, hurling himself off the gurney and sinking his teeth into her calf. Then he coded, and couldn't be revived.

Soon after, the bite became infected, necessitating the amputation of Hannah's leg below the knee.

She later discovered that his injuries had been self-inflicted. He'd stepped in front of a commuter train while streaming live on social media. His last words, barely audible over the screeching brakes and bleating horn, were, "Man is the disease. Death is the cure." Then he smiled into the camera until the train hit.

His was one of thirteen such deaths that day, in locales as varied as Brunswick, Maine, and Oakland, California—a coming-out of sorts for a group that called itself the Soldiers of Gaia.

Zoe—perhaps sensing Hannah's agitation—squirmed uncomfortably in Hannah's arms, her paper face mask crinkling. Hannah, barefaced, stroked Zoe's hair, and her fevered body stilled.

Hannah looked at her watch, an analog Timex, pretending not to notice the stubborn flecks of dried blood on its face. It was eleven oh nine. A minute later than the last time she looked. Two minutes before Jake was scheduled to meet her at the pier—assuming, of course, that she'd deciphered his message correctly.

Last night, she and Zoe fled Jake's building via a poorly lit side door, in part to avoid being spotted, and in part so Hannah could keep Zoe far away from the dead cops parked out front. After thumb-typing a quick Bangarang post, she'd slipped her cell phone into a bag of trash left at the curb. Worst case, she figured it'd keep pinging the tower nearest Jake's apartment until it ran out of juice. Best case, it'd wind up leaving town in the back of a garbage truck, and take anybody trying to follow her with it.

In the car, Hannah cleaned herself up with napkins and hand sanitizer, then changed into the spare clothes she kept in her gym bag. She drove around the empty streets of Queens for half an hour, Zoe drifting in and out of consciousness in the backseat, before she came across a body shop with a free spot tucked among the wrecks outside.

Hannah parked the car, cracked the windows, and turned off the engine, then reclined her seat so she could catch some shut-eye while they waited out the curfew. Her doctor's plates might prevent the cops from hassling her, but not from taking notice, and the less attention they attracted, the better. Since the body shop was closed on Sundays, she figured they could hang out there until it was time to go meet Jake.

Now, as she and Zoe neared the bottom of the ramp, the slap of the approaching Endtimers' gum soles jangled Hannah's nerves. Her skin crawled. Her stomach churned. Her missing limb ached, an awful memory manifesting.

The pier was within sight.

Jake wasn't on it.

She checked her watch.

Eleven ten.

One minute left, Hannah thought, *so where the hell is he?*

The taxi had barely moved in seven minutes.

Up ahead, orange traffic cones narrowed Tenth Avenue from four lanes to one. In the blocked-off section, a road crew milled around an open manhole spewing steam.

The roadwork had caught Jake's driver unawares. Now they were pinned in an interior lane by everybody trying to merge. Horns blared. Drivers swore at one another in six languages.

"Listen," Jake said when his driver allowed another cab ahead of them, "I'm in a bit of a hurry here."

"You and everybody else. Not much I can do."

Jake eyed the clock on the dash. Ten fifty-eight.

"That thing right?"

"Hmm?"

"The clock. Is it right?"

"I dunno." His driver shrugged. "More or less."

Goddamn it.

As soon as Jake had spotted Hannah's signal, he'd thrown on the same disguise he'd worn to the Jade Dragon and headed out. Initially, he planned on walking to the pier, so he could avoid interacting with anyone who might remember him if questioned later. Problem was, even at a brisk pace, Riverside Park South was nearly an hour and a half away from the Croziers' apartment, and he soon discovered it was way too sultry outside for him to hurry in this outfit. Add to that the fact that wearing a windbreaker in this heat attracted funny looks, and he decided flagging down a cab was worth the risk.

Sure, most New York taxis were equipped with cameras, but he was wearing a disposable mask, and anyway, their cameras were unconnected to the city grid. They were more like dashcams or bodycams, storing footage locally for later download. Absent a good reason, the odds that anyone would ever look at it were slim—and, thanks to Jake's line of work, he habitually carried more than enough cash to cover the fare.

New York's surveillance grid was a peculiar beast. Installing a municipal camera system large enough to blanket the entire city would have been prohibitively expensive, so instead, government cameras—traffic and security—were augmented by networking them with private cameras via a voluntary, tax-incentivized program that provided decent coverage for a fraction of the cost.

The method did, however, result in gaps. New York's public parks, for example. At nearly thirty thousand acres—variously managed by the city, state, and federal governments—they were impractical to surveil in their entirety. Instead, the NYPD relied on a handful of mobile camera rigs, which they moved from park to park as demand required.

The rigs were typically employed after-hours to deter drug dealing and illicit sex, so they were obvious by design—making a show of photographing anyone who triggered their motion sensors, complete with a bright flash and a recorded announcement stating, "Your picture has been taken for suspicious activity by the NYPD!"

During daylight hours, however, such public spaces were largely unmonitored, and the mobile camera rigs inactive. That, and the fact that he could easily communicate it to Hannah without tipping anyone who might be listening in, is why Jake chose to meet at Riverside Park South's Pier I.

On their first date, Jake and Hannah met for coffee. Jake was transfixed. Hannah was unconvinced. He was a gun-toting omnivore; she was a vegetarian pacifist. Still, they texted afterward, and she assented to a second date, largely because he offered up her favorite taco joint unprompted. They were halfway to the restaurant when he caught a case: a transient stabbed to death on the pier in what turned out to be a dispute over a fishing spot. Since they weren't far, Jake dragged Hannah along—apologizing profusely all the while—and had a uni drive her home.

He was sure he'd never hear from her again. Instead, to his surprise, she found the evening charming. A surgeon's life didn't leave much room for dating—or, for that matter, squeamishness—so she was relieved to find someone who understood, and took his job as seriously as she did.

Last night, thinking on the fly, the pier had struck Jake as an ideal location. Now, he had his doubts. It was way too visible for his liking, and only had one point of access, which meant if either of them was followed, they'd be trapped. Still, it was the best that he could do on short notice.

The cab crept forward. Jake checked the time. Eleven oh four. Seven minutes until the meet. He prayed that Hannah and Zoe would still be there when he arrived.

Though Hannah wasn't typically the superstitious sort, she always made a wish when the clock read eleven eleven, a habit that she'd picked up from her granddad. Jake figured his pointed *whenever you wish* would be easy for her to decipher. It also gave them two cracks a day at meeting, although he didn't relish the idea of Hannah bringing Zoe to the park so late at night, since the place was already kinda dicey when the sun was shining.

The cab pulled even with the work site. Jake bounced a knee to dispel his nervous energy. His right hand was stuffed into the pocket of his stolen windbreaker, gripping his backup piece tightly enough to leave a textured imprint on his palm.

The driver looked at him in the rearview. "You really *are* in a hurry, ain't ya?"

"Believe me, I wish I wasn't."

"I'm guessing this has something to do with a girl?"

"Yeah," Jake said. "Two of 'em, in fact."

"Two of 'em," he echoed, shaking his head. "Shit." It came out *shee-it*.

The cones stopped. The road widened. The traffic spread out and began to clear.

"Well, would you look at that," the cabbie said. "Must be your lucky day."

Tires squealed as he hit the gas.

Jake sunk back into his seat.

The cab lurched north.

As Hannah and Zoe reached the bottom of the ramp, where the Endtimers loitered, the one with dreadlocks flashed Hannah a toothy grin.

"Hey there, mama."

She walked past without a word, her gaze fixed on a seagull that circled in the middle distance. Its plaintive cries sounded, to Hannah's ear, like a warning.

The Endtimers fell in behind her.

"Aw, c'mon. Don't be like that. We just wanna chat."

Hannah hazarded a glance at her watch.

Eleven eleven.

Make a wish, she thought—and she would have, but she was torn between wishing Jake were here and wishing she hadn't left his old SIG Sauer locked inside her glove compartment.

"What're you, deaf? Look at me when I'm talking to you, bitch!"

Reluctantly, she turned to face them.

Overhead, traffic rumbled by, oblivious to her plight.

Seven million people in this city, Hannah thought, *and I wind up facing these creeps all alone.*

"So you *can* hear," Dreadlocks said. "Makes me wonder why you mighta been ignoring us."

"Right?" This from one of the bald guys. Up close, Hannah noticed he had a chinstrap beard that somehow accentuated his thuggish vibe. "Seems downright hurtful."

"Like she thinks she's better than we are," said his cleanshaven buddy.

"I don't want trouble," she said. "I'm on my way to meet a friend."

"This must be your lucky day, then," Dreadlocks said. "You found three."

His flunkies chortled.

"The little girl," said Chinstrap, "she yours?"

Hannah adjusted her grip on Zoe, who seemed to grow heavier by the minute.

The Endtimers fanned out, surrounding her.

Hannah's pulse quickened when she realized she couldn't keep an eye on more than two of them at a time.

"The little girl is none of your business."

"The hell she isn't. We're all stuck on the same dying rock, breathing the same poison air, drowning in each other's waste. Speaking of, do you have any idea how many hectares of arable land your little parasite requires to sustain her, or how many tons of trash she'll produce in her lifetime?"

"Not offhand," Hannah replied, "but I have a feeling you could tell me."

"You think the systematic rape of our planet is some kind of fucking joke?" She whipped her head around in time to see Dreadlocks's face contort with rage. "Procreators like you make me sick. You're all so goddamn selfish, fornicating while our Mother suffers, birthing hungry mouth after hungry mouth without a thought as to the consequences."

Zoe wasn't hers, of course, but Hannah didn't bother correcting him. After all, she spent her work hours patching up her fellow parasites so they could live to mindlessly consume another day. She figured that'd probably piss them off at least as much as breeding seemed to.

Hannah snuck another peek at her watch. Eleven thirteen.

Damn it, Jake — where the hell are you?

"What's the matter, bitch?" asked Dreadlocks. "We boring you or something?"

When she failed to answer, he closed the gap between them and grabbed her face in a pinch grip — his palm beneath her chin, his bony thumb and fingers mashing her cheeks into her teeth — forcing her to look him in the eye. Zoe awakened with a start. Hannah tried to wriggle free. Chinstrap grabbed her from behind, holding her fast.

"I asked you a question," Dreadlocks said. His breath stank of ketones, fruity and acidic — his body digesting itself as a result of his brutally restrictive diet.

He squeezed Hannah's cheeks so hard that she tasted blood.

A bead of sweat slid down her back.

Zoe, delirious and frightened, began to cry.

Then, from somewhere behind them, came a pained yowl, a sickening thud, and a familiar voice — muffled slightly as if filtered through a paper mask.

"Hey, fellas? Unless you wanna find out what the inside of your buddy's brainpan looks like, I suggest you let the lady go."

28.

"Jake?"

Though her speech was distorted by the dreadlocked Endtimer's grip on her face, the relief in Hannah's tone was hard to miss.

"Sorry I'm late," Jake replied. "Traffic was a bitch."

By the time he'd arrived at the park, Hannah and Zoe had already been surrounded. The roar of the West Side Highway overhead had drowned out the Endtimers' words, but their body language—predatory, cocksure—made apparent their intent.

Feigning disinterest, Jake had sauntered toward them, hoping to get close enough to intervene without exacerbating the situation. Then two of the Endtimers grabbed Hannah, and Jake abandoned any pretense of stealth, freeing his Glock from the right pocket of his jacket and breaking into a sprint.

The bald, cleanshaven Endtimer—who'd hung back a little from his buddies, as if conflicted about terrorizing strangers, though not enough to put a stop to it—pivoted toward the sound of Jake's footfalls, and right into Jake's pistol. Jake had meant to hit the scrawny bastard in the back of the head, stunning him, but the combination of his swing and the Endtimer's rotation magnified the force of impact considerably. A crunch of bone and Cue Ball went down hard—nose gushing blood, eyes showing only whites.

Jake grabbed him by the collar and lifted him to his knees. He swayed like a boxer who'd been TKO'd, but, with a little assistance from Jake, managed to remain upright. Jake pressed the barrel of his gun to the dope's head and told his nutfuck buddies to leave Hannah be.

Dreadlocks, who appeared unfazed by the sudden turn of events, raised his head to look at Jake and smiled. Looming over Hannah and Zoe, his haunting rictus exposing yellow teeth, he put Jake in mind of a scarecrow fashioned out of human bones. "Daddy dearest, I presume?"

"Presume anything you like," Jake replied, "so long as you do what I say."

Dreadlocks released Hannah and straightened. The one with the chinstrap beard followed his lead, letting go of Hannah's shoulders and slowly turning to face Jake, palms raised as if this were a stickup.

"Put your hands down," Dreadlocks told him. "You look like an idiot."

"Says the white kid with dreadlocks," Jake said as Chinstrap complied.

Dreadlocks' expression darkened. "If I were you, old man, I'd watch my mouth. You have no idea who you're dealing with."

First Amy, now this dick, Jake thought. *What's with everybody calling me old man?*

He was confident that, as a cop, he had their measure, but he wasn't about to give them the satisfaction. "Lemme guess. Shitty metal band? Out-of-work baristas? Art school dropouts who bonded over your matching Che Guevara posters?"

"We're Soldiers of Gaia. All three of us have pledged our lives to curing our planet of the plague of humankind, and we would gladly sacrifice ourselves for the cause if need be."

"That true?" Jake asked Cue Ball.

His head lolled as he tried to look at Jake, eyes swimming in their sockets. A frightened wail rose up from the back of his throat.

"I dunno," Jake said to Dreadlocks. "Your boy here doesn't seem too keen on the idea."

"For shit's sake, Billy," Chinstrap pleaded, "just let it go."

Dreadlocks said nothing, but it looked to Jake as if he recognized a shift in power had occurred. Jake decided to take advantage before it shifted back.

"C'mon, Hannah. We're leaving."

Dreadlocks scowled.

Cue Ball tensed.

Chinstrap held his breath.

But no one prevented Hannah from complying.

Except, that is, for Zoe.

Mad with fever and exhaustion, she'd watched the standoff unfold with mounting terror. Now, she came unglued: limbs thrashing, eyes screwed shut, face reddening behind her mask as she let loose a piercing shriek.

"Seems your little one would rather stay with us," said Dreadlocks.

"Shut the fuck up," Jake told him.

Hannah, exasperated: "Zoe, honey, everything's okay!"

"No, it's not! I want my daddy!"

"Sweetheart," Jake said, "I'm right here!" Without lowering his gun, he released Cue Ball's collar and tugged his mask down to expose his face.

Zoe quieted, her brow unfurrowing.

"Big mistake, asshole," said Dreadlocks. "Now we know what you look like. We ever see your face again, you're a dead man."

Jake laughed, cold and sharp as an ice pick. "Please. You dipshits are the least of my worries. If you wanna come for me, you're gonna hafta get in line."

Hannah traversed the path to Jake, giving Cue Ball a wide berth. Jake took Zoe from her with his free hand. Then—Hannah beside him, Zoe in his arms—he backed slowly down the pier, his Glock still trained on the Endtimers.

Cue Ball slumped from his knees into a seated position, blood dripping from his ruined face, a hand against the concrete for support.

Chinstrap glared—jaw flexing, nostrils flaring.

Dreadlocks paced, his pale face pink with fury, his bony hands balled into fists.

Still, as angry as he was, he didn't follow.

NEWS

Tensions rise as New Zealand issues ultimatum to asylum seekers

Seven hours ago, a former fishing vessel carrying fifteen members of an online survivalist group was intercepted by New Zealand's Coast Guard two nautical miles west of the island nation's shore. The vessel's crew requested asylum. New Zealand's government instructed them to turn around.

The *Dauntless* departed Australia for New Zealand—a voyage of 2,155 kilometers through driving rain and choppy seas—with a crew of eighteen. None of them were seasoned sailors; three reportedly perished on the journey. A senior member of New Zealand's ruling FreeNZ party, speaking on the condition of anonymity, explained that while he was not unsympathetic to the crew's plight, granting their request would set a dangerous precedent and put the lives of all New Zealanders...CONTINUE READING

Related Stories

Undaunted: Asylum seekers face long odds as they set sail for New Zealand

What we know about the *Dauntless* crew

Online betting sites see *Dauntless*-standoff boom

29.

"Hannah, something's wrong. Zoe's not breathing!"

Jake's voice echoed through the narrow foyer of the Croziers' building. His eyes were wide from panic. His daughter was rigid in his arms.

At Jake's insistence, they'd abandoned Hannah's Prius half a mile from his improvised safe house, and walked the rest of the way. It had seemed to Hannah an unnecessary precaution, since he'd already swapped her plates with those from a car of the same make and model before leaving the Upper West Side, but she'd been too tired and scared to argue. Now, she wished she had—because if they'd driven, they'd already be upstairs.

A low groan escaped Zoe's lips as her muscles clenched, squeezing the air from her lungs.

"Jake, I need you to remain calm and listen very carefully," Hannah said. "This is a seizure, triggered by her fever. Zoe will begin breathing again momentarily, but she'll also likely start convulsing. We need to lie her down before that happens."

"The elevator's right there. If we hurry—"

"There isn't time. We'll have to make do here. Give her to me, and take off your jacket, so we can use it as a pillow."

Without further delay, Jake did as Hannah instructed. As he shrugged out of Harold's windbreaker, Hannah removed the paper mask from Zoe's face, revealing lips of dusky blue. Together, they lowered her to the floor, and Jake slipped the jacket beneath her head. Soon after, Zoe began to tremble—and, to Jake's obvious relief, breathe again.

"You don't seem too surprised by this," he said, as they crouched beside Zoe. "Has it happened before?"

Hannah nodded. "Once, last night."

"Is it...normal?"

"Febrile seizures are not uncommon in kids her age," Hannah replied carefully. "Nor are they typically indicative of anything serious."

"Then how come you look so concerned?"

Hannah chewed her lower lip and exhaled sharply through her nose.

"Zoe's seizures are the result of an unchecked bacterial infection," she said. "Four years ago, I could've helped her. I could have *cured* her. Now, I'm next to useless. All I can do is keep her comfortable and hope she turns a corner on her own. It's fucking barbaric." Hannah's words tumbled out, unbidden. When she heard them aloud, she was mortified, and worried that they'd set Jake spiraling.

Instead, he took her hand—their fingers interlacing effortlessly as if the acrimony of the past few months had never happened—and said, "Go a little easier on yourself, would you? I know you're doing everything you can. Besides," he added as her eyes brimmed with tears, "we're not out of options yet."

Jake's sudden optimism regarding his daughter's prognosis was more perplexing than it was reassuring, but before Hannah could ask him where it was coming from, they were interrupted by a blond woman stepping off the elevator—a canvas tote slung over her left shoulder, a cell phone in her right hand.

"Excuse me!"

Her tone was impatient, accusatory, as she attempted to squeeze between them and the mailboxes. Then she spotted Zoe thrashing on the floor.

"Is . . . is she all right?"

Jake and Hannah shared a glance.

By unspoken agreement, Hannah answered.

"She will be, once her seizure passes."

"She doesn't *look* all right. I'm calling nine one one."

"No!"

At Jake's outburst, the woman's eyes narrowed.

"What my husband means is, that really isn't necessary. Our daughter's epileptic, so we're used to dealing with this sort of thing. There's no need to get a hospital — or, more precisely, their billing department — involved."

The woman looked at Zoe, who jerked spasmodically, and then at Jake, who did his best to project an air of looming insolvency. Then she met Hannah's gaze and said, "If you're absolutely certain—"

"I am." Hannah forced a smile. "But thanks so much for your concern."

The woman frowned.

Hesitated.

And reluctantly continued on her way.

"Jesus, that was close." Jake's heart clanged against his sternum. "If that goddamn narc had called the cops—"

"Cut her some slack," Hannah said. "She was only trying to help."

Cold comfort if she sics the DBS on us after all we've done to avoid leaving a trail, he thought — but instead, he said, "You're right. I'm sorry."

Jake's free hand rested lightly on Zoe's shoulder. After what seemed like an eternity — but was, in fact, only two minutes — she stilled, the tension in her muscles easing. Moments later, her eyelids fluttered open.

"Hey there, baby girl," Jake said. "Welcome back."

Zoe parted her dry, cracked lips as if to speak. For a moment, Jake dared to hope she was about to take exception to being called baby girl, as she'd been doing since her last birthday. Instead, her eyelids drooped, and she lapsed once more into unconsciousness.

Jake frowned. "Is she okay to move?"

Hannah reaffixed Zoe's mask and said, "She should be."

"Then let's get her upstairs."

Amy must've been watching for them through the peephole ever since she buzzed them in, because the apartment door swung inward before they had a chance to knock.

She'd freshened up since Jake had seen her last, and now wore one of Harold's button-downs untucked over a pair of Marjorie's jeans, cuffed at the ankle and doubtless belted as well. She'd swapped out her dirty hijab for a scarf of emerald-green raw silk.

Her color was good, her smile unforced. The only indication Jake saw of her recent injury was the fact that she favored her left arm when she greeted Hannah with a hug.

"Are you okay?" Amy asked. "I've been worried about you ever since Jake got your signal."

"Honestly? Not really," Hannah replied, "but I'm getting there."

"She had a run-in with our friends in black last night," Jake told Amy, "and some Endtimers this morning—not to mention a concerned citizen downstairs who, after one look at Zoe, would've dialed nine one one if Hannah hadn't intervened."

"You've been busy."

Hannah smiled weakly. "A little too, for my taste."

Mat, who'd been reading in the living room when they arrived, set down his book and stood. Hannah eyed him with curiosity, but Mat's eyes were locked on the unconscious girl in Jake's arms.

"Hannah, meet Mat," Jake said. "Mat, meet Hannah. And Sleeping Beauty here is Zoe."

"Nice to meet you," Mat said, awkwardly, to Hannah. Then, to Jake: "Can I, uh—"

"Please."

"Can he what?" Hannah asked.

"You wouldn't believe me if I told you," Jake replied, handing Zoe over to the boy. "I'm not even sure if I believe it yet myself."

Mat, stronger than he looked, carried Zoe to the couch and set her down. Then he brushed her hair aside and removed her mask.

"You shouldn't do that," Hannah told him. "She's very sick, and possibly contagious."

"It's okay," Mat replied. "I'll be fine."

"But—"

"Hannah, listen," Jake said, "I know this is a little...unorthodox...but trust me when I tell you that Mat knows what he's doing."

Hannah looked at Amy, her expression incredulous. "Are you on board with"—she gestured vaguely in Mat's direction—"whatever this is?"

"Yeah. I think I am." Amy seemed surprised by her own answer.

"Great, so either you two have gone nuts, or I have."

"Jake?" Mat interrupted. "Can you get me a clean rag and a bowl of water?"

"Sure thing." Jake rummaged through the linen closet until he found a washcloth. Then he fetched a bowl from the kitchen cupboard and filled it halfway from the tap.

Mat set the bowl on the coffee table and placed the washcloth on his lap. He submerged his hands in the bowl one by one and rinsed them, his pace deliberate, his focus acute. When he finished with them, he moved onto his forearms. Then he lowered his face to the bowl and splashed it several times. Finally, he slurped a mouthful of water with cupped hands, swished it around, and let it fall back into the bowl.

"I don't know what's going on here," Hannah said, "but as a doctor—"

"Hannah, please, just let him work."

Mat toweled himself off with the washcloth, dipped it into the bowl to wet it further, and used it to dab at Zoe's exposed skin. His movements were precise, unhurried. He swabbed her forehead, neck, and ears. Dragged the washcloth across her eyes, nose, and lips. Followed her arms down from the hems of her short sleeves to her pudgy, dimpled hands, and gently scrubbed each finger in turn. Then he wetted the washcloth one last time, held it just above her parted lips, and squeezed. Zoe's throat worked as she swallowed in her sleep.

This'll work, Jake thought. *It* has *to.*

God, please let this work.

The process, if you could call it that, took about an hour. Jake and Amy watched with something approaching reverence, while Hannah made no effort to disguise her skepticism.

When Mat finished, he set the cloth aside and maneuvered Zoe into a seated position. Then he fetched his book from the side table and climbed onto the couch beside her so that her head rested on his shoulder.

"I don't get it," Hannah said. "What happens now?"

After a long pause, Mat replied.

"Now we wait."

30.

By the time Ian stepped into the lobby of the Jacob K. Javits Federal Building, he was breathing heavily and drenched with perspiration. His undershirt clung uncomfortably to his skin. The back and armpits of his dress shirt were soaked through. Even his sport coat hung limp and heavy with humidity.

Ten minutes prior, he'd received a phone call from the deputy commissioner, ordering him to report to the Department of Biological Security's New York field office ASAP. When Ian asked why, she rather testily reminded him of their respective positions on the totem pole. After that, he didn't press, although he couldn't help but wonder while he walked.

Had Paget and Medina somehow caught wind of his illicit conversation with Jake last night? Maybe, but he doubted it, if only because they seemed the type to drag him out of HQ in handcuffs, rather than bothering to lean on his superiors to produce him.

Perhaps they'd come across some information they felt obligated to pass along—but if so, what? They clearly weren't big believers in professional courtesy. And why insist on doing it in person?

Again and again, Ian's thoughts circled back to the reason Jake had called. *Amy . . . took some shrapnel when the building blew, and yanked it out before I could stop her. I got her bleeding under control, I think, but I'm scared to shit about infection.* He'd asked for

Ian's help in getting Amy to a hospital, but Ian had been too god-damn worried about his own career to risk it.

If she'd succumbed to her wounds, Ian thought, *and they found her body, it'd sure as hell explain why I've been summoned.*

He banished the idea from his mind. Amira Hassan was a good detective, a good friend. The thought that he might, by his inaction, be complicit in her death was too terrible to contemplate.

The DBS occupied two floors of the monolithic federal building—which, like NYPD headquarters, was located within the secure perimeter of the Civic Center Pedestrian Zone. It was a sweltering Sunday afternoon, the sun bright enough to wash out the sky, so PeZe was largely deserted. Ian encountered no one on his march between the buildings, following St. Andrews Plaza north to Foley Square. The redbrick plaza may as well have been an oven; absent shade, the austere stone square was hotter still.

The building's interior was tired and dated, in the way of count-less government facilities. A mustiness that Ian associated with bureaucracy permeated the space. In addition to the Department of Biological Security, the wall directory included listings for the Centers for Medicare and Medicaid Services, Department of Homeland Security, Federal Bureau of Investigation, General Services Administration, Social Security Administration, and US Citizenship and Immigration Services, among others. Most of them were closed today, so the lobby was quiet as a church.

The speed with which Ian cleared security and caught an elevator only served to amplify his unease. Like many law enforcement officers, he was methodical by nature. Spontaneity was antithetical to his existence. He disliked having no idea what he was walking into—or, in this case, hurtling toward—and abhorred situations he was unable to control.

As the elevator car lurched to a halt, it occurred to Ian that, although he'd visited the New York offices of the DHS and FBI many times, he'd never set foot inside the DBS's before. He discovered, to his surprise, that its reception area was sleek and modern—more befitting a well-capitalized startup than a government agency. A young woman in a navy suit sat behind the gleaming black front desk, her chestnut hair twisted into a bun. The clatter of an unseen keyboard paused as Ian stepped into the room.

"Can I help you?"

Her tone was cool and clipped, as if his presence had somehow inconvenienced her.

"Ian Bavitz," he said. "I believe I'm expected."

"Put this on and take a seat. An agent will be along shortly to escort you."

She slid a visitor pass across the desk before returning to her typing. It consisted of a white card attached to a black lanyard and emblazoned with a large red V. Ian slipped the lanyard around his neck and dropped into one of the waiting area's low-slung armchairs.

A minute or so later, his escort—a fit, thirtysomething male whose every detail screamed Ivy League—emerged from the hallway to the right of the reception desk.

"Bavitz? Dessner. Good to meet you."

He offered his hand, if not his first name. Ian shook it.

"Likewise," Ian said. "Care to tell me what I'm doing here?"

"I'm afraid that's above my pay grade. All I'm supposed to do is keep an eye on you while you're here. Speaking of, follow me, and don't wander off. Anyone caught unaccompanied on the premises without prior clearance is considered a trespasser, and prosecuted to the fullest extent of the law."

"Don't wander," Ian repeated. "Got it."

Dessner led Ian down the same hallway through which he'd

appeared. All the doors in sight, save for the restrooms, required key-cards. Dome cameras were mounted every few feet overhead.

"Here we are." Dessner unlocked the door he'd paused beside—which, apart from a room number, was unmarked—by waving his access card at its proximity sensor. Then he depressed its lever handle and pushed. "After you."

Ian stepped through the doorway and found himself inside a high-tech command center. Three long, semicircular desks, each divided into four workstations, were arranged to face a massive wall display that bathed the room in cool blue light. Though only half of the work-stations were currently occupied, the atmosphere inside the room was tense, and prickled with the ozone scent of working electronics.

A detailed map of New York City took up much of the display, red dots pulsing in a handful of locations. Several tiles along the right side rapidly cycled through various surveillance feeds. The top left corner featured a heat map of the United States, though Ian wasn't clear on what, specifically, its colors were meant to represent. A smattering of medical reports, complete with gruesome images, pop-ulated the middle left. And a steady stream of information zipped across the bottom of the screen, too quickly for Ian to make sense of.

"Believe me," said Dessner, noting Ian's mystified expression, "you're better off not knowing. It took me forever to get the hang of reading it, and when I finally did, I had nightmares for a week. C'mon, we're headed this way."

Opposite the enormous screen was a conference room. It was sep-arated from the command center by a wall of glass, the middle third of which was frosted to create the illusion of privacy.

Dessner rapped on the conference room door—twice, politely—and opened it without waiting for a reply. Once Ian entered, Dessner closed the door behind him, but remained outside.

The room was dominated by a conference table of glass and brushed nickel. Black leather office chairs surrounded the table, while chairs of molded plastic rimmed the room's perimeter on three sides. A flat-screen display was mounted on the fourth, and presently featured a grainy image of Jake holding a child at gunpoint while his injured partner attempted to intervene. Ian recognized it as a still from the cell phone video that had gone viral shortly after the explosion in Tribeca.

As he entered, every face in the room turned Ian's way. Though the people seated along the outside of the room were largely unknown to him—aides and staffers, most likely, relegated to the kids' table—he recognized several of those occupying leather chairs. Agents Paget and Medina of the DBS; Commissioner Stahlberg and Chief Dolan of the NYPD; Alan Lieu, who ran the FBI's New York field office; Julia Vidal, from Homeland Security; Mayor Heberling's chief of staff, whose name Ian couldn't recall.

At the head of the table stood Lionel Mercer, director of the Department of Biological Security.

"Captain Bavitz," he said, "how good of you to join us. Please, take a seat."

Ian, stunned silent by Mercer's presence, shuffled over to the nearest unoccupied chair—plastic, naturally—and sat down.

"Now, where were we?" Mercer glanced at the display and frowned. "Ah, yes. Obviously, given the limited evidence at hand, it's difficult to ascertain whether Hassan is an accomplice or, like the child, being held against her will—"

"Sir?"

When Ian interrupted, an undercurrent of disbelief rippled through the room. The very idea of a police captain cutting off a cabinet member was almost laughably insubordinate. Truthfully, Ian was as dumbfounded as the rest of them. He hadn't realized that he was going to speak until the word had left his mouth.

Mercer sighed luxuriously. "Yes?"

"With all due respect," Ian said, "an accomplice to what?"

"The nature and severity of Gibson's crimes, as well as Hassan's level of complicity, are among the many things my people are currently working to determine. A word of warning, though, Captain: you're here as a courtesy to your commissioner, because the officers in question are at least nominally under your command. As such, your input is neither necessary nor encouraged."

Agents Paget and Medina snickered. Chief Dolan and Commissioner Stahlberg shifted uncomfortably in their seats.

"Fast-forward to today," Mercer said, once more addressing the entire room. "At approximately 1:30 a.m., PSAC II logged a call from an Adelita Jimenez of Jackson Heights, Queens, who reported hearing gunfire. Unfortunately, Ms. Jimenez is known to emergency operators as something of a frequent flyer, and claimed to be in no immediate danger. That, coupled with an absence of corroborating reports—which we're now attributing to her building's low occupancy rate—resulted in a response time of more than seventeen minutes. Had dispatch realized that Ms. Jimenez's apartment shares a wall with Jacob Gibson's, perhaps the responding officer would have arrived sooner. Regardless, this is what he found."

Mercer pressed a button, and the grainy cell phone image was replaced with a crime scene photo of a nondescript sedan parked beneath a maple tree on a residential street, taken from the vehicle's front left. The driver's-side window was spiderwebbed with cracks. Blood and brain matter coated the interior of the windshield.

"The decedents in the vehicle have since been identified as Officers Gordon Hager and Arlen DeCaro of the NYPD. They were presumably surveilling Gibson's residence in the hope that he might return, since a second team was found unharmed outside Hassan's—although we've yet to ascertain who ordered them to do so."

Ian's vision tunneled and his mouth flooded with saliva.

He's the one who'd ordered the surveillance detail.

He'd sent Hager and DeCaro to their deaths.

"Agents Paget and Medina assumed control of the scene shortly after its connection with the Central Park investigation was discovered." He clicked a button, and the screen displayed a residential hallway spattered crimson. "This was taken inside Gibson's apartment. As you can see, there were obvious signs of struggle, including shell casings from two different weapons. No additional bodies were found, although drag marks indicate at least two may have been removed postmortem. Why and by whom are, at present, unclear. We're still piecing things together as best we can, but we're hampered by the lack of CCTV cameras in the area, and the fact that the blood evidence was tainted with chlorine bleach in an apparent attempt to thwart DNA sequencing. The bottom line is, until we have Gibson in custody—"

"Wait, what?"

"Captain Bavitz," Mercer said icily, "I thought I made it clear that you were not to interject."

"What's clear is, someone's out there hunting my detectives, but you're too busy making scapegoats of them to find out who or why, much less put a stop to it."

"Careful, son. You're on thin ice."

"And you're an idiot if you think two decorated officers would go AWOL without good reason."

Half the occupants of the room gasped in unison. Mercer's face twisted with fury. Rather than engaging Ian further, however, he turned his attention to Commissioner Stahlberg. "Jesus, Rick, what kind of shop are you running here? I'm beginning to think insubordination is baked into the culture."

Stahlberg rose from his seat, face brick red beneath his shock-white buzz cut. "Bavitz. Outside. Now."

Once they'd exited the conference room, Stahlberg grabbed Ian by the upper arm and dragged him into a quiet corner. Dessner followed, hovering a discreet distance away, presumably so the two of them wouldn't be arrested for trespassing.

"For Christ's sake, Bavitz, what the hell was that? Are you out of your fucking mind?"

"I'm sorry, sir, but—"

"No. You've said your piece. Now you're gonna shut your yap and listen. I don't know if you noticed, but the department is up to its tits in shit right now, and sinking fast. Two mass murders in as many days. A child abduction caught on camera. A pair of cops gone rogue. Oh, and by the way, Mercer's pretty sure the kid's a Park City escapee, so there's a solid chance he winds up patient zero for the city's worst outbreak since 8/17."

Dessner, nearby, cleared his throat. Stahlberg's volume had risen steadily as he spoke, attracting attention from the agents staffing the command center. He leaned in close, and dropped his voice.

"Look, it's not that I'm unsympathetic to your position. Hell, your loyalty would be admirable, if it extended up the chain as well as down—but I don't take kindly to being publicly humiliated. Right now, our best hope of weathering this shitstorm is to make it clear that we're cooperating. If that means backing Mercer's play to bring in Gibson and Hassan, then so be it. If they're as innocent as you claim, we'll sort it out once they're in custody. Am I understood?"

Ian's jaw flexed. "Yes, sir."

"Good, because I swear to Christ, if you ever step out of line like that again, I'll have your badge." Stahlberg mopped his brow with a sleeve and smoothed his suit coat. "Now, I've got a meeting to get back to. Get the hell out of my sight. I'm sure our babysitter here can show you the door."

31.

Jesse Rochdale filled his lungs with acrid smoke and prayed the weed would take the edge off of his headache.

Two hours ago, he was strolling north along the Hudson River Greenway with his buddies Keith Vlasek and William McGowan. Then Billy had the bright idea to fuck with that procreator bitch who'd been clueless enough to bring her daughter to the pier.

Next thing Jesse knew, he was on the ground with two black eyes, a broken nose, and a throbbing between his temples that wouldn't quit. He was still a little fuzzy on how he got there, but to hear Keith tell it, some asshole came out of nowhere and pistol-whipped him in the face.

Felt more like a goddamn dump truck.

Now Jesse reclined beneath a yellow flag emblazoned with the Soldiers' Masked Mother in the back room of David Gunter's shop. A joint that Dave had rolled for him was wedged between his lips. A dog-eared translation of a Julio Cabrera treatise lay open in his lap.

Jesse wasn't really reading it. He was too distracted by the brutal chug of Vegan Reich blasting from the cassette deck, the clatter of Keith unpacking boxes of secondhand rifle parts with a pair of new recruits, and the rhythmic squeak of Billy handloading ammunition on Dave's rusty old press.

The bleary flat-screen mounted above the radiator was tuned to

CNN, but muted, per Dave's yoozh. *Knowledge isn't power,* he was fond of saying, *because it's useless to those who lack the conviction to wield it. Knowledge is a* weapon—*and, as Soldiers, we need all the weapons we can get.*

Dave was way older than Jesse and his buddies. Exactly how much older was a frequent topic of debate. Keith put him somewhere in his early thirties. Billy was convinced that he was forty-five at least. Jesse figured the truth was somewhere in the middle, although Dave's shaved head and placid, unlined features made it hard to tell.

Dave ran a junk shop on West 113th Street called Paradise Lost. The sign out front read ODDITIES AND EPHEMERA BOUGHT AND SOLD, but Jesse was pretty sure Dave bought way more than he sold.

The shop was stuffed from floor to ceiling with toys (action figures, die-cast miniatures, and fast food promotions), books (comic, hard-cover, and paperback), games (board, tabletop, and video), records (33s, 45s, and 78s), tapes (Betamax, cassette, and VHS), discs (compact, floppy, and laser), army surplus (Nazi, Soviet, and midcentury American), and electronics (computers, gaming consoles, portable media players, stereo components, and televisions)—the more offbeat or hard to find, the better. Any vertical surfaces that weren't obscured by the shop's dusty wares were plastered with old movie posters and flyers for punk shows long past.

Potential customers attempting to determine the Lost's hours of operation would be out of luck, because Dave had never bothered to post any. He only opened when he felt like it, which wasn't often. The Lost probably would've shut down years ago, if not for the fact that Dave's family owned the building.

They—and, by extension, Dave—were rich as fuck. Made their fortune in plastics and other petrochemicals, which probably explained why Dave turned out the way he did.

A radical environmentalist.

An elder statesman of the Endtimes movement.

The founder and chief architect of the Soldiers of Gaia—a decentralized brotherhood, dedicated to hastening the twilight of mankind, whose membership spanned continents and numbered in the thousands.

Hell, Jesse and his pals were positive that Dave was ShadowVox's infamous, unidentified thewhiterider—but whenever they pressed him about it, Dave just smiled that knowing smile of his and changed the subject.

At the workbench, Billy yowled, penetrating Jesse's mental haze. He'd somehow managed to catch one of his dreads in the reloading press midcrank. Now he was stuck, his head wrenched sideways, his neck cocked at an odd angle.

"Uh, guys? A little help?"

Keith pressed a box cutter into Billy's hand.

"Help yourself," he said. "It ain't our fault your ratty dreads got in the way."

Jesse snorted with laughter, causing his broken nose to twinge. Billy's dreadlocks were a frequent point of contention. Jesse, Keith, and the rest of their unit had followed Dave's lead by shaving their heads, but Billy had adamantly refused. He said his dreads had taken him forever to grow, and anyway, it wasn't like he wasted water washing them—as if solidarity wasn't half the fucking point.

Now, Keith needled Billy about his dreadlocks every chance he got. Jesse—who didn't give a shit about Billy's hair either way—loved it, because Billy was an egotistical prick who needed smacking down from time to time.

Eventually, Billy managed to hack through his trapped dreadlock. He straightened, rolling his head left and right to stretch his neck, then got all up in Keith's face. The severed dread hung, sad and limp, from the reloader.

"Why you gotta be such a goddamn dick?"

"I dunno. Why's your hair look like a hat made of 'em?"

Billy's face reddened. His fist tightened around the box cutter.

Then he lashed out, slicing Keith's left cheek.

Keith yelped in pain and surprise. Blood seeped from the wound.

That, Jesse thought idly, *is why I leave the teasing to Keith.*

"Gentlemen!" Dave bellowed. "Enough."

"Sorry," Keith mumbled, a palm pressed to his injured cheek to stanch the bleeding.

"He started it," Billy protested.

Dave ignored their replies, his focus occupied by the flat-screen on the wall. It seemed CNN had interrupted their regular programming with live footage of a press conference in Foley Square.

"Wait," Keith asked him, "is that Lionel Mercer?"

"It is."

Mercer stood behind a podium emblazoned with his department's seal, flanked by several dour-looking men and women in business suits. One of them was the police commissioner, so Jesse assumed the rest were law enforcement too. "What the hell's he doing in New York?" he asked.

"I don't know yet," Dave replied. "Kill the music, would you? And someone find the damn remote."

Billy stopped the Vegan Reich cassette. Jesse spotted the remote control on the desk beside his feet and tossed it wordlessly to Dave, who pressed Mute.

"*...at present, Gibson and Hassan are merely persons of interest, but they should be considered armed and dangerous. The child they're traveling with has been tentatively identified as Mateo Arturo Rivas, who recently went missing from the Sheep Meadow Emergency Refugee Center—more commonly known as Park City. Given the conditions within the encampment, Rivas must be treated* *as highly infectious—and, given their prolonged exposure to the boy, so too should Gibson and Hassan. If you see them, do not engage, and contact the authorities immediately…"*

The image onscreen was replaced by three photographs—two staged, one a blurry video still—each labeled with a name. The staged ones looked to Jesse like ID photos. Jacob Gibson: white dude, thirties, shirt and tie. Amira Hassan: Black chick, twenties, headscarf. In the video still, which was labeled Mateo Rivas, the white dude held a brown-skinned kid at gunpoint, while the Black chick looked like she was trying to talk him down.

"Holy shit," Billy said. "That's the guy!"

"What guy?" Dave and Jesse asked in unison.

"The guy!" Billy gestured vaguely in Jesse's direction, then mimed smacking himself in the face. "The fucking guy!"

Jesse felt as if he'd just dry-swallowed a D battery. "Are you shitting me?"

"Nah, dude. I'm telling you, that's him. He didn't have no spic or raghead with him, though."

"You're positive that's the man you saw?" This from Dave, who'd rewound the feed and paused the TV with the photos on the screen.

"The fucker damn near shot me, and messed up Jesse pretty bad," Billy replied. "I'm not likely to forget him."

"Keith?"

Keith looked at Gibson's picture long and hard before nodding.

For a moment, Dave just stood there, lost in thought. Then he said, "Put the word out. I want them found."

"Uh, Dave?" Jesse said. "I don't mean to speak out of turn or anything, but are you sure that's a good idea? I mean, the DBS—"

"The DBS has no idea where they are, or they wouldn't be on TV begging for help. Their New York field office contains, what, a few hundred employees? Our local membership is easily twice that, and knows this city better than they ever could. Besides, this Gibson fellow attacked a Soldier of Gaia. I, for one, refuse to let that go unanswered."

Jesse blushed and looked at the floor. "Thanks, Dave. That means a lot."

"Think nothing of it," Dave replied. Then, as if it were an afterthought, he added, "Oh, and make it clear we want the kid as well."

"The kid?" Keith said. "How come?"

"If Mercer's right, the boy is highly infectious, which would make him a marvelous addition to our arsenal. The anniversary of 8/17 nearly upon us, after all, and I can't imagine a better way to honor Brutsch's sacrifice than by unleashing an army of diseased martyrs upon an unsuspecting world."

Billy grinned.

The newbies blanched.

Jesse puffed his joint and nodded slowly.

"What about the Hassan chick?" Keith asked.

Dave's nose crinkled with distaste.

"Not my type. What you do with her is your business."

32.

As night fell, foreboding spread like fog throughout the Croziers' tiny, overstuffed apartment.

Dusk had enveloped the city some time before, but—except for the bulb beneath the microwave that illuminated the cooktop—Amy, Jake, and Hannah had yet to turn on any lights. Partly, they worried doing so would rouse Mat and Zoe, who were still sacked out on the couch. Partly, they feared it might alert the Croziers' neighbors to their presence, an eventuality Jake was doubly eager to avoid after the close call downstairs this afternoon.

In any case, the three-watt LED was bright enough to get around by, but not much more, and the outsized shadows it cast lent the space an air of menace that reminded Jake they were trespassing on a crime scene, surrounded by framed photos of the dead.

For much of the afternoon, the adults sat around the kitchen island, trying to hash out some kind of game plan while the children slept. While Jake was grateful for the time spent with Hannah, having missed her desperately in the three months since they'd split, the discussion didn't amount to much. The likelihood that Mat's pursuers were government operatives made the prospect of surrender untenable, because they couldn't guarantee his safety—and even if they could, Zoe's illness was sure to run afoul of the DBS.

Now, they sat in nervy silence: tired, cranky, and consumed by their own thoughts.

Despite Amy and Hannah's protestations, Jake couldn't help but blame himself for the mess they were in. If he hadn't phoned Hannah—a call he had no right to make, to ask a favor he knew she'd be unable to decline—she wouldn't have been forced to kill two men and flee into the night with his sick daughter. And if he hadn't stormed out of HQ when Cap suspended them, Amy wouldn't have stumbled into harm's way chasing after him, so she'd be home right now instead of hiding out in a dead couple's apartment with a chunk missing from her arm.

Then again, if the past two days had played out differently, Zoe might be languishing in a sanitarium, and Mat would likely have been captured—or worse.

Jake was so preoccupied by this cycle of doubt and remorse, he failed to register the sound of footsteps in the darkness until they were upon him.

"Daddy?"

When Zoe spoke, Jake nearly fell off of his stool. He wheeled to find her staring up at him, hair mussed, tiny fists rubbing sleep out of her eyes. She groaned in protest as he scooped her into his arms. For a moment, as he held her, the world fell away. She smelled of sleepy child, of happiness, of home.

"You're squeezing too hard!"

Zoe's grumbling was halfhearted, but Jake set her down nonetheless, and gently smoothed the clothes that Hannah'd dressed her in.

"How you feeling, baby girl?" he asked.

"Okay, but I'm *not* a baby—I'm four and a half!"

Jake smiled, a lump forming in his throat. "I know, honey, but you're still my baby girl."

Zoe looked around, befuddled. "Where are we? Why is it so dark?

What are Aunt Amy and Aunt Hannah doing here? Who's that boy snoring on the couch? Can I have a glass of water?"

Amy smiled. Hannah laughed. To be honest, Jake was so relieved to see Zoe up and about, he'd momentarily forgotten they were there. When he saw tears brimming in their eyes, he quickly looked away, as if they might prove contagious.

"That's a lot of questions," he said. "How about we tackle the last one first, then circle back?"

Zoe nodded, her expression solemn, her eyes wide and clear.

"Okay. One glass of water coming up."

"So," Hannah said, "when did you realize you could, uh—"

"Heal people?" Mat offered.

"Yes. I suppose that *is* what I mean." Even though Hannah had witnessed it firsthand, she still struggled to say the words aloud.

"I dunno. Maybe a year or so after me and Gabriel wound up in Park City? For a while, it was, like, an inside joke. My uncle's way of explaining why we hadn't caught any of the nasty stuff that was going 'round the camp. He said he used to get sick all the time before I came along."

"Looking back, do you think you've always been like this, or has something changed?"

"Something must've changed. I mean, I don't remember getting sick much when I was little, but my mom and brother totally did."

"Fascinating."

Amy cocked her head quizzically. "Wait—do you know how he's doing it?"

Amy, Mat, and Hannah were huddled around the kitchen island, so they could converse quietly. Zoe was in the recliner, watching a movie on the Croziers' tablet, the volume turned low. Jake sat propped against the couch back, facing the kitchen, so he could follow the conversation without ignoring his daughter.

Though Hannah had cautioned Zoe to drink slowly, she'd finished two glasses of water while Jake answered her questions as best he could without scaring her. Once Hannah was satisfied Zoe was capable of keeping water down, she let Jake make her a bowl of leftover Chinese—white rice, mostly, with a little tofu and brown sauce mixed in—which Zoe tucked into with zeal.

By then, it was as close to fully dark outside as New York ever got, so they shut the curtains, placed a towel along the bottom of the front door, and turned on a few more lights.

"I'm not sure yet," Hannah said, "but I have an inkling."

"Then it's not…magic?" Jake's tone was jokey, lighthearted, but his expression indicated he hadn't ruled it out.

Hannah smiled. "No magic. Just science." Then, to Mat: "The way you treated Zoe seemed awfully complicated. How did you know to do all that?"

"Once we realized my powers or whatever were legit, we tried all kinds of stuff to figure out how they worked. Me and Gabriel had been stuck together in a tiny tent for months—sharing everything from dishes to blankets, and breathing the same air—so that's where we started."

Amy frowned. "You didn't do all that crazy stuff for me, though, did you?"

"No. I only do that when I'm treating something really scary. Hanging out together's enough to keep most wounds from getting infected."

"The people you help," Hannah said, "are they like you afterward? Can they do what you do?"

Mat shook his head. "We thought of that. Doesn't seem like they can fix anybody. And whatever I'm doing must wear off, because lots of people I've treated wind up catching something new eventually."

"If that's the case," Jake said, "then how come everybody in your village was so healthy?"

"Our village was like family. They took care of us. Protected us. We tried to do the same for them."

"Is that why you and Gabriel chose not to leave when healthy detainees could still petition for release?" Amy asked.

"Yeah. The plan was, we'd help everybody in our village leave one at a time, to avoid suspicion—but the program shut down before we finished, so we wound up stuck."

"Forgive me for asking, but have you ever"—Hannah paused, searching for the most delicate way to phrase her question—"encountered anyone you couldn't heal?"

"Yeah. A couple people have been too far gone to save. And there are some things I just can't fix."

"What kind of things?"

"Sniffles, mostly. And I'm hit-or-miss on stomach bugs. Our neighbor Harry down the path from us had hepatitis, and died of liver failure even though I tried for weeks to fix him."

"I'm sorry to hear that," Hannah said, "but if it's any consolation, I think Harry just provided us the clue we needed to make sense of your abilities."

"Really? How?"

"Do you guys know about the human microbiota?"

Amy frowned as if the term rang a faint bell. Mat and Jake shook their heads.

"Okay. We'll take this slow. A microbiota is a community of microbes—bacteria, yeast, and fungi, mostly—that shares a particular habitat. Every plant and animal on Earth has one, including humans, and no two are alike."

"These microbes"—Mat handled the unfamiliar word carefully, as if it might break—"live inside us?"

"Some of them, yes. Others live outside of us—in our hair and on our skin. Still others float around us like a cloud, only they're so small you can't see them."

"Where do they come from?" Mat asked.

"All kinds of places. From your mom, before you're born. From the food you eat, and the water you drink. From all the people and places you're exposed to. For a long time, scientists thought these tiny critters served no purpose, that they were just along for the ride. In the past few decades, however, we've come to realize our microbiota is as much a part of us as our own cells. It affects our thoughts, our feelings, our behavior. When it's working right, it helps us digest food, and—most importantly for the purposes of our discussion—protects us from diseases."

"Hold up," Jake said. "Are you saying Mat's so goddamn healthy, it's contagious?"

"Language, Daddy," Zoe said without looking up from her tablet.

"Kind of, yes. It's not as crazy as it sounds. There's ample evidence in the scientific literature of the microbiota's role in preventing all sorts of diseases, from obesity to infections to schizophrenia—and it stands to reason that the Harbinger virus would accelerate the evolution of beneficial microbes as well as harmful ones."

"But why me?" Mat asked. "What makes me so special?"

"A combination of biology and circumstance, most likely. Biology, in that your unique genetic makeup must've created the ideal environment for a healthy microbiota to thrive. Circumstance, in that you've been exposed to lots of challenging environments that forced your critters to adapt, the same way that pathogenic bacteria learned to beat our antibiotics."

"Are Mat's abilities...permanent?" Amy asked.

"It's hard to say. The stability of interspecific mutualism—that is, relationships between two or more species in which all sides benefit—

is notoriously tricky to predict. Historically, though, most cata-strophic disruptions of healthy microbiotas were caused by antibiotics. Now that antibiotics are off the table, who knows?"

"So, okay, he doesn't have to worry about nuking his critters with antibiotics," Jake said. "What about, I dunno, depleting them by overuse?"

"I doubt it. Happy microbes multiply. It's what they do."

Mat frowned. "If happy microbes multiply, how come the people I give them to don't end up like me?"

"Chalk it up to differences in body chemistry," Hannah replied. "An infection is kind of like an invasion. Your critters make for excel-lent reinforcements, but they're not interested in sticking around, because they're only happy when they're home with you."

"How come I can't fix the sniffles?" Mat asked. "Why couldn't I fix Harry?"

"The common cold and most forms of hepatitis are caused by viruses, not bacteria. A healthy microbiota can prevent viruses from taking hold, which is why you don't catch them, but can't do much to help somebody who's already got one."

"So Mat's a living, breathing antibiotic in an era without any," Jake said. "No wonder these assholes are on his tail."

"Language, Daddy," Zoe repeated.

"The question is," Hannah said, "what do we do about it?"

"My uncle was in contact with the Resistance," Mat said. "Our friend Brian was trying to get me to them when he..."

The boy trailed off, gaze distant, eyes gleaming.

"Actually," Amy replied, "that isn't a bad play."

"How do you figure?" Jake asked. "Those guys are criminals."

"I hate to break it to you, partner—but, these days, so are we. Besides, all they're really guilty of is providing undocumented immi-grants the healthcare they so desperately need."

"Yeah, using supplies stolen from hospitals and drug companies."

"Private hospitals," Hannah clarified, "that cater to the rich."

"And pharmaceutical conglomerates with deep pockets," Amy continued, picking up the thread, "both of which can easily absorb the loss."

"Okay, okay." Jake raised his hands in surrender. "Say, for the sake of argument, I agree with you. What good does it do us? I mean, it's not like we have any way to get in touch with the Resistance."

Hannah reddened and stared at a speck of nothing on the kitchen island for a long moment.

Then she said, "That's . . . not entirely true."

33.

"How, exactly, do you know this guy again?"

Jake and Hannah stood outside the Community Church of New York—a modernist redbrick structure, all right angles and clean lines, on East 35th Street between Madison and Park Avenues.

It was a little after seven Monday morning, and the streets of Midtown were already clogged with commuters. The sidewalks likewise hummed with activity, a blur of business suits and coveralls that parted around Jake and Hannah without a glimmer of acknowledgment.

"Andre and I are old friends. We went to med school together. I'm sure I mentioned him to you when we were dating."

A gust of wind kicked grit into Jake's eyes. It smelled of coming rain. The barometric pressure had fallen overnight, and a low ceiling of pewter clouds had blown in from the east. Jake regarded the sky with suspicion—it seemed to darken by the minute—but at least the weather made their jackets less conspicuous.

"Did you? Because that sounds like the sort of thing I'd remember." Jake's words came out surlier than he'd intended.

Hannah eyed him appraisingly. "Don't tell me you're jealous."

"Okay. I won't tell you."

"You've got no right to be, you know."

Jake reddened. "I never said I did."

"As I recall," she continued tetchily, "you're the one who broke things off."

"That," Jake said, "I remember."

Although it had happened three months prior, the memory was still as fresh and painful as an open wound. Jake could picture Hannah's coffee table, littered with remnants of the evening's takeout, a pair of empty champagne flutes presiding over the mess. Her new definitive prosthesis, which they'd picked up that afternoon, lying on the floor beside, its carbon fiber socket gleaming in the candlelight. And Hannah, in a satin cami and pajama shorts, scowling drunkenly at him from across the couch. "You're joking, right?"

Jake cocked his head. His cheeks were flushed. His thoughts, fuzzy. Thank God Mrs. Jimenez had Zoe for the night. "What makes you think I'm joking?"

"All the shit I've been through these past seven months—endless hours of strength training and physical therapy, countless tweaks to my meds and temporary prosthesis, more setbacks than I'd care to admit—was to get me to the point where I could finally practice medicine again. Now you're saying you want me to fucking quit?"

"Whoa. Who said anything about quitting medicine? All I'm saying is, maybe you should consider stepping back a bit." Hannah glanced unconsciously at her residual limb, which for months she'd been reluctant to let Jake see. "Sorry. Poor choice of words."

"Okay, then. Spell it out for me. What would a step back even look like?"

"I dunno—a private practice, maybe?"

"Jake, I'm a surgeon, not a goddamn GP."

"Then how about a nicer hospital?"

"Oh, I see. You think I should sell my soul to some heartless corporation that caters to rich douchebags. What the hell is up with you today?"

Jake sighed. "Look. This is coming out all wrong. It's just, that warzone you call a hospital took your leg, and damn near killed you. After everything that Zoe's been through, I can't stomach the thought of her losing another parent figure."

"Oh, please. Don't try to pin this on Zoe. If you were really so worried about her losing someone else, you'd find a safer way to make a buck than chasing murderers around the city. No, this is about you. The least you could do is muster up the courage to admit it."

"So what if it is? When Olivia died, I thought I'd never be happy again. Can you blame me for being terrified of losing you?"

"No," she replied, "but I can sure as shit blame you for pushing me to walk away from the only thing in life I've ever really cared about."

It wasn't until Hannah saw Jake's stricken expression that she realized the implication of her words.

"Jake, listen, I didn't mean—"

"The problem is," he said, "I'm pretty sure you did."

Jake wasn't proud of the argument that followed, or the fact that he stormed out afterward. When he left, Hannah didn't bother trying to stop him. He wasn't sure it would've made a difference either way.

A few blocks from her apartment, he hailed a cab—vision swimming, emotions reeling. Curfew was fast approaching, so the ride home was quiet, mournful. Jake closed his eyes, rested his head against the window, and listened to the lullaby of rubber against asphalt, his right fist curled around the velvet ring box in his pocket.

He'd called Hannah a few times since, when booze and loneliness conspired to shout down his bruised ego. It went about as well as you'd expect. Now, here he was, accompanying her to meet some mystery guy with ties to the Resistance. You're damn right he was a little jealous.

The church's main entrance was up a flight of concrete steps.

213

Hannah skipped them in favor of an unobtrusive door at sidewalk level. A bulletin board encased in glass hung to its left. Nestled among handbills advertising poetry circles, Spanish lessons, and antiracist action meetings was a small pride flag, its colors long since washed out by the sun.

Jake's family was Catholic. This place was nothing like the churches of his youth.

Once inside, they descended a staircase to a quiet hallway lit by overhead fluorescents and studded with red fire alarms. It reminded Jake less of a house of worship than an academic building closed for summer.

Meeting rooms of various sizes lined the hall. Most of them were open, empty, unlit. One appeared to be in use. MEDITATION IN PROGRESS, read the piece of paper taped to its closed door. DO NOT DISTURB.

"This is it." Hannah knocked, removed her mask, and nodded toward the nearest fire alarm. "Smile—you're on *Candid Camera*."

Jake's eyebrows raised in surprise. He stuffed his mask into a jacket pocket and waved halfheartedly at the alarm.

The door rattled against its jamb as a series of locks were unfastened, then swung open to reveal a man too tall and handsome for Jake's liking.

"Hannah freakin' Lang!" He scooped her into his arms, lifting her briefly off the ground before releasing her. "Goddamn, it's good to see you! Who's the fella?"

"Andre, Jake. Jake, Andre."

At the mention of Jake's name, Andre's body language took a turn for the guarded.

"Don't worry," Jake assured him. "I'm off duty—and even if I weren't, what you do here is no business of mine."

"In that case, it's great to finally meet you, man! Hannah's told me all about you."

He offered Jake his hand.

Jake shook it.

"See?" Andre said to Hannah. "I always said you crazy kids would work things out."

Hannah looked away. "We're...not together."

"Oh. My bad."

"No," Jake said, "I'm pretty sure it's mine."

Hannah cleared her throat. "Listen, Andre—"

"Hey," he interrupted, "you speak French, don't you?"

"Well, yes, but—"

"Thank God. Come with me."

Andre took Hannah by the hand and dragged her inside.

Jake followed. "Since when do you speak French?"

"Since, like, seventh grade?"

Jake wasn't sure what he expected to find beyond the door, but this wasn't it. The space—which, if the bookcases and bland inspirational art were any indication, had begun life as an ordinary conference room—had been converted into a tiny but sophisticated clinic, complete with padded examination table and portable handwashing station. The shelves were overflowing with equipment and supplies. Diagnostic instruments hung from brackets on the walls.

A privacy curtain, open at the moment, ran on a track across the ceiling. A cluster of chairs in the corner nearest the entrance served as an ad hoc waiting room. A painted metal hatch, much newer than the floor itself, disrupted the pattern of the wood parquet—an escape route, should the DBS come knocking, Jake supposed.

Andre set the locks and said to Jake, "Grab a seat. We won't be long!"

Before Andre yanked the curtain closed, Jake glimpsed a young couple of African descent. The woman—visibly pregnant beneath her vibrant wrap dress—sat atop the examination table, bare legs dangling. The man—wearing a pale tunic and dark pants—stood nervously beside it, his hand in hers.

The next twenty minutes passed at a crawl. Jake, perching on an uncomfortable wooden chair that seemed a holdover from the clinic's conference room days. Andre, painstakingly describing a regimen of prenatal vitamins, medications, and exercises in ever simpler English. His patient and her partner, peppering Andre with questions in French. Hannah, translating the three of them as best she could.

Eventually, the curtain swooshed aside and the expectant parents emerged beaming. Andre handed them two paper bags stuffed with prescription bottles and opened the door for them. Hannah tried to keep up with the pleasantries they exchanged.

"Now," Andre said as he set the locks behind them, "you two wanna tell me what you're doing here?"

Jake and Hannah shared a look.

"We need to talk to somebody who's authorized to speak for the Resistance," she said.

"Hannah," he said dubiously, "what the hell have you gotten yourself mixed up in?"

"Honestly, it's safer for all three of us if I don't answer that, but we wouldn't be here if I didn't think it was important."

Andre licked his lips—nervous, darting. "Look, I'd love to help, but I'm a doctor, not a revolutionary. All I'm authorized to do, if that's even the right word, is treat patients."

"Can you at least point us in the right direction?" Jake asked.

"That's harder than it sounds. It's not like I can just consult my fucking org chart. The Resistance is anonymous by design, and heavily compartmentalized, so we can't rat each other out if we get busted."

"What about the person who recruited you?"

"We only met the once, at a dive bar half a block from my apartment, a couple weeks after I got shitcanned for trashing the DBS on social media. He introduced himself by his handle, and assigned me one as well. All our communications since have been electronic."

Hannah frowned. "Why can't you write him and request a meeting?"

"The first rule of Fight the Power Club is, anybody who breaks protocol is presumed compromised. It's how we've managed to survive this long despite the best efforts of the Whitmore administration to take us down. If I request a meeting, I'm as good as burned, which means my clinic can kiss all future resupplies goodbye."

"You said you guys communicate electronically," Jake said. "How do you keep the DBS from listening in?"

Andre eyed Jake warily.

"Are you sure this guy is off the clock?" he asked Hannah.

"Positive," she replied.

"We use a hidden chat service accessible only by a garlic-routing mixnet." When Jake blinked at him uncomprehendingly, he added, "It's kind of like the secure drop boxes that newspapers maintain on the dark web, to communicate with sources."

"Ah. Gotcha. We're gonna need to know how to access it."

"Haven't you been listening? Even if I gave you the address, it wouldn't do you any good. The Resistance is too careful. I can't arrange a face-to-face, and I've got a legit handle. What makes you think they're gonna hop to for some rando?"

"Andre, please," Hannah said, "I'm begging you. It's life and death."

Andre grimaced. His shoulders sagged. Then he snatched up a scrap of paper, took a pen from his shirt pocket, and scribbled something down.

As he handed it to Hannah, she smiled. "Thanks. I owe you big-time. We both do."

"No, you don't," Andre replied, "because you two were never here."

34.

When she and Jake returned from Andre's clinic, Hannah was relieved to find the building's entryway unoccupied. Amy buzzed them in, and they beelined for the elevator. It opened within seconds of Hannah summoning it—empty, thank God.

As Jake hit the button for the Croziers' floor, Hannah heard a jangle of keys from the direction of the entrance, and a gust of wind swept through the narrow foyer.

"Hey, hold that thing a sec, would you?"

A man in running gear trotted into view, dripping sweat. Jake feinted toward the Door Open button, instead tapping the brushed-steel panel right beside.

The man thrust an arm—veiny, sunbaked, glistening—into the narrowing gap.

The doors closed on it, gently, and began to part.

Damn it, Hannah thought. *We were so close.*

He stepped into the elevator, face damp and blotchy, dark hair plastered to his forehead. Hannah caught a whiff of gym socks and yesterday's cologne. Her nose crinkled behind her mask.

"Sorry about that. Button didn't work. Where you headed?"

"I'm on three." The man looked them up and down suspiciously. "Are you two sick or something?"

"Not sick," Hannah replied, "just careful."

"Ah."

The elevator car lurched upward.

The man bounced on the balls of his feet as if unable to stand still.

"So, you guys live on four?"

"Yup." This from Jake.

"Weird that this is the first time we've run into each other."

Jake eyed him warily. "Not really. We just moved in."

"Gotcha," he said. "You know, I've got a buddy, lives on four. If you want, I could—"

"We're good, thanks."

"Oh."

"Don't mind my husband." Hannah shot Jake a warning look. "He forgets his manners when he's hungry."

The elevator coasted to a halt.

The man cleared his throat awkwardly. "Well, this is me."

"Nice meeting you," Hannah said.

"Yeah." He glowered pointedly at Jake. "You too."

Then the doors opened, and he bolted from the elevator.

As the car resumed its ascent, Hannah wheeled on Jake, intending to scold him for his curt behavior. That's when she spied the grip of his Glock, peeking from the pocket of Harold's windbreaker.

"How'd it go?" Amy asked, once they were back inside the apartment, the chain and deadbolt set behind them.

Hannah winced. "Honestly? Not great."

"Don't listen to her. Hannah's guy gave us a solid lead."

"Andre's *not* my guy," she said, reddening, "and I worry that the information he gave us won't be enough to justify the awkward run-in we just had with another of the building's lawful tenants."

"Awkward?" Amy's brow furrowed. "Awkward how?"

"Hannah's pretty sure he noticed I was carrying," Jake replied, "and he knows what floor we're on, which isn't ideal."

"Crap."

"Yeah," Hannah agreed, "crap."

Jake handed Amy a paper cup in a recycled cardboard sleeve.

"What's this?"

"One large oat-milk latte."

Her eyes widened with delight. "You're a saint."

Mat and Zoe sat catty-corner at the kitchen island, ensconced in a board game. Amy had apparently been combing news feeds on the Croziers' tablet when they arrived, because it was still clutched in her left hand, its screen a riot of competing headlines.

Hannah gestured toward the tablet. "May I?"

"By all means." Amy gave Hannah the tablet. "At this point, I'm just doomscrolling."

On the couch, Hannah consulted the piece of paper Andre had given her, and downloaded the browser he'd specified—a handy bit of freeware that afforded users anonymous access to the dark web via a process known as garlic routing. Then, flanked by Jake and Amy, she typed in the chat service's address.

The site took forever to load. A consequence of the routing software, Hannah supposed. When it finally did, its landing page was spare and unadorned, consisting of two buttons near the center of the screen—NEW MESSAGE and CHECK REPLIES—and an attribution at the bottom that read "Powered by DedDrop v8.5.9."

Hannah clicked NEW MESSAGE, which brought up a submission page dominated by a blank text box. Above the text box was the randomly generated passphrase they'd need to access their responses.

"Write this down," Hannah said to Jake. "All lowercase, no punctuation."

Jake's field notebook was on the coffee table, a cheap ballpoint pen clipped to its cover. He picked them up, clicked open the pen, and said, "Whenever you're ready."

"Radium bisect ensign platypus tapioca."

"Jesus. That's our password?"

"Language, Daddy," Zoe said.

"Looks like," Hannah replied. "You get it all?"

"Depends. Is this how you spell *tapioca*?"

He tilted his notebook toward Hannah.

She smiled, shook her head, and corrected him.

"So," she said, "what do we want to say to them?"

"Unfortunately, what we want to say and what we can get away with saying are two very different things," Amy said.

"How so?"

"Obviously, our goal is to convince these guys to meet with us, right? Problem is, we need to figure out a way to do so without using any keywords the DBS might be monitoring for. At this point, that almost certainly includes our names—mine, Jake's, and Mat's, at least—as well as any mention of Tribeca or Park City."

"Isn't the whole point of this chat service that it's secure?"

"There's a world of daylight between anonymous and secure. The browser, coupled with DedDrop's software platform, should prevent anybody from tracing the messages we send back to us, but since we're trying to set up a meeting, they wouldn't have to—"

"—because they'll know exactly where we plan to be," Hannah finished, catching on.

"Bingo," Amy replied.

Jake massaged the bridge of his nose with thumb and forefinger. "This'd be a whole lot easier if the Resistance had just given Mat a goddamn handle."

"Lang—"

"Honey, I know," he interrupted, "but these are special circumstances, so you're gonna hafta cut your dad some slack."

"Why would they have given me a handle?" Mat asked.

"Not, like, a door handle—an alias, a code name."

"Oh." A thoughtful scowl settled on the boy's face. "Maybe they did!"

"What do you mean?"

"A couple weeks ago, Gabriel was talking to Brian on the phone, and our tent's so small, I couldn't help overhearing. Anyway, I heard him say something about pelicans, which seemed weird, so when he hung up, I asked him why. He told me not to worry about it. I figured it was none of my business. But, back then, I didn't know that Brian was part of the escape plan Gabriel had cooked up for me."

"Think carefully," Amy said. "Did he say *pelicans,* with an *s,* or *pelican?*"

"*Pelican?*"

"You're asking me?"

"No," he said, more forcefully, "it was *pelican.*"

She nodded. "Okay, then. What say you two?"

"I say it's worth a shot," Jake replied.

"Agreed," said Hannah.

After some back-and-forth regarding the contents of their message, they settled on a simple, direct approach: *Pelican requests meeting ASAP.* Hannah, feeling faintly silly, keyed it in, then muttered, "Here goes nothing," and clicked Submit.

The page didn't refresh automatically. Every time they wanted to check for a reply, they were required to enter their passphrase. It soon became a game of chicken. The tablet would sit on the coffee table until one of them lost patience, snatched it up, and painstakingly typed in all five words. Then, finding nothing, they'd set the tablet down, and the game began anew, until—

"Guys?" Hannah's voice was tight with excitement. "We've got something."

"What's it say?" Jake asked.

" 'Ghostwood Coffee. 1300 hrs. Accept/Reject?' "

Jake leaned in to read the message for himself. Hannah flushed. He was near enough for her to feel his body heat and smell his scent.

"Ghostwood Coffee...any idea where that is?"

"Lenox Hill," she said. "I sometimes pass it on my way to the hospital."

Jake eyed the clock.

It was twenty minutes shy of noon.

"Tell them we accept."

35.

Compared to much of the city, the Upper East Side neighborhood of Lenox Hill may as well have been another planet. Pretty au pairs pushed ostentatious strollers down broad sidewalks free of refuse and street vendors. Dog walkers clutched bouquets of purebred canines by multicolored leashes clipped to designer collars. Expensive women in expensive clothing made expensive plans on expensive phones. Few in sight wore masks. Nearly everyone was as pale-skinned as the limestone faces of the buildings that surrounded them.

As Mat and Jake zigzagged northeast toward the coffee shop — hat brims worn low over paper masks, bodies obscured by shapeless clothes — Jake couldn't help but marvel at how little the area had declined. Sure, its population had contracted some, and many of its buildings now sported enhanced biosecurity features — but if you didn't look too closely, you could almost convince yourself that 8/17 had never happened.

In the weeks following Olivia's death, Jake found himself on the receiving end of all manner of dubious wisdom, none more odious or unwelcome than *time heals all wounds*.

For one thing, it was demonstrably false. Some wounds festered. Some wounds killed.

For another, Jake took no comfort in the notion that his pain might one day fade, because it felt disrespectful to his wife's memory.

As far as he was concerned, *time heals all wounds* was useless pablum, mindlessly regurgitated—but, looking around, it was clear that nothing papered over them like money.

He and Mat had left the Croziers' place about an hour ago. Before they set out, Hannah pulled Jake into the guest room for a little privacy.

"Are you sure I can't come with you?" she'd asked, sotto voce. "I don't like the idea of you doing this alone."

"And I don't like the idea of putting you in any more danger than I already have," he said. "Besides, somebody's gotta look after Zoe and Amy, make sure they don't backslide."

"That's not going to go over well with Amy."

Jake smiled. "Which is why I plan on telling her I need her to stay here to protect you two. You know as well as I do she's in no shape to be gallivanting around."

"She may not have a choice. If any of the Croziers' neighbors call the cops—"

"They won't," he insisted, but the emotion in his voice belied his words.

Hannah took his hand in hers. "Just promise me you'll come back soon, okay?"

Jake surprised them both by kissing her, long and slow.

"I'll do my best," he said.

"How much farther?" Mat asked now, his voice tight with worry. With 1 p.m. fast approaching, Jake wasn't sure if the boy was stressed about the meet itself, or the prospect of being late.

"Not much," Jake replied. "A couple blocks. Are you sure that you're okay with this?"

"I...I think so."

"You don't have to be, you know. There's still time to turn around."

Mat took a steeling breath. "No. This is what Gabriel wanted."

"Maybe so," Jake said, "but is it what *you* want?"

To that, Mat said nothing, which Jake figured was an answer of a sort.

A few minutes later, they found themselves at Ghostwood Coffee, as instructed.

Problem was, the place was closed.

Permanently, by the look of things—gate rolled down, FOR RENT sign on the front door.

"Now what?" Mat asked.

"I dunno. Lemme think."

As Jake stood there, hoping for a signal of some kind, a man in reproduction Knicks warmups shouldered past, nearly knocking Mat down in the process.

"Watch it, asshole!" Jake said reflexively, but the man continued on without a glance.

"Uh, Jake?" Mat said, producing something from the front left pocket of his jacket. "What's this?"

Jake took it, turned it over in his hand. It was a device of black textured plastic, a little smaller than a deck of cards, with a rudimentary display on one side, and a belt clip on the other.

"It's a pager. That guy must've planted it when he bumped into you."

Jake peered down the sidewalk in the direction the man had been headed, but he was impossible to pick out from the crowd.

The pager vibrated. Directions to a second location, this one in Chelsea, blinked onto its screen—along with a warning not to attempt to contact anyone, because they were being watched.

As Jake read the message, a fat raindrop smacked against it, making rainbows of the LCD display. Soon after, another landed on his head.

"New marching orders?"

"Yeah." Jake looked skyward. "Let's get out of here before we wind up drenched."

36.

Mat froze and eyed the tunnel mouth across the street with dread. "You've gotta be kidding me."

"I wish I were." Jake held the pager up for him to see. "Unfortunately, our instructions are pretty clear."

They stood beneath a flimsy umbrella Jake had purchased from a hawker in East Harlem. Heavy rainfall blurred the world around them, and drowned the city's clamor in white noise. Assuming the time stamp on their latest page was accurate, it was almost 4 p.m. Three hours had elapsed since they left the coffee shop in Lenox Hill, during which the Resistance had yanked them all over town—much of that amid a deluge.

Now they found themselves, sodden and exhausted, on a desolate stretch of Broadway in Washington Heights. Ripe trash bags lined the puddled sidewalks. A burned-out hatchback sat, abandoned, along the curb. Bland, utilitarian brick buildings jutted from the hilly landscape to either side, their CCTV cameras smashed, their facades vandalized. The only people in sight were either junkies or the corner boys who sold to them, the former seemingly impervious to the elements, the latter huddled under awnings to stay dry.

As devastating as 8/17 had been to the city at large, the months that followed were even worse for the working-class Hispanic enclave located at Manhattan's northern tip. The area, comprising the neighborhoods of Inwood and Washington Heights, was crippled by the suspension of mass transit, which remained in effect long after the citywide quarantine was lifted, and prevented many of its residents from commuting.

Eventually, subway service resumed, but consolidations shuttered the IRT Broadway–Seventh Avenue line between Riverdale and the Upper West Side, dramatically curtailing the number of trains that stopped in Upper Manhattan.

Crime spiked as unemployment soared. Those who could afford to relocated, erasing decades of revitalization in a matter of weeks. Those who couldn't discovered that they—unlike, say, the entrenched wealthy of the Upper East Side—held little sway over city hall. As a consequence, the area was written off, consigned to ruin. These days, even sanitization crews rarely ventured this far north, and police patrols were sporadic at best.

"Can't you, I dunno, suggest somewhere else?" Mat asked.

"Would if I could," Jake replied, "but I'm pretty sure this hunk of junk's incapable of sending messages."

"Pretty sure? You mean you don't know?"

"Hey. Gimme a break. I've never used one of these things before today."

Truth was, Jake suspected the Resistance hadn't chosen this style of pager by accident. Unlike cell phones, or fancier two-way pagers, passive receivers were impossible to track—and that's assuming the DBS even considered such an obsolete technology worth monitoring.

"I'm sorry," Mat said. "It's just...I don't know if I'm ready to go back underground yet."

Jake couldn't blame him. Getting lost inside the city's sewer system would be enough to mess anybody up, much less a kid of twelve. Hell, venturing into an abandoned subway station sixteen stories belowground during a monsoon wasn't Jake's idea of a good time either. But, unless they wanted to blow off their only chance to meet with the Resistance, it seemed they didn't have much choice.

Prior to its decommissioning, the 191st Street Station had been the deepest in the city's subway system. Now—thanks in part to the lawlessness of its location, and in part to the fact that it was buried deep enough to shield it from electronic signals—it played host to an underground bazaar known as the Devil's Market, where all manner of illicit goods and services were bought and sold.

The station's elevators were nonfunctional, so the market's only access point was the pedestrian tunnel they stood outside. Twelve feet tall, twelve feet wide, and three football fields in length, the tunnel had been bored and blasted through the island's bedrock more than a century ago. More recently, an enterprising street artist had transformed its entrance into a gaping maw, streaked with gore and slobber, over which was scrawled ABANDON HOPE. Jake thought it was a little on the nose.

"You can do this," Jake said. "It won't be anything like last time, I promise."

"What makes you so sure?"

"This time, you've got me."

Mat filled his lungs, then let the air out, slow and shaky.

"Okay," he said, nodding once. "Let's go."

The air inside the tunnel was clammy and stank of mildew. Because the dormant station lacked electricity, the tunnel's overhead lights were out. Gray daylight reflected dully off graffitied walls for twenty feet or so before surrendering. A smattering of glow sticks—some fresh, others dying—marked the path ahead in ghostly green but provided scant illumination.

Jake shuffled forward cautiously. Mat followed, clutching a fistful of Jake's windbreaker. Broken glass crunched underfoot. Water dripped from somewhere up above.

At first, Mat was puzzled by the heaps of dirty laundry that had gathered at the edges of the tunnel. Once his vision acclimated, however, he realized they weren't piles of clothes, but people. Grimy skin and matted hair obscured their features and nearly robbed them of their humanity. Mat discerned them only by the whites of their wide, searching eyes.

They must've come here to get out of the rain, he thought.

He and Jake continued on. Rats scurried out of their way, more heard than seen—a click of nails, a sniff, a chitter. A brackish, dead-fish smell emanated from somewhere below, the ghost of storm surges past.

Three lights appeared at the far end of the tunnel and began bobbing toward them. Cell phones, in flashlight mode, belonging to three teenagers: two male, one female. They wore hostile, arrogant expressions as they hurried by, but Mat wasn't fooled. He recognized posturing when he saw it. Bluster aside, they were probably as spooked as he was.

You guys think this tunnel's scary now, he thought, *you should try walking it without lights.*

Halfway down the tunnel was a long break in the dotted line of glow sticks. As they passed through it, darkness enveloped them, and the dank atmosphere seemed to congeal. Mat suddenly felt like he was trying to breathe mucus or wet sand.

His lungs ached as he struggled to fill them. His hand tightened on Jake's windbreaker. His feet stopped following his brain's commands.

"Mat, what's wrong?"

"I—I can't breathe."

"Yes, you can."

Mat shook his head, a useless gesture, since Jake couldn't see him.

"I'm dizzy," he wheezed. "My hands are prickly."

A rustle of fabric as Jake turned. The clatter of a dropped umbrella. A pair of hands on Mat's shoulders. Then gentle pressure as Jake touched his forehead to the boy's.

"Listen to me. You're having a panic attack. I know it's frightening, but it'll pass, and I'll be right here with you until it does. Just unclench your muscles and take slow, deep breaths."

Mat did as Jake told him. Eventually, his breathing steadied.

"You okay to keep going?" Jake asked.

"Yeah. I'm all right."

Arm in arm, they continued on, the umbrella lost to darkness behind them. Mat, thinking of the huddled figures near the tunnel's mouth, hoped whoever found it put it to good use.

Up ahead, the tunnel jagged left. Light spilling from whatever lay beyond made the going easier. As they approached, color bled back into the world, revealing walls crammed with elaborately painted tags, and Mat could hear the rise and fall of many voices overlapping.

They rounded the corner, and the tunnel gave way to a long, narrow mezzanine, the bulk of which extended to their right. Its turnstiles, token booth, and vending machines had been stripped away. Now the space was crammed with vendors' blankets, tables, and tents. Some of the displays were ramshackle; others were surprisingly sophisticated. The result looked less like a subway station than a street fair, and a busy one at that.

Mat found it so strange, and so beguiling, he couldn't help but stop and stare—his anxiety momentarily forgotten.

Jake's eyes crinkled as he grinned behind his mask.

"Welcome to the Devil's Market," he said.

37.

Jake couldn't blame the kid for being awestruck. Though he'd never ventured into the Devil's Market before today, he'd heard plenty of rumors, so he had some idea what to expect—and still, he found himself impressed.

The mezzanine was clotted with activity. Since the station's overhead lights were out, many of the vendors supplied their own illumination. Flickering candles threw distorted shadows throughout the space. Gas lanterns projected domes of gold onto the water-damaged ceiling. LEDs glared blinding white, each bulb a tiny star. A blinking string of Christmas lights—battery operated, Jake assumed—looked more manic than festive, under the circumstances.

Customers of all stripes navigated the warren of displays. Peddlers vied for their attention, or haggled with those already engaged. Music, thudding and repetitive, emanated from the far end of the mezzanine. A makeshift grill to the immediate left of the entrance blanketed the market in a gauzy haze that smelled of char, jerk seasoning, and rendered fat.

"Is that *meat*?" Mat said aloud, to no one in particular.

"Sure is," replied the pit master, who had one eye of cold gray, and another of milky white. His grill was an old oil drum, sliced in half, to which a greasy cutting board had been affixed. The grates inside it looked suspiciously like industrial stairwell treads. He'd set up at the

233

mouth of the station's elevator alcove, and propped open the doors to the shafts behind for ventilation. "Squirrel and pigeon, fresh today. Want a taste?"

"He's fine, thanks." Jake placed a hand on Mat's back and gently guided him away.

The Resistance's instructions were to give their pager to a man in a black leather plague mask, which had sounded easy enough aboveground. Down here, in the chaos of the market, it was more challenging than Jake had anticipated.

As they squeezed through a narrow gap in the crowd beside a plywood table strewn with bladed weapons, Jake collided with a skeletal young man whose bald head gleamed in the dim lamplight. A jolt of recognition quickened Jake's heart rate, but he relaxed a little when he realized this wasn't one of the Endtimers he'd encountered on the pier, simply another of their number.

"Watch it," the Endtimer snarled. His breath smelled like rotting fruit. A feral, unwashed stench emanated from his threadbare army surplus clothes. Both penetrated Jake's flimsy mask with ease.

"Sorry," Jake said, stepping aside so the Endtimer could continue on his way.

When the Endtimer failed to move, Jake took Mat by the hand and led him past.

The Endtimer stood his ground and glared at them until they vanished from his line of sight.

"Who was that guy?" Mat's tone evinced concern.

"Nobody you need to worry about," Jake replied.

A few minutes later, Mat stopped before a booth stocked with mason jars containing liquids in a variety of shades from pale yellow to bright orange and dark brown.

"What're those?" he asked, intrigued.

"Those," said the vendor, a grubby man in a velvet dinner jacket and a porkpie hat, "are the cure for whatever's ailing you!"

Jake rolled his eyes. "They're full of piss," he said.

Mat's face lit up with the sort of pleasurable disgust that only someone with a preteen's wit was capable of expressing. "Really?"

"Darn right, they are, and you won't find better within five hundred miles of here, I guarantee! I've got a source inside Elysian Tower who hooks me up with the best single-source rich-folk pee, diverted straight from their fancy, no-flow toilets. Them people are the healthiest in the city, on account of they can afford the snazziest new drugs, and most of what they take is just as useful coming out as going in."

"Time was," Jake said, "the rich only alluded to pissing on the rest of us. Guess they got sick of metaphors and decided they'd try trickle-down for real."

"Laugh all you want—but, my hand to God, it works. Heck, doctors've been doing this since World War II, when they collected wee-wee from GIs treated for the clap, 'cause there wasn't enough penicillin to go around."

"So people...drink it?" Mat asked.

"They sure do, and happily, at that!"

"And it actually helps them?"

"You bet your bottom dollar it does! I seen customers come in with TB, desperate for a dose of Mello Yello, only to bump into 'em a month later on the street, and *poof*—they're right as rain."

"Sure you have," Jake replied.

"Hey, I ain't claiming those results are typical. Caveat emptor, and all that. But I don't mind telling you a mug or two of Orange Crush cleared up a nasty little rash I got last month."

"Honestly, I kinda mind you telling me."

The vendor rolled his eyes theatrically. "Don't listen to your old man," he said, addressing Mat. "Whatever's wrong with you, I've got the fix."

Mat's eyes narrowed. "Who says there's anything wrong with me?"

"Look around, kid! Everybody's got something wrong with 'em these days."

"Not everybody," Jake replied, dragging Mat once more into the crowd.

They wandered another fifteen minutes before spotting their man, leaning against a railing at the far end of the mezzanine. The railing overlooked an open staircase to the northbound platform. A vertiginous mosaic of a couple dancing in midair—*or maybe falling,* Jake thought—extended from landing to ceiling on the wall opposite.

The Resistance contact wore a zippered sweatshirt, hood up, and dark jeans. His posture—hands in sweatshirt pockets, one foot propped against the rail behind—suggested bored watchfulness. His beaked mask made him look disconcertingly like a raven. Its tinted lenses gleamed black in the soft light, and tracked their progress as they approached.

"I'm guessing you're the guy we're looking for," Jake said, leaning close and speaking loudly to be heard over the music.

"That depends. You got something for me?"

Jake handed him the pager.

The masked man pocketed it and jerked his head toward the stairway.

"Follow me."

"Whoa. Hang on a sec. We're not going anywhere with you until—"

But Jake broke off, because there wasn't any point in finishing his thought. The man ignored him, hitting the stairs at a trot and vanishing down them without so much as a backward glance.

"Nice guy," Jake deadpanned. "Chatty, though."

Mat tried a smile. It didn't take.

"You okay?" Jake, serious now.

"Honestly? Dunno."

"Look, if you're not sure you wanna do this—"

"No. I'm sure."

In truth, Mat sounded about as sure as Jake felt, which wasn't very—but the boy was trying to honor his uncle's wishes, so Jake didn't think he had the right to intervene. "Fair enough."

Jake offered Mat his hand again.

Mat took it.

Together, they descended.

38.

Light from above reflected off the landing's tile mosaic, illuminating a small island of dingy gray at the bottom of the stairs. Mat and Jake halted at its center. The northbound platform vanished into inky black on either side of them. The southbound platform, opposite, was a formless void punctuated by two rectangles of dim light where its staircases terminated.

A breeze whipped, cool and musty, through the darkened space. The platform's concrete ceiling blunted the market's tumult, allowing Jake to hear a susurrus of flowing water. It reminded him that the station's sump pumps were as dead as its lights and elevators, and conjured images of a river where the tracks should be.

Their Resistance contact, at the light's edge, lowered his hood and removed his mask. He was pretty much your basic white guy—trim, cleanshaven, and forgettable, his close-cropped hair dishwater brown.

"Sorry for blowing you off back there," he said, "but I couldn't run the risk of being overheard. The fact is, I'm not authorized to answer your questions—all I'm supposed to do is bring you to the meet."

"Bring us?" Jake's temper flared. "You mean this isn't it?"

"Hey, man. Don't shoot the messenger. I'm just doing what I'm told."

"Yeah? Join the club. We've been doing as we're told for three fucking hours, and all we've got to show for it are wet clothes and blistered feet."

"You're frustrated. I get that. I'm even sympathetic, to a point. But remember, you came to us, not the other way around. Seems to me, you want our help, you can't get pissed at us for taking reasonable precautions."

"Okay, okay. Point taken." Jake sighed. "How much farther do we have to go?"

"Not very." The man unclipped a small flashlight from his belt and turned it on. "But first, I've been instructed to frisk you."

"You're welcome to," Jake replied, producing his backup piece from his coat pocket, "but I can tell you what you're gonna find."

The man held out his hand, palm up, revealing a glimpse of reddened skin beneath his sweatshirt sleeve. When Jake hesitated to hand over the pistol, he said, "Nonnegotiable, I'm afraid. You have my word you'll get it back once our business is concluded."

Mat's gaze flitted back and forth between the two of them.

Jake squeezed the boy's hand reassuringly and surrendered his weapon.

"Good choice." The man slipped the Glock into his sweatshirt pocket. "This way."

They headed left, their footfalls echoing. The flashlight's narrow beam swept left and right ahead of them, providing glimpses of a station abandoned years ago in haste. A high-heeled shoe, taupe. A pair of glasses, frame bent, lenses cracked. A tiny, lifeless form in a floral dress that gave Jake a momentary shock before he realized it was a baby doll.

As they approached the end of the platform, a faint line of yellow became visible up ahead: light showing through the gap at the bottom of a door. The flashlight's beam revealed the door to be the entrance to the station's scrubber room—a broom closet, essentially, notched out of the platform along the side wall.

Beside the door stood a Black man of the same general description as his colleague, save for the matter of his ancestry. He and their escort exchanged nods—subtle, economical—after which he opened the door and stood aside to let them enter. Jake felt a twinge of unease, instinct plucking a discordant note, although he couldn't say precisely why.

He and Mat stepped across the threshold. Their escort followed. The other man remained outside.

The scrubber room was maybe four by twelve and tiled from floor to ceiling, with a drain set in the middle of the floor. The cleaning equipment it was meant to house had been replaced by three lightweight, collapsible camp stools. An electric lantern dangled from the wire cage that encased the dead fluorescent light overhead. A backpack leaned against one wall.

Two of the stools were empty. A man of thirty or so occupied the third, knees splayed, hands resting in his lap. Black buzz cut and blue eyes. Heather-gray tee, olive cargo pants, black boots. Like his buddies, he was tidy, compact, nondescript—or, at least, he would have been, were it not for the crescent of glistening pink that traced the left side of his face from jaw to temple.

Jake had seen burn injuries like that before. Treated them, in fact, back in his army days. Incendiary weapons had a knack for finding gaps in body armor.

Too late, Jake realized what his instincts had been trying to tell him.

These men weren't civilians. They were soldiers. Just like the men who'd razed Mat's village, and laid waste to that building in Tribeca.

Jake tensed himself to lunge. "You son of a—"

"Easy." The man rose from his stool and trained an ugly little .45

at Jake's chest. It had been resting on his lap, obscured from sight by his hands, while he was sitting. "Let's not make this any messier than it has to be."

"Jake?" Mat said, frightened, as the door clanged shut behind them. "What's going on? Who is this guy?"

The man smiled, thin and tight, his burned skin stretching.

"I'm sorry. Where are my manners? It's awfully nice to finally meet you, Mateo. You can call me Pike."

BREAKING NEWS

Vessel carrying asylum seekers destroyed off New Zealand coast

New Zealand authorities confirm that a fishing vessel carrying asylum seekers has been destroyed after its crew ignored repeated warnings to retreat to international waters. All fifteen crew members are presumed dead. Three others reportedly died on the journey from Australia to New Zealand.

"This action, though regrettable, was necessary to protect the health and safety of all New Zealanders," the Prime Minister declared in a brief written statement. "It sends the world a forceful message that our nation's sovereignty is nonnegotiable; we will not be held hostage." Her office directed all questions to Lieutenant General Reginald Lancaster of the New Zealand Defence Force.

This story is developing and will be updated.

Related Stories

Undaunted: Asylum seekers face long odds as they set sail for New Zealand

What we know about the *Dauntless* crew

Tensions rise as New Zealand issues ultimatum to asylum seekers

39.

Mat and Jake sat shoulder to shoulder on the other two camp stools, their combined width nearly identical to that of the narrow scrubber room. A damp chill radiated from the tiles. A foul odor wafted upward from the floor drain at their feet.

Pike slouched atop the stool opposite, forearms resting on his knees, pistol aimed at nothing in particular—but the rhythmic flexing of his jaw muscles belied his apparent nonchalance. The man they'd met upstairs, whom Pike called Ringo, crouched before Jake, binding his wrists and ankles with zip ties.

"I've gotta hand it to you, kiddo," Pike said. "You gave us one hell of a chase. There aren't many people, alive or dead, who could say the same."

"Go screw yourself," Mat replied.

"C'mon. Don't be like that. I'm paying you a compliment! Besides, you're as much to blame as I am for the mess we made. If you'd just stayed put, a whole lot of bloodshed could've been avoided."

Ringo, finished with Jake, got to work binding Mat's limbs.

"Speaking of," Jake said, "what happened to the Resistance contact we were supposed to meet with? Did you kill them too?"

Pike laughed. "Man, you're in so far over your head, you don't even know what you don't know."

"I know that murder's still illegal in all fifty states."

In a flash, Pike rose from his stool, grabbed a fistful of Jake's hair, and pressed his pistol to the underside of Jake's chin.

Mat's heart pounded. Blood roared in his ears.

Ringo pinned him where he sat with an iron grip on his thigh.

"Yeah? Let me tell you what *I* know. I know that if I were you, I'd be very careful about running my mouth. Our priority is the kid. You're an afterthought at best. At the moment, my boss thinks you might prove useful, but it wouldn't take much to convince him that you're more trouble than you're worth."

Without letting go of Jake, Pike turned his attention to Mat, who cowered in his seat.

"As for you, you little shit: don't think, just because you're valuable, you can get away with mouthing off like that again. Packages get dinged up in transit all the time, and I'm already pissed at you for costing me six good men, so you'd do well to remember there's a world of hurt between pristine and broadly feasible. You get me?"

"Y-yeah," Mat said, "I get you."

"Good." Pike released Jake and straightened.

Ringo stood and wiped his hands on the thighs of his jeans. "We're all set here."

"Copy that." Pike rapped on the scrubber room door. It swung open, and the man who'd been standing guard outside entered. "You two," he said to Mat and Jake, "on your feet. Ringo, you're on point. Crank, you take the kid. Me and the cop will bring up the rear."

Ringo stowed the camp stools in the backpack and slipped it on. Then he removed a pistol from the shoulder holster beneath his sweatshirt. As he left the scrubber room, he unclipped the flashlight from his belt with his left hand and turned it on.

Crank threw Mat over his shoulder as if he were a sack of flour. Crank's clavicle dug into Mat's stomach. The zip ties around Mat's wrists and ankles cut off circulation to his hands and feet.

At least my hands are tied in front of me, he thought, *and not behind.*

That'd make it easier for Mat to catch himself if this asshole dropped him—or to defend himself, if need be.

Pike grabbed the electric lantern overhead, affixed its carabiner to one of his belt loops, and jabbed the barrel of his gun into Jake's back. "Move."

Mat watched Jake shuffle forward haltingly. It was clear that the zip ties around his ankles—one each, cinched tight, and linked together by a third—made walking difficult.

A discreet set of stairs at one end of the platform led to the tracks below. Crank handled them with ease, despite the added weight, but Jake's restraints made navigating them a struggle.

As he descended, he overbalanced, and teetered on the edge of wiping out.

Pike snatched at Jake's windbreaker in an attempt to keep him upright, but Jake shrugged him off angrily and continued unassisted.

Caked with grime and partially submerged, the tracks looked to Mat more like natural phenomena than anything man-made. Oily water, its surface iridescent in the dim light, lapped against Crank's boots.

Mat craned his neck and saw the concrete overhead was veined with cracks and darkened by rainwater leaching through. Fat drops plinked uncertain melodies as they fell.

To the north, Mat spied a faint dot of stormy gray, where the tracks went aboveground at Dyckman Street. To the south was only darkness.

They went south, feet sloshing, rats scuttling all around.

The noxious odors of black mold and rodent musk caught in Mat's throat. The electric lantern on Pike's hip swayed as he walked, making the tunnel seem to pitch and roll like a boat on stormy seas.

Pike and his men largely steered clear of the tracks, but deep puddles and fallen debris occasionally made doing so impossible. Intellectually, Mat knew that the tunnel was inactive, that the third rail was inert—but his limbic system remained unconvinced. His fight-or-flight response felt like a living thing, all wings and claws, inside his chest: manic, fluttering, desperate to escape.

As they left the station behind, the world narrowed, and Mat's breath began to quicken. Soon, his face tingled, and his panicked wheezing echoed off the tunnel walls.

"Easy, buddy," Jake said, "you're all right."

"Shut the fuck up," Pike snapped.

"Come on, man. Can't you see he's freaking out?"

"You're right," Pike said. "I'm sorry." Then, louder: "Hey, little man! Nut up and handle your shit, or I'm gonna shoot your cop friend in the back of the head—comprende?"

Mat, draped over Crank's shoulder, swallowed hard and nodded. Phantom spots swam before his eyes.

He couldn't feel his hands or feet.

Just unclench your muscles and take slow, deep breaths.

This time, the voice inside his head wasn't Gabriel's, but Jake's.

He heeded it and felt his terror abate.

"See? Problem solved." Though it was too dark for Mat to make out Pike's expression, his tone suggested a malevolent smile.

Eventually, they reached a catwalk, which they followed to a yellow door labeled EMERGENCY EXIT. Behind it was a metal stairwell, gone to rust. They clanged upstairs single file, Jake using the handrail for support, and soon found themselves on a small landing that terminated at a dusty ladder, above which was an iron hatch.

Pike glanced at his watch. "Hopscotch should be in position," he said to Ringo. "Get up there and give him a hand."

Ringo holstered his weapon, clipped his flashlight to his belt, and started up the ladder. When he reached the hatch, he banged on it three times, and received what sounded like three boot stomps in reply.

Ringo pushed on the hatch. With a rusty groan, it opened, but only a crack. Outside, Hopscotch grabbed ahold of the hatch by its exposed lip and yanked. The crack widened. Working in tandem, they forced it open. Gray daylight and slanting rain pummeled Mat's upturned face as Ringo climbed through.

"You next," Pike told Crank, "and be careful with the kid."

Crank ascended, his right hand sliding along the outside of the ladder's vertical support, his left arm holding Mat to his chest. As he neared the hatch, he handed the boy off to Ringo, then clambered out himself.

"Your turn, asshole."

Jake did as Pike said, albeit clumsily. With his wrists bound tight to one another, and his ankles given only a few inches' play, his ascent seemed to take forever. Eventually, he flopped onto the puddled sidewalk—blinking in the brittle daylight, the cleansing rain.

A black SUV idled at the curb, with Hopscotch at the wheel. Ringo stood beside it, Mat squirming in his arms. Crank loomed over Jake to discourage him from running—as if, with his legs bound, it were even a possibility.

Pike emerged from the sidewalk hatch and slid into the SUV's passenger seat. Crank hauled Jake to his feet. The vehicle's liftgate swung open, and Ringo deposited Mat inside. When Jake reached the cargo area, Crank offered a steadying hand, but Jake shrugged him off, just like he'd done when Pike tried to assist him on the stairs between the platform and the tracks.

"I don't need your fucking help," he spat.

"Suit yourself."

Crank watched with amusement as Jake, affecting wounded

pride, flopped awkwardly into the vehicle. Then Crank and Ringo shut the liftgate and climbed into the backseat.

As the SUV pulled away from the curb, Mat sighed inwardly, relieved that Pike and Crank had taken Jake's mulishness at face value.

They still believed that Ringo had frisked him, after all.

It wouldn't do to have them find Amy's concealment holster, and her impossibly tiny backup piece, tucked into the waistband of Jake's jeans.

40.

The SUV splashed through the Bronx's rain-soaked streets, taking a route so circuitous and nonsensical that Jake would've assumed they were lost, had he not noticed the red guideline projected onto the windshield from the dash.

It must be tied into the city's grid, he thought, *which is why we haven't hit a single red light since we got off the highway—or seen a single cop.*

They'd been on the road awhile, wipers sloshing, rain tattooing the roof over their heads. Traffic had bottlenecked on the Washington Bridge, but it began to flow at a decent clip once they reached I-87.

Eventually, they wound up in the South Bronx neighborhood of Hunts Point—although neighborhood, in this instance, was something of a misnomer.

A peninsula bordered by the Bronx and East Rivers, Hunts Point was once home to the world's largest wholesale food market. Prior to the emergence of the Harbinger virus, half the city's meat and poultry passed through it, as well as the majority of its seafood.

As a result, Hunts Point was more commercial than residential, an ugly hodgepodge of low-slung buildings separated by vast stretches of pavement. Most of them sat empty now, their windows gapped, their walls defaced, unchecked frost heaves creating fault lines in their parking lots. Entire properties at the water's edge were overrun by scrub brush, their only inhabitants the raccoons, rats, and seagulls that feasted on whatever washed ashore.

The red line guided the SUV to a narrow concrete drive. To its left was a corrugated structure of some kind. To its right, a rocky downslope led to a shallow inlet, blanketed with kelp and rockweed, that looked as if it had once served as a boat ramp.

Access to the property was restricted by a chain-link fence topped with barbed wire. As the vehicle rocked to a halt in front of it, Ringo hopped out, unlocked the gate, and swung it wide. Once the SUV passed through, he relocked the gate and trotted after.

The concrete drive was crumbling, uneven. Crabgrass and dandelions pushed up through the cracks. Junk lined it on both sides: old tires, wooden pallets, coiled lengths of heavy rope.

They jounced along until the drive gave way to a small parking lot. Then Pike and Crank piled out of the vehicle, while Hopscotch popped the SUV's liftgate.

"Ringo, go ready the boat. Crank, you grab the kid."

The men did as Pike instructed.

"A fucking boat?" Jake, incredulous.

"That's right," Pike said. "Now get out, nice and slow."

"You mean you're not gonna carry me?"

"Be careful what you wish for," Pike replied.

Jake swung his legs out of the vehicle and stood. They appeared to be on an old wharf. Through the chain link to his right, he saw rotted pilings jutting from the turbid water, pale gray above the high tide line, and deep russet below—the remnants of a wharf that had run parallel.

They entered the building via a dented steel door that had been painted green some time ago and left to flake. Jake, chilled by the vehicle's AC, was grateful to get out of the rain.

The room inside was spacious and dim. Exposed beams and dirty windows. Rough-hewn wooden floors covered with dark, blotchy stains. Jake detected odors of stale coffee and spent iron, a combination he associated with crime scenes.

"What *is* this place?" Mat muttered.

To Jake's surprise, Pike answered. "Some kind of fish-processing facility — or, at least, it used to be, before they folded. The bank that took possession of it folded, too, so I guess it's as much ours as anybody's now. Don't worry, though. We won't be staying long."

Jake had figured as much. The room contained no furniture, no sleeping bags. The only indication that it was occupied was the cheap coffeemaker in the corner, a tin of grounds and stack of paper cups beside.

"Hey, kid," Pike said, "you hungry?"

"No." Mat glared at him defiantly.

"Oh. Then I guess I won't bother offering you one of these." He removed a protein bar from his pants' right cargo pocket, opened it, and took a bite.

Mat's eyes widened. His stomach growled.

"That's what I thought." Pike took two more out of his pocket. Handed one to Mat. Waggled the other at Jake. "You want?"

"I'm good."

"Take it anyway," he said. "You'll need your strength."

"For what?"

"You're going to run a little errand for us."

"And why would I do that?"

"Because you value your life?"

Jake cast a sidelong glance at Mat, who was momentarily preoccupied with his snack, and dropped his voice. "Cut the shit. We're both professionals. You wanna keep things friendly for the kid's sake, that's fine by me, but let's not pretend you plan on letting me walk away when all is said and done."

"Fair enough," Pike replied. "How about this? If you do what I ask, I'll have no reason to go after your little girl. Your friends can only hide her from me for so long, after all."

Jake felt a sudden urge to wrap his hands around the bastard's neck and squeeze. By force of will, he tamped it down. He knew that Pike's men would take him out before he had the chance to do any lasting damage, and he was of no use to Mat or Zoe dead.

"Stay the hell away from my daughter."

"Happily — provided you cooperate."

"Fine," he said through gritted teeth. "Tell me what I need to do."

Pike smiled. "See? I knew you'd come around. The mission's simple, really. Your target's name is Jessica Vandermeer, although her lawyer kindly informed us she's been hiding out under her maiden name of Williams, which explains why it's been such a bitch to find her."

"Hold up. Did you say target? Because there's no way in hell—"

"Easy, tiger. We're not asking you to kill anybody. All we want is information."

Jake eyed the man skeptically. "Information."

"No more, no less."

"About what?"

"Shadow Reckoning."

"What the hell is Shadow Reckoning?"

"If I knew that, I wouldn't be sending you to ask, now, would I?"

"You must have *some* idea. Otherwise, why go to all this trouble?"

Pike laughed. "I'll tell you why. Money, and lots of it."

"Seriously? You're a fucking merc?"

"You make it sound like such a dirty word. Fact is, I've served my country, and by the time they spit me out the other end, all I had to show for it was an empty bank account, a broken marriage, and a whole bunch of dead friends. I'd like to tell myself they died for a worthy cause, but I've spent enough time downrange to know better. The guys you're training one day, you're shooting at the next, and for what? So whoever writes the biggest checks to the hypocrites and liars in DC can see a fat return on their investments? Seems to me, I'm better off cutting out the middleman and chasing paper my damn self. It's a transaction I can wrap my head around, at least."

"That's...dark."

"That's life."

"Not much of one."

"Says the captive to the captor."

Jake shrugged, as if conceding the point.

"If I find out about this Shadow Reckoning," he said, "you'll leave my daughter be?"

"That's the long and short of it, yeah."

"I don't get it. What's the catch? Why can't you just go talk to her yourself?"

"Oh, did I forget to mention?" Pike smiled. "Jessica Vandermeer is on Rikers Island."

Tidewater Sanitarium

Treating people, not diseases.

———

The staff of Tidewater Sanitarium at Rikers Island knows there's nothing you wouldn't do for your sick loved ones. That's why we offer the highest quality of compassionate care, customized to meet each patient's unique needs, in a tranquil seaside setting—so you, and they, can rest assured they're in good hands.

FOR MORE INFORMATION,
VISIT WWW.DBS.GOV/TIDEWATER

41.

The boat—**a** matte-green rigid-hulled inflatable dinghy—skipped across the water like a flat rock expertly thrown. Its bow sliced through the East River's chop, sending brackish spray skyward whenever they connected.

The sting of drying salt on Jake's cheeks brought to mind something his high school science teacher used to say. *The East River isn't actually a river but a tidal estuary, formed by a drowned valley.* Funny how that nugget stuck when he couldn't even recall the woman's name.

Jake was sitting on a bench in the middle of the vessel, his arms and legs no longer bound, his borrowed windbreaker snapping like a warning flag in a hurricane. Jake's minder, Ringo, manned the outboard engine. It was quieter than Jake expected, barely audible over the roar of the wind in his ears—some kind of military tech, he supposed.

The rain had stopped, thank God, but the evening sky was overcast, gray fading to black from west to east. Jake was grateful that the light of day was waning. It made the lump of Amy's gun beneath his clothes harder to see.

This dumbass missed it once before, Jake thought. *It'd be a shame if he were to spot it now.*

They were headed south. Manhattan's cityscape was to their

right. The humbler silhouette of Queens was to their left. Planes roared in and out of LaGuardia straight ahead.

Though their route meandered some to avoid running afoul of other vessels, the trip was short. Rikers Island was less than half a mile from Hunts Point as the crow flies.

Over the centuries, Rikers Island had served many purposes: as a training ground for Union soldiers during the Civil War; as a landfill so crammed with refuse that it quadrupled the island's size; as the largest penal colony in the world.

Contrary to popular belief, Rikers Island hadn't actually been a prison, but a jail—or, rather, ten of them. The island's four hundred acres once housed ten thousand inmates, the vast majority of whom were pretrial defendants. Some had been denied bail due to the severity of their crimes. Far more were simply unable to afford it.

Despite the fact that many of its residents awaited trial for minor offenses, the complex had a reputation for being among the most violent corrections facilities in America. That's why, for decades, the city worked toward its closure.

Five years ago, they succeeded, leaving the facilities in limbo. Even in a market as saturated as pre-8/17 New York's, most developers had little appetite for trying to flip a literal pile of blood-soaked garbage in the East River, and the few who bothered looking into it soon discovered that the remediation required would be a nightmare. For a while, a popular online retailer considered using the island as a hub from which they could launch shipping drones into the city, but the FAA nixed the deal, citing its proximity to the airport.

As a result, the island's facilities sat empty until the Harbinger virus created a dire shortage of hospital beds. By the fledgling DBS's estimation, Rikers Island was the perfect solution: isolated, turnkey, and—most of all—cheap.

Now Rikers Island hosted greater New York's sickest patients—

those so far gone, and so communicable, they needed to be sequestered from the population at large. There'd been talk of transferring the residents of Park City to the island as well, but lawsuits from several prominent human rights organizations halted progress on that front—and before they could be adjudicated, the facility ran out of beds, rendering the proposal moot.

Ironically, much of the island's support staff consisted of nonviolent inmates housed on-site, the result of a controversial work release program. The DBS considered it safer than allowing civilian workers to commute to and from. Jake couldn't help but wonder how the inmates felt about it. Lord knows he was less than thrilled at the prospect of setting foot inside the facility.

"Vandermeer's on Rikers?" he'd asked Pike. "What's wrong with her?"

"Tuberculosis. To hear her lawyer tell it, she doesn't have long left, not that anybody does once they're shipped off to that hellhole."

"Is that why you're sending me? You're afraid of getting sick?"

Pike shook his head. "Not exactly. The fact is, we could suit up and go get her, but the fragile nature of her condition makes her... difficult to interrogate."

"Hard to torture without killing, you mean."

"Tomato, tomahto. Point is, a soft approach—while more challenging, from a logistical perspective—is likelier to yield a favorable result. That's where you come in."

"Super."

Pike ignored Jake's obvious sarcasm. "My boss thought so too. See, he's eager to test the boy's abilities, and your close contact with him over the past few days provides the perfect opportunity."

"Oh, yeah? How's that?"

"I won't lie. Most of the math he threw at me sailed right over my head. Still, I understood enough to get the gist. The bottom line is, there's no way you could spend any length of time in an enclosed space with that many active TB patients and not contract it—unless, of course, Mateo's everything that he's cracked up to be."

"So I'm your guinea pig, is that it?"

Pike smiled. "That, or our sacrificial lamb."

Ringo piloted the boat to a small, crescent-shaped beach in the shadow of a decommissioned pier. Upslope from the beach, stadium lighting blanketed the campus in false daylight. Nearby smokestacks belched acrid gray into the evening sky, conjuring in Jake a sense memory of the charred bodies in Park City.

When they reached the shallows, Ringo shut off the boat's engine and tilted the hinged transom it was mounted to so that the engine was no longer in the water. For a moment, they coasted silently toward shore. Then Ringo hopped out of the boat and ordered Jake to do the same.

The water was cold and foamy and knee-deep. Together, they stashed the boat among the pilings, Jake's nerves jangling all the while. Rationally, he expected the island's perimeter security to be light—after all, there weren't many people dumb enough to break *into* a quarantine facility—but still, he worried he'd be putting Zoe in danger if they were caught.

Ringo removed a hand-drawn map of the island from the back right pocket of his jeans, unfolded it, and pointed to a building circled in red. "I'm told this is where they keep the lungers. Vandermeer should be somewhere inside."

"I don't suppose you've got her room number."

"That, you're gonna hafta find out for yourself."

"Because you don't know," Jake asked, "or because you wanna make sure I spend long enough inside for your little experiment to work?"

"Hey, man. I'm just the hired help. Any beef you've got is with the man in charge, not me."

"Then I'll be sure to take it up with him. Remind me—what's his name again?"

"Cute. Now quit stalling and get a move on. The sooner you get what we came for, the sooner we can both get out of here."

"Easy for you to say."

"The fuck're you worried about? I thought the kid's force field or whatever was supposed to keep you safe."

"It's not a force field," Jake replied, "and who said I was worried?"

Thing is, he *was* worried.

Believing Mat had helped his daughter beat a fever was one thing.

Betting his life on the untested theory that hanging out with Mat had given Jake a bubble of happy microbes to protect him was another matter entirely—particularly since, even if it turned out to be true, there was no way to know how long he had until that bubble popped.

42.

When Billy's phone buzzed, he was lying facedown on a patch of sun-baked dirt, his dreadlocks twisted into a knot at the nape of his neck, a pair of day-and-night HD smart binoculars pressed to his face.

A rusty chain-link fence shot through with weeds enclosed the unpaved lot that he was lying in. The lot belonged to an auto salvage company that didn't seem to have much use for it, since it was badly overgrown, and empty but for Billy.

Though his position was far from cozy, it afforded Billy a partial view of the dilapidated building in which Mateo Rivas—and, until recently, Jacob Gibson—was being held. The sun had set some time ago, but the sky was not yet fully dark. The vegetation that surrounded Billy was still damp from the day's rain, and smelled how he imagined a jungle might: sharp, earthy, overripe.

A few hours ago, a fellow Soldier of Gaia clocked a white dude and a brown kid sneaking around the Devil's Market, and called it in. Both wore masks, but the description he gave for Gibson was consistent with what Billy had seen him wearing on the pier, so Billy put the troops nearby on high alert.

Not long after, one of Billy's pals was on a smoke break outside his uncle's barbershop at the corner of St. Nicholas Avenue and West 186th Street, when an unmarked SUV screeched to a halt outside the grocery store diagonal. Next thing he knew, a bunch of guys with guns crawled out a goddamn hole in the sidewalk, dragging Gibson and Rivas along with them. Then the guys with guns forced Gibson and Rivas into the car, and it peeled out, headed north.

By then, Upper Manhattan was crawling with Soldiers, who quickly mobilized in search of the SUV. It wended, seemingly at random, through the city—but the Soldiers caught a break thanks to a snarl of traffic on the Washington Bridge, which bought them time to position several vehicles on the far side. From there, tailing the SUV to Hunts Point was a breeze.

Billy's phone buzzed again. He rolled onto one bony hip and removed it from his pocket. On its lock screen was a message from Dave Gunter that read *Sitrep.*

Shit.

While Billy's fellow Soldiers had done yeoman's work locating Gibson and Rivas, laying hands on them was proving harder than anticipated. For one thing, the guys who'd taken them were clearly armed. For another, they were holed up on a private wharf, which meant that Billy and his raiding party would either have to take a swim or bust through a locked gate to gain access. And then there was the fact that Gibson was no longer on the premises—he left via inflatable dinghy while Billy was waiting for reinforcements to arrive.

Billy, you fuckwit, he thought. *Why couldn't you just shut your stupid mouth for once, instead of volunteering to lead the charge?*

Truth be told, though, Billy knew the answer. Last time they crossed paths, Gibson had humiliated him, and he would rather die than let that stand.

Billy pecked out a cagey nonresponse to Dave's text: *Our men are in position and standing by.*

Then what exactly is the holdup???

He hesitated.

Dave wasn't gonna like this.

JG+1 hostile left via boat before we got our team in place, he said. Then, because he couldn't help but try to contain the damage, he added: *MR still inside.*

For a long while after he hit Send, a set of ellipses pulsed onscreen, causing Billy's stomach to tighten like a fist. Dave's trust was as easy to lose as it was difficult to gain, and Billy had seen firsthand how steep the descent from his good graces could be.

The ellipses vanished.

Then reappeared.

Then vanished again.

Finally, Dave replied, *A FUCKING BOAT???!!!*

Yeah. Little one. Inflatable. Can't be going far.

You'd better hope not, Dave replied. *Move on them the second he* returns.

THE 8/17 COMMISSION REPORT
APPENDIX H

The following is an archived snapshot of a private https://www
.shadowvox.net/messages chat as it appeared on August 19, 2028,
01:13:00 GMT. Said web domain is now defunct, the result of a
federal seizure order executed on August 23, 2028. Username Plague-
Doctor has since been positively identified as Spencer Aaron Brutsch
(deceased). Username thewhiterider remains unidentified. For a
comprehensive list of all known /endtimes users, see Appendix N.

---

https://www.shadowvox.net/messages

ShadowVox: Speak Freely

PLAGUEDOCTOR (2H): heey man u therre?

THEWHITERIDER (1H): you rang

PLAGUEDOCTOR (58M): o thank darwn. i was beginigg to eondert if youd ever
grt back to me.

THEWHITERIDER (56M): you okay bro?

THEWHITERIDER (55M): your usually all anal about your spelling and shit

PLAGUEDOCTOR (51M): notreally

PLAGUEDOCTOR (50M): im all fukd up

PLAGUEDOCTOR (49M): feel like sht

THEWHITERIDER (47M): what do you mean you feel like shit

PLAGUEDOCTOR (45M): wat do u thnk

THEWHITERIDER (43M): y pestis?

THEWHITERIDER (43M): you said youd be careful

THEWHITERIDER (42M): that you could deliver it to me all safe and sound

PLAGUEDOCTOR (40M): yeah abt that

PLAGUEDOCTOR (40M): i wantd to suprise you

PLAGUEDOCTOR (39M): but hyou nwnot be needin gthat shopment we discussed

THEWHITERIDER (37M): youre talking crazy man

THEWHITERIDER (36M): theres no need to go off halfcocked

THEWHITERIDER (36M): just stick to the plan like we discussed

THEWHITERIDER (35M): you give me the biologicals

THEWHITERIDER (34M): ill handle the dispersal

PLAGUEDOCTOR (32M): lttle late forthat

PLAGUEDOCTOR (32M): litl e lat for me

THEWHITERIDER (30M): youre scaring me bro

THEWHITERIDER (29M): what did you do

PLAGUEDOCTOR (27M): what we tlked about

PLAGUEDOCTOR (27M): what we dreeamed about

THEWHITERIDER (25M): YOU DUMB FUCK WHAT DID YOU DO

PLAGUEDOCTOR (23M): i thought uoud be proud of me

PLAGUEDOCTOR (23M): i idd it for us

PLAGUEDOCTOR (22M): fr you

THEWHITERIDER (21M): DID WHAT

PLAGUEDOCTOR (20M): remade th world

THEWHITERIDER (18M): THIS IS IMPORTANT

THEWHITERIDER (17M): I NEED TO KNOW EXACTLY WHAT YOU DID

THEWHITERIDER (17M): AND WHERE YOU ARE RIGHT NOW

PLAGUEDOCTOR (15M): youll sfind out hwen you wach the news tmorrow;)

PLAGUEDOCTOR (14M): not me tho

PLAGUEDOCTOR (14M): ill be longg one by thn

PLAGUEDOCTOR (13M): chanses ar yuo nd eberybody elss on't bee far behind

PLAGUEDOCTOR (13M): think of ghiw beuatiful teh world wil be when were allgon e.

THEWHITERIDER (12M): GODDAMN IT TELL ME WHAT YOU DID RIGHT NOW

PLAGUEDOCTOR (10M): ur my best frend u kno

PLAGUEDOCTOR (10M): m y only frind

PLAGUEDOCTOR (9M): my name is spebxer by th way

PLAGUEDOCTOR (8M): *spncer

PLAGUEDOCTOR (8M): *spencer

PLAGUEDOCTOR (7M): seemd important uou shoild kno wthat

THEWHITERIDER (6M): spencer what

THEWHITERIDER (5M): what's your last name

THEWHITERIDER (5M): your address

THEWHITERIDER (5M): tell me

THEWHITERIDER (5M): tell me where you are

THEWHITERIDER (4M): you NEED to tell me NOW

THEWHITERIDER (4M): i'm SERIOUS spencer

THEWHITERIDER (4M): GODDAMN IT SPENCER I'M NOT FUCKING AROUND

PLAGUEDOCTOR (3M): lkndcdvvvjmk,.omokmkknklllllllllllllllll;./

THEWHITERIDER (1M): spencer?

THEWHITERIDER (30S): SPENCER???

43.

Jake trundled upslope from the beach beside the pier and ducked down a narrow drive between two buildings. The smokestacks towered over him to his left. As he passed them, an ashy taste caught in his throat, and he resisted the urge to spit.

Tidewater's campus was austere and eerily unpopulated. It was also much larger than Jake had anticipated—more Eastern Bloc dystopia than former jailhouse. Labyrinthine fences topped with concertina wire encircled the buildings, their gates thrown open, their guard stations shuttered and unoccupied. Though he knew that they were nothing more than artifacts of the island's former life, they seemed to Jake like haunting echoes of the Park City massacre.

The outdoor lighting—enormous banks of stark white bulbs held aloft by massive poles—swarmed with insects. The peculiarity and intensity of the illumination they produced seemed to flatten everything in sight and knock its color saturation out of whack, like a bargain-basement flat-screen. A low electric buzz filled the air, though whether it was from the insects or the lights, Jake couldn't tell.

Eventually, he came to a building studded with loading bays. Unoccupied delivery vans were parked at several of them, seemingly at random. A set of concrete stairs at the far end of the loading bays led to a heavy door inset with a square of crosshatched glass. A long ramp that folded back on itself beside the stairs led to the door as well.

He tried the door. It was unlocked. Inside, he found pallets stacked high with lab coats, towels, and bed linens. Each item was folded neatly and wrapped in plastic. They ranged in color from bright white to dingy yellow, the latter clearly a result of repeated bleaching.

Jake riffled through the lab coats until he found one labeled 42R. Then he tore open its plastic wrap and slipped it on. It smelled faintly of chlorine. Its cuffs and collar were discolored. A patch on the right breast said TIDEWATER SANITARIUM.

Nearby was an empty canvas laundry bin, wheeled, a number stenciled on its side. After looking around to see if anyone was watching him—near as he could tell, nobody was—he began tearing open bags and tossing their contents into the bin. Then he mussed them up a bit, making sure the yellowest items were on top, and wheeled the bin back out the door through which he'd entered.

Years ago, before he was assigned to homicide, Jake worked a string of burglaries in which the perps walked out of several Midtown office buildings with nearly a hundred grand in portable electronics. Turned out, they'd come in dressed like pest control technicians, put their haul into industrial-sized bait stations, and wheeled it out the front door unmolested. If they hadn't eventually slipped up by parking their getaway car in a tow zone, they could've easily made off with twice that.

Obviously, Jake wasn't trying to steal anything, but he didn't want anybody looking too closely at him, or demanding to see his nonexistent credentials. The way he figured it, the whole island was teeming with diseases, so a bin full of soiled laundry ought to keep nosy staffers at arm's length.

Jake wheeled the bin down the ramp and across the paved lot to a concrete footpath. Though the linens themselves weren't heavy, one of the bin's wheels was uncooperative, so he soon found himself sheathed in sweat.

Then again, that could've been a result of his jangling nerves.

He didn't see many people on his way to Vandermeer's building—which, according to the signage, was formally designated the E. A. Blair Tuberculosis Recuperation Center—and those he encountered gave him a wide berth.

Jake rolled by the building's main entrance without slowing, because he didn't like his odds of sneaking past the front desk unnoticed and thought he might have better luck around back.

As he approached a side door tucked between a pair of unkempt shrubs, a harried woman in a paper gown, hairnet, and safety glasses came into view. Her face was pale and bony. Her hands were dry and cracked. Though her gown was powder blue, its cuffs were bleached sickly green.

The woman dropped the cigarette that she'd been holding and ground it out beneath a patterned clog. Then she waved her badge in front of the proximity scanner to unlock the door.

"Hey, hold that for me, would you?"

"Sorry," she replied, "you know the policy."

"Which policy is that?" Jake said, plucking a couple details from a recent *Times* piece he'd read. "The one that's got me working mandatory overtime without a nickel to show for it, or the one that leaves dead patients in their beds 'til Monday morning because the assholes in charge don't feel like paying docs to work weekends?"

She flashed Jake a weary smile and opened the door wide. "You know what? Fuck it. But hurry up, at least. If I get caught, it's another fifteen days on my sentence, guaranteed."

"Thanks. You're a saint."

"That so?" She coughed into the elbow of her paper gown. "Then how the hell'd I wind up here?"

Just inside the entrance was a corridor. The woman headed right, so Jake went left, abandoning the laundry bin as soon as she disappeared from sight.

The hall in which he found himself was wide and beige, with a drop ceiling, bumpered walls, and a vinyl tile floor—all of it scuffed, stained, or otherwise tainted. Cool, recirculated air stank of mildew, bleach, and human waste. Fluorescent panels flickered overhead.

Beds dotted the hallway on either side. Several were empty and stripped of linens. The rest were occupied. Through open doors, Jake saw the rooms were crammed with beds as well, with little space between.

Some patients slept, their breathing noisy, labored. Others coughed, wet and hacking, without end. Still others whimpered, begged, and pleaded—with Jake, with God, with no one in particular. A few were quiet and still, their sunken eyes open, their pale faces slack. Jake wished he could convince himself that they were lost in thought, but years spent investigating homicides had taught him otherwise.

Hand sanitizer dispensers were mounted every fifty feet or so, but obviously hadn't been refilled in quite some time, because they were crusty from disuse. Instead, carboys filled with dilute bleach rested atop scavenged nightstands, filing cabinets, and TV trays at the end of every hall—spigots dangling over edges, vinyl flooring spattered white below.

That explains the sorry state of that poor lady's hands, Jake thought. *Although, by the look of her, it's not doing any good.*

Up the hall, Jake spied a nurse's cart, parked outside a women's restroom. On it was a tablet computer, its screen a blur of textured glove prints; a half-drunk bottle of Diet Coke; and a Snickers bar—still wrapped, thank God.

Jake grabbed the tablet.

Heard a flush.

Hightailed it up the hall and around a corner.

Once he'd checked the door to ensure it wouldn't lock behind him, he slipped into a nearby stairwell, and poked at the tablet until it gave up Vandermeer's—er, Williams's—room number.

Five minutes and three flights of stairs later, Jake found himself at the threshold of Vandermeer's room. The room contained four beds, although it looked as if it had been designed to hold no more than two. One of them was stripped down to its rubberized mattress. A trio of women—pale, skeletal, and seemingly unconscious—populated the other three.

As Jake stood there, trying to figure out which of them was Jessica Vandermeer, the one nearest the window opened her eyes and said, "If you've come to kill me, I suggest you hurry up."

Her voice was shaky and weak, but her pale-green eyes were clear. If Jake were forced to guess, he'd say that she was in her late forties, but her condition made it hard to tell.

"I'm not here to kill you," Jake said.

"Damn." She smiled faintly, her teeth tinged red. "It'd be a kindness."

"I'm sorry."

"Don't be..." She trailed off, her raised eyebrows a prompt.

"Jake."

"...Jake," she finished. "I'm Jess—but, then, I'm guessing you already knew that."

"I had a feeling."

The room's AC cycled on. Jess shivered and pulled up her blanket. Flecks of dried blood stained its hem, a morbid scatterplot around her chin.

"If you're not here to kill me," she said, "why *are* you here?"

Jake cast a glance at the women sleeping in their beds. Neither had stirred since he'd arrived. "I need to know about Shadow Reckoning."

Jess grimaced, triggering a coughing fit. Wet, hacking, and violent, it doubled her over—but when Jake rushed to her side to assist her, she pushed him away, her eyes wide with alarm.

Eventually, her coughing fit subsided. She wiped the blood from her lips with the back of her hand, which looked like crumpled paper stretched across a frame of dead, dry twigs.

"Are you insane? At this point, there's nothing you or anyone can do for me, and getting near me unprotected while I'm coughing is a death sentence." The fit had left her winded. She struggled audibly to find the breath to speak.

"I'm sorry," Jake repeated, "but I've been wandering these halls awhile now, trying to find you, so I think that ship's already sailed." Under the circumstances, it seemed cruel to tell her he might be temporarily immune—and could result in her dismissing him as a crank.

"Regardless, I appreciate the gesture, even though you might find me undeserving once you hear what I have to say."

This conversation wasn't going anything like Jake expected. It left him feeling rudderless, unmoored. "Then you'll tell me what I came to hear?"

"I've run out of reasons not to," she replied wearily, "and it seems wrong to take a secret this big with me when I go. I suppose you could consider it my last confession. How much do you already know?"

"Assume that I know nothing."

"I don't understand. How did you manage to find me, if you don't even know what you're doing here? It's not as if I made it easy."

"I didn't find you—or, at least, not exactly. I was sent by someone who threatened to hurt my daughter unless I could get you to talk. They told me where you'd be."

"Funny," she said, "I spent years thinking I was keeping quiet for the same reason—but, now that my husband and stepdaughter are

271

both gone, I'm forced to admit I never talked because I was ashamed. I suppose that's why I dared to hope that you were here to kill me."

"I'm—"

"—sorry, I know. Believe me, I'm sorry, too, because what I'm about to tell you can never be unheard."

Jake flashed a smile. "Hey, with a pitch like that, how could anyone resist?"

A surprised laugh escaped Jess's lips, followed by another bout of coughing. Once she regained her composure, she said, "I'd ask if you were sure about this, but—"

"—you already know that I don't have a choice," Jake said.

Jess nodded, her expression somber.

"I hope your daughter knows how much her father loves her."

"Thanks." Jake felt a surge of apprehension as he wondered how Amy, Hannah, and Zoe were faring in his absence. "I hope so too."

44.

"What the hell was that?"

Hannah bolted upright in her seat, the question escaping her lips before she had a chance to stop it.

Shit, she thought. *I must've nodded off.*

"Someone's at the door," Amy whispered.

Hannah sat on one end of the couch. Zoe lay beside her, fast asleep, her feet in Hannah's lap. Amy was in the recliner, the Croziers' tablet propped on one knee. Its icy glow cast her worry lines in high relief.

"You think it could be Jake?"

Amy shook her head.

Hannah checked her watch. It was a little after 10 p.m.

Far too late for this to be anything but bad news.

They knocked again.

Amy's right, Hannah thought. *Whoever's out there isn't knocking, they're pounding—violent, insistent.*

No sooner had the thought occurred to her than the pounding ceased.

For a moment, all was quiet.

Then the door began to rattle in its jamb.

"Open up, goddamn it, we know you're in there!"

Zoe sat up blearily. "What's happening?"

"Nothing, sweetie." Amy's expression softened. "Everything's fine."

"I don't think they're going anywhere until somebody talks to them," Hannah said.

"Are you suggesting we answer?" Amy, incredulous.

"We may not have a choice. Take Zoe to the guest room while I go get rid of them."

"No way. I'm coming with you."

"Amy, you're a wanted woman. If anybody were to recognize you—"

Amy raised her hands in acquiescence. "You're right. I know you are. That doesn't mean I have to like it. Promise me you'll keep the chain fastened?"

"You got it."

"C'mon, Zoe! You and I are gonna hang out in the other room for a minute, okay?"

Zoe nodded. She and Amy padded to the guest room, hand in hand.

The pounding started up again.

"Hold your horses," Hannah yelled, "I'm coming!"

She checked the peephole, which afforded her a fish-eye view of four people—three men, one woman—gathered around the door. The jogger with whom she and Jake had shared an elevator was front and center. The blonde who'd nearly called in Zoe's seizure stood to one side.

Hannah made sure the chain was fastened.

Disengaged the knob lock and the deadbolt.

Then, with a steeling breath, she opened the door.

"Can I help you?"

"Yeah, you can start by telling us what the hell you're doing in our building." The man from the elevator leaned in, close enough to touch. He stank of whiskey and stress sweat. A dusting of cocaine clung to the dark stubble beneath his nose. An aluminum baseball bat dangled from his right hand.

"I didn't realize you owned the place." Hannah struggled to project an air of nonchalance. She didn't want to sound conciliatory, for fear they'd take it as a sign of guilt or weakness, but she wasn't sure how far to push.

"Don't get cute. We know you're not supposed to be here." This from the blonde, who clung fearfully to the man beside her, like they were walking through a haunted house. His right arm was wrapped around her waist. In his left hand, he carried a meat mallet.

"Excuse me?" Hannah feigned offense. "This apartment belonged to my Uncle Harry and Aunt Marge. They died just shy of two weeks ago. My family and I are staying here while I sort out their affairs."

The third guy frowned. "Harold never mentioned having a niece." He wore an open bathrobe over boxers, and appeared to be unarmed. The jogger's friend, no doubt, roped into this because he lived on the Croziers' hall.

"Actually, he has three. I'm not surprised he didn't mention us. He and my mom weren't close."

"If all that's true," said the man from the elevator, "you shouldn't mind us coming in to take a look around."

"Are you insane? Of course I mind. It's late, I'm tired, and my little girl is sleeping. Meanwhile, you're armed, drunk, and spoiling for a fight. You can't seriously expect me to let you in."

"The guy I saw you with this morning was carrying a gun," he replied — petulant, defensive.

"You mean my husband? He's got a permit." She eyed the bat in his hand pointedly. "I don't know if you're aware, but this city's not as safe as it used to be."

"You think this is fucking funny?"

"I promise you, I really don't. Look, if you wanna call the cops on me, feel free. I'm sure they'd be interested to hear what you planned to do with that baseball bat. In the meantime, though, I'm going to bed."

Hannah closed the door, or tried.

The man from the elevator stopped it with his foot. "The hell you are."

He shouldered the door, hard. His companions launched into a cacophonous medley of alarm and enthusiasm. Hannah, thrown off-balance, staggered backward.

The chain held.

He slammed into the door again.

This time, the chain snapped.

Terror gripped Hannah's heart and squeezed.

45.

Broken seashells crunched underfoot as Jake walked, backlit, toward the water's edge. To the west, the city's skyline glimmered against a field of purple velvet.

"Took you long enough," Ringo said, materializing from the shadow of the pier. "I was beginning to think you fucked up and got pinched."

"Sorry to disappoint."

Jake's tone was brittle, strained.

If Ringo noticed, he didn't let on.

"You get what we came for?"

"Sure did."

"Then help me put the boat back in the water so we can get outta here."

"I'm afraid there's been a change of plans," Jake replied. "I'm leaving. You're staying."

"That so?"

An uncertain smile twisted Ringo's lips, like he halfway thought that Jake was putting him on. It faded when he saw the pistol in Jake's hand.

"Son of a bitch," he said. "I shoulda realized, when you gave up your piece so easily, you had another on you somewhere."

"Yeah. You probably should've. Now sit the fuck down."

Jake's voice was cold and hard, a byproduct of what Jess Vandermeer had told him, he supposed. On his way back from her room, he'd considered taking Ringo hostage, only to dismiss the idea as impractical. As Ringo said himself, he was a hired gun, which made him a lousy bargaining chip—as disposable to his employer as he'd be dangerous to transport. Jake figured it was better to subdue him here than run the risk of bringing him along.

"Easy, buddy. Let's talk this through."

As Ringo spoke, he showed Jake his palms, a gesture intended to pacify—but Jake wasn't fooled. He noticed that Ringo had timed it to obscure a subtle pivot that simultaneously narrowed the gap between them and presented Jake a smaller target.

"The only thing we're talking through is you sitting down, removing two of those zip ties from your belt, and putting them around your hands and feet, all nice and slow."

"Or what?" Ringo shuffled a little closer. "You're gonna shoot me?"

Jake stepped backward in an effort to maintain his distance.

Loose sand shifted beneath his feet.

"If I have to."

"C'mon, man. You're not a murderer. Just put the gun down, and we'll pretend this never happened, okay?"

Jake squeezed the grip of Amy's Glock so hard, his forearm ached. His body quaked with rage and grief. The awful truth of Shadow Reckoning swelled like a malignancy inside his chest. Ringo, oblivious, inched nearer—palms up, arms outstretched.

"Please," Jake said, "don't make me do this."

"Gibson, listen, I know you're in a tough spot right now, but I need you to be smart, for *both* our sakes."

"Meaning what?"

"I'm a working stiff, man, same as you. This gig is nothing but a paycheck to me. Pike, on the other hand, is a sadistic motherfucker.

This ain't a job to him, it's...I dunno...a primal urge. He uses pay-days as an excuse to scratch the itch—and, given half a chance, he'll scratch until it bleeds."

"What's your point?"

"My point is, if you don't do exactly as he says, he'll jump at the opportunity to go after your poor, sweet Chloe, and *neither* of us wants that."

"Is that so."

"I'm telling you, dude. Makes me sick to even think about."

Jake's jaw flexed. "Zoe."

"Huh?"

"My daughter's name is Zoe."

"Shit." Ringo smiled. "You think if I hadn't botched her name, you woulda bought it?"

"Honestly? Not really."

Ringo shifted his weight onto the balls of his feet, like a runner getting ready to steal a base.

"Ah, well," he said. "Can't blame a guy for trying."

Ringo leapt.

46.

As darkness settled over the East River, a crack of gunfire split the night, startling a mated pair of herons from their nest, and briefly catching the attention of a young dreadlocked man who lay prone in a nearby lot. But when the echoes of the first shot died without it being followed by a second, the man and birds began to relax. Soon, it was as if they'd never been disturbed at all.

47.

Holy heck, Amy thought as she listened in on Hannah dealing with their interlopers. *She might actually pull this off.*

Then a heavy thud caused the entire apartment to shudder.

Did one of them just hurl himself against the Croziers' door?

"Stay put," Amy said to Zoe, who nodded, eyes wide.

Amy drew Jake's SIG Sauer from her waistband and yanked open the guest room door, her injured arm protesting. As she burst from her hiding place into the hall, the door chain snapped; Hannah caught a heel on the runner in the entryway and toppled backward; and the man who'd broken down the door, carried inside by momentum, landed hard atop her—an aluminum bat clenched in his right hand.

Hannah raked her fingernails across his face.

With a snarl of rage and pain, he raised his bat.

Amy would've put him down, but she didn't have a clean shot. Hannah and her attacker were too entangled. If she aimed low, she could hit her friend. If she aimed high, or the bullet passed through him, she might wing one of the morons who watched, dumbfounded, from the hall.

No time to overthink, Hassan.

She grit her teeth and pulled the trigger.

When Jake's old backup thundered, the blonde in the corridor shrieked, and the man beside her dropped his mallet. Six inches to the right of Hannah's assailant, the wall between the entryway and kitchen puckered, coughing drywall dust—and the refrigerator on the other side began to hiss.

"You three," Amy said to the idiots in the doorway, "run."

She didn't need to tell them twice. The couple took off down the hall, headed left. The other guy broke right, his bathrobe trailing behind him like a cape.

Amy closed and locked the Croziers' door, her weapon trained on Hannah's attacker all the while. "Your turn. Drop the bat and get off her. Now."

Dazed, confused, he didn't move. "You almost shot me!"

"If I wanted to shoot you," Amy said, "you'd be shot. That said, there's still time, so don't test me. You have no idea what I've been through in the last few days."

"She's not bluffing," Hannah managed. "I'd do as she says." With the guy's weight bearing down on her chest, it was clear that she was struggling to draw breath.

He dropped his bat and slumped beside her, the fight gone out of him.

"Are you okay?" Amy asked Hannah.

She sat up, wincing. "Peachy."

"Good. There's a ball of butcher's twine in the utensil drawer. Go grab it so we can tie him up. I'll make sure he behaves while you're gone."

"What? That's not fair! You didn't make my friends—"

"Your friends didn't assault anybody," Amy said. Then, to Hannah: "While you're at it, see if you can find something to gag him with. I'm already sick of listening to him whine."

Hannah returned with butcher's twine, kitchen shears, and a tea towel.

Amy held the man at gunpoint while Hannah trussed him.

Once the man was bound and gagged, Hannah rose and asked, "What now?"

Amy tucked the gun into her waistband and rummaged through the coat closet until she came across a duffel bag. "Here. Pack up anything that might come in handy. Not the tablet, though—it's too risky. I'll go get Zoe. We're out the door in two minutes, max."

"But if we leave now, how will Jake—"

"I don't know. I haven't thought that far ahead. What I *do* know is, we have to go—it's not safe here anymore."

48.

The wharf loomed over the undulating surface of the water. As Jake approached it, he cut the outboard engine, and let momentum carry the dinghy to the floating dock beside.

Finding the place again had taken longer than anticipated. Hunts Point's waterfront looked very different at night, particularly since so many of its buildings were vacant and unlit. Although light pollution imbued the clouds above with an unearthly glow, it provided scant illumination by which to navigate—and Jake, a novice sailor, was learning on the fly.

The floating dock knocked rhythmically into the wharf's pilings, a woozy lullaby of wood on wood. Water lapped, high and tinkling, against the shore. Crickets, frogs, and katydids filled the night with myriad chirps, croaks, and rasps. As Jake wrestled the dinghy into parallel position with the dock, he hoped that the combined racket was loud enough to mask the sounds of his exertion.

He tied off the boat as best he could, wrapping the nylon line around a rusty cleat in several clumsy figure eights. Then, after an iffy moment straddling the gap, he managed to hop onto the dock.

The boards beneath Jake's feet were sodden and spongy. The platform bobbed with every step, causing his stomach to lurch.

A rough-hewn ladder crusted with lichen and tumorous barnacles led to the wharf above. Jake had secured Amy's pistol before fleeing

Rikers Island because he didn't want to run the risk of dropping it into the water. Now he freed it from its holster and began to climb.

Obviously, Jake hadn't expected the meeting with the Resistance to go as disastrously as it had, but he *had* anticipated the possibility that they'd attempt to confiscate his weapon—which is why he brought Amy's tiny backup piece along as well, and resigned himself to surrendering his bulkier weapon if need be.

She'd nearly emptied it during the shootout in Tribeca, but thankfully, Jake's old backup was also a 9mm, so they were able to reload it using ammunition from the spare magazines Hannah had brought with her.

The Glock 26 that he'd surrendered held eleven rounds.

So did the SIG Sauer P229 he'd left with Hannah and Amy, provided it remained unused.

Until recently, the Glock 43 that he was carrying contained seven.

It'd taken every ounce of Jake's restraint not to keep firing until he was sure Ringo was down, as he'd been trained to do—but he was badly outnumbered, and couldn't afford to waste a single bullet.

He'd contemplated taking Ringo's compact tactical .45, but an unfamiliar weapon can easily prove a liability in the field, and this one in particular likely implicated Ringo in two mass murders. Jake's former colleagues might consider him a criminal, but he still thought like a detective, and couldn't bring himself to taint key evidence in an ongoing investigation.

He had, however, taken Ringo's cell phone. Thanks to facial recognition, gaining access was a snap, and once he was in, he simply set it to remain unlocked.

Good thing I hit the bastard center mass instead of going for a headshot, Jake thought—*although, if he'd been wearing body armor, I'd probably be the one lying dead on that beach.*

As Jake neared the top of the ladder, he paused and listened.

Hearing nothing amiss, he climbed another rung and hazarded a peek onto the wharf.

The floating dock was to the wharf's immediate east, opposite the concrete drive, which followed the wharf's western edge. The abandoned processing facility was situated between them, though it cheated eastward, creating a narrow walkway from the ladder to the building's rear entrance.

The walkway, lit indirectly by the pallid glow that spilled through the dirty windows from inside, was as untended as the rest of the property. Weeds pushed through buckled concrete. Junked equipment rusted where it sat.

To Jake's relief, the back door wasn't guarded. He made his way toward it at a crouch, mindful of the windows' sight lines and the broken glass that lurked among the weeds. When he reached the door, he pressed his ear to it, and heard a murmur of quiet conversation — two voices, maybe three.

As he stood there, wondering how best to play this, fate — or, more likely, too much coffee — decided for him.

"Deal me out," said one voice, growing louder, "I gotta drain the radiator."

Then, before Jake had a chance to react, the door swung open.

He and Hopscotch stood face-to-face, no more than two feet apart.

When Hopscotch saw Jake, he muttered "The fuck?" and went for his gun, only to freeze as Jake leveled Amy's pistol at his face.

"Hands up. All of you. No sudden moves."

The men inside complied halfheartedly.

Hopscotch responded with greater zeal.

"Now turn around," Jake told Hopscotch. "Nice and easy."

Once he'd obeyed, Jake grabbed him by his left shoulder, pressed Amy's Glock against the base of his skull, and maneuvered him back into the building, using his body as a shield.

The space was even gloomier by night, despite the soft glow of the electric lantern. Crank and Pike sat beside it, amid a spray of playing cards and three unequal piles of matches Jake assumed were meant to serve as poker chips.

Mat was several yards away from them, at the edge of the lamplight, his back to a wooden post, his wrists zip tied around it. He regarded Jake with wide, gleaming eyes, his expression a tug-of-war between hope and fear.

Jake's voice softened as he addressed the boy. "How you doing, pal? You hanging in?"

"I...I'm okay," Mat replied shakily.

"Uh, Gibson?" Pike said. "Where the fuck is Ringo?"

"Ringo's fine," Jake lied, "but I'm afraid he won't be joining us."

"The hell he's fine," spat Crank. "I *told* you that was a gunshot. This shitbag killed him."

"If that's the case," Pike replied, "maybe you should reconsider your tone, given that he's got a gun to Hopscotch's head." Then, to Jake: "I thought you and I had reached an understanding."

"We did—and, so far, I've held up my end."

"You spoke to Vandermeer?" Pike sounded surprised.

"Yes."

"And she told you about Shadow Reckoning?"

"She told me everything, and I'm willing to pass it all along to you, provided you agree to my conditions."

"Do you seriously expect me to negotiate under duress?"

"Why not?" Jake asked. "You expected it of me."

Pike adopted an indulgent tone. "Okay, then. What are you proposing?"

"On my way back here, I thumbed through Ringo's contacts, and spotted your call sign among them." In fact, Ringo's phone contained precisely nine contacts, each of them a call sign. Assuming Pike hadn't lied to Mat when he claimed he'd lost six men, that meant these assholes were the last three breathing.

"Ringo gave you his phone," Pike replied, not a question, not quite not.

"What can I say? He must've been feeling charitable. Point is, I've got it and you're in it, so here's what I propose. You cut Mat loose. He leaves by boat with me. Once we're on the water, I call you up and tell you everything you want to know—and believe me, this story is a barn burner."

"Say, for the sake of argument, we're willing to part with the boy. Why should I believe you'll bother calling?"

"Because I don't want you coming after my family."

Jake's answer, while truthful, wasn't the *whole* truth. The fact was, he had no intention of keeping this secret to himself. Once he was out of here, he planned on telling everyone he could. What did he care if Pike was among them?

Pike steepled his fingers in contemplation. "And what makes you so sure I won't just kill you, keep the boy, and ask Vandermeer what she knows myself?"

"You mean apart from the gun I'm holding to your buddy's head?"

"Yes, apart from that."

"I guess you can shoot me if you like, but I guarantee you won't get Vandermeer to talk."

"How can you be so sure?" Pike said.

"Because I watched her die."

Jake was bluffing. When he'd left Vandermeer, she was still very much alive—although, with her permission, he'd swapped her chart with the one hanging from the empty bed in case anybody thought to look.

"Do you have any proof of this, or am I supposed to take your word for it?"

"Proof? No, but you're welcome to go check. Of course, there's a chance they've found Ringo by now, in which case the island's probably locked down and crawling with cops."

"Ringo's corpse, you mean." This from Crank.

"Stand down," Pike snapped at him. Then, to Jake: "I confess, Gibson, you're ballsier than I gave you credit for, but—"

Pike paused, distracted by a noise outside, coming from the direction of the parking lot.

It sounded like...howling?

"What the fuck is that?" Pike eyed Jake with suspicion.

"I have no idea," Jake said, mystified.

A diesel engine roared, then dropped into gear with a mechanical *ka-chunk*.

Tires squealed.

Metal jangled against concrete.

Jesus Christ, Jake thought, *whoever's out there just broke down the front gate.*

"If this is your doing, Gibson, I swear on my mother's gra—"

Jake never heard the rest of Pike's threat.

It was interrupted by a crash of breaking glass, followed by a thunderclap.

Everything inside the building went white.

49.

Amy, Hannah, and Zoe were less than two blocks from the Croziers' place when the first police cruiser screamed by—lights on, sirens blaring.

"That didn't take long," Hannah said.

"They'll be looking for us soon." Amy, in a hooded sweatshirt that obscured her headscarf, spoke through gritted teeth. "We need to get off the streets."

Zoe frowned. "Aunt Amy, are you okay?"

"I'm fine, honey, thank you."

Hannah eyed Amy appraisingly by the glow of the streetlights. Her eyes were sunken, her expression wan. A dark stain discolored her left sleeve. "You're not fine, you're bleeding."

"It's nothing."

"Now, maybe, but that doesn't mean it's going to stay that way."

"Mat's critters—"

"—won't prevent you from bleeding out, if it comes to that, and we have no idea how long they'll protect you from infection. We need to get you somewhere safe, so I can irrigate your wound and change your dressing."

"No, we need to find a perch nearby with decent sight lines to the entrance of the Croziers' building, so we can wave Jake off before he walks into an active crime scene."

"He's been gone eleven hours, Amy, and curfew's fast approaching—which means the chances he'll be back tonight are slim."

"Then what are you suggesting?" Exasperation crept into Amy's tone.

"We left my car not far from here. I doubt it's been towed yet. We could use it to get out of the city."

Amy shook her head. "Too risky. If they've connected you to Jake, plate readers will alert them the second we get on the highway."

"Jake swapped my plates with someone else's before we left the Upper West Side."

Amy looked impressed. "Still, traffic cams—"

"—won't be a problem if I'm masked, and you two ride in back."

"Where would we even go?"

"My family's got a cabin upstate. It's not fancy, but it'll do, provided you don't mind eating from expired cans."

"So, what, we just abandon Jake?"

"We're not abandoning him, we're keeping Zoe safe. It's what he'd want. You know it is. Once we're there, we'll figure out a way to contact him, I swear."

"Fine." Amy swayed a little on her feet. "Where's this car of yours?"

"Maybe five blocks?"

"In that case, what are we waiting for?"

They didn't get far before Amy began to slow. When she paused to catch her breath outside an empty storefront encased in scaffolding and plywood, Hannah said, "You know what? I'll move faster, and attract way less attention, on my own. Why don't you and Zoe hide out here while I go get the car?"

Amy's face, though blanketed in shadow, showed relief. "I'll admit, that's not the worst idea I've heard all day."

"I guess faint praise is better than no praise at all." Hannah knelt beside Zoe and said, "Can you take care of Aunt Amy while I'm gone?"

"Only if you promise to come right back," Zoe replied.

"I promise."

Before Hannah left, she hugged Zoe tight, and prayed it was a promise she could keep.

50.

When the stun grenade smashed through the filthy windowpane and skittered across the floor, Jake shoved Hopscotch toward it and dove out the open door onto the wharf.

A fraction of a second later, the flash-bang went off.

Though he'd immediately recognized the perforated cylinder, with its trademark blue stripe, Jake had never experienced one detonating before. The NYPD's use of stun grenades was curtailed decades ago, after police executing a no-knock warrant predicated on faulty intel startled an innocent Black woman named Alberta Spruill into a fatal heart attack.

While it was unlikely that Pike and his men would suffer the same fate, Jake knew that they'd be functionally deaf and blind for several seconds, and disoriented for some time after that.

Jake, owing to his quick reaction, fared marginally better. He climbed shakily to his feet—ears ringing, vision tinted green—and staggered over to the back door. Then, leaning against the building's corrugated exterior for support, he peered cautiously around the jamb.

Oily smoke hung in the air—from the grenade itself, Jake thought at first, until he saw the curling shapes of flame-licked playing cards to his right, and realized the explosion had ignited the matchsticks that had served as ersatz poker chips. The mercs were on the floor, struggling to right themselves. Mat, apparently unconscious, slumped against the post that he was zip tied to, his eyes closed, his head lolling to one side.

Please, God, let him be okay, Jake thought.

The front door slammed open and rebounded off the inside wall. Jake caught a glimpse of a faded yellow box truck, its high beams on, its front end a tangled mass of crumpled grill and broken chain link. Then a teeming horde of braying lunatics in gas masks pushed inside.

Jake pegged them as Soldiers of Gaia in an instant.

Their shaved heads gleamed white by the glow of the truck's headlights. Their tattered army surplus clothing hung loosely on their scrawny frames. Their gas masks—shabby, vintage, and mismatched—appeared to be for show, because many lacked filters or had cracked lenses.

Some brandished handguns. Others carried rifles. Still others wielded makeshift weapons: steel chains, tire irons, sledgehammers. None appeared to be wearing armor of any kind.

Crank snatched up a nearby automatic and loosed a spray of gunfire in the general direction of the main entrance—cleaving wood, glass, and flesh.

The Endtimers, incensed, returned fire. Crank convulsed as bullets perforated his body, then stilled as Pike unleashed a salvo of his own—mowing down the first wave of intruders.

Soon, a logjam of fallen Endtimers at the front door prevented their brethren outside from gaining entry, so they began clearing the window frames of glass and boosting each other through, whooping and hollering all the while.

Fresh air poured into the building, causing the fire to spread.

Though Jake's head was fuzzy, and his balance slow to return, he didn't dare wait any longer—he had to get Mat out of there. He patted his pockets, looking for his folding knife, before remembering he'd left it on the Croziers' countertop in Soho.

Shit.

He entered the building at a crouch. Bullets splintered the wood-work all around. Between the smoke and the long shadows cast by the headlights, visibility was poor, so Jake had no idea if they were shooting at him or firing wildly. The stun grenade had dulled his hearing, so the sound of their reports, and the Endtimers' deranged battle cries, registered as far away.

A man materialized from the gloom a few feet ahead. Silhouetted by the truck's headlights, his details were indistinct, but there was a pistol in his left hand—and it was swinging toward Jake.

Jake squeezed off two quick shots.

The man tottered and fell, landing inches from Jake's feet.

It was Hopscotch—badly wounded, but alive.

Jake kicked Hopscotch's gun across the floor, knelt beside him, and removed his combat knife from its sheath. Then he rose and headed toward Mat, or tried.

In all the chaos, it was hard to get his bearings.

As Jake paused, trying to figure out where he was in relation to the boy, a hatchet cut the smoke a hairsbreadth from his face.

He turned and fired. A rawboned young man in a rubber gas mask hit the floorboards, a bloody hole in his chest. His hatchet clattered out of reach across the rough-hewn planks.

Somewhere to Jake's left, Mat yelped. Jake hurried toward the sound. It seemed the boy had regained consciousness, but not his wits. He thrashed uselessly against his restraints, making it difficult for Jake to cut him loose.

"Hey, asshole! Where the fuck you think you're going with our kid?"

Pike, shouting from behind the partial cover of a post across the room, seemed reluctant to shoot at Jake, for fear of hitting Mat.

Jake opened fire on his position, squeezing off three shots before the borrowed Glock clicked empty.

Then the smoke between them thickened, obscuring Pike from view.

Jake tossed the empty gun aside, thinking *Amy's gonna kill me for that if we survive*. The knife in his right hand, he steadied Mat with his left, so he could saw through the boy's bindings without hurting him.

Once Mat was free, Jake picked him up and headed for the back door at a sprint.

By some miracle, their exit was unimpeded. In moments they were on the narrow walkway, headed toward the floating dock.

But as they neared the ladder, an emaciated figure rounded the corner of the building—a knot of ratty dreadlocks spilling over his gas mask, a lever-action rifle in his hands.

"Howdy, Gibson." He worked the rifle's lever, chambering a round. "Long time, no see."

51.

"I've gotta tell you, dude, I'm kinda hurt. I went to a lot of trouble to throw this shindig in your honor. Now I find you slinking off without so much as a goodbye?"

"I'm sorry," Jake replied. "That was insensitive of me." He spoke with exaggerated calm, mindful of Dreadlocks' volatile temper, of his finger wrapped around the rifle's trigger—and of the innocent child that Jake held in his arms.

"Goddamn *right* it was insensitive. I mean, I thought we really *connected* yesterday." He paused and cocked his head dramatically, causing fat ropes of hair to rustle against the lenses of his gas mask. "No, wait. My bad. That was your pistol and my friend's face."

"Is . . . is that why you're here?" Incredulity crept into Jake's tone.

"You assaulted a Soldier of Gaia. We weren't about to let that go unanswered."

A nearby window spilled orange firelight into the night's deep blue. Its few remaining panes were spiderwebbed by bullet holes. Smoke billowed through the empty muntin squares.

"You're telling me you did all this—that you led a literal truckload of men to their deaths—because I broke your buddy's nose?"

Dreadlocks shrugged. "I wouldn't expect the likes of you to understand."

"The likes of me?"

"A mindless drone. A procreator. A tiny cog in a gargantuan machine."

Mat, who'd gone limp when Jake picked him up, stiffened in his arms and began to cough. Jake patted his back and said, "Easy, kiddo. You're all right. I've got you."

When Mat's coughing fit subsided, he opened his eyes. They moved involuntarily in their sockets. His head wobbled like he'd just gotten off a Tilt-a-Whirl. "I don't feel so good," he muttered, burying his head against Jake's shoulder.

Dreadlocks took a big step backward. "What's wrong with him?"

"Are you serious? You hit the kid with a flash-bang grenade, and set the building he was trapped inside on fire."

"But he's, like, safe to be around? For now, I mean. I'm not scared or anything. Just curious."

"I don't follow. Safe how? Scared of what?"

"It's just, to hear the DBS tell it, the kid's a walking petri dish—and, given how hard they're looking for him, he's probably got something even nastier than they're letting on."

Suddenly, the picture in Jake's mind snapped into focus. "You're not really here for me, are you? Or, at least, not entirely. You're here because whoever you take orders from wants Mat. So, what's the plan? Do you guys think that you can use him as a weapon?" *If so,* he thought, *imagine how pissed they're gonna be when they find out what he really is.*

"Our intentions are none of your goddamn business. Now shut the fuck up. The three of us are getting out of here."

Dreadlocks sidestepped toward the building and jerked the barrel of his rifle toward the water, clearly intending Jake to carry Mat past him, so they could leave the way that he'd arrived.

Jake struggled to hide his disappointment. He'd hoped Dreadlocks would prove dumb enough to put himself between Jake and the wharf's edge, thereby giving Jake the opportunity to knock him into the water, but no such luck.

With little choice but to comply, Jake hitched Mat a little higher on his hip and shuffled forward, only to halt when a voice called out behind him, smoke-roughened and dry as fired clay.

"Hey, dirtbag! Find your own damn captives. Those two are spoken for."

Pike leaned against the building's exterior a few feet from the back door, a trail of blood streaking the wall from jamb to shoulder.

Looking at him, Jake wasn't surprised he needed help remaining upright. Pike's eyes were glassy, bloodshot. His face and clothes were covered in soot. A deep furrow bisected his right deltoid. A puncture wound oozed blood down his left thigh.

Jake hoped he was responsible for at least one of them.

Pike had a .45 in his right hand, but it was pointed toward the wharf. It was unclear to Jake if he was capable of lifting it, much less firing.

"Who the fuck are you?" Dreadlocks replied.

"I'm the guy speaking for them."

"Dude, c'mon. You're a fucking mess. Unless you're looking to be put out of your misery, your best bet is to turn tail."

He raised his rifle to accentuate his point.

To Jake's surprise, Pike responded in kind with his .45.

"Cute popgun," Pike said. "What is it, a thirty-thirty?"

After a brief hesitation, Dreadlocks answered, "It's a twenty-two."

"Huh. I shoulda known. I had one just like it when I was five."

He shambled closer.

Dreadlocks tensed. "Not another fucking step."

"You wanna stop me, you're welcome to try."

While they jawed at one another, Jake turned his head toward Mat's and muttered, "Still with me?"

Mat nodded, his face buried against Jake's neck.

"Good. When I give you the signal, hold your breath and hang on tight, okay?"

Another nod.

"Ready..."

Pike took another lurching step forward, his shoulder painting the wall red.

"Don't test me, man. I'm serious!"

"I'm sure you are," Pike replied. "Of course, that rifle of yours is better suited for varmints than big game."

"...set..."

"Oh, yeah?" Dreadlocks scoffed. "Which are you?"

"Pull the trigger and find out. Unless, of course, you're too chickenshi—"

"...go!"

Jake locked his arms around Mat and leapt off of the wharf.

For a fraction of a second, they hovered, weightless, the rising flames bathing them in heat and light. Then they were swallowed whole by the shadow of the wharf.

A moment later, they plunged feetfirst into the East River.

The brackish water, though far cooler than the August air above, was less a shock than Jake expected. At no more than eight feet deep, it was shallower as well.

When Jake touched bottom, he bent his knees to absorb the energy of their fall, then pushed off, releasing Mat when it became clear that he was paddling on his own.

They surfaced to the sound of gunfire. A high, thin crack from Dreadlocks' long gun. Three assertive claps from Pike's .45.

Then, for several seconds, nothing.

Jake treaded water, listening, as his eyes adjusted to the low light. A small swell hit him in the face, and he sputtered.

Mat whispered, "Are you all right?"

For all his dizziness, Jake thought, *the kid swims like a champ.*

"I'm okay," he replied, whispering as well. "You?"

"A little better now, I think."

"Glad to hear it. C'mon. Our ride's this way."

They swam side by side to the floating dock, but before they could hoist themselves out of the water, Pike shouted at them from above.

"Gibson! You and Rivas can come out now! The evil Endtimer's all taken care of!"

Great, Jake thought. *He survived.*

He looked up in time to see Pike's head poke out over the wharf's edge and look around. Adrenaline hit his system like a narcotic. He fought the urge to panic.

"Seriously, you colossal asspains, where the hell are you?"

Jake smiled. Pike couldn't see them—the wharf's shadow was too deep, and the firelight above too bright.

Jake put a finger to his lips and gestured for Mat to stay put. Mat, who'd steadied himself with a palm atop the floating dock to save himself the trouble of paddling, responded by giving Jake a thumbs-up with his free hand.

Slipping between the dinghy and the floating dock, Jake unwound the dock line from the cleat that it was wrapped around. Then he curled an arm around the boat's port side and began maneuvering the boat around the dock.

Mat watched him work a moment, then pitched in when he realized what Jake was doing. Soon, they'd positioned the dinghy underneath the wharf. Fusty darkness lurked above. Pilings jutted from the water on all sides.

"I'm not fucking around, Gibson! Surrender now, or I swear to Christ that when I find you, I'll yank your teeth out one by one, and make the kid watch."

Jake boosted Mat into the boat, then slithered in himself. As quietly as they could manage, they began paddling with cupped hands, headed toward deeper water.

"That's far enough," Jake whispered when they neared the end of the wharf. "Try and hold position if you can. I'm gonna see if I can get the engine started."

Jake knew that, as soon as he did so, Pike would realize precisely where they were. Their only hope was to get up to speed before he could reach them.

Last time, on Rikers Island, it had taken Jake a while to figure out how the engine worked. Turned out, it was an electric start, and pretty simple—but down here, he couldn't see well enough to determine the appropriate throttle position.

With a silent prayer, he took his best guess, and pressed the Start button.

The engine caught.

Pike hurled a curse at them from somewhere overhead.

"Hold on to something," Jake said, and twisted the throttle.

The dinghy jetted forward.

52.

The boat skittered across the uneven surface of the East River, its throttle cranked as high as Jake dared. Wind whipped at his sodden clothes. Sea spray stung his narrowed eyes.

The vessel's bow was angled skyward. Its hull juddered as it slammed into peak after choppy peak. Any faster, and Jake worried they would flip.

Pike's pistol thundered behind them.

Jake goosed the throttle and screamed, "Get down!"

He could barely hear himself over the night air buffeting his ears, but Mat obeyed nonetheless, flattening his body between the benches.

Another gunshot, quieter than the one before.

Then two more, each quieter than the last.

Eventually, Pike's gunfire ceased, and Jake allowed himself a smile. He backed the throttle off and said, "You can come out now! I think we're in the clear."

"Yeah?" Mat replied. "Then why's the floor all wet?"

Jake put a hand against the deck. The kid was right. They were taking on water—and, unless Jake was much mistaken, also listing to starboard.

A quick inspection confirmed it: they'd taken a bullet to their starboard air chamber, and another to the chamber on the bow. If one were compromised, they might've been able to make a go of it; with two damaged, it was clear to Jake that they didn't have long before the dinghy sank.

He'd hoped that they could use the boat to get out of the city—as far as Greenwich, maybe, or North Hempstead. Now they'd be lucky if they weren't forced to swim to shore.

As they chugged south, something blotted out the lights of Port Morris, to their right. A landmass, Jake realized, unlit and apparently uninhabited.

He steered them toward it. The boat was sluggish now, and sat so low Jake was sure that it would slip beneath the surface any moment. Instead, its hull ground to a halt against the island's silty shallows, ten yards or so from land.

They waded ashore—shivering, exhausted—and found themselves on a rocky, unkempt beach, not far from the ruins of a small outbuilding. Beyond the ruins, Jake could make out nothing but thick vegetation, which looked like a mass of solid black in the low light.

"What is this place?" Mat asked.

"I have no idea," Jake replied, adding, "but maybe I can find out!"

He fished Ringo's cell phone out of his pocket. It came out dripping wet, causing Jake to fear the worst, but the screen blazed to life without a care.

"Thank God these assholes sprung for military-grade cases. If this were my phone, no amount of rice would save it."

Jake opened Ringo's GPS app just long enough for it to tell him where they were, then toggled off location services so Pike's people couldn't use the phone to find them.

"We're apparently on North Brother Island."

"Seriously?" Mat replied.

"That's what it says. Why? You know it?"

"Sure do. I learned about it in school."

"Park City has a school?" Jake was ashamed to admit that, until this moment, he'd never even wondered about Mat's education or lack thereof.

"Nope. There aren't enough kids, and we're all different ages, so they just enrolled us in online charter schools and gave us tablets."

"Sounds...depressing."

"I dunno. It was all right. Actually, Park City's why I remember reading about North Brother Island. A long time ago, there was a hospital here, where the city would send people who had stuff they were afraid of. Typhoid Mary spent twenty years here before she died."

"I confess, I didn't know that Typhoid Mary was a real person. I figured she was, like, a boogeyman or something."

"She was real. Her name was Mary Mallon. She was an immigrant, like me, who came to the US as a kid. She didn't know it, but she was also an, uh, asym—"

"Asymptomatic carrier?"

"Yeah! An asymptomatic carrier of typhoid fever. For her whole life, probably, because her mom had it when she was born. It's sad to think about. I mean, she couldn't help the way she was, but it robbed her of the chance to lead a normal life." Mat's expression darkened.

"Mat, listen. That's not going to happen to you. I won't let it. One way or another, we're gonna put things right, okay?"

"Okay," Mat replied.

"Does anybody use the island now?"

"Nah. It was abandoned a long time ago. I think it's, like, a bird sanctuary or whatever. Any chance you know somebody with a boat?"

"Afraid not," Jake said, "but I may have an idea."

Mat regarded him dubiously. "What kind of an idea?"

"I'll tell you in a sec." Jake handed him the phone. "First, see if you can find me a detailed map of this place."

"Why me?"

"Because I'm old, and it'll take you half the time."

Mat poked around and found a couple maps that, while outdated, seemed as if they might be useful. He showed them to Jake, who muttered to himself for a moment, then filled Mat in on his plan.

"You think that'll work?" To his credit, Mat didn't look aghast, but neither was he terribly enthusiastic.

"Beats me," Jake replied. "What do you think?"

"Might. Might not. Seems kinda crazy either way."

"Well, then, at least we're agreed. Wanna try it anyway?"

Mat pursed his lips. "What happens if I say no?"

"Then we'll figure something else out."

"Really?"

"Really. Far as I'm concerned, we're a team. I'm not going to make you do anything you're not comfortable with."

"Okay, then." Mat smiled. "Let's do it."

53.

When Lionel Mercer's stomach growled, he glanced reflexively at his watch, and was startled to discover that it was after 2 a.m.

Christ, he thought. *How long's it been since I last ate?*

For security purposes, the New York field office's command center was located at the interior of the building, far away from any windows—which meant that Lionel hadn't caught a glimpse of natural light since he'd arrived that morning.

A musky scent hung in the air. The command center was crammed beyond capacity with agents, analysts, and technicians, many of whom hadn't seen a bed or shower in days.

"Any recent sightings?" he barked.

"Dozens," Paget said, "most of them bullshit—unless you believe that Gibson's tossing back shots at a VFW in East Rockaway, or Hassan roughed up some random Soho cokehead with a laundry list of priors."

Mercer sighed. "What about known associates?"

"Hassan's brother-in-law is now in custody," Medina replied. "We're leveraging his visa status to sweat the family, but so far, they haven't given us anything actionable."

"And Gibson's?"

"Could be nothing," said Paget, "but we're having trouble locating the ex he rang up on the night of the Park City attack."

A junior officer hovering at Lionel's side attempted to break in. "Uh, sir?"

Lionel, ignoring her, asked Paget: "You think Gibson's ex is helping him somehow?"

"Hard to say. SIGINT dug into their text history. Seems they parted on bad terms, and he's drunk-dialed her a few times since."

"Sir?" she tried again.

"What about her socials?" Lionel asked.

"She posted something Saturday, on Bangarang, about leaving the city awhile. That's consistent with her phone's last known location—some bumfuck town in Eastern Pennsylvania—but it went dark not long after, and we've been unable to reactivate it remotely."

"Maybe it died. Tell SIGINT to keep trying. We'll circle back as the evidence dictates."

"Director Mercer!"

"What?" Lionel snapped.

"You have a phone call."

"Is it the president?"

"No, but—"

"Then take a fucking message. It may have escaped your attention, but I'm coordinating a goddamn manhunt here."

"That's just it, sir." She swallowed hard. "The caller identified himself as Jacob Gibson."

Lionel blinked in surprise, his anger evaporating as he tried to process what he'd just been told. "You can't be serious."

"I am."

"Where's he calling from?"

"The phone is pinging off a tower in the South Bronx. Its signal strength is steady, which indicates he isn't on the move, but Wi-Fi and A-GPS are disabled. We're scraping data from its gyroscope and accelerometer, as well as analyzing background noise, but converting that into exact coordinates is going to take some time."

Lionel jabbed a finger at the conference room. "I'll take it in there. Notify me the moment you get a fix on him."

"Yes, sir."

At the center of the conference table was a speakerphone. Lionel tapped the blinking line and said, "Mercer here."

"Hiya, Lionel. Can I call you Lionel? On second thought, fuck it. I'm on the lam—a person of interest, to borrow your phrase, who should be considered armed and dangerous—so I'm just gonna go ahead and call you Lionel."

"Lionel's fine. To whom do I have the pleasure of speaking?"

"Oh, come on, Lionel, you already know the answer to that, or you never would've bothered picking up."

"Still, I'd like to hear you say it."

The voice on the other end of the call laughed. "Of course you would—and preferably nice and slow, so you can use the time to pinpoint my location."

Mercer fell silent for a beat. "The thought had crossed my mind."

"Lemme save you the trouble. I'm on North Brother Island."

"North Brother Island? What on earth are you doing there?"

"Thinking, mostly."

"Okay, I'll bite. What about?"

"A fascinating conversation I had with an old colleague of yours by the name of Jessica Vandermeer."

Lionel's mouth went dry. He opened it to speak, but no sound came out.

"You remember Jess, don't you?" Gibson continued. "Because she sure as hell remembers you. In fact, she told me all about this operation you handpicked her for a few years back. Said you called it Shadow Reckoning."

He cleared his throat. "Never heard of it."

"That's funny. The drop box full of records Jess squirreled away tells a different story. Now, I've been kinda busy lately, so I haven't had a chance to read through everything—but, from what little I *have* seen, your life's gonna take an ugly turn if this shit leaks."

"What do you want, Gibson?"

"Tell you what: why don't you come ask me that in person? Say, an hour from now, at the beach between the coal dock and the gantry?"

"You can't expect me to—"

"The hell I can't. If you don't show, every journalist on the planet with a public email address is gonna be reading about Shadow Reckoning over their morning coffee. Ditto if, to pick a crazy hypothetical, I wind up dying in a drone strike between now and then."

"You're bluffing," Lionel said. "You don't have a goddamn thing."

"Only one way to find out," Gibson replied. "See you soon, Lionel."

The phone went dead.

54.

Hopscotch, semiconscious, gasped for air.

His throat was parched.

His mouth tasted of smoke.

His stomach felt like it was stuffed to bursting with hot coals.

A ragged exhalation, followed by another labored breath.

What the fuck happened to me?

Hopscotch's thoughts were muddled, his memory occluded—and, for some goddamn reason, he couldn't seem to fill his lungs.

His eyes fluttered open. He was supine, a stark white ceiling overhead, two bare fluorescent bulbs running parallel down the middle.

"Welcome back to the land of the living."

Hopscotch propped himself up on one elbow and looked around. He and Pike were in a self-storage unit, not far from the fish-processing facility—one of several bolt holes like it scattered throughout the city.

The space was small and spartan, but well stocked with food, water, munitions, and emergency medical supplies. A portable chemical toilet sat in the far corner. Heavy moving blankets tacked to the walls blunted the sound of sirens wailing nearby.

Pike sat on a folded moving blanket, his shoulders against the wall. Hopscotch lay atop yet another blanket, this one stained with blood and iodopovidone. His torso, he noted with surprise, was bare.

The shirt that he'd been wearing was in tatters on the concrete floor beside.

"How long...have I...been out?"

"Dunno exactly." Pike's voice was hoarse, his eyes glassy, his expression weary. "Gotta be a couple hours now."

That explains how he had time to clean himself up and change his clothes, Hopscotch thought.

"Did you...carry me?"

"Nah. You were awake when I dragged your ass outta the building, and made it here under your own power. I'm not surprised you don't remember, though, because you passed out shortly after we arrived. Those Endtimers fucked you up pretty good."

A look of concentration gave way to fury as a flash of memory pierced Hopscotch's mental haze. "Not Endtimers. Gibson."

"Y'know, I'm beginning to think we shoulda killed that asshole when we had the chance."

"Agreed." He nodded gingerly toward his bandages. "How bad?"

"You took a bullet to the left forearm, and another to the gut. The arm wound is superficial—no damage to your bones or major blood vessels—but the gut shot's pretty gnarly. I think you passed out because your abdomen was filling up with air. I disinfected both injuries as best I could, wrapped your arm in hemostatic gauze, and slapped a vented chest seal on you so you wouldn't suffocate. I figure, you woke up, so it must be working."

"Did Crank—"

Pike's expression darkened. He shook his head.

"Fuck." Hopscotch swallowed hard. "What about Gibson and the kid?"

"Slippery bastards got away when shit went pear-shaped—but, on the plus side, you're making complete sentences again."

He's right, Hopscotch realized. *Every breath feels a little deeper than the last.*

"Sure, but for how long? Without the kid, and his magical whatever, I'll probably be dead within the week."

"C'mon, man. Don't talk like that. I'm dinged up too. One problem at a time, okay?"

Pike's cell phone began to buzz.

"Well, I'll be damned."

Hopscotch frowned. "Who is it?"

"Caller ID says Ringo," Pike replied, a smile of grudging admiration on his face.

He set his phone down on the floor between them and answered it on speaker.

"Gibson," Pike said, "if you're calling to gloat—"

"I'm not," Gibson replied. "This conversation is strictly business."

"What kind of business?"

"Mat and I would like to negotiate a truce."

"Okay, then: negotiate."

"Not with you. With your boss."

Pike laughed. "And you expect me to, what, give you his name and number? Maybe text you his address, so you can drop by?"

"No. I expect you to get his ass to North Brother Island's western shore in exactly forty-five minutes, so we can do this face-to-face."

"You're kidding."

"I'm not."

"That's an awfully tight deadline."

"Too bad. It's the only one you're gonna get."

Pike sighed. "Look, Gibson. I'll be straight with you. If you're willing to hand over Rivas, I can probably convince my boss to leave you and your little girl be—but there's nothing you can offer him that'll offset the cost of giving up the boy."

"Not even incontrovertible evidence that Lionel Mercer is guilty of mass murder?"

Silence stretched across the line as Pike and Hopscotch shared a look.

"Yeah, that's what I thought. This offer expires in forty-four minutes."

Gibson disconnected.

"What the fuck was that about?" Hopscotch asked. "You think he's serious?"

"Beats me—but he's a wanted man, so if he's trying to dick us over, I can't see how."

"You gonna call the boss, then?"

"Fuckin' A, I'm gonna." Pike fished two packets of go pills from his pocket and tossed one of them to Hopscotch. "If we play this right, we'll grab the kid, get the dirt on Mercer, and put Gibson down for good."

Hopscotch tore his packet open, downed its contents, and grinned.

Maybe this day wasn't a total shitshow after all.

55.

North Brother Island was an earthen comma, twenty acres in size, situated between the mainland Bronx and Rikers Island in the East River. As its name implied, the island had a sibling to the immediate south—six acres of dense scrub brush unbroken by any sign of human intervention.

Even during its heyday, North Brother Island was accessible only by ferry, making it an ideal site to quarantine contagious patients. The ferry's decrepit gantry slip remained, in the modest bay formed by the island's western shore, but the coal dock that ran parallel had partially collapsed.

The two were separated by a thin sliver of beach, no more than fifty yards long, that all but vanished when the tide was at its highest. At the moment, however, the beach was visible—or would have been, were there any light to see it by.

The island's interior was lush, wild, and overgrown. Its buildings had long since been engulfed—and, in many cases, felled—by the relentless vegetation. The paths that linked the ruins to one another were often treacherous and occasionally impassable, a fact that Mat and Jake discovered when they'd explored the island prior to Jake's phone calls with Mercer and Pike.

Now they stood atop a stout redbrick structure, two stories high, that overlooked North Brother Island's western shore. Once the campus morgue, it had thus far escaped the ravages of time intact. Jake questioned the logic of placing the morgue so near the ferry slip, where arriving patients couldn't help but see it, but he was grateful that its crenellated roof provided decent sight lines of the bay, as well as a measure of cover.

He tried not to take the building's morbid history as an omen.

A small skiff approached from the west, its sidelights glowing red and green, its center console bathed in white by the lights mounted on its T-top overhead. There were two men aboard. One was at the helm. The other rode on the cushioned seat in front of it.

"We're on," Jake said. "You ready?"

"Guess we're about to find out," Mat said. "Which one's that, you figure?"

"Mercer."

"Yeah?"

"Gotta be. Pike's a soldier. He'd never bring his boss in all lit up like that."

The vessel—civilian, Jake noted, not law enforcement—slowly circumnavigated the diminutive bay, lingering awhile beside the busted gantry slip, before dropping anchor a little ways offshore. A spotlight blazed to life, illuminating the narrow beach. Then Lionel Mercer hopped, cursing, out of the boat—his pants pushed up past his knees, his socks and shoes hugged to his chest.

Jake's fingers tightened around the grip of the flare gun he'd rescued from the beached dinghy. Sadly, the extra flares he'd found alongside it were sodden and unusable—which meant he had, at most, one shot. He couldn't afford to waste it prematurely lighting up this piece of human garbage.

When Mercer reached the shoreline, Jake flicked on Ringo's flashlight app and said, "That's far enough."

Mercer raised a forearm to shield his eyes. "You could've warned me there wasn't anywhere to land."

"You're right," Jake said. "I could have."

"The kid up there with you?"

"Sure am," Mat replied.

"You two wanna come down here so we can talk?"

"If it's all the same to you," Jake said dryly, "I think we'll pass."

"And if it isn't all the same to me?"

"We'd still pass. Then I'd tell you to fuck off. It's not like you're in any position to be making demands."

A weary sigh escaped Mercer's lips. "You can drop the tough-guy act, Gibson. You don't need to remind me you're in charge. I know the playbook. I'm law enforcement too."

"Is *that* what you are."

Mercer ignored the gibe. "Why don't we skip to the part where you tell me what happens now?"

"Now we wait."

"For what?"

"For the remainder of our party to arrive."

Three interminable minutes later, a matte-green dinghy slipped into the bay, smooth and quiet as a sharpened blade. As Jake predicted, it was unlit. Though its helmsman skirted the spotlight's illumination, Jake thought he spied the vague outlines of four men aboard.

Only two waded ashore.

The first was Pike. Though he'd cleaned up somewhat, he was limping badly, and bleeding through a fresh set of fatigues.

The second was oddly familiar—but, absent context, Jake struggled to place him. Truth be told, the guy wasn't much to look at, but he moved with an easy confidence that spoke of money. His white linen shirt was unbuttoned far enough to reveal a tuft of chest hair.

His chinos were rolled neatly to midcalf. A pair of boat shoes dangled from two fingers of his left hand. A braided leather belt circled his waist.

As he approached, Jake noticed a molded leather pouch on his right hip that matched neither his shoes nor his belt. Something about it tickled at Jake's memory.

Apparently, Mat's recall was better still.

"Holy crap," he muttered, "that's Ethan—"

"Rask?" Mercer exclaimed. "What the fuck are *you* doing here?"

"Evening, Lionel. I confess, I was about to ask you the same thing."

"You're here," Jake said, projecting to be heard from the rooftop, "because Mat and I have concrete evidence tying Lionel to a catastrophic failure of an operation called Shadow Reckoning, and you're each desperate to get your hands on it—Lionel, so he can bury it forever, and Ethan, so he can use it to bury Lionel."

Mercer scowled. "So this is, what, an auction?"

"If that helps you."

"What, precisely, would constitute a winning bid?" This from Rask.

"Mat and I are running low on friends these days, so we're in the market for a new one. The ideal candidate would, at minimum, have the clout to guarantee our freedom going forward."

"That's a big ask."

"We'll see if you still think so when you find out what it buys you. Shall we get down to business?"

"Pump the brakes a second, Gibson," Pike growled. "We're not getting down to shit until you ditch that cell phone you're holding."

Jake hesitated a moment before responding. "Fair enough."

He tossed Ringo's phone off the roof.

It landed in the sand at Pike's feet.

"Happy now?"

Pike crushed the phone beneath a dripping bootheel and kicked the pieces into the water. "Ecstatic."

"Glad to hear it. I should probably start by thanking you, Ethan. If your men hadn't pointed me toward Vandermeer, I'd be out of moves to make, and none of us would be standing here tonight."

That got Mercer's attention. "Been digging for dirt on me, Ethan?"

"Seems, I dunno, ironic," Jake said, "him looking for dirt, when he's already got so much of his own."

"Oh, yeah?" Mercer said. "Like what?"

"For starters," Mat replied, "he had his people wipe out my whole village."

"And a building full of squatters in Tribeca," Jake added.

The shock on Mercer's face was genuine. "But...why?"

Amusement, inexpertly stifled, tugged at the corners of Rask's mouth. "You mean to tell me you really don't know? I thought, when you assumed control of the investigation, you must have finally figured it out—but, apparently, I gave you too much credit. The boy spent three years in your custody, and you still haven't got a clue."

"Who, Rivas?"

"Yes, Rivas!"

"I don't get it. He's nobody—a grubby illegal, not yet old enough to shave. What could possibly be so special about him?"

Mat opened his mouth to object to the casual bigotry of Mercer's description, but Jake stilled him with a hand.

"The boy's immune to bacterial infections, Lionel. What's more, he can heal the sick."

Mercer scoffed. "You're joking."

"He's not," Jake said. "I've seen it myself."

"So all those people in Park City—"

"—were an unfortunate but acceptable loss, when weighed against acquiring the most valuable IP in human history. For years, I've been convinced that ProTx was on the verge of harnessing the potential of the human microbiota. Now it's clear to me that Rivas is the key. The only problem was, his fellow villagers knew firsthand what he was capable of. Hell, most of them were living proof. I couldn't risk them coming forward and accusing me of kidnapping—or, worse, calling the ownership of my patents into question."

"That's monstrous."

"Please. I'm trying to remake the world, Lionel. To disrupt so complex a system, one must think in economies of scale. Besides, those people weren't really living, they were simply passing time, trapped in a purgatory of *your* design. Now, at least, they died in service of something greater—and, when you consider all the lives our new technologies will save, their sacrifice may as well be a rounding error."

"And the squatters?"

Rask shrugged. "In the way."

Mercer made a face.

"What? Nobody's going to mourn for them. They were drug-dealing miscreants. Societal parasites."

"Say, for the sake of argument, that I believe any of this. How did you find the boy in the first place?"

"I didn't have to. His uncle found me."

"By way of the Resistance," Jake prompted.

Rask's eyes narrowed. "You know what, Gibson? You're not as stupid as you look."

"He's right, then?" Mercer said. "You're Resistance?"

"Not exactly. We merely have a mutually beneficial relationship. Their client base survives, and occasionally thrives, in the most abhorrent of conditions. I'm interested in understanding how. So I fund their clinics in return for information. Most of it is pretty dry. Medical records, migration data, that sort of thing. Now and then, they'll pass along something juicier—a wild story about a child who cures people with his bare hands, for example, as related by the distraught relative desperate to protect him—if they think that it'll pique my interest."

Jake rolled his eyes. "You mean open your checkbook."

"That too."

"Can I ask you something?" Mat, sheepish.

Rask looked up at him in surprise. "Sure."

"Why *pelican*?"

A smile bloomed on Rask's face. "Are you familiar with Saint Thomas Aquinas?"

Mat shook his head.

"He was a brilliant man who lived a very long time ago, when many of the world's most gifted minds were priests. Among his writings is a famous hymn explicating his devotion, in which he describes Christ as a divine pelican, capable of saving the entire world with a single drop of blood."

"And who's the Holy Father in this scenario—you?" Mercer's face twisted into an expression of contempt. "Just once, I'd like to meet a man with a billion dollars in the bank who didn't think himself a god."

"I hate to break it to you, Lionel, but you're short a couple zeroes," Rask replied.

Jake let out a low whistle. "I always figured, if I hit the lottery, I'd buy myself a '58 Corvette. The idea of bankrolling my own private army never even occurred to me."

Mercer snorted.

"You think *that's* funny," Jake replied, "you shoulda been here when the guy behind the biggest intelligence fuckup since 9/11 had the stones to accuse some other dude of playing God."

"All I wanted was to keep our country safe!"

"Well, then, you did a bang-up job."

Rask said, "I assume you two are talking about Shadow Reckoning?"

"That's right," Jake answered.

"Care to fill me in?"

"How much do you already know?"

"Not much," he admitted. "Mostly whispers in the dark corners of the internet."

"Funny; that's kind of where our story begins. See, Shadow Reckoning was a sting operation of sorts—an attempt to infiltrate the most notorious breeding ground for violent extremism on the internet: ShadowVox's /endtimes forum."

Rask's eyebrows climbed in surprise.

"Thing is," Jake continued, "this was shortly after the emergence of the Harbinger virus, so the forum wasn't yet a household name. In fact, at the time, it seemed like Lionel was the only one who took it seriously. He'd spent the better part of his career warning that an attack like Brutsch's was inevitable, but Bureau leadership ignored him at every turn, so—tired of waiting for them to come around—he set out to get proof. And when that proved harder than anticipated, he decided to take a more active role. Isn't that right, Lionel?"

"Of course not. It's conspiracy theory bullshit. The bipartisan 8/17 Commission concluded that Brutsch acted alone."

"Maybe so, but their report makes repeated mention of a ShadowVox user named thewhiterider—who, despite the best efforts of the FBI, was never positively identified. Remind me, who was in charge of that investigation again? Oh, right. It was you."

"We were unable to identify thewhiterider because a good deal of ShadowVox's data was corrupted when we executed our seizure order, but the material we *did* recover indicates that he or she was, at best, an unwitting accomplice. Brutsch was in the driver's seat the entire time."

"Yeah. Real bummer about that corrupted data. Funny thing, though. Jess Vandermeer's copies of thewhiterider's chat logs are nice and clear—but then, hers are contemporaneous screenshots."

"She . . . kept copies?"

"You're goddamn right she did, and they paint a very different picture from the one contained in the official report. Turns out, thewhiterider was no hapless sidekick. He was a manipulative bully who egged Brutsch on at every turn—mocking him when he expressed a modicum of sympathy for his potential victims, questioning his manhood whenever he faltered in his convictions, even offering him technical assistance when his ambitions outstripped his abilities. Of course, I shouldn't have to tell you that, since you and your team were thewhiterider all along."

"Jesus, Lionel, is that true?" Rask's voice was scarcely louder than a whisper.

"I didn't know . . . I mean, he wasn't supposed to . . ."

"Bullshit," Jake said. "Your team spent months creating a psychological profile of the guy. You knew what buttons to push. You preyed on his loneliness, his narcissism, his insecurities. You dared him to impress you, to prove his worth. And, in the end, that's exactly what he did."

"You don't understand." Mercer's voice had taken on a peevish tone.

"No, *you* don't understand. You killed my *wife*. Because of you, my little girl will never know her mother."

His face paled. His shoulders slumped. "I . . . I'm sorry about that, but—"

"No, you're not. If you were sorry, you would've come forward, instead of using the attack as a springboard to a position of power. If you were sorry, you wouldn't be eyeing the Oval Office the way a lion sizes up a gazelle. If you were sorry, you wouldn't have threatened

Jess's family to keep her quiet, or killed the members of your team you couldn't buy off or blackmail."

"You can't prove that."

"You're right. I can't. But once the rest comes out, I won't have to. It'll simply be assumed. A...what did Ethan call it earlier? A rounding error."

Mercer licked his lips and mopped his brow with the sleeve of his suit jacket.

"Listen, Gibson. You're a practical man. Think this through. The best Ethan can promise you is a one-way ticket to some shithole country without a US extradition treaty, and a pile of money that—once bribes, legal fees, and private security are taken into account—will never go as far as you'd expect."

"Lionel underestimates the pile of money I'm willing to offer for the evidence you've described," Rask replied.

"Be that as it may," Lionel continued, "it's only money. I, on the other hand, can give you your life back. Make a hero of you, even. Think about it: you stood up to the big bad businessman, saved the innocent kid that he's been chasing, and discovered a bona fide miracle cure along the way. So, what do you say?"

"I've gotta hand it to you, Lionel. That's one hell of a pitch. And I'll admit, Ethan, a giant heap of cash sounds awfully nice. Thing is, Mat and I would rather swallow broken glass than cut a deal with a mass murderer, so I guess all four of us are out of luck." Then, louder, "You can fire 'em up now, Cap!"

The night air was disturbed by an insectile buzz, too sudden to be of natural origin.

A constellation of quadcopter police drones rose as one into the sky.

56.

Mat watched the drones take flight with a queasy mix of terror and exhilaration. He and Jake had sprung their trap. Now all they had to do was hang on until help arrived—provided it was actually on the way.

The drones hovered twenty feet or so above their former perches: the ruined gantry, the overgrown transformer vault, the partially collapsed coal house, the tall grass along the shoreline. Their undercarriage lights strobed out of sync, bathing the island below in variegated shades of red.

Just offshore, the skiff's spotlight went dark, and its anchor thudded onto the deck. Then its engine sputtered to life and the boat lurched forward, carving a tight arc through the black water as it sped out of the bay.

"You sons of bitches set me up," Mercer spat.

Jake affected a wounded tone. "Hey, man. It's your surveillance state. We're just living in it."

"And Vandermeer's evidence..." Rask trailed off, as if unable to vocalize his question.

"Is nonexistent, so far as I know—although she obviously told me plenty."

Rask's face dropped.

Mat smiled despite himself.

When Jake had first explained his plan, Mat thought it sounded nuts. Jake had already called his captain once and been rebuffed. Wouldn't they be inviting arrest if they rang him up a second time and told him where they were?

That, Jake said, was the whole point. Bavitz had made it clear his loyalty to Jake didn't extend to helping them evade the law—but what if, in return for his assistance obtaining evidence of their claims, Mat and Jake offered to come in peacefully?

Jake swore the guy was honorable, and said he'd be as interested as they were in bringing Rask and Mercer to justice, but Mat remained dubious until the drones that Bavitz promised them arrived.

Bavitz said the only way he could prevent Mat and Jake from being scooped up prior to the meet was to keep the circle small. That meant they'd be forced to hang tight while he used any evidence they gathered to convince his superiors to dispatch backup. He also warned them that he was obligated to disclose the operation afterward, regardless of its success—so, to avoid arrest, they'd need clean audio of either Mercer or Rask incriminating themselves.

Finding a suitable location wasn't easy. The drones' microphones were temperamental, and their first few sound checks—coordinated via phone—were a disaster. Thanks to the wind through the trees, and the endless lapping of the East River against the shore, Bavitz struggled to make out what they were saying if they spoke any quieter than full voice.

That, coupled with the need for a defensible position, is why Mat suggested they station themselves on the morgue's roof. Now he prayed it had paid off. He couldn't stand the thought of being locked up while these monsters roamed free.

"Hey, boss?" Pike said to Rask. "I hate to say it, but it's time to go."

"The hell it is," Mercer snarled. "If I'm going down, you're damn sure coming with me."

His right hand darted toward the gun inside his suit jacket.

Pike—who, even injured, was quicker on the draw—fired twice, hitting Mercer in the left knee and right shoulder.

Mercer crumpled, screaming.

"I've no intention of leaving empty-handed," Rask told Pike, conversationally, as if Pike hadn't just shot a man on his behalf. "Rivas is our ticket to a soft landing in the country of our choosing. Once they realize what he's capable of, they'll line up to offer us asylum in exchange for early access to any resulting technologies—not to mention a percentage of the profits."

"I'm not going anywhere with you," Mat said.

"Oh, I think you are."

"Yeah? Why's that?"

"Because if you don't," Rask replied with the smug confidence of someone laying down a royal flush, "I'll order my man on the boat to put a bullet through your uncle's head."

Mat's head swam.

His breath caught in his chest.

Is it possible? Could Gabriel be alive?

"You're lying. My uncle's dead. Your men killed him."

"That will be news to him," Rask said mildly. "Hopscotch! Kindly bring our guest ashore."

Two figures, barely visible in the dim red light, climbed out of the dinghy and splashed toward the island.

As they approached, Mat saw that one's face was obscured by a black hood. His clothes were torn and bloodstained. His hands were zip tied at his waist.

The hooded figure moved haltingly, muscled along by Hopscotch, who—despite looking like a walking corpse—had a vicious grip on his left triceps.

When they reached the shoreline, Hopscotch released the man, who stumbled to his knees.

Then Hopscotch grabbed his hood and yanked.

"Mijo?"

The word—warped by the swollen lips and misshapen jaw that formed it—was just shy of inaudible, but it shook Mat like a detonation nonetheless.

Gabriel was alive.

"See?" Rask said. "I told you."

Rickety and draped in shadow though they were, Mat couldn't recall heading down the morgue's stairs. One moment, he was on the roof, and the next, he was outside—Jake shouting after him from what sounded like a million miles away.

"But…how?" he stammered.

"One does not become as successful as I have without learning how to bend others to one's will," Rask said. "To paraphrase Archimedes, give me the proper lever, and I'll move the world. Today, it seems, your uncle is that lever, which is precisely why I've allowed him to continue drawing breath."

Jake spilled, winded, out of the morgue. He froze when he saw Pike's .45 pointed at him.

"Mat, please, I'm begging you," Jake said, "don't let this creep get what he wants."

"I'm sorry. I have to." He flashed Jake a sorrowful smile. "People like me don't get to live normal lives. I appreciate you trying, though."

"Then you'll come?" Rask said.

"Yeah, I'll come, on one condition."

"What's that?"

"You let my uncle go."

"Mijo, no!"

"It's okay, Gabriel. I promise." Then, to Rask, "Do we have a deal?"

"We do," Rask said. "Now get on the goddamn boat."

"No way. Release him first."

"And, what, just take you at your word that you'll come willingly?"

"For fuck's sake, Rask, we've gotta motor!" Pike's head was cocked to one side. His expression showed alarm.

Mat held his breath and listened. Outboard engines whined in the distance, their volume growing louder by the second. Rask's eyes widened as he heard them too.

"How about a simultaneous exchange?"

"Sold," Mat replied. "Count of three?"

Pike and Hopscotch hauled Gabriel to his feet.

"One..."

Jake placed a hand on Mat's shoulder and squeezed.

"Two..."

Hopscotch, moving stiffly, waded back into the water to ready the dinghy, leaving Pike holding on to Gabriel.

"Three!"

Pike shoved Gabriel, who staggered forward.

Mat began to walk.

They met in the tall grass between the shoreline and the morgue. The boy shook uncontrollably. Tears streamed down his uncle's bruised, swollen face.

"I love you, mijo," said Gabriel in Spanish, as he wrapped Mat in his arms.

"I love you too," Mat replied.

Then, reluctantly, they separated.

When Mat reached Rask's side, the man smiled. "I knew you'd make the right decision."

He draped an arm around Mat's shoulders to guide him toward their waiting boat—and, as he did, Mat unsnapped the molded leather pouch on Rask's belt.

Rask wheeled toward the boy in alarm.

Mat elbowed him in the stomach.

Rask doubled over, wheezing.

Then, suddenly, his autoinjector was in Mat's hand.

"NO!"

Mat jabbed the autoinjector into his thigh, flooding his body with a megadose of broad-spectrum antibiotics.

"You selfish little shit," Rask said between gasps. "Do you have any idea what you've done?"

"Yeah. I just ruined your soft landing."

"And destroyed a precious gift that could've shaped the course of human history!"

"Some gift," Mat said, "winding up a rich douchebag's lab rat."

Rask, enraged, cocked back his hand.

Jake screamed, "Mat, look out!"

The boy dropped, covering his head with his hands.

Jake pulled the flare gun's trigger.

A tiny comet split the night and slammed into Rask's chest, engulfing him in flames.

Pike took aim at Jake, who held Gabriel upright with an arm around his waist.

Jake released him. He landed in the tall grass with a sickening crunch.

A handgun roared.

To Jake's surprise, Pike staggered backward, chest welling red.

For a moment, Jake couldn't figure out what happened. Then he spotted Mercer lying on the beach, his knee and shoulder pulsing blood, a pistol clenched in his right hand.

Hopscotch—apparently deciding he'd rather flee than join the fray—fired up the dinghy's engine and brought the boat around, but he was too late. Police boats swarmed the bay, blocking his path.

"Gabriel?" Mat shouted. "Where are you?"

"He's over here!" Jake waved at Mat until the latter closed the gap between them.

Gabriel sat, wincing, in the tall grass.

"Careful," Jake told Mat. "I think he cracked a rib when I let go of him."

"Better...than taking...a bullet," Gabriel managed through gritted teeth. "Thank you."

The boy took his uncle's hand. "Are you okay?"

"I'll be fine...but mijo...what did you do?"

"I did what I had to, to protect us both."

"I don't understand."

"I'm not different anymore," Mat said, "so there's no reason for anybody to come after us."

57.

Rask's charred corpse was fished out of the East River an hour later.

Mercer was medevac'd to a private hospital nearby. He clung to life for two days, drifting in and out of consciousness, before sepsis claimed him. Those who heard his deathbed confessions dismissed them as the delirious ramblings of a fevered mind.

Hopscotch ruptured a blood vessel resisting arrest and died on-site.

Mat, Jake, and Gabriel were taken into custody by the DBS and transported to an undisclosed location, where they were placed in separate negative pressure rooms and subjected to a barrage of diagnostic assays—a TB test among them.

Jake was delighted to discover his was negative.

Shortly afterward, the questioning began. A parade of agents—each more incredulous than the last—marched Jake through his story repeatedly for hours on end. Paget and Medina were the cruelest of the bunch, accusing Jake of treason and telling him that, if they had their way, he'd be executed for what he'd done.

When he insisted that they had it all wrong, that Bavitz's recordings would exonerate him, they assured him that there were no such recordings.

He asked for a lawyer. Citing the Wellness Act, they denied him.

He asked to see Mat. They laughed.

He asked about his daughter. They claimed that she, like Amy, was still missing—which made him grateful that he hadn't mentioned Hannah yet.

Two weeks later, Mat, Jake, and Gabriel were released.

They found the streets roiling with antigovernment protests.

Paget and Medina weren't kidding when they said that there were no recordings—at least, not officially. They'd apparently vanished sometime after Jake and company were apprehended, much like the drones themselves. It seemed the Whitmore administration wasn't wild about Mercer's transgressions coming to light.

Eighteen hours before the trio were freed, however, the recordings surfaced on Bangarang and immediately went viral. NYPD traced the leak to Bavitz, who was dismissed, only to be granted immunity by the former chair of the 8/17 Commission before he could be brought up on charges. Last Jake heard, he'd taken a job working security for the American Museum of Natural History. His kids, both dinosaur fans, were over the moon.

Amy, Zoe, and Hannah came out of hiding shortly after Mat, Jake, and Gabriel were released. Like Bavitz, Jake and Amy wound up testifying before the reconvened commission. Mat, being a minor, was spared the public spectacle.

Though Jake answered the commission's questions to the best of his ability, he allowed one particular misapprehension to stand, at Gabriel's request: namely, the assumption that Rask had injected Mat against his will before he died.

The moment wasn't captured by the drones, because they were airborne at that point—their microphones useless, their red anticollision strobes insufficient for recording low-light video.

Jake felt no guilt over the omission. The way he figured it, what happened to Mat's critters was no one's business but Mat's anyway.

Once they'd finished testifying, Jake and Amy were both cleared for duty. She, more determined than ever to change the department's culture from the inside, returned to work. He didn't. Truth was, he'd grown weary of carrying a gun, and thought he'd be more useful elsewhere.

Six months later, Jake was employed as an EMT. The salary was for shit, but on the plus side, he sometimes got to see his fiancée, Hannah, at work.

Thanks to the ACLU, the courts awarded Mat and Gabriel a tidy settlement but fell short of insisting on Park City's closure. The two of them wound up renting a place not far from Jake, Zoe, and Hannah. Mat even babysat for them from time to time.

Zoe loved him.

Jake and Hannah loved him too.

Mat was an amazing kid—brave, kindhearted, and inquisitive.

Though Mat's healing abilities never returned, Jake believed he'd one day change the world.

58.

The line snaked through the narrow alleyways of Mumbai's Dharavi slum, doubling back on itself so many times that its length was difficult to estimate.

Some waited alone. Others cradled babies to their chests. Still others were helped along by grown children or grandchildren. Many carried modest offerings: food, textiles, wood carvings.

The line terminated at a patchwork shanty of plywood and corrugated tin, with a blue tarpaulin where its front door should be. Its interior was cluttered, but tidy: three cots, a camp stove, a small refrigerator, some floating shelves, a cathode-ray TV. Clothes hung several layers deep from a series of mismatched hooks along one wall. Three neatly folded prayer rugs were stacked beneath them. A bare electric lightbulb dangled from the ceiling, illuminating the space.

Fourteen-year-old Fatima Usmani yawned and stretched, briefly rising to her bare tiptoes. Then she nodded to her mother, who watched her expectantly from the cot nearest the ad hoc door.

Her mother rose and held the tarpaulin aside so that the old man next in line could shuffle through. His eyes were rheumy and wet. His face and neck were knotted with angry boils.

"Please," he said, "I've come so far."

He was hard of hearing, and spoke a dialect of Hindi with which

335

Fatima—a native Urdu speaker—was unfamiliar, but she did her best to assure him that he'd be okay.

Fatima guided him to the cot farthest from the door, and gestured for him to lie down. Once he did, she looked over his boils, evincing neither horror nor disgust.

Then, gingerly, she laid her hands atop them.

AUTHOR'S NOTE

When I was younger, I wanted to be an Epidemic Intelligence Service officer with the CDC. You know: a bug hunter, a disease detective, one of the brave (and some—not I—would say, foolhardy) souls who travel the world containing outbreaks of Ebola, cholera, and the like.

My wife, as you can imagine, was thrilled.

At the time, I was in thrall to Richard Preston's *The Hot Zone* and Laurie Garrett's *The Coming Plague*—two books I still highly recommend—but I was serious enough about it to pursue a PhD in microbiology at the University of Virginia's School of Medicine, with a focus on infectious diseases.

The program turned out to be a poor fit for me, because I lacked the dedication to devote every waking hour to science. How could I, when I had all these stories nattering in my head?

So I dropped out of my grad program, took a job in a laboratory, and devoted my nights and weekends to writing.

For the first thirteen years of my writing career, science kept the lights on, but rarely found its way into my work. I've often wondered why that was, since my passion for it never waned. I suspect it was partly a matter of church and state—when you do science all day long, thinking about it on your off time is no fun—but it was also partly fear. In the land of fiction, bad science abounds, and thrilling tales built on good science are few and far between. Could I present a scientific premise in an entertaining way without compromising the factual underpinnings on which it's built? Would I, in my quest for verisimilitude, be sucked into a black hole of research, never to return?

The answer to the first question is kinda up to you. The answer to the second is, yeah, almost.

The book you're holding in your hands is the result of countless hours of research. Though it's obviously a work of fiction, the science behind it is very real, as is the existential threat that it portends.

My selected bibliography—while acknowledging several publications to which I'm particularly indebted—represents a tiny fraction of the resources, scholarly and otherwise, that have informed my thinking throughout the course of this book. That said, the story I chose to tell required no shortage of interpretation, interpolation, and extrapolation, all three of which are riddled with potential pitfalls. If, despite my best efforts, you happen across any errors in this text, I assure you that the fault is mine.

You might be wondering, as you read this, why bother showing your work? You're writing fiction, not a textbook; who cares what's real and what's made up?

The fact is, *I* do—and, if you place any value in modern medicine (or the occasional steak dinner), so should you. The grim vision of our future that *Child Zero* represents is all too plausible, given the path we're headed down, but I wouldn't have spent so much time and effort writing it if I thought that future was impossible to avert.

Thing is, the time to act is now.

We need to become better stewards of the antibiotics at our disposal by curtailing unnecessary prescriptions and agricultural overuse. Better sanitation and increased vaccination rates would go a long way toward reducing the number of bacterial infections in humans and animals, while faster, cheaper diagnostic tools would ensure our antibiotics are more strategically employed.

We also need to get new treatments into the pipeline, which means incentivizing the development of novel antibiotics and vaccines, as well as research into such promising avenues as probiotics, immunotherapy, and phage therapy.

And we must reject the nationalist tendency to assume our interests and responsibilities end at our own borders. As COVID-19 chillingly demonstrated, we're all in this together, so it's high time we started acting like it. Moral obligations aside, the incubation period for pneumonic plague is one to two days—far shorter than most diseases, but still long enough for someone carrying it to circumnavigate the globe.

Speaking of moral obligations, I'd be remiss if I didn't take a moment to discuss a topic at the beating heart of *Child Zero:* namely, the intersection of race and public health.

Many readers are likely familiar with the Tuskegee syphilis experiment, in which proper diagnoses and effective remedies were denied to hundreds of impoverished African American men with latent syphilis infections, so that doctors could observe the disease in its untreated state. I wish I could tell you it was an isolated incident, but the fact is, our nation's history of violating the bodily autonomy of minorities in the name of science dates back centuries—and continues to this day.

James Marion Sims, often referred to as the father of modern gynecology, developed new surgical techniques by operating on enslaved women without anesthesia. The American eugenics movement resulted in the forced sterilization of tens of thousands of minorities throughout the twentieth century, including an estimated 25 percent of Native American women, and there's evidence that similar abuses have been perpetrated against undocumented immigrants in recent years. Immortal human cell lines (so named because they're capable of dividing indefinitely) are a vital tool in biomedical research; the first of them (which Salk used to test his polio vaccine, and is still in use today) was created using cells taken from an African American cancer patient named Henrietta Lacks without her knowledge or permission. And a 2018 study indicated that African Americans are enrolled in clinical trials that don't require patient consent (such as those comparing various CPR methods) at a disproportionally high rate (29 percent, despite comprising roughly 13 percent of the total population).

Writing a child migrant of mixed race isn't something that I entered into lightly. Mat's identity is essential to the story for a number of reasons, both scientific and thematic, but I'd be lying if I said the responsibility of portraying him (or, for that matter, several of the novel's supporting characters) respectfully from a place of privilege didn't weigh on me.

I bring this up in part because, by story's end, Mat is forced to make a choice—one so difficult, I suspect many readers will question his decision. For what it's worth, I think he chose correctly— although, in truth, it's not worth much.

Mat's choice was his alone to make.

And that, dear reader, is very much the point.

SELECTED BIBLIOGRAPHY

Browne, H. P., Neville, B. A., Forster, S. C., & Lawley, T. D. (2017). Transmission of the gut microbiota: Spreading of health. *Nature Reviews Microbiology, 15*(9), 531–543. doi:10.1038/nrmicro.2017.50

Dill-McFarland, K. A., Tang, Z., Kemis, J. H., Kerby, R. L., Chen, G., Palloni, A., Sorenson, T., Rey, F. E., & Herd, P. (2019). Close social relationships correlate with human gut microbiota composition. *Scientific Reports, 9,* 703. doi:10.1038/s41598-018-37298-9

Domínguez-Díaz, C., García-Orozco, A., Riera-Leal, A., Padilla-Arellano, J. R., & Fafutis-Morris, M. (2019). Microbiota and its role on viral evasion: Is it with us or against us? *Frontiers in Cellular and Infection Microbiology, 9,* 256. doi:10.3389/fcimb.2019.00256

Hoffman, R. E., & Norton, J. E. (2000). Lessons learned from a full-scale bioterrorism exercise. *Emerging Infectious Diseases, 6*(6), 652–653. doi:10.3201/eid0606.000617

Jung Lee, W., Lattimer, L. D., Stephen, S., Borum, M. L., & Doman, D. B. (2015). Fecal microbiota transplantation: A review of emerging indications beyond relapsing Clostridium difficile toxin colitis. *Gastroenterology & Hepatology, 11*(1), 24–32.

Keen, E., Bliskovsky, V., Malagon, F., Baker, J., Prince, J., Klaus, J., & Adhya, S. (2017). Novel "superspreader" bacteriophages promote horizontal gene transfer by transformation. *mBio, 8*(1), Article e02115-16. doi:10.1128/mBio.02115-16

Landecker, H. (2016). Antibiotic resistance and the biology of history. *Body & Society, 22*(4), 19–52. doi:10.1177/1357034X14561341

SELECTED BIBLIOGRAPHY

Lathrop, P., & Mann, L. M. (2001). Preparing for bioterrorism. *Proceedings of the Baylor University Medical Center, 14*(3), 219–223. doi:10.1080/08998280.2001.11927766

Meadow, J. F., Altrichter, A. E., Bateman, A. C., Stenson, J., Brown, G. Z., Green, J. L., & Bohannan, B. J. (2015). Humans differ in their personal microbial cloud. *PeerJ, 3,* Article e1258. doi:10.7717/peerj.1258

Muzzi, A., Seminari, E., Feletti, T., Scudeller, L., Marone, P., Tinelli, C., Minoli, L., Marena, C., Mangiarotti, P., & Strosselli, M. (2014). Post-exposure rate of tuberculosis infection among health care workers measured with tuberculin skin test conversion after unprotected exposure to patients with pulmonary tuberculosis: 6-year experience in an Italian teaching hospital. *BMC Infectious Diseases, 14,* 324. doi:10.1186/1471-2334-14-324

Riedel, S. (2005). Plague: From natural disease to bioterrorism. *Proceedings of the Baylor University Medical Center, 18*(2), 116–124. doi:10.1080/08998280.2005.11928049

Ross, A., Ward, S., & Hyman, P. (2016). More is better: Selecting for broad host range bacteriophages. *Frontiers in Microbiology, 7,* 1352. doi:10.3389/fmicb.2016.01352

The Office of the United Nations High Commissioner for Refugees. (2015). *UNHCR Emergency Handbook* (4th ed.). https://emergency.unhcr.org/

ACKNOWLEDGMENTS

A heartfelt thank you to my agent, David Gernert, who believed in this book—and my ability to write it—long before I did.

To my editor, Josh Kendall, who has the instincts of a whetstone and the patience of a saint.

To David's crack team at the Gernert Company, and Ellen Coughtrey in particular.

To Ben Allen, Gregg Kulick, Xian Lee, Gabrielle Leporati, Liv Ryan, and the rest of the Mulholland / Little, Brown family.

To my copyeditor, Leslie Keros, who wrestled my bibliography into shape without complaint.

To Lou Berney, Lee Child, Matthew FitzSimmons, Tess Gerritsen, and Matthew Quirk for their early words of encouragement.

To Hilary Davidson, for a startlingly specific editorial note.

To my family—Burns, Holm, and Niidas—for their unflagging support.

To the vibrant community of readers, writers, booksellers, reviewers, and librarians who've embraced me as their own.

And to the educators whose words and deeds illuminated my path, of whom Nick LaPre and Susan Morgan are but two.

As ever, my deepest gratitude is reserved for my wife, lodestar, best friend, first editor, and ideal reader, Katrina. Thanks for letting me ride shotgun with you, love. You're more beautiful and talented than you'll ever know.

About the Author

Chris Holm is the author of the cross-genre Collector trilogy, the Michael Hendricks thrillers, and around thirty short stories in a variety of genres. His work has been selected for *The Best American Mystery Stories,* been named a *New York Times* Editors' Choice, appeared on more than fifty Year's Best lists, and won a number of awards, including the 2016 Anthony Award for Best Novel. He lives in Portland, Maine.